CHRISTMAS
Among the Gum Trees

JENNIE JONES

SUSANNE BELLAMY

LAUREN K. McKELLAR

NICOLE FLOCKTON

AINSLIE PATON

mira

Christmas Among the Gum Trees © 2020

12 Days at Silver Bells House
© 2014 by Jennie Jones
Australian Copyright 2014
New Zealand Copyright 2014

First Published 2014
Second Australian Paperback Edition 2020
ISBN 9781867215820

Her Christmas Kisses
© 2019 by Susanne Bellamy
Australian Copyright 2019
New Zealand Copyright 2019

First Published 2019
First Australian Paperback Edition 2020
ISBN 9781867215820

Naughty or Nice
© 2019 by Lauren K. McKellar
Australian Copyright 2019
New Zealand Copyright 2019

First Published 2019
First Australian Paperback Edition 2020
ISBN 9781867215820

Christmas in Ghost Gum Springs
© 2018 by Nicole Flockton
Australian Copyright 2018
New Zealand Copyright 2018

First Published 2018
First Australian Paperback Edition 2020
ISBN 9781867215820

Tinsel in a Tangle
© 2018 by Ainslie Paton
Australian Copyright 2018
New Zealand Copyright 2018

First Published 2018
First Australian Paperback Edition 2020
ISBN 9781867215820

Except for use in any review, the reproduction or utilisation of this work in whole or in part in any form by any electronic, mechanical or other means, now known or hereafter invented, including xerography, photocopying and recording, or in any information storage or retrieval system, is forbidden without the permission of the publisher.

This book is sold subject to the condition that it shall not, by way of trade or otherwise, be lent, resold, hired out or otherwise circulated without the prior consent of the publisher in any form of binding or cover other than that in which it is published and without a similar condition including this condition being imposed on the subsequent purchaser.

All rights reserved including the right of reproduction in whole or in part in any form.

This is a work of fiction. Names, characters, places, and incidents are either the product of the author's imagination or are used fictitiously, and any resemblance to actual persons, living or dead, business establishments, events, or locales is entirely coincidental.

Published by
Mira
An imprint of Harlequin Enterprises (Australia) Pty Limited (ABN 47 001 180 918), a subsidiary of
HarperCollins Publishers Australia Pty Limited (ABN 36 009 913 517)
Level 13, 201 Elizabeth St
SYDNEY NSW 2000
AUSTRALIA

® and TM (apart from those relating to FSC®) are trademarks of of Harlequin Enterprises (Australia) Pty Limited or its corporate affiliates. Trademarks indicated with ® are registered in Australia, New Zealand and in other countries.

A catalogue record for this book is available from the National Library of Australia www.librariesaustralia.nla.gov.au

Printed and bound in Australia by McPherson's Printing Group

Contents

12 Days at Silver Bells House   1
Jennie Jones

Her Christmas Kisses   185
Susanne Bellamy

Naughty or Nice   381
Lauren K. McKellar

Christmas in Ghost Gum Springs   483
Nicole Flockton

Tinsel in a Tangle   591
Ainslie Paton

Also by Jennie Jones

Swallow's Fall Series
The House on Burra Burra Lane
The House at the Bottom of the Hill
The House at the End of the Street

Daughters of Swallow's Fall Series
The House on Jindalee Lane

The Rangelands Series
A Place to Stay
A Place With Heart

A Dollar for a Dream Series
Last Chance Country

12 DAYS AT Silver Bells HOUSE

JENNIE JONES

*For everyone who loves Chardonnay,
shooting stars and the country.*

Chapter One

Katherine Angelica Singleton tapped her fingers on the steering wheel of her hire car and threw all thoughts of murder onto the New South Wales Monaro Highway behind her.

Losing her life plan just as she was about to turn thirty hadn't been on her spreadsheet. Now there was a hard choice to be made. But Kate wasn't referred to as Snappy Singleton for her dress sense alone. Kate had brains and she'd decided to push them to the limit, albeit at a time when she hadn't expected to explore the spontaneous side of her nature.

The thought of why she was in this predicament caused gushes of steaming fury to rise to the surface of her skin.

Five days ago she'd been drawn to New York for a fashion shoot that would have seen her young Australian designers flourish in the way she wanted them to, in a manner that had been wearing her heels down for the last decade. By groundwork and gumption.

A measly one hundred and twenty hours away from home soil — and what happens? Her world tumbles into something she's never faced before: Mayhem, folly, madness.

This morning she'd stepped off the plane from New York in hometown Sydney and made her first rash decision *ever*. She caught the next flight to the political hub of Canberra, booked a hire car and drove into the Snowy Mountains.

This December, she was going without Christmas.

Stuff the turkey. She'd ding-dong merrily on her own. With Chardonnay.

She breathed deeply and attempted to blow her worries out and away; gathering enlightenment and insight with her next intake of breath with all her Zen might. If she hadn't been driving which necessitated staying focussed — as in eyes open — she'd have got into the Lotus position.

She sighed. Twelve days of freedom; no tinsel. Four hundred and fifty kilometres south of society and Singleton's Sassy Sensations fashion house; no parties, no fake smile, no juggling canapés on cocktail sticks.

While shepherds watched their flocks by night, Kate would be cosied up in a stone cottage all by herself in the Snowy Mountains, courtesy of a last-ditch wish on a shooting star in New York and a surprising suggestion from her best friend, Sammy.

She glanced at her pale arms, her pale slim fingers topped with dusky-rose nail polish, and made another rash decision. *She'd get a tan.* Stuff having to slather herself in 30+ sunscreen and take Vitamin D supplements to compensate for the lack of ultraviolet radiation. This was Australia where sunshine abounded. Even smallest, remotest Swallow's Fall township had sunshine.

She smiled in satisfaction and licked her top lip, tasting her dusky-rose lipstick.

How about another rash decision? She frowned behind her polarised oval-framed sunglasses. She didn't make impetuous decisions, it was difficult pulling one from nowhere. She slapped her hand on the wheel. 'No dieting.' Dump the eternal calorie counting. Her days would be filled with endless summer walks and her evenings spent with Chardonnay and pretzels — the full fat, don't-hold-back-on-the-salt variety.

She pressed the window button and stuck her arm out into the country air which rushed over her skin with more heat than she'd reckoned on. This was the *Snowy* Mountains for God's sake. It was supposed to be a little chilly even in summer.

She closed the window and concentrated on Highway B23 spreading before her.

Look out country, here comes Kate.

Kate brought the car out of cruise-control and slowed to make a right turn into All Seasons Road. She'd purposefully missed the town's turn off at Main Street ten kilometres back. No need to head into the little town until tomorrow morning. The only thing she didn't have was food, but she'd gone without food most of her adult life, what would one night without pretzels matter? And anyway, she wasn't ready to face any holiday cheer that might be going on in town. They probably already had a big fat fir tree in place outside the pioneer cemetery, with plump carol singers standing around its base, handing out homemade mince pies while going off-key with a rendition of 'Deck the Halls'.

The last thing Kate wanted was optimism of the Christmas variety. Which is why Silver Bells House would be her safety net. '*Key's probably under the door mat,*' Sammy had said. '*Or someone will be there to let you in.*' The lack of administrative orderliness about the whats and hows of this away-from-it-all holiday worried Kate but she'd grown accustomed to weekly reports about rural life from Sammy, and had herself witnessed the quaint curiosity of the people of Swallow's Fall when she'd visited to attend Sammy's wedding. Over a year ago now. Her friend had married a vet. Her artist friend had chosen the country instead of the city. And her friend was so bloody happy. If Sammy could find happiness in the country, why couldn't Kate?

Driving along All Seasons Road calmed her disorderly emotions. The long, wide road led to relief. The hedgerows guided her. White, purple and yellow wildflowers sprung in tufts along the verge and wandered into the undulating grassy plains beyond. So quiet. So isolated. So bloody perfect.

Yes, siree. The twelve days of Kate. Should be plenty of time to make The Decision, as she'd christened her problem. 'Heck, darn and shucks,' she said, practising her country vernacular. She'd been practising from the moment she stepped off the plane from New York, having sat next to an elderly couple from Texas and learned all about which vittles were best for a Sunday sundowner after a long, hot day of branding, and how to attract a whisky-swilling ranchero — should one want to. She'd been a'bushel and a'peckin' all through Customs, right through baggage collection and straight into her hire car.

She jolted in her seat and gripped the steering wheel as a deafening, squawking noise erupted above and around her. The early evening sky darkened as though the devil himself had swung the cape of evil from his shoulders with a wrathful flourish.

Hark! The herald of the country. *Parrots.* Hundreds of them.

'For God's sake,' she yelled as she slowed the car. They swooped so low that for a second, she couldn't see the road in front of her, just a sea of slate-grey wings and red topped heads. She pounded the horn.

'No,' she hollered as globs of dinner plate–sized parrot poo hit her windscreen. White mess. Lots of white mess. *What the hell did the birds eat around here?* She hit the wiper-washer — no water. 'You're joking!' She pulled the arm again — still no water, just a squelchy squeak as the blades made a Picasso of the poop on the windscreen. And the car was still moving.

She slammed the ball of her foot onto the accelerator instead of the brake and screamed as the car veered sideways and crashed through something that splintered, cracked and popped like an exploding barrel. *Must be a gate.* The slam knocked her backwards in her seat. She hit the brake — and almost snapped a four-inch heel — but the vehicle slid, and kept on sliding, the glopping sounds and bouncing informing her that the car was skimming along mud.

Kate had little idea how to steer a runaway car but she kept her hands on the wheel in case something brilliant happened, like a sudden downpour of rain on the near-blanketed windscreen. No such luck. Just a tree. *Great.*

The car came to a thumping stop when it bumped into the tree trunk, a shower of twigs and leaves falling on the roof and the bonnet of the car.

Then the airbag exploded, pushing the breath out of her lungs. *Timing!* Would have been too late if the car had hit a brick wall. She'd have been crushed. They'd have found her buried beneath twisted metal, smashed windscreen and parrot poop.

Time stood still, except for the squawking parrots as they flew overhead and on towards the next unsuspecting motorist. *Good luck finding one.* She hadn't encountered another car in the last forty-five minutes.

She pushed the airbag down, helping it deflate faster with hard slaps; punching her fury into it. She gripped the steering wheel and watched billowing white powder float in the air and all over her figure-hugging indigo and eggshell-coloured business dress, designed by herself. Now she smelled like talcum powder. *Why me?* Life had changed too fast and she wasn't referring to the last five minutes. Kate had changed. She turned her head and looked out at the sprawling green and brown paddock through the side window. No — she hadn't changed, she'd been kicked out of her own skin. She'd lost herself.

And now she'd ditched her bloody car.

Welcome to the country.

She gathered her breath in gulps, hoping she wasn't going to pass out — something else that had never happened before — and considered her options. It was after six o'clock and although she had her mobile phone, who would she call? Sammy and her husband Ethan, the local vet, were away, taking the opportunity for a long-delayed honeymoon, and their house on Burra Burra Lane was locked up. They were building a new veterinary surgery and stables on the lower paddock which for some reason meant the water and power to their house had to be shut down for a week. She couldn't even call Sammy and ask who to ask for help. For one thing, Kate was a super-powered businesswoman who never asked for assistance with anything, unless it was to fire short sharp orders to her team at Sassy Sensations. For another — Sammy and Ethan Granger would currently be thirty-thousand feet high, flying north-west to the Kimberley in Western Australia.

But Kate hadn't called her business Singleton's *Sassy* Sensations for nothing. She'd bought country equipment in Canberra before driving down here. She had torches and firelighters. She had matches and a lighter. She had rope. What she'd need the rope for only God knew, but it was a pretty black and yellow weave, so she'd plopped it onto the counter of Hillsides & Waysides mountaineering shop along with the rest of her gear. She had more than Chardonnay too, she had Wellington boots. The pretty kind, with blue rosebuds and although she hadn't wanted to get them covered in mud, she supposed that was their original purpose and she'd have to buckle up and ride that beast.

Except all that equipment was in the boot. A two-metre walk through gluggy mud without her rosebud wellies.

She undid her seatbelt and twisted to the back seat to check her tortoiseshell leather carry-on bag, packed neatly and tidily with the full seven kilograms cabin allowance. She might not know how to deal with parrots but she knew how to pack. Except she hadn't packed her flat pumps. They were in the boot, in her larger suitcase, alongside the Chardonnay and the wellies.

With a sigh and a reminder that she was now in a courageous and countrified state of mind, she opened the door and stared down at the glop. Dark brown muddy mire, along with the turf her car had torn up after it collided with the gate. She'd ruined someone's paddock.

Another sound punctured the air. Not parrots. Kate lifted herself from the seat until she stood on the edge of the opened door frame. She held onto the top of the car and looked over the roof and over the gate and the stone wall to the road. Thank God she hadn't crashed into the wall. She concentrated on the sound.

A truck? A bus? Too mechanically rickety-sounding. Too loud. Not chugging fast enough. The sound was heavy and metallic, and vibrating on the road.

The top of a yellow cab came into view, rumbling down All Seasons Road. A crane or a digger or something. With a workman!

'Hello,' she called, waving madly at the workman driving the huge yellow digger.

It slowed, and Kate sighed in relief. He'd seen her — or perhaps he'd seen the broken gate which was now shattered over the road and the muddy paddock. She flinched as the digger-excavator steamrollered parts of the broken gate and then came to a shuddering stop.

The workman opened the cab door. 'Are you alright?' he called, getting out and jumping off the conveyer-belt tread.

Kate knew all there was to know about designer style and this guy had none of the style she was used to. But he did possess muscles. Beefy ones that matched his height and his work boots. Kate ran an expert eye over him, deciding he was a 48-inch chest, a 36-inch inside leg and a size thirteen shoe. About six foot three, all up.

What did people *eat* in the country?

Kate waved. 'I'm fine,' she called back. 'But I'm stuck. Can't get out.'

He stopped at the stone wall and looked down at the ground around her vehicle. 'From where I'm standing it looks like you can walk out of there.'

From where he was standing he obviously couldn't see the *mud*. She offered him her most pleasant smile. Perhaps it was his gate and his mud and he didn't like his paddock ripped to furrowed shreds by her hire car.

She pointed to the gate. 'I'm so sorry about your gate. I'll pay for a new one.'

'Isn't my gate. It's part of the property on Burra Burra Lane.'

'Sammy and Ethan. Yes — my friends.' Sammy wouldn't mind a bit of damage to one little gate. They didn't keep sheep or anything that would wander out of the paddock.

'The Grangers aren't home,' he said.

'I know. They're on their way to the Kimberley.'

'So why are you here? You can't live up at the house. The water's turned off along with the electricity.'

'Are you the man digging the ditch?' Sammy had said some guy was working up at the homestead, digging ditches for the cabling and plumbing for the new veterinary surgery.

'I was today, probably will be tomorrow.'

A ditch-digging workman. What did he need the excavator for when he had shovelling shoulders so wide he probably had to buy his shirts from Bigger & Bigger Work Wear?

'Do you work for them?' she asked.

He shook his head. 'I work for myself. How'd you manage to crash through the gate?'

Kate fought the signs of frustration as he stood there, not moving, not rescuing. 'I didn't *manage* it, it was an accident.'

'How?'

'A flock of parrots.'

He stared at her for a long time as though considering her answer and any response he might make to it. Or perhaps he hadn't heard her.

Kate had to admit a flock of parrots probably didn't usually give motorists cause for concern but she was in the *country*, for God's sake. There were parrots everywhere. 'Parrots,' she said again, louder. 'And now I'm stuck.'

'Well, if you're not prepared to help yourself, there's only one way out.'

Kate looked around, searching for stepping stones or planks of wood to use as a bridge. 'Which way?' she asked.

'Over my shoulder.'

In a swift, heave-ho manner, he put one hand to the top of the stone wall and leapt over it. Mud splattered up his work boots and onto his khaki-trousered legs.

Oh, good heavens. He was enormous. She teetered on the door frame, and grabbed the roof of the car to steady herself.

'You drive in those things?' he asked, pointing at her eggshell-coloured sling-back stilettos.

Kate nodded. 'Automatic car,' she told him. 'More difficult in a manual, but not impossible for the most tenacious of women.' Like herself. So let *that* be a lesson, Mr Bigger & Bigger. Try driving your digger in four-inch heels.

He shook his head and squelched towards her. 'Madness.'

The man did a lot of muttering. But he was about to rescue her so Kate kept her mouth closed until she remembered she was alone. In a paddock. With a strange man.

'Okay,' he said, holding his arms out and beckoning her with his fingers. 'Come on.'

He wanted her to leap over his shoulder? Just like that? Without an introduction?

'Wait.'

He dropped his arms to his sides and looked at her.

Kate looked at his face. She'd recognise barbed and ugly if she saw it in his gaze. She'd seen sly and snarky too and knew what signs to look for: dead eyes, lips curled in a tight, controlled smile and… Oh.

Hello country.

Chapter Two

Bigger & Bigger's eyes were a leather-brown colour and his gaze had a comfy look to it, as though nothing disturbed him, even if you were to throw yourself at him. He had one of those strong, square faces. The ideal shape to work with. Interesting to see a natural six o'clock shadow on his jaw too, instead of one that had been barbered into perfection. She made a mental note of this for when she next did a shoot for jeans and boxer shorts. Don't let the make-up guys add too much glamour. Keep it earthy. And try to get the male models to aim for a natural tan and not the sprayed-on kind. It worked on this guy. He was extremely handsome, for a ditch digger.

She held out her hand. 'Kate Singleton. Nice to meet you. And you are?' Hopefully not some ruffian who looked like Superman but had the brain of a turkey.

'Jamie Knight.' He took her hand and shook it.

Kate ignored the fact he hadn't wiped his shovel-sized hand first and withheld the need to wipe off the dried, dusty dirt now on hers.

She glanced over her shoulder and the roof of her car to his yellow excavator and saw *Knight Works* painted in bold white signage, although a bit mud-splashed.

'My knight in khaki,' she said with a smile, and ran an eye down his torso, over his khaki-clad hips and down his legs. All that thrust and heave-ho would get her out of the mud. If she was nice to him. *Must remember to talk in country mode.* 'Golly galoshes but you look strong.'

He raised his brow and said nothing, but the comfy expression in his eyes turned a kind of wary-looking. No time to dither on that point in case he changed his mind and left her to the mud.

Kate pointed to the boot of her car. 'I don't suppose you'd be able to rescue my Chardonnay too, would you?' If he had her slung over his hefty shoulder, she'd be secured and he'd be hands-free. 'If I carry my carry-on bag and my shoes, you could probably carry my wine.'

He wiped his mouth with his big, dirty hand and looked off into the distance. 'Why me?' he asked in a quiet tone, but by the look on his face Kate didn't think the question was directed at herself.

'Pop the boot,' he said.

Kate did so, then took her shoes off. Holding them by their slingbacks she knelt on the driver's seat and reached over to the back seat for her carry-on. She placed the bag and the shoes on her seat so she could pick them up once she was…over his shoulder.

'Ready,' she said, turning to him.

He took hold of her by the waist, lifted her off the seat, flung her over his shoulder and turned so his back was to the car.

'Grab your gear,' he told her.

Okay, not quite ready. She tensed as she found her balance on his shoulder, and then stretched down. 'Got them,' she said. And… *off we go.*

Heavens.

It was a little worrying having her backside to the sky and had she been armed with foresight, once she'd got off the plane from

New York she would have changed out of her slimline dress into her track-pants. Scrap that thought. She would have remembered to *buy* track-pants. She hoped to God the grocer's in town stocked more than coffee, milk and pretzels.

The boot of her car slammed and Kate angled her head to check, as best she could around the broad back she was hanging against, that Jamie Knight had her wine. He did. He also had her big suitcase. Holy cowboy, what strength. What long arms. Twenty-three kilos of checked baggage, seven kilos of cabin bag, *ahem* kilos of Kate and…how much would twelve bottles of wine weigh?

His shoulder was broad enough for her midriff to settle on the width without sliding off but she couldn't hold on due to her hands being full of her tortoiseshell-leather bag and her favourite shoes. She jammed her elbows into his sides as a means of clinging on as he moved off. 'Um…are you sure you can carry the wine *and* the suitcase?'

He didn't answer so Kate sucked it up and held onto her courage, her carry-on and her sling-backs. At least this way, she'd have her pyjamas and her Chardonnay for her first solo night in the country. Not the arrival she'd envisaged but life wasn't easy in the country. Sammy had told her that.

Once on the road, he let her down by swinging her around and levering her down his arm so her luggage and her shoes didn't fall. A He-Man with a capital H.

'Thank you so much,' she said, slipping her feet into her shoes. 'How are we going to get the car out?' She held her hand up in a placating manner, and added a smile. 'Obviously I don't expect you to tow it with your excavator, you've done so much already — but do you know if there's a mechanic around?' Kate wasn't sure if roadside assistance operated this far into the Snowy Mountains. Perhaps they winched bogged hire cars out of distress with a helicopter.

'Your car's here for the night. Can't use the excavator to tow it, and anyway, I'm on my way home.'

The night. One night. Not too bad then. He must know someone who could help her retrieve the vehicle. Probably a farmer with a tractor. At least she had her own tow rope. That might appease any farmer with a tendency to think city women drivers were more trouble than their feminine wiles were worth. And she doubted any of them would believe the parrot story.

'I'll bring my ute down tomorrow morning and tow it out for you.'

Kate clapped her hands together. 'Thank you so much.' Country manners. A woman didn't get this sort of assistance in the city. 'So are you able to drop me off at Silver Bells House on your way home, or is it out of your way?' She glanced down All Seasons Road which led to nowhere she could see. 'That's where I'm staying.' She'd got herself, her luggage and her wine safely saved but there was no way she'd be able to lug it all to wherever this house was. Up a hillside, Sammy had said. Take All Seasons Road as far as you can heading east until you come to the No Through Road sign, then take the winding track up to the house. Sammy had also said to make sure she arrived in daytime and it was now nearly dusk.

'You're what?' he asked.

'Sammy arranged for me to live in the holiday house. I think the key's under the mat — or something.'

'She what?'

'Silver Bells House,' she said, pronouncing each word carefully. Perhaps he'd gone deaf over the years from driving his excavator.

'Right,' he said, studying her as though she were a puzzle where the pieces didn't fit.

'I can recompense you for fuel and your time.'

He frowned. 'No need.'

'So could you give me a lift?'

Nothing, except that deep, now forbidding frown.

He took a breath. 'Looks like I'll have to.' He climbed onto the metal traction thingies on the excavator, her large suitcase in one hand, her wine under his other arm. *So strong.* 'I can take you to the house,' he said as he stored her luggage behind the driver's seat. 'Then we need to talk.'

Talk? About what? She hadn't envisaged sharing her wine with him as they chatted about world peace under the stars. She just wanted a lift.

Kate noticed three man-size pedals attached to long levers, sitting to the left of the driver's seat. 'Is it like driving a car?' she asked as she passed him her carry-on.

He didn't answer her question. He'd put her suitcase behind the seat, and placed the box of wine beside it. Her carry-on went in next, on top of the wine.

Then he got out and held out both hands for Kate to step onto the traction thingies. Before she had time to wonder about how high her slimline dress would ride up her legs and how much thigh he'd get a look at, he'd taken hold of her outstretched arms and pulled her up and onto the digger.

'Good heavens,' she said, teetering on the balls of her feet so her heels didn't get caught in the metal rollers. Had he needed to be that vigorous?

'You're going to have to perch on your suitcase — behind me,' he said. 'You need to hold onto my shoulders, please. And don't tell anyone I did this.' He pulled her up into the cab and — quite forcefully, Kate thought — coerced her into the cab behind the seat.

'Did what?' she asked, squeezing herself behind the seat, twisting her legs to one side and perching on the suitcase.

'Gave you a piggyback in my fourteen-tonner.' He hauled himself up into the seat and closed the cab door. 'My insurance wouldn't cover it.'

He turned the key in the ignition and all the lights came on. Then he released a handbrake and Kate grabbed the back of his seat in case they shot off. But nothing happened until he moved one of the long levers with a pedal attached and…they were off. She was rather charmed by the thrill rumbling through her. Who'd have thought she'd get to ride in a fourteen-tonner?

'What a view from up here. I can see over the hedges. Spectacular.'

He mumbled something.

Kate leaned forwards over his shoulder. 'What did you say?' She angled her face so that her ear was next to his cheek.

'Hold onto my shoulders,' he said.

Touchy. She straightened, as much as was possible. Her head was tilted forwards and her body twisted to one side in order to fit. She gripped the back of his seat.

Kate listened to the rackety noise in the cab. Perhaps Mr Bigger & Bigger *was* a little deaf. He hadn't answered any of her questions directly.

She drummed up some sweetness. 'What a lovely excavator,' she called above the drone. 'You must be so proud.'

He moved his head slightly as though about to look at her, but apparently changed his mind. He studied the road ahead.

'How do you move the big arm?' she asked, pointing to the digger's big arm.

No response.

Kate sighed. It might take hours to get to the cottage. She wondered how fast they were going and whether or not his fourteen-tonner was at full steam ahead.

She sat back and shut up. For at least thirty seconds.

Maybe he only spoke man-talk. She could do man-talk. Singleton's Sassy Sensations had done hundreds of shoots on industrial sites and in car yards, making tall, lanky male models look dirty and oily enough to sell jeans and boxer shorts by the millions. She slapped her hand onto the knob of an unused lever at his right-hand side. 'How many to the litre?' she asked him.

He grabbed her hand and held it firmly up and away from the lever. 'Don't touch anything,' he said, sounding peeved.

She pulled her hand out of his. Just her luck. In the bleak midsummer with Excavator-man.

After another ten minutes he turned the excavator onto the No Through Road track and Kate's heart bounced like a puppy off the leash as they drove uphill. She leaned forwards slightly, in case the additional weight to the front of the cab helped ensure the bloody fourteen-tonner didn't topple backwards.

'Oh, look.' She pointed through the side window to a row of stones of various shapes and sizes, all neatly stacked between A-frames and string plumb lines. 'Somebody's building one of those dry-stone country walls. Isn't is fabulous?'

She didn't expect a response, but got irritated by the lack of one anyway. 'Is something wrong?' she asked snappily.

'I'm just trying to work a few things out,' he ground out.

She ignored him after that and concentrated on her future destination. Her heart swelled like an inflatable pillow. A remote country lane, shaded with gum trees. The eucalyptus aroma up here, high on the hill, mellowing her vexed frame of mind. She sighed. Twelve days of nothing coming right up. Yes, siree.

'Oh, my God.' She tapped him on the shoulder. 'Look. Look — we're here. That's the house.'

Stunning. Such potential. Two-storey, old-stone, weathered and wonderful. Slightly European in design, which was a surprise but it blended into its surroundings with ease. The front portion of the house jutted out from the back part with a dynamic sloping roof on the left and a shorter slope on the right.

'Holy moly.'

Six square windows, each of different size, suggested cosiness and contentment waited for her. And someone had switched the lights on inside. How thoughtful. Two coach lights, one either side of the sturdy pale-blue wooden door were also lit, shining a welcome on the arched, stone paved portico.

'Oh, it's just dripping in gorgeous.'

'Thank you,' he said, loudly and resolutely.

Kate leaned forwards to check his features. Why would he thank her? He glanced her way.

Kate sat back, not wanting to be held captive by that serious frown, and took another look around. Oh-oh. A monster white ute with tyres as big as a bear was parked on the driveway. On the side of the monster ute were the words: *Knight Works*.

She fought a sudden agitation and looked out of the other window. Did Excavator-man live in the area too? Maybe there was a hut around the back, and Sammy and Ethan had kindly allowed him to stay there while he was digging their ditches.

Her heartbeat knocked against her ribcage. She didn't like the idea of sharing her patch of country with Jamie Knight.

'What in bejeezus is going on here?' she asked.

'Bejeezus?' he asked, quizzically. 'Where are you from? Ireland?'

'Sydney.'

'So what's with all the…Never mind.' He switched everything off in the cab, opened the door and got himself out. 'Come on then. Home sweet home.'

As though in a dream, Kate levered herself out of the confined space and put her arms out to him.

'Don't lose your shoes,' he said as he swung her onto the metal rollers. 'I haven't got time to fix the traction because of a four-inch spike.'

What had happened to the country manners?

He jumped off the excavator, reached up for her, took hold of her waist and swung her off the rollers and onto the ground.

Kate's body was taut and her brain seemed to be sparking. 'Where are *you* staying?' she asked. *Oh, please, God, don't let him say it. Don't let him say it.*

'Where do you think?'

Excavator-man's constant, low-drawled, unhelpful responses were beginning to get on her executive nerves. 'This is my holiday home,' she told him in the brusque tone she used when one of her newcomer designers got too big for her wedges. 'It's my twelve-day getaway. Thank you for the rescue and all that, but I hope to God you're not staying here too.'

'I'm afraid it's worse than that.'

Like how much worse? Wasn't there supposed to be a choice? *Do you want the good news first or the bad?*

'I don't know what's going on here,' he said steadily, 'but Silver Bells House isn't a holiday home. It's mine. I own it. And I don't take guests.'

Chapter Three

Kate's mouth wouldn't work. It was open, because the warm evening air partied with her tongue, but... *What had he said?*

She swallowed the air and salivated her mouth. 'I thought you were the ditch digger.'

'I am. I'm also the owner of Silver Bells House.'

'Since when?'

'Since four weeks ago.'

'But what has... I mean why did...' She shrugged her shoulders to her ears. 'I don't understand.'

'Neither do I, but there's been a mistake.'

'Sammy doesn't make mistakes. Are you sure she didn't mention me?'

He shook his big, workman's head.

'Not even a little? As in, "Hi, Mr Knight, my best friend is coming to stay at your house".'

'Not even a smidgeon.'

'I thought you worked for Ethan.'

'Correction. I accepted Ethan's contractual offer to build the new stone veterinary surgery. I'm a stonemason.'

'But I thought you were a...' Workman passing through. She ploughed on, not caring what he thought about her rapid-fire questions. 'Why did you buy this house? Are you a local?'

'I liked it. And I'm now local number eighty-eight.'

'Well I like it too, and it's supposed to be my twelve-day retreat from everything your flippancy is reminding me too much of.'

'Too bad.'

She released her shoulders which were still stuck up around her ears, and pulled them back. He hadn't gone at all male-affronted at her questioning, which she admired. The man had tenacity. And her holiday house. 'I need to call Sammy.' Except Sammy, her *once* faithful friend, would still be thirty-thousand feet high. 'Don't bother getting my luggage out — you'll have to give me a lift into town.' And she wasn't about to say please.

'In the excavator?' he asked with a wry lift of his eyebrow.

In his wheelbarrow if need be. 'I'll stay at the B&B.' She'd stayed there for the night of Sammy and Ethan's wedding, along with Verity Walker, Sammy's difficult mother. 'The Cappers',' she said. 'They own the B&B. They know me.'

'The B&B is closed,' he informed her. 'The Cappers have gone west to visit their son.'

'Closed?' It couldn't be. Where the bloody hell was she going to stay? 'I need to talk to Sammy.' Not that giving Sammy a good talking-to about this fiasco would leave Kate with anywhere to sleep, unless she curled up for the night in the waterless, powerless homestead on Burra Burra Lane. 'What am I going to do?' God-damn the country. No hire cars. No taxis.

No bloody room at the inn.

'You won't reach Sammy and Ethan until tomorrow.'

'I know that!' Okay, so her own tenacity had worn thin. *Was there a wheelbarrow?* She turned from him to take a look, already envisaging herself pushing it all the way down All Seasons Road. In the dark. No streetlights because *this was the bloody country.*

'Obviously, you'll have to stay here.'

Kate spun to him so fast she nearly tripped as the heel of her sling-back twisted beneath her. Which annoyed her even more. She never tripped. She was the *steady at heights* kind of stiletto-wearing executive. 'Stay here?' she demanded as something horribly like panic bubbled inside her chest. 'I don't know you. I know nothing about you. You might be a ditch-digging murderer. Is that why you bring your fourteen-tonner home each night? So you can dig holes to bury the unsuspecting visitors?'

Oh, now he decided to smile.

'I brought the excavator back because I don't need it up at the homestead tomorrow, and I've got a job I want to use it for here. At my house. Silver Bells House. Jamie's house.'

If she hadn't already been given a shoe-about-to-break warning, she'd have stamped her stilettoed foot on the slab paving.

'Stop quaking and come on in,' he said. 'Looks like we'll be getting to know each other.'

He needn't have made it sound like he'd been forced into sharing his house with his mother-in-law.

Kate tried to keep the panic at bay and her temper under boiling point but the softer senses inside her speedily came to the fore when she stepped inside the house.

The wall on her left was mellow-yellow stone, like the outside. Must be a foot thick. The wall on her right was plastered and painted a French-linen colour. Two plastic builder's buckets, a set of trowels and a red wheelbarrow — ah! there it was, her possible transportation — sat in the hallway to one side of the pale-blue front door. He must have been repointing the stone wall in the hall, Kate thought, noting the slight difference in colour between the old grouting and the new, but that was probably because the new needed time to dry out and weather.

Kate's apartment in Sydney was modern and functional but one day she planned on finding the time to buy and do up one of the Federation bungalows still to be found in the Sydney suburbs so she knew a thing or two about renovation.

Jamie left her suitcase in the hall, at the base of a reddish-brown wooden staircase with wrought-iron railings.

'Okay, come on through.'

She followed his big, broad back into the kitchen and any stony parts still in her heart melted like chocolate chips in a warm bakery.

Dark floorboards again, like the ones in the hall and on the staircase. They probably went throughout the house. Plastered walls in antique white, one feature wall with a big window left as stone above a square white-enamel sink, surrounded by black granite bench tops. An old blackened range stood in a stone-encased alcove. It must work; there wasn't another stove in the room. The ceiling gave the room its greatest appeal. Breadth and length. Thick, squared beams painted in dove-grey ran the length, fitted and slotted into crossing beams. The entire space was countrified with flare. Not feminine, not entirely masculine.

What had once been a separate dining room now extended into the kitchen, making it one long room. The plasterboard wall still in its just-knocked-down state. It's exactly what Kate would have done. The man had taste.

She glanced his way and as he busily moved things on shelves in the pantry, or looked for something she gave his physique her full attention. What would this khaki-clad, work-booted man look like in a suit? The first assumption she made when perusing shots of male models her young designers might use. Surprisingly she discovered she didn't want to know how Jamie Knight would look in a designer suit. Instead, she saw him in cream chinos and a slate-grey shirt. A black belt and black shoes. Relaxing on his Chesterfield sofa in his stone-built house with his Sunday newspaper.

The masculine greys would complement his nutmeg-brown hair, the deep, natural tan on his arms and the sprinkling of dark hair at his throat, where his khaki work shirt sat untidily, three buttons undone. Nothing about him — his clothes, his style, his demeanour — said predisposed to trend. This was a naturally-honed man and she had a feeling his personality matched. Rough and ready when called on. Big-hearted and gentle when needed.

A bit of a yummy package. She took her eyes off him. Pointless trying to listen to the part of her personality that demanded she stay frosty. Jamie Knight was a lot yummy. She'd seen thousands of glamorous, handsome men in her job, although she didn't date models. A rule. She didn't date at all, really. Well, now and then. More then than now. And of course, she wasn't even considering a date with Excavator-man. Her thoughts were simply a comparison of what she was used to and what she faced.

She took a deep Zen breath. She wasn't in the country to ponder the lack of gentleman escorts in her life. She was in the country to make The Decision.

'It's a lovely house,' she said, a slice of envy carving a space inside her because she wouldn't be enjoying it in solitude. Wouldn't be enjoying it at all. She'd have to leave. Go back to Sydney where she'd be plagued with business. Gone were her chances of peace while she contemplated which way to murder *you know who* and get away with it. There'd be no running from business or *him* now. It was Christmas. All the cute country holiday lets in New South Wales would be fully booked. She'd wanted twelve days. She had eleven, after tonight. She didn't stand a chance of finding somewhere to nurture her solitude. 'I take it you're an ace builder as well as a stonemason.' He must be the one building that dry-stone wall.

He smiled. 'You sound peeved about that.'

There was something comforting about the ever-present slight crease of a frown between his eyebrows. As though he'd always be on the lookout, always be alert and prepared to rescue, or have a concise answer to a problem.

'This was supposed to be my hideaway house, remember?' she told him.

'What are you hiding from?'

'Business,' she said, not about to go into details. 'I run a fashion house in Sydney.'

'That explains the skyscraper heels and the elegant attire, then.'

Was he being suggestive or rude? Difficult to tell. He just looked comfy. Big and comfy. And secure.

Jamie let her study him. She'd be more than peeved about the accommodation problem, she'd be wary about staying here with him. He might have helped her out of a muddy paddock, but one small rescue didn't constitute safety. What was it about this city woman that made him feel sorry for her or compassionate or something?

The last thing he needed was a damsel in distress. He'd spent the previous four years worrying about another damsel and he doubted his nerves would hold out on another. Especially one who appeared to be in an emotional flap. Maybe she was just tired and a little frustrated. She certainly hadn't known the house was his.

What the hell was going on? Why had Sammy arranged for her friend to stay at Silver Bells House?

'I'm afraid there's not much to eat,' he said, dropping the bag of potatoes he'd taken out of the pantry onto the bench top. 'Grocery shopping is overdue.'

'That's alright, I'm not hungry.'

He turned to look at her as she ripped at the lid on the box of her wine. Slim build. Slim. Not *thin*. Not ultra-thin. He noticed these things. He had reason to note collarbones and elbows and wrist circumferences. She had a whippet-slim waist which enhanced her hips, making her look like she had some. Yet Kate had curves too. He'd felt them when she'd been pressed over his shoulder. She didn't look like a wire coathanger fashion guru in some magazine. Well, maybe the softly padded variety.

'I'll cook us some baked potatoes. Cheese and chives topping okay with you? I've got some lettuce and a couple of tomatoes too.' He closed his eyes briefly and turned from her, a little irked he'd settled into coercion mode so fast. It wasn't anything to do with him if she didn't want to eat.

'I just want a glass of wine,' she said, struggling to open the cardboard box.

'It'll be warm,' he said, picking up a kitchen knife and walking over to her.

She shot back when she saw the knife. Jamie slit the cardboard on the box, took a bottle out and put the knife down onto the kitchen bench at a range where she was closest to it, not him. 'I'll put this in the fridge,' he said, holding her bottle of Chardonnay up. 'I've got a good Shiraz if you'd like a glass of that.'

He slid her Chardonnay into the near-empty fridge. *Must do shopping tomorrow.* Especially now he had a guest. He pulled a bottle from the wine rack he'd built into the recess above the bench top. He'd spent every evening and weekend of the last four weeks, since the sale had settled, sanding, remodelling the bathroom and the kitchen, knocking down the dining room wall and doing a spot of repointing and painting. Nothing else to do in the evenings or at the weekends, and he wasn't the sort who liked having nothing to do. Neither was he the sort to have bought the house on some Goddamn whim. But he had. He was still trying to come to terms with why.

Now he wished he'd done up one of the spare bedrooms upstairs. Where was he going to put her? He'd taken the master bedroom for himself and had stripped the other two bedrooms. They were four walls. No furniture. She'd have to take his bedroom. He'd sleep in the small spare room. The only other room that had a bed.

She had her hand around the cap on the bottle of Shiraz he'd handed her, her face angled away and her features telling him she was concentrating hard, but not on the wine.

Everything about her was all shades of chestnut — apart from her blue eyes. Her hair, her eyebrows, even her eyelashes. But he had a feeling most of the make-up, the dress and the shoes were for show. Like a candy bar. Peel off the snazzy wrapper and what would you find? Nougat; sugar and honey with the odd hazelnut thrown in for bite and flavour. He had an inkling most people in her executive world wouldn't look for the softer side of her. Why was he seeing it then? Because of Megan, probably.

She'd styled her chestnut-coloured hair into what he thought of as a ponytail with glamour. She'd secured the ponytail, somehow, with her own hair. Her long fringe swept across her brow in a dramatic way, concealing one eyebrow and almost touching her eyelashes but — again, somehow — it looked smart and casual all at once. The fringe part flopped forwards and the executive ponytail swung around her shoulder.

He walked over to her and took the bottle off her. 'Look,' he said, twisting the cap in the palm of his hand and cracking the seal. 'We can figure things out in the morning, so why don't you calm down?'

He wanted to put his hands on her shoulders and anchor her. He'd like to run a hand over the top of her head too, and smooth her ponytail in his fist, right down to the tip at her shoulder blades, to check if it was as soft as it looked.

Instead, he turned and took two wine glasses out of a cupboard beneath the island bench. The glass rang with a dull tinkle as he put the stems onto the bench.

He poured wine into one glass then paused as she moved. He looked across at her as she picked up a house renovation magazine from a stack on the dining room table and flicked through the pages.

She put the magazine down and ran her fingers through her fringe, eyes downcast, as though ironing out her thoughts. Or strumming through her worries.

Jamie went back to the wine, poured one for himself.

'What am I going to do tomorrow?' she asked. 'I've got to get the hire car out of a paddock and that might take all day to arrange. Then what do I do? Get the evening bus out of here?'

'Well obviously, it's going to take a couple of days. So stay a couple of nights.' He walked around the island bench and handed her a glass.

She sighed softly as she took it, with what was obviously an unwilling acceptance of her situation. 'I don't have much choice.'

She peeked up at him. Stunning eyes. Almond-shaped dark-blue boats, framed with long brown lashes. Her pale-skinned face looked more theatrical because of the blue-toned eye make-up and the rose-coloured lipstick.

'Although I tell you now,' she said, glass of Shiraz aimed in warning. 'One weirdo move, one miniscule sexual innuendo and I'll be picking up that nail gun over there and zapping you in your Bojangles.'

Jamie's grin almost hurt his cheeks. 'Bojangles?' he asked. 'Isn't that a song?' He wandered back to the bench where he'd gathered the makings for their impromptu evening meal, and sipped his wine. 'And before you get any nicer than you already are, I'd like to talk to Sammy about a couple of things too. But since we can't do that until tomorrow, why don't you drink your wine and settle down?'

Jamie put the two plates of microwaved baked potatoes onto the dining room table next to the bowl of salad he'd prepared. He'd filled the potatoes with the cheese, chopped chives and put a dollop of sour cream on top.

He sat opposite Kate, and picked up his knife and fork. 'Eat,' he told her, pointing to her plate with the tip of his knife.

'Not hungry.'

He studied her while she studied her glass of wine. *Please eat*, he wanted to say. He shook his head. It wasn't his place to worry, and he didn't want to have to worry.

His eyes burned, even now, when he thought about Megan and what she'd gone through.

'So how come you're taking time off from your fashion business and holing yourself up in the country?' he asked.

'That, Mr Master Builder, is none of your business.'

Dead right. And if it wasn't for the discomfort still veiling her eyes Jamie shouldn't have cared less. Shouldn't, but did.

'What's the name of your business?' Maybe some general conversation would calm her down.

'Singleton's Sassy Sensations.'

Jamie couldn't help his roar of laughter that sounded like a crack of thunder, even to his own ears.

She looked instantly affronted, her brows drawn and her rosy mouth crimped. 'It's not funny. It's my business. And I'll have you know it's a successful business due to my brains.'

'And sass?' he asked. 'How much of the sassy part of you can I expect to see while you're here?'

'You might be a master but let me tell you right now, I'm a mistress.'

Her dark blue eyes shone dusky and dangerous and Jamie had a sudden vision of the mistress side of her. Wearing a corset and killer heels. A white corset, with a couple of neat white bows down the front — and maybe a pair of bold, red, four-inch man-killers on her feet.

'I am sassy,' she told him. 'And Singleton's young designers are sensational. Hence the business name.' She picked up her wine and sipped. 'I mean, you called your business *Knight* Works. I doubt that means you work at night.'

'Not if I can help it.' Except for on his own property. This property. The one he'd bought on a whim. And why the hell was he contemplating that all over again? Hadn't he decided it was just one of those things?

'Do you think my Chardonnay will be cold by now?' she asked. 'Your Shiraz is good and all that, but I don't usually drink red.' She picked up her knife and fork, cut into the potato and raised a piece to her mouth. 'Not that I'm a creature of habit,' she told him after swallowing, and, Jamie was pleased to see, slicing off another piece of cheesy potato. 'So don't start making remarks about any contrariness you might think I possess. Because I don't.'

Katie, Katie quite contrary,
How does your garden grow?
With silver bells and cockleshells…

And a temperament he was going to have to watch out for.

'I hope you didn't poison my baked potato,' she said as she raised a third forkful. 'Because it's really rather delicious.'

For no particular reason he could think of, apart from maybe compassion for the city woman lost in the country, Jamie started liking Katie Singleton.

'If you'd like to, Contrary-Katie, you can stay the whole twelve days.'

She paused, fork halfway to her mouth, and stared at him.

Jamie's heartbeat pummelled his ribcage. Where the hell had those words come from? *Take it easy, pal.* He hadn't cooked his goose yet, he'd simply made her an offer. One she'd probably refuse.

'Pass the salt, would you?'

'Right. This is the bedroom.' Jamie opened his bedroom door. 'You can have it. I'll sleep in the spare room.'

'Where's the spare room?' she asked, turning full circle on the upstairs landing.

'Behind you.'

'I'll take it.' Her heels clacked on the wooden floorboards and Jamie winced. Good job they were hardwood jarrah. The weight of her discontent would put serious dents into pine.

He let her open the door to the spare room and watched as she gasped. It was small, no more than a store room and it was also currently stacked with the boxes and crates he'd carted from the family home in Sydney but hadn't yet got around to unpacking.

'Right,' she said. 'Lovely.'

'You can have my room.'

'No thanks. This will do.'

She hadn't responded to his offer to stay the whole twelve days with more than a pause and a stare. Jamie hadn't known why he'd suggested it in the first place, apart from the compassion that seemed to have stuck to his innards like a fast-hardening bonding glue. He hadn't reiterated the offer because he wasn't one hundred per cent sure why he'd presented her with the notion in the first place. Not even twenty per cent sure.

'Is there a bathroom?' she asked.

'Already renovated, you'll be glad to hear. Hot water, the works.' As long as she didn't take up all the bathroom time with five-hour-long bubble baths. Not that he stocked bubbles, but he'd bet the right front tyre on the fourteen-tonner she had some in her luggage.

'It's the only bathroom?'

''Fraid so.'

She seemed a little deflated by this.

Jamie turned for the hall linen cupboard, opened it and pulled out a couple of sheets, a thin coverlet and a pillow. 'I'll nip in and shower now, while you unpack and make up your bed. Then the bathroom's all yours. Here.' He handed her the bed linen.

She put her carry-on down just inside the door of the spare room and took the linen off him. 'Thank you.'

'You're welcome.' Given the misery on her face and the tiredness in her eyes, it looked like she'd be catching the first bus out of Swallow's Fall tomorrow morning after all. No doubt leaving the locals to deal with the mess she'd left alongside her hire car. 'We'll make better arrangements tomorrow. Make things more comfortable for you. I'll shift those boxes.'

'No need.' She stepped into the room and looked back at him, over her shoulder. 'Thank you,' she said quietly. 'You have actually been very... You know — helpful.'

'Goodnight, Kate.' He almost said 'sleep tight' until he remembered he still needed to nip downstairs and lock up that nail gun.

Jamie sat on his king-size bed, forearms on his thighs, hands hanging. What was he doing? People had helped and coerced Megan, whether she'd wanted it or not. One thing Jamie recognised was the insistent, independent quality some women had. Megan had it. And Kate Singleton had it. By the fourteen-ton bucketful.

He stood, left the bedroom, walked across the hall and knocked on her door.

'Yes?'

'Can I open the door?' he asked.

'Um...'

He heard scrambling noises. Boxes being shifted, the scrape of a chair. Her suitcase being wheeled across the wooden floorboards. Was she trying to barricade herself in? 'There's no lock on the door, Katie,' he called. 'I can walk in any time. If I was going to do you in with my sledgehammer, I'd have done it by now.'

The door wrenched open. 'If you wish to call me something other than Kate, please call me Katherine.'

She wore navy-blue pyjamas with white bunny rabbits on them. Shorts and a short-sleeved jacket style top. Didn't quite match the starch in her voice. Jamie's mouth curled in a smile. He looked down at her feet, half expecting the man-killers, but she was barefooted.

Her toenails were painted the same pink colour as her fingernails. Same colour as the lipstick she'd worn.

'Maybe I'll call you Sweet-Katie.' He grinned. Her face looked fresh and dewy, as though she'd just woken up. No make-up. She'd let her hair down too. 'Or Katie-pie. Maybe Sugar-Katie.'

She pursed her mouth and Jamie tasted lemon.

'Please leave my bedroom.'

'Sorry,' he said. 'No can do.' He hooked a thumb, indicating she get out of the spare room. 'I'll take this. You're having my bed.'

Chapter Four

Kate woke with the sun warming her cheeks. She hadn't closed the curtains on the windows in the bedroom last night because she'd loved the face of the moon shining in on her as she closed her eyes and prayed for sleep. Amazingly, she had slept. For eight hours by the look of her travel alarm clock sitting on Jamie's bedside table.

She lifted herself to sit, propping herself up on the mattress with her hands behind her. The sheets smelled clean, but she'd fallen asleep with a slightly tantalising aroma of Jamie Knight. Stone walls, summer-dry fields and a surprising hint of lime. Not the mortar kind, the aftershave kind.

She pushed the covers back and stood, stretching her arms up to the ceiling, lifting her head and waking her body. *Nice* ceiling. More beams. In need of a touch up though, the grey-blue paint flaking here and there.

She checked out the rest of the room in the morning light. Large. At the front of the house. The navy-checked curtains on the four little square windows tucked neatly behind iron holdbacks. The walls were plastered and painted antique white, as was most of the house. A feature wall wouldn't go amiss here and there. The wall behind the king-size bed would give the large room a stately feel if it was painted a darker blue-grey.

She wandered to one of the windows and took a look at the driveway. Both the excavator and the Knight Works ute were parked. He hadn't gone to work yet.

She grabbed her lavender-coloured summer-light dressing gown, her toiletry bag, and headed for the bathroom. Last night she'd done nothing more than take her make-up off and freshen up a bit. This morning, she wanted more.

Water, hot and gushing from a powerful top mounted showerhead above, drowned her in pleasure. What a shower. Big enough for three. Big enough for Jamie to slosh all the stone dust and mortar and excavator grease from his six-foot-three body.

Stop that right now, Kate Singleton.

Oh alright. One more thought. All six wall-mounted jet sprays directed at his upper body, pulsating vigorously over those squeaky clean muscles.

Okay. Stop it.

She turned the shower off and stepped out of the large, damask-coloured tiled recess onto a dark-brown bath mat. Kate would change that for white. She'd have white towels and hand cloths stacked on the beechwood shelves. Maybe interspersed with treacle-coloured towels.

She combed through her hair in one of the mirrors above the double vanity. A His and Hers. Who would Mr Knight choose to share his bathroom? Funny he wasn't married already. A good-looking guy, a successful business, a brilliant handyman on tap. There were women in the world who'd missed out. Kate wondered what Jamie had done wrong, until she remembered she wasn't married either. And she hadn't done anything wrong, had she?

The Decision. *Dang.* She'd been so busy imagining Jamie Knight soaped up in his shower, she'd forgotten about The Decision. And if she wanted to get her life in order before she turned thirty, she only had a few days to do so.

This was day two of her twelve-day sojourn. So from which angle was she going to approach the problem? Holy heck, she still had no idea. And was she going to stay at Silver Bells House until she turned thirty?

Kate knew the best way to enter a room was to breeze in with a smile as though you owned it. Sadly, she didn't own Silver Bells House but she swept into the kitchen as though she did anyway. Couldn't quite drum up the smile due to the nerves tickling her insides.

He was at the bench, scraping butter on toast and looking scrubbed and sexy. And it wasn't only his looks that tickled the nerves in Kate's stomach. It was his quiet, Superman strength. The internal kind. Confidence, discreet but effortless. Intimate even. *Wonder what would make him lose his cool?* There had to be a forceful, gritty side to a man that big and that wide.

'Good morning,' he said as he looked up at her. His eyes widened for a second then he rotated a shoulder and looked away. 'Sleep well?'

'Probably better than you did,' she said, tightening the belt on her dressing gown and wondering if perhaps he'd have preferred she was dressed. At weekends or on holidays, she rose early but never got dressed until late morning, working from home in her pyjamas or her dressing gown. 'That's one comfortable king-sized bed you have.'

'Isn't it?' When he looked up this time, his features were impassive. 'Breakfast?'

'Toast would be great. Thank you.' Kate took a seat at the table, ensuring her dressing gown was safely wrapped around her legs.

The aroma of fried temptation wafted throughout the kitchen. Bacon.

'Help yourself to coffee.' He nodded at the pot on the table. 'There's tea, if you prefer.'

'Coffee's perfect.' She poured from the percolator into a china cup and added a dash of milk from a china jug. Holy galoshes. A man who set the table. 'Aren't you going to work today?' she asked him. 'Please don't worry about me. I'll get myself organised. And I promise not to steal anything from your house.'

'Thought I'd go to the homestead later. Wanted to make sure you were okay with your plans.'

'Plans?' she said with a derogatory huff at herself and her situation. 'I'm full of them.' All spontaneous and none of them currently working.

He put a plate of toast in front of her. Three slices. Did he expect her to eat all that?

'Like what?' he asked as he took a seat opposite her with his plate of bacon. And two eggs. Fried. And toast. Four slices. Superman needed sustenance, obviously.

'I have a monumental decision to make which I'm dithering about,' she told him and immediately wondered how she could have fallen into the trap of truthfulness with him. This must be a new side of her. She normally kept her plans to herself until ready to fling them at her world when they were in meticulous order. Maybe Jamie lived up to his surname. A modern day knight. He'd been particularly careful to ensure she wasn't scared of him last night. Again, all that comfortable kindness with a dash of firm masculinity. 'I'm going to test-run a few things to take me out of my usual modus operandi and see what happens.'

'Like what?'

'Like not dieting.' She cut a square of toast in half, pulled an opened jar of jam towards her and slathered jam over one piece. 'Watch this.' She bit into it and closed her eyes, squishing her shoulders up to her ears as the deliciousness of the blueberry jam and the hot dripping butter spread throughout her. 'Yum,' she said after she'd finished it. She pushed the plate away and picked up her coffee.

'One half slice of toast is not dieting?'

'You betcha. Did you see how much jam I put onto that?'

She took a surreptitious look at Jamie's breakfast plate. Her stomach rumbled. Maybe tomorrow morning she'd have bacon too. One rasher, slapped between two slices of buttery toast. If she was here tomorrow morning.

Her mobile rang. Kate plucked it from the pocket of her dressing gown and checked the caller ID. 'Oh, darn.' Work. Not *you know who* but his assistant. She answered the call.

'Kate Singleton, Singleton's Sassy Sensations.' She listened as conceited Sarah — pronounced Sahra — informed her they'd received her message yesterday about not coming back to the office and how shocked they were and had she changed her mind because work was piling up. Ms Up-Herself Sahra probably needed murdering too. She was undoubtedly in on *you know who*'s underhand doings. The personification of a young manager who thought she had more skills than she'd ever possess. 'Well, you're going to have to rattle the office cage without me,' Kate said, cutting Sahra off in the middle of her tirade about timesheets and invoices and errant designers not turning up on time for shoots. 'That's right. Uh-huh. Golly, shall I repeat myself? I said I'm not coming back until after the holiday season.' She punched End Call and put the phone down.

'What's going on?' Jamie asked.

'Nothing.' That she wanted to discuss.

'So you're not going back to the city?'

'Don't know yet, I just said that to keep them guessing.' And hopefully choking on the influx of telephone messages and emails piling up. Perhaps tempers would get so hot the office would ignite and annihilate Sahra and *you know who* in one roaring backdraft. Then Kate wouldn't have to make The Decision and could walk away with half of the insurance money. 'Well,' Kate stood. 'Excuse me. Think I should be able to get hold of Sammy by now.' She pushed her chair under the table, picked up her mobile phone and walked into the hall.

She hit the selected speed dial and stood at the far end of the hall, next to what she presumed was the back door. It had little paned windows on the top half and gave Kate an excellent view of the gardens behind the house. She tapped the phone with her index finger as she listened to it ring, and ring and ring. Lovely garden. A whole paddock. Wouldn't get that with a Federation bungalow in Sydney.

At last Sammy answered.

'Okay, girlfriend — what's going on?' Kate asked.

'Hi, Kate. How are you?'

'I'm stuck in the country with an excavator-driving stonemason. I bogged my hire car. I don't have that cute cottage all to myself. You remember? The one you said I was living in for twelve days. Instead, I'm stuck, Sammy. *Stuck.*'

'Oh heck. I totally forgot. How dumb.'

'Five miles high dumb, Samantha. That's how dumb.' Forgot? *How could she forget?*

'Where are you now?' Sammy said in a tone suggesting she was smiling.

'I'm in Silver Bells House.'

'It's gorgeous, isn't it? Do you like the stonework inside?'

'Oh, I love it. Peachy.' Kate paused. 'Was that a giggle?'

'Now calm down, Kate. Let's figure this out. What did Jamie say?'

'He said I could stay a few nights until I get organised to get out. And then he said I could stay the whole holiday, if I really wanted to.'

'Oh, did he now?'

'Don't go reading anything into that. He's got the charm of a bulldozer.' Not true, but she had to arm herself with something derogatory about him. He'd looked a lot yummier last night than her nearly thirty-year-old body had been happy about. She'd expected him to be fully dressed when she opened the spare room door. Instead, he'd looked like a freshly showered, virile machine. Bare-chested. Barefooted and bewitching. If she'd been able to take a photograph of him standing there in nothing but his tanned, stonemason's muscly skin and his clean khaki trousers she'd have brought khaki out of the work-wear world and into the glittering arena of top fashion houses. 'I daren't stay,' she said. In case she found herself unable to take her eyes off him. In case all that comforting protection stuff he possessed got to her and she forgot the reason she'd come to the country. To make The Decision.

'Why not? You'll hardly see him.'

'Because... Because...' Kate leaned her forehead against a glass pane in the back door and stared out at the garden. 'Am I safe?' she asked quietly.

'From Jamie? Are you mad? He's the most reliable man I've met — apart from Ethan.'

She hadn't meant it that way. After her riotous thoughts in the shower about how he'd soap the dirt off his body she'd wondered if perhaps Jamie Knight might be unsafe from the clutches of Kate. 'What's his story?' she asked.

'Haven't got a clue what his whole story is.' Sammy paused. 'But…'

'Yes?'

'I think he's the retiring, reluctant type — and he's shy.'

Kate considered this. Shy? At six foot three and built like a brick outhouse? 'Why?' she asked.

'Not my place to say.'

Kate nodded, her mouth tugging to one side. 'Woman trouble?' she asked, keeping her voice low. Had he been hurt in love? Maybe some woman had wounded him and he'd buried his poor stonemason's soul in the country. In what should have been *her* holiday house.

Kate pulled a face. Jamie's scenario wasn't too far from her own. Lost and lonely, looking for…well, not love but some other word beginning with L if the alliteration in the sentence was going to work. If she did stay, perhaps she could help him. Ease him out of his misery. Be a good house guest and cheer him up. It would be something to do. He had been big-and-burly helpful, apart from the initial peeved tone, which she now understood the reason for. Woman trouble.

What kind of female troubled Jamie Knight? The petite bouncy blonde? The Jessica Rabbit redhead? Or the executive brunette?

Kate squeezed her eyes shut. She hadn't meant herself. Yes, she was a brunette and she happened to be an executive but she hadn't meant herself. No way, José.

'Promise me you won't go digging for whatever it was that hurt him,' Sammy said. 'Be jolly and happy around him. Don't push and don't ask him personal questions.'

Was Sammy out of her mind? One of Kate's best skill sets was figuring out what made people tick. She ran a fashion house, for

God's sake. Human beings ticked differently and in the fashion world you met all types of beings. Not always human. 'Alright,' she said to Sammy. 'I'm feeling safer.' About not ogling Mr Knight too much, and about being brave enough to concentrate solely on The Decision.

'You've got nothing to worry about,' Sammy said. 'You probably won't even see him. He'll be out early morning and back late afternoon.'

'I think I might stay then.' Because where else was she going to go to get away from it all? She'd have to wait at least two more days due to the damage on her hire car anyway. Or get the bus into the next big town with hire car prospects. Talk about stuck.

'Okay,' Sammy said. 'Your choice — but don't forget that shooting star. It was magic. Magic happens when shooting stars appear, Kate. Don't forget the star.'

Kate had forgotten about the shooting star. It had appeared in the night sky in New York and she'd made a wish. She'd also forgotten that she'd told her best friend about the star — and the wish.

'You're a fine one, telling me what not to forget, Samantha Granger. You've forgotten that you're the one who *forgot* to tell me I'd have nowhere to stay for my magical twelve-day holiday.'

Jamie looked up as his house guest walked back into the kitchen. 'Did you get hold of Sammy?'

'Yes.'

'And?'

'And… I do need to stay for a few days. I'll call the hire car company now and ask them what they want to do. I suppose they'll send a tow truck down.'

'That'll probably take forty-eight hours. I don't want to leave the car where it is though, so I'll go this morning and take photos of everything, for the insurance, then tow the car out of the paddock. It'll be safe on the side of the road.'

'I ought to buy a new gate too,' she said, and flicked through the screens on her mobile phone, as though searching for the nearest shop to buy one.

Jamie smiled, although she wasn't looking at him. He'd got the fright of his life when she'd walked in for breakfast earlier, wearing a dressing gown that ought to be termed a morning ball gown. She wore it still. An ankle-length silky lavender-coloured dressing gown. She sat on the arm of the Chesterfield sofa by the fireplace. The gown slipped open revealing a smooth pale-skinned portion of her thigh and Jamie's brain scrambled.

What day was this? What was his name?

He blinked a few times, attempting to sooth the heat in his eyes. 'I'll clear up the broken gate and fix up some wire fencing for the moment,' he said, concentrating on physical activities he could engage in with— No, dammit. Not physical as in…not with… Oh hell, who was he kidding? The woman didn't knock his socks off, she ripped them off.

'You can discuss paying for a new gate when Sammy and Ethan get home.'

'Right,' she said. 'All sorted then.'

Jamie raised his brow. 'You're staying?'

She looked up from beneath her long chestnut lashes. 'If you're sure it's okay.' She smiled, and all that honey nougat caramelised his brain all over again.

It should be okay. It really should. But she hadn't said for how long he'd be in the oven, getting cooked. Two days or the whole holiday?

Her mobile phone rang. 'Oh, darn.'

The morning ball gown slipped open as she uncrossed her legs. Looked like she had long legs. Nice thighs. Soft skin. Hell. *What was his name?*

'"Oh darn"?' he said, as moisture returned to his mouth.

'Country vernacular for "oh shit".'

'So why not say "oh shit"?'

Jamie didn't get an answer. She pressed a button on her phone. 'Kate Singleton, Singleton's Sassy Sensations.'

Jamie smothered a smile. Good job she didn't have a lisp.

'Don't know,' she said. 'Mm-mm. Uh-huh. Really no idea. You'll have to figure it out for yourself.' She ended the call by snapping a pink-nailed finger on the End Call button, and slid the phone back into the silk pocket of the gown that made Jamie feel… Pretty much peeled, sliced and roasted.

'You get a lot of calls,' he said. 'You don't want to take them?'

'You're darn tootin' I don't.'

'Business?'

'Yup.'

'Well, talking of business, I need to make a call. Excuse me.'

'Okay. I'll wash up. Since you cooked.'

She floated across the kitchen, dressing gown flowing between her legs.

Jamie left the room, eye sockets stinging.

He walked to the end of the hallway to the back door, opened it, stepped outside into the already warm morning air and punched in the speed dial for Sammy's number. She answered it within one ring.

'Hi, Jamie.'

'Hi, Sammy.'

'How's it going? What's new your end?'

'Um. Well…'

'Those ditches aren't giving you trouble, are they? Don't tell me there'll be no water or electricity for Christmas.'

'No, no. Everything's going to plan. All on time.'

'Great. So...what do you need?'

Oh, come on. What game was Sammy playing here? 'Well, I'm sort of wondering about your friend Kate.'

'Oh that! Of course. I'm really sorry about the mix-up. My fault, Jamie. I don't know how it happened — although, truthfully, it would have been hard for her to have to spend this time back in the city.'

'Really?' Like — why? What problems *did* she have with her business?

'Actually, Jamie — can I speak to you in confidence?'

Jamie hoped like hell this confidence wasn't going to involve woman-stuff. Like broken hearts and two-timing boyfriends.

'Alright,' he said deliberately slowly. Might as well learn what sort of nail gun wielding, morning ball gown–wearing woman he was giving his bed to.

'Kate has a problem.'

'Oh?' Reluctance to hear the answer crawled up the back of his neck. Sammy wasn't going to ask him to take care of the problem, was she? Sammy wasn't going to ask him to do things for Kate, was she? Like befriend her. If he got that close he'd be toast.

'She's shy.'

Jamie thought about this for a few seconds. Kate Singleton, city woman with skyscraper heels was shy? He had to admit his interest piqued. 'Doesn't seem that way.'

'Oh, she'd never let you know. I bet she's showing you her gregarious side.'

'Don't know about gregarious, but she's...' Offbeat. Trying too hard. A little desperate around the edges. All that *golly galoshes* talk.

'Thanks for saying she could stay, Jamie. It would be fantastic if you were able to get her to open up.'

Jamie straightened. Open up to what? The woman didn't stop talking. But Sammy must mean the problem Kate was facing. 'She hasn't said she'll stay the entire time.'

'I don't suppose you'd try and persuade her?' Sammy asked. 'Maybe until the power's back on at the homestead? Then she can move in there if you're uneasy having her around.'

Oh, uneasy had him by the scruff of his neck. Not to mention his Bojangles. 'Power'll be off for another five days.'

'Oh…of course. I forgot.' Sammy sounded deflated.

Jamie sighed. 'Okay,' he said. 'I'll see if I can persuade her to stay.' If she really wanted to.

'Thank you, Jamie, thank you! You're a star.'

The immediate vision in his head was the tail end of a bright light he'd seen in the night sky ten weeks ago as he'd dithered with an unexplained urge to buy Silver Bells House and settle into Swallow's Fall. He was a journeyman builder. He was supposed to journey. He had an apartment in Sydney which had hardly been used over the last two years, as he travelled the sunburnt country rescuing stone houses from disrepair and assisting in heritage works. He wasn't supposed to buy a house and settle down for at least another decade. Thirty-three-year-old men had a lot of single-life left in them. But this thirty-three-year-old man must have gone soft in the head. He'd bought Silver Bells House on a whim. On the tail end of a shooting star. Madness.

He shook his head as he disconnected the call to Sammy. If Katie stayed and this was day two, he had ten to go. Somehow, he didn't think he was going to make it through without something major happening. He only hoped this major event didn't involve a heart attack and the emergency services.

Chapter Five

Nothing to do. Nothing to do. *Nothing to do.*

Kate roamed the house, folding her arms as she studied Jamie's chosen artwork, most of it impressionist with auras of restfulness which suited the languid, French feeling of his house. Unfolding her arms, she wandered from the living room to the hall and into the open-plan kitchen-dining room. She plumped the cushions on the big deep-brown leather Chesterfield sofa. The colour of Jamie's eyes.

The beechwood shelving and the mellow-yellow stone created a haven, she decided. Somewhat masculine but not male enough to deter a woman from wanting to throw herself on the Chesterfield and fall asleep.

She'd slept most of yesterday and missed an entire day. When had she ever been this tired? Maybe she needed fresh air. And she had no intention of staying indoors while outdoors summer beckoned in such a spectacular manner. She still had no car and Jamie had been at work all day yesterday, and today, so no lift. She'd walk into town then.

She'd moved her luggage into the main bedroom and set her rose-bud wellies next to a wooden chest of drawers. If all this furniture was Jamie's, he'd either had unexpected good fortune when buying the house, because it slotted in beautifully with the architecture, or he'd bought the house, furniture and all. Must remember to ask him.

She unzipped her large suitcase and plucked out her designer denim shorts in bloodshot red and a white capped-sleeved top. She'd been given heaps of next summer's clothing range by the shoot guys in New York. Just as well, or she'd have been sweating in angora and fleece for the next eight days.

Oh, darn. No socks. Kate sighed and glanced at the chest of drawers. Jamie would have socks. Surely he wouldn't mind if she borrowed a pair to wear with her wellies? She opened one of the top drawers. There they were. She pulled a rolled pair apart. 'Holy bulldozer.' Size thirteen thickened wool. Workman's socks. Well, they wouldn't be seen once she had her wellies on.

While she changed and put on the socks and wellies, her mind waged war. Should she take a peek in his wardrobe? In the other drawers in the chest? In the bedside tables? No, of course she shouldn't. But her mind's counsel did nothing to appease her curiosity. It would be rude to search through his possessions. However, she did need a hat and maybe Jamie had a baseball cap somewhere. Like on the top shelf of the wardrobe. No. Just boxes and folded jumpers. Maybe he'd tucked a hat in his bedside drawer.

As she pulled at the drawer, she knew she wasn't looking for a hat, but hey, the handle was in her fingers, and hey — the drawer was open. Her heartbeat pounded as she rifled through pens and notepads filled with notes about equipment and mathematical calculations. He must work at all hours. He had a huge chalkboard in the kitchen, and that too was peppered with lists about metal fixings and epoxy resins.

Her fingertips rested on a photograph frame. Plain silver, usual plywood backing and flip-out support. Upside down though, so she couldn't see the picture of who or what was in the frame. She tapped it. This *was* rude. Downright intrusive. She should leave it. She shouldn't be looking in his bedside drawer in the first place.

She pulled the photo frame out and turned it over.

Her heart danced with a surprisingly resentful tempo. She took a breath, swallowed the unease about her nosiness and gave herself a moment to adjust to the funny nausea inside her which had now reached her stomach. Jealousy. Because Jamie had a photo of a beautiful young woman in his bedside drawer?

She ran her finger over the edge of the frame. No dust. Perhaps he'd put the photo into the drawer before offering her his bedroom last night. Or maybe he kept the photo in his bedside drawer so as not to be hurt by looking at it every night. Maybe he took it out and gazed at it just before he went to sleep. Maybe he spoke to the brunette beauty in the photo, telling her about his day and what he'd done.

She put the frame back into the drawer; carefully. Concealing it as best she could with the notepads and pens, making it look like it hadn't been disturbed.

If the lady in the photo was the one who'd broken his heart, his heart must hurt like hell. Younger than Jamie though. A good ten or twelve years younger, Kate guessed. But oh, so beautiful. Wind blowing her long brown hair, dark-brown eyes smiling, and a flush of pleasure on her cheeks.

Darn. Kate didn't do jealous. Kate had no need of jealous. No, siree. But as she wandered back downstairs, still hatless, her mind burned to know more about the woman Jamie kept a secret in his bedside table. Perhaps she only came to life in his dreams.

She opened the cupboard under the stairs. A coat closet. Gnarled walking sticks, a couple of golf umbrellas and an array of hats. The baseball cap too big and with no way of tightening it. The purple beanie a definite no in a heatwave. The straw hat then. She plucked it off a peg and shook the dust off the crown and the large brim. She'd slathered herself in sunscreen, force of habit, but certainly didn't want to burn her face. It might be an hour's walk into town.

She stuffed the hat on her head and checked her reflection in a mirror on the inside of the cloakroom door. She decided she looked different and perhaps a bit eccentric, but if she didn't want to burn she'd have to wear the dang thing. Her fingers itched to yank off the two fake white daisies but it wasn't her hat to improve. Anyway, this was the country. She'd probably just blend in.

The land either side of All Seasons Road wasn't too parched yet, but it was dry. Like Kate was beginning to feel. The sheep were resting in flocks, nibbling the green bits of grass still left, looking all cute and cuddly and in the shade. Unlike Kate.

Bad move with the wellies. For one, there wasn't any mud, the roads were bitumen. Two; Jamie's socks were too thick. They might also have melted and stuck to her feet which now felt like two bricks in an electric blanket.

At last, a crossroads. *Main Street*, the sign said. *Swallow's Fall 6k*. Six kilometres? She did the maths. Ten minutes to walk one kilometre. One hour to go. 'Holy bloody gumnuts.'

She took a slug from her water bottle, then trudged on.

Later, her heat-induced tiredness turned to anticipation as she rounded a bend and walked into the sanctuary of Swallow's Fall. The town seemed to spring open before her in a splash of welcoming calm. A cool, colourful array of late nineteenth and early twentieth century buildings lined the one-street town. The chosen colours for the half-dozen shops on the raised walkway along the right-hand side were mostly traditional Australian heritage. Yellows, greens, dove-greys, hints of red and a splash of pink at the northern end of town from the closed B&B. A sort of sad bumpiness settled in Kate's chest at the sight of the churned-up lawn and the broken railings on the veranda. What on earth had happened to the B&B?

She glanced up at the population sign hanging off a bracket on the historic and rather dilapidated Town Hall. Swallow's Fall, Population Eighty ~~Six~~ ~~Seven~~ Eight. Sammy had told her that she was number eighty-seven, Jamie must be eighty-eight. Kate pulled at the brim of her hat, shading her eyes in case someone suddenly pounced her from nowhere and made her honorary townsperson number eighty-nine. Swallow's Fall was too small for Kate. She was used to an expansive world. This little town was too isolated for her industrious mind. Cute and all that, with its never-changing atmosphere. But it wasn't for Kate. Should she decide to move to the country, there'd be other towns, close to the city. And if she moved to the country she'd have made The Decision to let *you know who* have it all.

Fat Jacques Burch. And she wasn't referring to his waistline. She meant fat as in greedy and petulant and downright nasty. Jumping jalopies, Jacques made her blood boil and her mind seethe.

Putting that scumbag to the back of her mind she stopped outside the petrol station and stared at a beautiful, pressed metal sign. A wonderful, welcomed and mouth-watering sign: *Ice Cream*. She nearly went down on bended knee in front of it to sing a halleluiah.

'Good heavens. You walked all that way?'

Kate swung to the only fuel bowser at the station and the lady standing next to it. She recognised the short, plump, smiling person with her hair piled high in a bun. Still-jet-black hair, even though she must be close to retirement age. Mrs Z? Mrs P? 'I've walked from Silver Bells House,' Kate said, throwing a hand behind her to indicate the excessive kilometres she'd journeyed by Wellington boots.

The lady, whose smile hadn't left her face, beckoned her inside the petrol station shop. 'Come on in, dear. You must be exhausted. What are you wearing wellies for?'

Don't ask.

Once inside the air-conditioned little shop — no more than a clean white room with a counter, a twirling rack of postcards and metal shelving full of all the expected mechanical oils, jump leads and car air fresheners — Kate's heated skin and dehydrated internal organs breathed a sigh of relief.

'Kate Singleton,' Kate said as way of introduction while the lady peered under the rim of Kate's straw hat. 'I'm Sammy's friend. I think I met you at the wedding.'

'I know. I remember you. Heard you were in town. Jamie's girlfriend, is it?'

Excuse me?

'Sammy and Ethan are away,' Mrs P or Z said. 'But you know that. Jamie's been at Silver Bells House for over two months now. Fancy you and Jamie being together. Did you walk?'

'Yes,' Kate replied to the last question, and, 'No,' to being Jamie's girlfriend. 'I'm not his girlfriend.' Sweet lady, but oh, so wrong about the situation. 'There was a bit of a misunderstanding. I came down to rent the cottage for Christmas, not realising it had been bought, then I bogged my car because of a flock of parrots, and Jamie got me out and there was nowhere else to go.'

'How kind of him. Such a gentleman. Were they gang gangs?' She held her hand out. 'Mrs Tam. And I meant the parrots.'

'Hello again,' Kate said, shaking Mrs Tam's little hand. 'Lovely to see you. Not sure what kind of parrots they were but there were thousands of them.' Slight exaggeration but this was the country. Anything could happen, and for all Kate knew, probably did.

'Fancy Sammy forgetting to tell you that Jamie bought the house.' Mrs Tam shook her head. 'Most unusual.'

Wasn't it? Kate had been thinking along the same lines during the last two hours' trudge into Sammy's township. *Have you been playing me, Samantha?*

'Can I buy an ice cream?'

'Of course, and no buying. It's on me. Can't have Jamie's girlfriend wilting from heat exhaustion. Homemade, you know. Which flavour?'

Kate followed Mrs Tam to the ice cream refrigerator. Rainbow colours of ice-cold ice cream made her forget about the girlfriend remark. 'Two scoops of raspberry-ripple please.' Pile it up. Bring it on.

'Oh, good choice.' Mrs Tam got her metal ice cream scoop out of a little bucket and lifted the lid on the freezer.

Kate inhaled the cold and welcomed the momentary freeze on her skin.

'People are like children, you know, when they choose their flavours.' Mrs Tam piled the ice cream into a waffle-wafer cone. 'I'm trying a new recipe actually. Strawberry-marshmallow. There you go.' She patted the top with the back of the ice cream scoop. 'I've got the strawberry, of course, but I'm having trouble blending the marshmallow flavour in.'

Kate licked the top scoop. 'I wish you luck with it, Mrs Tam. Sounds delicious and this is, honest to God, the best ice cream I've ever tasted. Anywhere. In the whole world.'

'Thank you, dear. Oh! Excuse me a moment.'

Kate followed Mrs Tam outside as a lone car pulled up for petrol. While Mrs Tam dealt with the petrol pump — personal service, the country was full of such delights — Kate took a good look down Main Street. So quiet. The poor little town didn't have much.

She nodded down the street towards the pioneer cemetery when Mrs Tam came to stand next to her. 'Where's the Christmas tree?' Kate felt sure they'd put the tree up there. Best place for it. It could be viewed from both entrances to town — or exits, depending on which way you'd entered.

Mrs Tam tutted. 'There's a bit of a to-do this year due to the newly formed town committee. Mr Penman, our grocer, has a condition.'

'For the committee?' Kate asked.

'Oh no, dear. Waterworks.'

'Plumbing problem in the shop?'

'He can't pee.'

Gee whiz, thanks for the explanation. 'Poor man,' Kate murmured. 'Was he supposed to chop the tree down and haul it into town?'

'Not at his age. Jamie's doing that. As soon as the feud's been settled.'

'What feud?'

'Mr Penman always plays Santa when we hand out the Christmas presents to the locals. But due to his condition, he can't sit for too long.' Mrs Tam patted the bun on top of her head. A big, black pie of a bun. 'Can't stand for too long, either, come to think of it.'

'Shouldn't he see a doctor?'

'Already has. Nothing they can do but let nature take its course.'

Kate didn't want to imagine how. It would totally ruin the flavour of raspberry-ripple in her mouth. 'So what's the feud about?' Sammy was forever giving her snippets of information about Swallow's Fall and its passions, its glories and its gossip mill.

'Ted Tillman,' Mrs Tam said. 'He runs the stock feeders' and he's our committee chairman. He wants to play Santa in Mr Penman's stead. But that means the costume will have to be let out quite considerably and Mrs Penman refuses to give it to Mrs Tillman.'

Kate stood under the shade of the petrol station's veranda and studied Main Street as Mrs Tam spoke. The claret ash trees lining the street were countrified gorgeous. Glossy green foliage glinting in the sunlight. They'd look beautiful at night, covered in sparkly white lights nestling against the darkened leaves, like cheeky, bright-eyed elves in a forest.

If you were in to that sort of thing.

'The families aren't talking,' Mrs Tam continued. 'Which means we haven't got the decorations up yet. What a to-do. Never known the like of it before.'

Kate didn't mind there being no decorations. She wasn't doing Christmas this year but it was a shame for the townspeople, not seeing Main Street draped in tinsel.

'I need to do some shopping,' she said, looking across the street. 'Does Mr Penman sell pretzels?' She wouldn't be able to carry much more on the long trek home. 'And sandals?'

'You can buy all modern conveniences in Swallow's Fall,' Mrs Tam informed her with a smile. 'So long as it wasn't created or produced after 1990.'

Kate grinned. Another great thing about the townspeople here. They didn't seem to have any misgivings about their lot. 'What happened to the B&B?' she asked.

'It was hit in a big storm we had just over a year ago. The Cappers haven't got the money to renovate yet.'

'What a shame.' A pretty little house. Out of date décor inside, but it had a warm feeling. Even Sammy's mother, the ferocious Verity Walker, seemed to calm down from her never-ending complaints when she stayed there.

'And what about the pub?' Kate asked, aiming her ice cream cone at Kookaburra's Bar & Grill across the street. It looked quiet. Dead. Lifeless. Closed. Thank God Jamie had rescued her Chardonnay.

'Shut for the moment. We've got a new owner though. A young man. He's been here for the handover, gone back to Queensland to collect his things and promised us the bar would be open by Christmas. He'll be resident number eighty-nine, you know.'

Oh good. That saved Kate from taking up the position.

'And there's Grandy,' Kate said, looking across to Morelly's Hardware store and the old man sitting on a bench out front. He was talking to a blonde teenager who had a pad or a sketchbook in her hand, and her foot on the tilted edge of a skateboard. Kate not only remembered Grandy, she felt she had the right to say she knew him. The grand old patriarch of Swallow's Fall. The man had more sense than most people gained in a lifetime. Kate had been truly interested in the letter Sammy had sent her, detailing Grandy's ninetieth birthday party and the ruckus of yet another feud about who was going to bake the cake and how many tiers it ought to have. If only Kate's business world had been filled with such funny, abstract problems, she might not be in the position she was in now.

'Why don't you go say hello, dear. He'll be pleased as Midas to see you.'

Kate put the paper wrapper from her now eaten ice cream into a rubbish bin. 'I will, thanks for the ice cream, Mrs Tam. I'll see you later.'

'Cheerio, dear.'

Kate wandered across the street. Mrs Tam had been spot on with her Midas analogy. From what Sammy had told her Grandy seemed to have the ability to turn folly into sensible gold.

'What's with the heat?' she asked Grandy as she trudged up the stairs to the wooden walkway which supported the shopping side of Main Street. The pub, the grocer's, Cuddly Bear Toy & Gift shop and Morelly's Hardware store. 'I thought the Snowies were supposed to be ten degrees lower in temperature than the rest of Australia.'

'Sun must have come out to welcome you,' Grandy said. He lifted his cane and pointed the end at her feet. 'Like your wellies.'

Kate noted Grandy wore trainers. As did the young girl standing at his shoulder. 'Hello,' Kate said, holding her hand out to the teenager.

'Hi. I'm Gemma Munroe. You're Jamie's girlfriend.'

'Oh, no.' Kate laughed the remark away but, as this was the second person to remark on her girlfriend status, thought it best to quash all rumours now. 'I'm not his girlfriend. He's not my boyfriend. We only met yesterday. A mix-up in holiday arrangements.' One she'd be seeking further answers to from Sammy. She looked at the sketchpad in Gemma's hand.

'Oh, did you do those?' she asked, pointing to the open page.

'I did. Not my best work though. I was just asking Grandy's opinion.'

Kate took the offered sketchpad and flicked through the pages. 'These are amazing.' Sammy had told Kate about one of the young girls in town who had a truly magnificent talent. Kate recognised the style of Gemma's drawings instantly, and although there were no direct associations in the work, she knew each piece represented various aspects of the mystical philosophy, Karma. 'Good heavens, you're good.' Blue pools with dancing dolphins sending ripples on the water to four corners. Representing the earth.

'I haven't travelled yet,' Gemma said. 'So I wasn't sure if I'd got the meaning right.'

Another drawing showed the dolphins beneath the water, as though in an ocean of complex undercurrents. A third showed a beach, full of people watching the ocean and the dolphins. Some pointing, many holding hands. All gathered in a semi-circle, sending their varied karmic ripples in all directions. 'This represents the community,' Kate said. 'And the altruistic effect of so many lives coming together and blending, regardless of the problems.'

'Wow. How'd you know that?'

Kate smiled, and looked up at the blue-eyed girl. Wow right back. The kid wore ripped shorts, an old T-shirt and a broad, chirpy smile. She would be a stunner in about five years, once she'd grown into her athletic slim frame.

Kate closed the sketchpad and handed it back. Talent. Pure and trustworthy. 'What are you going to do with this skill?'

Gemma shrugged. 'Don't know. I'm experimenting at the moment. I'd like to go to Paris though. One day. Maybe.' Another shrug, and a darkening of her blue eyes. Perhaps she didn't believe in herself, Kate thought. Or perhaps her parents would never be able to afford to send her to college, let alone Paris.

Kate made a firm mental note to discuss Gemma Munroe with Sammy and make sure the girl was given a chance. Somehow. Anyhow. Before someone like Fat Jacques got hold of her. He'd pounce. And probably destroy the natural ability while pimping it out to the highest bidder. Another reason she was torn about The Decision and whether to let her hard work go, or to fight for it. Her world had been coloured by greed, and she wasn't sure she wanted to be part of it anymore. Her own karmic pond had many ripples, all criss-crossing.

'Nice to meet you,' Gemma said, flicking her skateboard with the toe of her foot and flipping it up in the air. She caught it neatly with her free hand. 'Best go. Bye, Grandy.'

'Watch yourself on the road,' Grandy said.

Kate sat on the bench next to Grandy as Gemma bounced down the steps to the road and sprinted down Main Street, waving at Mrs Tam as she passed the petrol station.

'That's serious talent.'

Grandy nodded. 'The best kind. Still untouched. Needs to see the world a bit though.'

Kate glanced his way. She'd only known Grandy for a short time, but he had a way of appraising all around him with an astounding accuracy. Grandy Morelly, the soul of Swallow's Fall.

'You're looking well, Grandy. How's life?'

'Happening. How's yours?' he asked.

Kate pulled a face. 'Topsy-turvy crazy.'

He chuckled. 'Thought it might be. Got the look of the lost and lonely about you.'

Kate pulled her straw hat off and ran a hand over her head, checking her ponytail was still tailed. 'I'm okay,' she said in an offhand way. 'So what's been going on in town? I hear there's a feud.'

'The sun wouldn't know which side of town to set without a few sparks to light its way.' He glanced at her, his watery-blue eyes full of humour. 'We're movers and shakers here in Swallow's Fall though. Two new things have happened in the last three months.'

Kate curled a leg beneath her on the bench and turned to face Grandy.

'Your Jamie moved in, and we're expecting another young man soon. The one who's just bought Kookaburra's.'

Kate glanced to her right, at the closed-up pub.

'Wouldn't do you any harm to move into town,' Grandy said.

Kate laughed. The townspeople were quaint and inquisitive. Curious and cautionary. No way would Kate become number ninety. 'Is there a quicker way back to Silver Bells House?' she asked. 'It took me almost two hours to walk here.'

'I imagine it did. I heard that your car's wrecked. Apparently you were doing a hundred down All Seasons Road.'

'I was not,' Kate said, aghast.

'And that you'd scared the wings off two dozen parrots, crashed through Ethan's gate and let ten of his horses loose.'

Kate sighed. 'How do stories get out so fast anyway?' she asked. 'Nobody knows I'm here.'

'Jamie was in town earlier. Told me you were here.'

Jamie had spoken of her? Kate wondered what he'd said. How he'd explained. Whether or not he'd described her.

'Since Ted and Mr Penman were around, all ears, I suppose that's how the news spread,' Grandy said.

'Spread? It's like greased lightning.'

'So what does bring you to town?'

'A greedy scumbag, a quest to get something right inside me, and a shooting star.' Kate smirked. Work that one out, Swallow's Fall. Hang on. If they tried, God only knew what sort of stories they'd make up.

Grandy said nothing but he placed his hands on the handle of his cane, as though he were waiting for Kate to say more. The old man had light and depth. Made Kate want to sit and talk to him. Maybe tell him her problems with Fat Jacques, The Decision and her dilemma about that quest to get something right. Tell him she'd lost her *raison d'être*. He might have some answers. She'd come to the country to get away from it all, desperate to find *something* or *anything* that would make her feel worthwhile in her own skin. Talk about torn. Talk about a messed up life. Talk about…

'Shooting star, huh?' Grandy said, lifting his chin and gazing across the street as though he had some inner knowledge. 'Now that's what I call interesting.'

'Why?' Kate asked, wanting to know why he'd said that. Did the man have second sight? Could he see into her future?

'Ask Jamie.'

Jamie?

'Funny how Sammy forgot to tell you the house was no longer available for holiday lets, isn't it?'

'Isn't it?' Kate agreed.

'And she's normally such an organised woman, too. Makes you wonder what she's up to.'

No. Sammy wouldn't have arranged this. *Would she?*

'Are you going to help us with the town's decorations at the weekend?' Grandy asked. 'Feud should be settled by then.'

'I won't, if you don't mind,' Kate said, taking her leg from beneath her bottom. Sitting on a hot wellie wasn't pleasant. 'I'm here to get away from all things Christmas.'

'Too much jolliness for you?'

'I'm turning a certain age and I've currently got nothing jolly going on.'

'So you're here to review your life then, are you?' he asked, then nodded, pursing his mouth in contemplation. 'Good idea. Spit it out, chart it out and sort it out.' He shifted on the bench. 'Some people do the hardest things first.'

'Like what?' Holy polony, the man must be a wizard.

'Like not making the list before they start throwing things out of their lives.' He turned to look at her. 'If you've got stuff going on in your life, and you're not sure how to handle it, make your list and identify the things about yourself you disguise from others.' He nodded, with a smile. 'Got to see yourself, Katie, before you can be seen by others.'

Hot dog! Bang on. Where did he get this wisdom from? Kate's mouth dried out instantly. Maybe this was why she'd hung her hopes on a shooting star. She was supposed to be in Swallow's Fall, to talk to Grandy.

Grandy nodded down the street, towards the southern side. 'Looks like your boyfriend's here to give you a lift.'

Kate glanced up and saw the Knight Works ute pull into town.

She looked sideways at Grandy as Jamie brought his vehicle to a stop on the road in front of the hardware store. 'He's not my boyfriend.'

Grandy chuckled. 'I hate to tell you, Kate, but by the end of today the whole town will know about the wellie-wearing city girl Jamie has hidden away up at the house.' He winked. 'They'll have you married by dawn. They'll be planning Wellington boot-throwing competitions for the reception.'

'Oh, ha ha.' Grandy was jesting, but really, did Kate look like the sort of woman who'd end up in Swallow's Fall? Did she?

'What's with the wellies?' Jamie asked Kate, coming up the stairs to the walkway. 'Grandy.' He tipped his head at the old man.

Yes, what was with the wellies, Kate? Nobody in town wore them. Alright, they probably did when working the paddocks and in winter. One thing she'd got wrong. The other was her interference in Jamie's life. Finding the photo. Correction. Kate shifted on the bench. She hadn't found the photo, she'd gone looking for something and hadn't really known what to think about what she'd found. Serve her right if she was blushing as Jamie watched her.

He took his attention off Kate and to Grandy, chatting about the new surgery at the homestead on Burra Burra Lane. He must have already been home and showered. He'd changed. Some guys wore T-shirts and some guys made T-shirts wear them. Jamie Knight was the latter. His dark grey short-sleeved T-shirt fitted him comfortably. It wasn't skin-tight, something Kate never liked, but neither was it loose. His 48-inch chest made her sigh inwardly. She imagined how his powerful-looking shoulders, and those triceps and biceps, would move beneath his skin as he heaved stones and boulders while building his wall.

'Thought you must have walked into town,' he said to Kate. 'Or got lost.'

He'd come to collect her? A gentleman in work boots. The type of man who would always have a hand ready to place at the base of a woman's spine to gently guide her across the road, or through a bar or restaurant. And a fist big enough to knock a bloke's block off if a situation demanded such an event. Something Kate wouldn't mind seeing her rescuer doing. Especially with Fat Jacques… Scumbag.

'Habit is a dragon breathing fire,' Kate said, thinking back to the incredible representational drawings of karma young Gemma had shown her. 'I'm hostage to my own way of thinking. I need to take action.'

'Want a lift home first?' Jamie asked.

Heat crawled up Kate's neck and crept onto her face. She hadn't meant to speak out loud. She nodded. 'Yes please. These wellies are killing me.' And he'd said *home*. So was she going to stay the whole holiday and make Silver Bells House her temporary home? Grandy had given her enough stimulation of the mental variety to get cracking on The Decision. Jamie inspired other mental pictures. On which she ought not to ponder. She was pretty sure she'd already blushed once too often in his company.

After saying their goodbyes to Grandy, Kate settled into the cool interior of the Knight Works ute, buckling her seatbelt and admiring the choice of music playing on a low volume in the cab. Country rock.

'I forgot to do some grocery shopping,' she said, looking back at Mr Penman's store and wondering if he was currently standing in agony or sitting on it, then deciding she didn't need to know details.

'Don't worry,' Jamie said as he pulled out and performed a U-turn on Main Street, heading his monster truck southwards. 'I did the shopping this morning.'

'Didn't get pretzels by any chance, did you?'

Jamie pulled the ute up by the petrol station as Mrs Tam came out, waving at them and holding…a pair of mauve-coloured rubber thong-between-the-toe sandals.

'Here you go, Kate,' she said, handing them through the window Jamie had wound down.

'How thoughtful, Mrs Tam. Thank you,' Kate said, stretching her arm over Jamie's 48-inch T-shirted chest. Smooth. Firm. Lime-scented muscles. Kate pulled her arm away and sat back in her own seat.

'You're welcome, dear. Now you two have a lovely evening. And don't forget the decorating at the weekend. Might as well make it something special this year. We've waited long enough for the decorations to go up.' She wagged a finger at Jamie. 'Behave. Remember, Swallow's Fall appreciates courteousness and civility.'

Jamie pulled away once Mrs Tam went back to the petrol station. 'Was she talking about my driving?' he asked in a perplexed tone.

'No. She was talking about you and me.'

'How come?'

'We're boyfriend and girlfriend.'

'Are we now?' he said after a slight pause.

Kate grinned. 'You didn't get the town committee email?'

Jamie shot her a look. 'Something else Sammy forgot to send.'

Kate's laugh bubbled out. 'Didn't she just?' She settled into her seat. 'Oh well. Can't go accusing her of matchmaking when we don't know for sure if she was.' Although Kate would be interrogating Sammy about the possibility. 'Anyway, the townspeople are just gossiping and Sammy's wrong about the match. So everything should be put right soon.'

Kate didn't get a response. She glanced his way. His features were impassive, the slight frown probably concentration on driving. Or perhaps he hadn't heard her.

Chapter Six

Jamie watched the road ahead, driving mostly by reflex, his thoughts processing the girlfriend–boyfriend scenario.

Swallow's Fall townspeople were liberal enough for his liking. Isn't that why he'd decided to settle down here? Settle down. More thought needed on that concept too. Shooting stars had a lot to answer for. Like — why now? Why settle for a town with a quiet ambience? Why settle at all? And yeah. What about that girlfriend–boyfriend thing?

'It's cute, yes?' Kate said, obviously referring to her remark about matchmaking which Jamie hadn't felt needed a response. 'An old-fashioned terminology for people our age though, don't you think?'

She was prising an answer from him. Maybe looking for an idea about what he thought. 'Well, that's the country for you,' he said, by means of no answer at all.

Swallow's Fall townspeople tended towards the ultra-conservative when they looked at boyfriends and girlfriends. No matter their ages. Like, no pashing in public. Nothing French, anyway. Hopefully they'd seen Kate's arrival for what it was — an accident, albeit they'd already tied the two of them together in some sort of romantic knot.

His 'girlfriend' bent over in her seat, catching Jamie's eye with her movement.

'Are those my socks?' he asked as she pulled her pretty Wellington boots off her feet with a huge sigh.

'Yes, hope you don't mind but I borrowed them. I don't have any socks.' She arched her feet, stretching her toes the way ballet dancers did and for some goddamn unknown reason, Jamie thought of sex. Her feet were pale skinned and elegant. Why she bothered with the heels, he didn't know. Yes he did. What man wouldn't look at a beautiful girlfriend wearing four-inches of look-at-me shoe and not admire her and them?

He cleared his throat and told his mind to wander elsewhere. Like to the road ahead.

Kate's mobile rang. Jamie glanced over again when she pulled it from the pocket of her red denim hipster shorts. He caught a glimpse of the skin on her waist as her little white top rode up her midriff.

Don't look, he said to himself, as his gaze flicked over the length of her legs. Don't look there, either.

Suddenly, in eight short weeks he had a house and a guest who'd become his girlfriend. He'd shopped with care that morning and planned for meals. Next thing he knew, they'd be getting a cat.

'Hmmm,' Kate voiced as she looked at the screen of her phone. She hit a button with her rosy-pink tipped finger, obviously not happy about the ID of the caller and slipped the phone back into her pocket.

'Business?' he asked.

'Yup.'

'Still don't want to take the calls?'

'Nope.'

Jamie clamped his mouth together. But hell, Sammy's voice rang in his head anyway. *Try to get her to open up, Jamie. It would have been hard for, staying in the city at this time.*

'So who are your calls from?' he asked as he turned the ute into the No Through Road to his home.

'Fat Jacques,' she said. 'Fat in the greedy, covetous department, that is. Scumbag-style.' She turned in her seat to face him. 'Who in bejeezus do some people think they are, Jamie?'

'That's Irish,' he reminded her. 'So Fat Jacques is...?' *Her boss? Her boyfriend?*

'Varmint.'

His mouth curved in a smile. 'Now you're crossing continents. Varmint is southern USA. You mean vermin.'

'I mean rat.'

Jamie took a breath, something inside his chest getting worried on her behalf. 'Aren't you concerned about losing your business, by not taking the calls?'

'Might have lost it anyway.'

She spoke so quietly Jamie wasn't sure if he was supposed to have heard. He didn't question her further, but the scenario played on his mind all the way up his No Through Road driveway.

She had the bunny pyjamas on. Jamie took his concentration off the short shorts and the nipped in jacket and back onto the summer lamb casserole he'd been preparing. 'Dinner'll be a couple of hours yet.'

'Don't care. I need wine first, anyway. Ooh.' She padded across the kitchen to the fridge, barefooted and looking as though she was walking on hot coals. Jamie gave the lamb casserole a last stir, and put the cast-iron dish into the heated range oven. He hadn't expected Kate to be a dressing gown and pyjama-wearing woman. Not around him, anyway. He'd imagined his immaculate executive guest to remain clothed in her power-wear. The bunny PJs and silky robe were a surprise. As were the wellies and the ridiculous straw hat. Kate the enigma.

'Living in the country is agony,' she said, lifting her feet, one after the other and scrunching her toes as though to relieve the tension or joint pain.

'Don't tell me,' he said. 'You're plumb tuckered out.'

'You guessed it. You have no idea what fourteen kilometres has done to my feet. This never happens on the running machine.' She unscrewed the cap on her Chardonnay, pulled a wine glass across the bench top and poured wine. She lifted the bottle and her eyebrows his way.

Jamie shook his head. 'I'll have a beer.'

She grabbed one out of the fridge, closed the door with a kick of her backside and hobbled over to him.

'Thanks.' He unscrewed the cap and took a slug. And couldn't hold back his next question. 'Are you going to stay the whole holiday, Katie?'

She paused, obviously mulling over her answer. She sipped her wine. 'Yes, please,' she said softly, not looking at him. 'If it's still okay.'

'It's still okay.' Fine. It was okay. This was day four — he'd mostly missed her yesterday because she'd slept all day. Now he knew he had a full eight days ahead of him, he'd handle it. He wasn't going to count the nights. He'd think about those another time. When she didn't look so adorable in her pyjamas. When he'd quit imagining her out of her pyjamas.

He took another slug of his beer, and downed nearly half the bottle.

'You know, in some ways, Jamie, being thrown together like this might be a bonus for both of us.'

He narrowed his eyes. The bonus would be seeing her out of her…

'Come on,' she said, swinging her glass his way and looking as though she'd taken his pause as a negative about what she'd said. 'Really. We're so different — perhaps we can learn from each other's perspectives on life.'

'You have a perspective on life that I need to know about?' he asked, topping his remark with a grin.

She pulled a face. 'Well, it's not going to work if you're not going to play.' She frowned at him in a stuffy manner. 'Thing is, you've got it all.' She indicated the house with her raised glass. 'I have to go without a few things before I can decide which things I want to pick up and run with.'

'Like what?'

'Don't know yet. It'll come to me. That's what Grandy suggested I do. Chart it out. I think he might be the reason I was drawn to town.'

'Really?' Again, Jamie searched for the elusive reasons of why he'd chosen this town.

'He's a wise barn owl.'

'Yes, he is.' Jamie liked the old man. Reminded him of his own grandfather. And also of his father and the lengths James Knight had gone to protect his family from the elements of change. Which, of course, reminded Jamie of Megan.

'I don't have it all,' he told Kate. Although he had enough, and he'd have more, if Megan would let him call her and speak to her. But she wouldn't, so what he had for now was a house he'd never imagined buying, an intention to settle down he'd never before desired and a beautiful fashion executive wearing bunny pyjamas he wanted to get her out of. Yeah. Right. All he needed now was for the cat to make an appearance and he'd be in the middle of home-sweet-homey-ness.

'So I've decided I'm going without it,' she said.

For the love of God, why did he immediately think sex? 'Without what?'

'Arg!' She flopped onto the Chesterfield and wiggled her toes.

Jamie put his beer down and strode over to her. 'How come you can wear killer heels and not have any problems, but walking in flats is killing you?'

'Lack of practice.'

'Here.' He bent on one knee, took hold of her foot and pressed the pad of his thumb into the ball of her foot.

'Oh, Mr Knight Works,' she said, her voice tumbling from softly satisfied to deep and sexy. 'I'm going to let you do that because you have no idea how good it is.'

Jamie knew caution at this moment would be his saviour but he couldn't help himself to save himself. He pressed both of his thumb pads into the sole of her foot and waited for her to writhe.

'Oh, God, yes. That's good. Don't stop. Don't stop.' She slithered further down the sofa, her backside tucked into the cushion behind her. 'This is definitely something I don't want to go without.'

Since he'd been without what *he* was thinking about for some time, he let her foot slide out of his hand and back to the floor. There was only so much self-inflicted torment a man could take.

'You stopped,' she said, in an accusatory tone.

'More wine?' he asked.

'So what shall we talk about?' she asked as she poured herself a second glass of wine.

How you look without your pyjamas?

Jamie gathered some pre-dinner foodstuffs from the pantry. She might not be hungry but he was starving. Dinner would have been earlier if he hadn't had to go into town in search of Kate.

'We've got eight nights ahead of us at Silver Bells House,' she said. 'What do you do for evening fun?'

'Strip walls, sand wood and knock down walls.'

She wiggled her fingertips at him. 'Sorry. Manicure. No can help.'

'How about a board game?' They'd better find something to do. Or at least, he ought to. *We've got*, she'd said. *We*. As in *our* place. Our home. Jamie shook his head to get himself out of the cloud his mind had wandered into.

'Great. What games have you got?'

He stepped through the wooden partitions of the wall he'd ripped out between the kitchen and the dining room and pulled out a couple of boxed games from the sideboard. Anything to take his mind off her damned pyjamas.

'Exasperation or Monopolise,' he said as he placed both board games onto the dining room table.

She grinned at him. 'I haven't played Exasperation since I was ten years old. I love it. I love popping the plastic bubble and watching the die bounce.' She moved from the Chesterfield and pulled out a chair at the table. 'I'm gonna beat your stonemason's hide.'

Jamie held up his hand, index finger pinched to thumb. 'And I was *this* far from a getaway.'

'Come on, boyfriend. Sit down and prepare to be annihilated.'

Jamie chuckled. 'Hope you don't cheat, girlfriend.'

'I'll set up,' she said, taking the lid off the box of Exasperation. 'And I'm the guest, so I choose red. You can be blue.'

'Thanks.' He'd have chosen that colour anyway, although Megan usually gave him the green game pieces to pop into their clear plastic slots as the game progressed. It had been the only game that kept her occupied. They'd played it over and over. She hadn't wanted to read and Jamie hadn't wanted her to watch television or DVDs. Nothing that could remind her of what she thought she had to look like.

He stood, went to the kitchen bench and ripped open a bag of cheese and onion chips. He emptied them into a bowl and slid it across the dining room table, next to the Exasperation game. 'Help yourself.' He sat.

'What flavour?' she asked, scrunching her nose and looking at the chips as though they might jump up and bite her.

'Take a handful and find out.'

She munched on two slivers of broken cheese and onion chip. 'Are you trying to make me fat?' she asked.

His heart almost sliced in two right there and then. 'Please yourself,' he said, and ignored her in the way he used to ignore Megan when he'd tried to get her to eat something and she refused.

Kate took a handful and grinned. 'I will,' she said, and layered three chips so that they sat perfectly curved, one on top of the other, then bit into them. 'Yum.' She wiped a crumb from the corner of her mouth with her finger. 'Absolute bloody calorie-heaven.' She swallowed the rest and grabbed some more. 'Are these the only flavour we've got?'

The muscles of his torn heart melted and then mended at her words. He pushed the bowl towards her and she took another handful. Why hadn't Megan been able to do that?

'Do you think I'm snappy?' she asked, pressing the bubble down hard with the palm of her hand.

'Hey,' Jamie said, pointing at the game. 'You pressed it twice.'

'I did not.'

'You did. You got a three and a two on the first pop — which would have taken you nowhere fast — so you popped again.'

She held her hands up. 'I didn't pop again, I got a six and a five on the first pop. You're seeing things and hearing things, Mr Knight Works.'

Jamie stared her down. She grinned, but didn't look away from him. Jamie gave in.

'I don't think you're snappy,' he said, answering her question. 'But I think you probably make snap decisions. Especially when you cheat.'

'I *don't* cheat but I do make snap decisions. That's exactly what I do and most of the time they work.'

'Yeah, but those are business decisions. How many times do you make snap decisions on what you're going to do next? I mean the personal decisions.'

'It's not good to make hasty decisions of the personal variety. Don't know where you'll end up.'

'So perhaps that's what you can focus on while you're here. Figure out the difference.'

'That's good. I will. After all — I made a hasty decision to come to the country, didn't I? And that's working out.' She lifted her glass of wine. 'You know, if I like the country and it likes me — I might stay.'

Jamie raised his brow. 'Holy moly, Katie. Not sure we're ready for you.'

She laughed. He'd meant to put fun into the conversation and to get her to open up, but hearing her laughter, listening to her discuss her wants, needs and possibilities — Jamie hoped like hell everything did work out for her. Whatever *it* was.

After their fifth game, one of which he'd won, Jamie tucked into his lamb casserole. She'd only eaten a small bowlful, which he supposed he couldn't blame her for. She'd eaten her way through most of the family-sized packet of chips and half a tub of guacamole dip.

'How do you know Sammy?' he asked.

'I was her boss. She's a fabulous artist. She used to finalise my designers' sketches. Turned them into art, believe me. Then she married the vet and gave it up to do her own art stuff. But she's my best friend above everything else. At one point — before she and the vet sorted themselves out into a true love match — I had it in mind to come down to Swallow's Fall and punch him.'

'Why do keep calling Ethan the vet?' Jamie asked.

'Because I love him and he likes my jokes.'

'I didn't take you for a joke-maker.'

'He's the master vet. Like you're the master builder. Maybe I love men who are masterful.' She raised a finger. 'In the nicest possible way, of course.'

Jamie's thoughts swung to being masterful in the bedroom.

'Damn,' she said, frowning as though a thought had struck her.

'What now?'

'I'm jealous of my best friend.'

'Because she has a masterful man in her life?' He expected Kate to throw him one of her well-placed executive looks but instead, she nodded.

'Not of Sammy having Ethan,' she said. 'Just that she's got someone wonderful in her life.' She peered at him. 'I'm going to have to do something about this.'

Jamie raised his eyebrows. Looked like he was going to be told what. Just his luck. 'Like?' He hoped to God it didn't involve him.

'Like start getting my act together. I've only got eight days.' She looked across the kitchen. 'Can you spare a small area of your chalkboard?' She uncurled her long bare legs from her chair and hobbled to the board he'd put up on one wall, closest to the pantry.

She picked up a piece of chalk and drew an off-centre line down the board. Jamie's chalked notes about additional lifting tackle and the types of dowels and clamps he intended to use on the veterinary surgery now took up a quarter of the space, with Kate's section taking up the remaining three-quarters.

Things for review, she wrote as a header, then drew another line down the board so she had two columns. *Things to go without*, she wrote as a header in the second column.

'That's a small area of my chalkboard?' he asked.

'Ssh,' she said. 'I'm thinking. You see, I have to strip down…'

Oh, please.

'…and get to the earthy side of me. Then I can rebuild myself, being true and all that.' She stood looking at her columns for minutes. Then wrote under the Things for review heading: *country vs city (big change!), my life (a mess), my business (and you know what), my sudden desire for a masterful man (could just be the country air).*

Jesus. Why couldn't women figure things out by nipping down to the local pub, throwing a few darts and talking sport?

She raised the chalk in her hand to column two and Jamie held his breath. What things would she go without? The Chardonnay might be a good idea. Or the pyjamas.

High heels (don't need them), she wrote, then, *Lipstick (hard but necessary). The need to control (probably impossible).*

'There.' She plopped the chalk onto the board holder and turned to him with a smile that pronounced she'd been successful. 'It's a start. What do you think?'

'Do I have to answer?'

'Yes, you do. Unless you'd prefer to play Exasperation again and get your hide beaten. Again.'

Chances were she'd cheat, again, and do it so well he didn't notice. Again. 'Okay,' he said, sounding as reluctant as he felt. 'How does the Things for review column relate to what you're going to try to go without?' What the hell did it matter if she wore lipstick or not? And what about the heels? Did she mean go without them forever? He'd sort of miss them. Like a lot.

'Jamie, Jamie, Jamie,' she said, shaking her head with every utterance of his name.

She walked over to the Chesterfield and sat, legs pulled up to her chin, feet on the seat. She contemplated the chalk board as though God himself had written a new commandment. One only for Eve, obviously. Poor Adam, Jamie thought. The man hadn't stood a chance in a paddock with a naked woman and an apple. If Eve had looked anything like Katie Singleton and Adam had had anywhere near the appreciation for Eve that Jamie had for Kate, why the hell had anyone dithered over the apple?

'Don't you get it?' she asked.

No. Hadn't got a goddamn clue. And neither could he focus. He was caught in how she looked. Trapped in her soft sensuality. She had eight days. He wasn't going to last forty-eight hours.

Chapter Seven

Kate stuck the tip of a fork into a cold potato in last night's lamb casserole, pulled it out and bit into it. *Mmm.* Delicious. A man who could cook.

She put the lid on the casserole dish and slid it into the preheated range oven. It had taken a while to work out how to operate the range, but she'd done it. Her housekeeping skills hadn't stopped there either. She'd found her long-lost homey side earlier this morning. Although she preferred to think that her natural ability to multi-task had risen to the fore in order to vanquish boredom. Everyone around her knew her predilection for orderliness. But today, she'd played house. What a great game. No deadlines. No-one interfering.

Jamie had gone by the time she'd got up and showered. Superman was a hit in the kitchen, the do-it-yourself department and with the gentleman qualities he displayed but he was after all, she'd discovered, a typical man. Cushions needed to be plumped and straightened, picture frames realigned where they'd tilted out of whack. A pile of paperbacks and trade magazines had needed to be put into order on the beechwood shelving in the dining area. And everything above floor level had to be dusted.

Her mobile sang with the birdcall she'd chosen to make her feel more at home in the country. She picked up the phone from the bench where she'd placed it next to the breadboard and the bread she'd unfrozen and warmed in the heating stove. The aroma of dough hitting her nostrils created an overwhelming hunger within her the like of which she'd never given into before.

Fat Jacques Burch, the ID told her.

She put the phone down, unanswered, her appetite waning fast. She didn't want the scumbag disturbing the peace and happy-go-lucky enjoyment she'd eventually found today as she sauntered through Jamie's house, tidying up and feeling like a real, ever-present, ever-loving country householder.

However, after the conversation with Grandy, the fun evening playing games with Jamie, and the initial chalkboard sort-out of the goals she needed to achieve, Kate had dreamed all night. One dream after the other and each as abstract and absurd as a dragon with two heads breathing fire in her face.

Jacques's and Sahra's faces had loomed at her within the psychedelic world of her dreams. Shouting demands, screaming for business recognition in the world Kate no longer felt she belonged to. Voices admonished her about lost goals and financial wreckage if she didn't sign the paperwork and help lead Sensations into the future. A future that she'd accepted in her dreams. Signing the documents that saw Jacques take control and relinquishing her personal endeavours to remain sassy and creative, and foreclosing any chance for her young designers to stay true to themselves and what they created. She'd woken soaked in terror, with a pounding headache. So much for the lie-in. Two extra hours' sleep had wrung her emotions through a mangle.

She'd devoted herself to the art of fashion and helping young designers, beginning her career as a fashion artist, just like the job she'd hired her friend Sammy for, and leading herself forwards to a damned remarkably good position and an industry presence. She'd brought Jacques into the business as a co-partner only last year, and only because she'd been at a point where she'd needed a financial bump-up in order to keep her desire to be straight and sincere in the fashion world going. To keep her designers employed. But Jacques had turned her business into an industry-gossip, celebrity-kowtowing nightmare. He'd already fired six of her designers and brought in what he termed were fresh talent with avant-garde flair.

Sensational bullshit. No truth. No eye for what women wanted or needed in order to remain feminine yet functional. Just money-making nonsense. Fashion no woman on today's street would dream of wearing, let alone be able to afford.

And then, in New York, a mere week ago, he'd hit her with his bombshell. Bastard.

She switched on the timer sitting to one side of the oven range and set it for an hour. Then chewed on her thumb. Decide or stew.

Difficult to believe she was hesitating by taking a huge twelve-day break. But this was the dilemma that had found her wishing on a shooting star.

Twelve days. Deals were brokered in twelve minutes but here she was, in the country. Looking for…something. Thank God for Chardonnay.

She'd had another nap this afternoon. Had lain on the Chesterfield, closed her eyes and waited for more sleep to cover up the lack of decision-making. *What was it with the air around here?* She'd never felt more exhausted in her life.

But eventually she'd risen, showered the smell of cleaning fluids and dust from her body and assembled the sensible parts of Kate.

And here she was making dinner and planning on a fruit platter for dessert. Outside, on the patio maybe. Kate — under the stars with nothing to do but relax. How cute. How so not Kate Singleton. Would she ever fit in here? Probably not. But it was a nice picture. For those who wanted that sort of thing.

Every way she looked at it, Kate wasn't in that country picture.

She pulled her shoulders back and her thoughts into order. Jamie would be home soon, a little weary from his day. Wanting sustenance and a quiet evening.

Okay. Kate could do that for him. What a guy he was turning out to be. God bless the country; even if it wasn't to be her field in life she recognised that it was Jamie's. It embraced him. It had sunk into his skin and his clothing, that summer-dry aroma of stone and earth. And she'd promised Sammy to be cheery around him.

She pulled butter out of the fridge and unwrapped it. She used a spoon to pull lengths off the pat, creating butter curls which she placed in a bowl. *You got through the nights, and here you are in on the evening of day five. You've still got time.*

Rise and shine, Katie. Smile. Put on the glitz.

As soon as Jamie stepped through his front door he noticed the difference. The aroma struck him first. Lamb casserole and warm bread. He swallowed the mouth-watering need to eat and closed the front door. He stood awhile, taking in the changes. Atmosphere, he decided. He wasn't alone. The house had a friend. He couldn't quite figure out what was different about the hallway as he studied it. Nothing had changed, nothing out of place but it felt as though it had been used today, not just walked through as a means of getting in or out.

He put his keys on the hall table, walked to the door of the kitchen-cum-dining room and paused.

There she was. His house guest. Tonight she wore ivory-coloured linen slacks that clung to her delectable bottom and a midriff-hugging pale green strappy top. Suitable clothing for a hot summer's night. Most unsuitable for a man who already had trouble *not* envisaging her naked.

'Hi,' he said.

She spun around, and smiled. 'Hi. How was your day?'

Such a positive, energetic yet warm, homey feeling pervaded the space, Jamie half expected the cat to appear.

'Can't lay claim to having slaved over your dinner,' she said, lifting a glass of white wine from the bench. 'Since you cooked it. But I'm heating it up. Hope that will give me points.' Another smile.

Jamie responded with a smile of his own. 'What else have you been doing?' He turned a slow, full circle, taking in the neatness of his usual clutter. 'You've been tidying.' Hell. Had she felt the need to clean up his mess? Was it a mess, his usual way of living? He cleaned, he cooked but…yeah — he hardly ever tidied up. Had a habit of stacking things where he'd last used them instead of putting them back in their proper places. Unlike his truck or his working gear and equipment in the shed, where he knew where every damn screw or trowel was.

He turned back to her. She had a hand on her hip, and the smile still bounced on her features. 'You look rested,' he told her, although her eyes were a little over-bright.

'Jamie, I've been playing house with your home. I hope you don't mind. You have some fabulous pieces of furniture and art. Are they all yours? Or did you inherit them from the previous owner of the house?'

Jamie turned and picked up one of the renovation magazines she'd stacked on the bookshelves. 'Mostly mine,' he said, absently flicking through the pages so he had something to occupy him.

'Some of it was my father's.' He hadn't kept any of Megan's things when he'd closed up the family home, not that she'd had much. Mostly just her bedroom furniture and a few pieces her mother had left her. Megan's stuff was in storage, waiting for Megan to want it.

Jamie looked up from the magazine. Kate obviously didn't feel the need for further enquiry because she began flitting around the kitchen again, pulling dinner plates and side plates from the cupboards. Slicing bread, setting the table. Looking at home in his kitchen. Looking damned good in his kitchen.

'I'll go shower,' he said, taking a step back from the cosiness she portrayed in case he suddenly sank onto the Chesterfield, hands behind his head, feet crossed on the arm and asked her to fetch him a beer.

'Okay.' She looked up, knives and forks in her hand. 'I'm not going to mention the glass-cleaner squeegee tool I found in your vanity unit, because of course, it isn't my bathroom and therefore I'm in no position to ask you to use it after you've finished in the shower.'

Jamie grinned. 'Ouch,' he said, and took another step back. 'I think you just grabbed the landlord by his Bojangles.'

She laughed. 'Nice one.' She'd kept her hair loose tonight. It fell neatly over her shoulders. 'You've got twenty minutes to clean up,' she told him. 'And if you're a really good landlord and use the squeegee tool, there'll be a cold beer waiting for you.'

'I'm outta here.' Jamie held his hands up in defence and left the room before he succumbed and laid himself out flat on the Chesterfield.

Even though he'd assembled the lamb casserole and shoved it in the oven yesterday, having it served by Kate this evening made it feel like she'd hunted, shot, skinned and cooked for her man. She'd set the table to perfection. Knives and forks aligned, water glasses and wine glasses to one side of the dinner plates. And a mat for his bottle of beer which dripped condensation.

'Beautiful, Kate,' he said, putting his napkin onto the table and pushing his empty plate to one side. 'Thank you.'

'There's fruit for dessert. Would you like some? No cream though.' She wagged her finger. 'Just as well. Don't want us getting fat.'

'Are you having fruit?'

She shook her head and put her hands onto her stomach. 'Couldn't fit anything else in.'

Jamie smiled. 'So what are we doing now? Fancy a game?'

She pushed her chair away from the table and stood. 'I'd only beat you.'

'You mean you'd only cheat and beat me.'

She laughed. Then sighed. 'I'm tired.' She looked away. 'I don't know why I'm so tired, Jamie.'

The use of his name held an appeal. One that had him wanting to put his arms around her and give her a warm sweet hug. She looked rested alright, but there was also an aura of mental exhaustion around her. The same one he'd seen when he first met her in the paddock. Her flapping emotions seemed to have settled down somewhat, but perhaps they'd only turned into something deeper and more expressively meaningful for her.

'Want to come outside?' he asked, standing.

She looked across at him, questioningly. 'I'd planned on maybe having the fruit salad outside on the patio.' She sighed and looked away. 'I think I've lost my hunger, Jamie.'

Jamie knew she didn't mean for food. He picked up the ice bucket with her wine in it and his bottle of beer and walked to the patio doors. He opened them, letting the night invade the kitchen. 'Come on, Katie. Let's go sit under the stars and you can tell me your story.'

She gave him a wry smile. 'You want to hear it?'

He nodded and stepped outside. 'Come on.'

She followed him. He held the door open for her. 'Amazing,' she said, lowering herself onto one of the sun loungers on the patio, sprawling flat out and staring up at the sky.

'Isn't it?' Jamie answered as he sat on the other lounger. He lowered himself a little more cautiously to a lying position and crossed his feet at the ankles.

'The ceiling of the country,' she murmured.

Jamie had to agree, although he said nothing. The night sky spread above them, an endless summer-blue shadow. Not a cloud in sight, the stars dusting the sky like a gentle snow storm in a glass bowl.

'So what's the story, Katie?'

She breathed deeply and put her hands behind her head. Maybe the dusky night and the meal she'd eaten had softened her senses. The way she was sprawled, so casually, so contentedly, made Jamie want to leap the distance and take hold of her. Put his arms around her and ask her softly to tell him what her troubles were.

'I did a stupid thing, Jamie. I allowed the industry I work in to slip by me. I lost it.'

'Lost what, exactly?'

'My love of it.'

She quietened then, probably contemplating, and Jamie let her be, waiting for her to continue.

'I had this dream from a young age. A dream that I fulfilled.' She looked across at him, her eyes darkened in the evening light. 'I was good.'

He nodded, had no doubt she would be. But she'd said *was*. 'How good were you?' he asked, and hoped the question would lead to why she no longer felt she was good enough.

'I know things.' She sat up on her lounger, suddenly vivacious and alive. 'I know what women today need. I know how they think. I know what they can and cannot afford. I know how hard it is to want to look great but to know that something has to be given up before you get that one little item...' She hunched her shoulders slightly and put her index finger and thumb together. 'That little gem of a piece of clothing — whether it's a pair of shoes or a skirt, or a scarf. That one thing that makes a woman feel like she's rewarded herself.'

Her enthusiasm caught a hold of him. He could practically envisage her in her office. At her desk. Designing. On the telephone. Laughing and coercing. 'Go on.'

'The trick is not to be super-matchy.' Her eyes sparkled, lit with eagerness. 'It'll look like you're trying too hard. And it's quantity over quality if you're going through a rough financial patch.'

'Is that why you've got so many outfits in my bedroom wardrobe?'

She laughed, and leaned back to the lounger, hands behind her head, all reflective again. 'I'll let you in on a secret, Jamie. The woman of your dreams is going to want a big wardrobe because eventually, she'll fill it. And if she doesn't fill it, she'll be happy while she's intent on filling it.'

'Just as well I don't have one then.'

'Well I know you don't have a big enough wardrobe,' she said, glancing over at him with a coquettish grin.

Jamie rumbled a cough in his throat and frowned at her. 'I think everything else I have is big enough for any dream woman that might walk into my life.'

She raised her brow and tilted her mouth in an oh-so-saucy manner. 'Are you being dirty-minded?'

Yes. Oh, yes. Somebody save him, yes. He smiled, and allowed the devil inside him loose. Just this once.

She shot up to a sitting position and slapped her hands on her knees. 'You are!' she proclaimed. 'This is great. You're loosening up.' She paused, and gave him a challenging look. 'Tell me a dirty joke.'

He laughed. He knew plenty, but didn't think the majority were suitable for a fashionista's perfect little ears. 'Can't think of a single one.'

'Go ahead,' she waved her hand at him. 'I'm not a prude. I work in fashion, remember? There isn't any part of a male body I haven't seen naked, half-dressed or even in some state of arousal.' That index finger of hers waved his way again. 'Some of the younger male models can't keep it tamed in their trousers when surrounded by half-naked young women.'

'Really?' He shifted his position as a twinge of jealousy poked at his gut. 'You're telling me you've slept with all these fashion boys?'

'Don't be ridiculous. I'm their boss. Rule number one, never sleep with the boss.'

'Whose rule is that?'

'Mine.'

Plenty of men must have wanted to sleep with Katie. Plenty had probably tried and failed. All ages. Eighteen to eighty.

'What about landlords?' The words were out of his mouth before his brain had time to register what he'd just asked her.

Even in the lamp-lit dusk he saw the blue of her eyes darken as awareness stilled her.

'I've never had a landlord before now,' she said softly. 'I'm not sure what rules I'd need to put in place.'

Her phone chirruped in the kitchen behind them.

She levered herself upright. Jamie reached across and took hold of her arm at the elbow. 'Leave it.'

She paused, studying him by looking him directly in the eye. The sky seemed to explode above them, filling the space between them with the light of a million falling stars. Jamie didn't lose eye contact, and neither did she.

After a few moments, she relaxed back on the sun lounger. The mobile phone chirruped three more rings then stopped.

'I wanted something tangible from my business,' she said quietly. 'And I had it, for a long time.'

Jamie sighed his relief as silently as possible. She'd chosen not to explore his question any deeper. Thank God. Because he didn't know where he might have taken things if she had. 'So when do you think you lost it?'

She laughed, but it was a dull sound, not one he'd expected from her. It's tone belittling. Of herself, he realised. 'I have two choices, Jamie. Either I give Jacques the go-ahead to send Sensations out into the up-beat, up-market world or I go under.'

'Surely not?' He couldn't see Katie going under for anything or anyone. Parrots or fashion moguls.

'He's got me by the Velcro curlers. Tight enough to need to snip off half a head of well-groomed hair in order to get free.' She angled her head his way, catching his gaze. 'I was in New York last week. At a fashion shoot. I knew things were tough and that he was doing the devious behind my back but I'd ignored it, hoping for the best — whatever I'd thought the best might be.' She shuddered slightly. 'I got a call from him on my last night in New York. He'd brokered a deal behind my back. A great deal. An enormous opportunity for my young designers to shine.'

'And the problem with that is?'

She looked up at the sky. 'It's not what I built my business to be. And I don't know if I can go along with it. He wants to forge ahead into the big-time. Hit the catwalks worldwide. But that means damaging my vision for what's real for the women in the world.'

'Do you need to go along with it?'

She nodded. 'If I don't, Sensations will go under and Jacques will broker the deal anyway.'

'With a new company,' Jamie said, figuring it out. 'A new company he's in sole charge of, taking your designer people off you and making the money anyway.'

She blew her breath out. 'You got it.' She shifted on the lounger. 'God, let's get off the subject. This starlight thing is making me feel exposed.'

Jamie smiled at her. She had an extraordinary tenacity. One she used to broker her emotions. Not necessarily a healthy way of dealing with problems, but who was he to say she should be reasoning with herself on a different level, a different plane?

'Let's talk about you.' She angled her head to look behind her, at the house. 'Wonderful house. I mean, it's so different from anything in town. It's not an Australian style.'

Jamie relaxed into the new conversation, happy to be away from personal causes, his or hers. He leaned across to the side table between them, pulled the Chardonnay bottle out of the ice bucket and topped up her wine. 'Oh, it's got its Aussie heritage here and there.' The basics of the build, the materials used, the plumbing. But she was right, the style was undoubtedly European.

'Who built it?' she asked.

'A couple who moved here fifty years ago. He was an astronomer, she was a gardener. She died first then five years ago he did. He left the house to their son, an amateur astronomer who apparently travelled quite a bit. He didn't want to be tied down with a house so he put it on the market.' Jamie hadn't gone into the happenstance of it too much although he'd recognised it as a coincidence; him being a journeyman, like the amateur astronomer, and since he'd seen the shooting star on one of his first nights in town.

He'd been in Kookaburra's — before it had been sold. He'd left before closing and had been standing on the walkway under a crescent moon when he looked up and caught sight of the flight of a shooting star.

'A stargazer,' Kate said. 'That's amazing. You'll never guess what.'

Jamie raised an enquiring eyebrow, pretty sure he was going to find out what.

'The reason I came here is because of a shooting star.'

The hair on the back of Jamie's neck prickled his skin.

'That night I told you about, after the shoot in New York. I stepped out onto the street and as the concierge was calling for a taxi I looked up and saw a shooting star. A real one,' she said with emphasis, as though such a sight had never before been seen. 'I was mesmerised. But the strange thing is — nobody else around me saw it. Nobody looked up. They were going about their business, heads down. Except me. I saw it.' She paused. 'And I knew it was mine.'

Jamie paused, remembering his own star. Yes, he'd claimed it as his. And the moment it disappeared, he'd made his decision to stay in Swallow's Fall. 'I'm sure your star was beautiful,' he said softly, imagining her standing on a busy night street in New York City, mouth slightly open, eyes wide with wonder.

He shifted on the lounger and grabbed his bottle of beer from the side table. She'd seen her star only a week ago. Jamie had seen his over two months ago. Nothing coincidental or fateful about that. Shooting stars rode the sky every night and somewhere in the world, someone saw one and imagined fate was leading them to something.

His thoughts went to Sammy. Was she matchmaking here? Sammy was a great one for breaking a guy down. Somehow she'd got him to tell her about the shooting star. They'd been discussing the new surgery and the heritage style both she and Ethan wanted, and Jamie had practically spilled his guts about Silver Bells House and his strange need to settle down. It had been easy talking to both Sammy and Ethan. They'd taken on a role of leadership in town. Everyone loved and admired them. They were a happy couple, and of course Sammy would still be seeing stars herself, having only been married a year or so. She'd have been pulling a fast one mind you, shoving him and Katie together. He ought to back away from the companionable sensations that were becoming more and more settling every hour he spent with Katie. Jamie wasn't staying in the country for the rest of his life. He was a journeyman. He'd use the house as his base, but wouldn't always be living in it. A lot depended on Megan, too. And Katie wouldn't leave the city. He'd bet on it. She'd go back.

'Why did the original owners call it Silver Bells House?' she asked.

'After the Christmas Bells plant. The one with the red bell-like hanging flowers.'

'I know the one. Tipped with saffron-yellow. But where does the silver part come from?'

'He liked the silver in the stars and his wife liked the Christmas blush in the flower bells.' Jamie closed his mouth before he confessed that he'd been so fascinated he'd asked around town and got the information he wanted. If he told her all this he'd make himself look soft. Romantic, if not a little soppy. 'How about we go inside now? Feeling the evening chill.' He levered himself off the lounger and stood.

She held her hand out to him. 'Are there any planted here?'

Jamie shook his head. 'I've seen some in Canberra, but I'm not sure if they'd be suitable for the soil here.' He took her hand, reluctantly, and felt the roar of attraction hit his veins the moment he touched her.

'But you're going to try and grow them, right?' she asked as he pulled her up to stand.

'I doubt I'll have time.' He didn't tell her he'd already sourced a nursery and researched the possibility of recreating a sandy limestone rockery. That sounded too damned soppy and he was already feeling way too romantic while standing with beautiful Katie under the stars.

Chapter Eight

'You're up. Thought you might've slept in again.' Jamie was stamping the dust off his work boots onto the doormat in the portico as Kate opened the front door to let him in.

'I'm all slept out,' she said. 'Where've you been?' She'd woken late again, at eight, and Jamie and his monster truck had gone.

He nodded behind him. 'Chopped down the Christmas tree for the town.'

'Oh.' Uncomfortable prickles settled inside her as saw the huge tree strapped onto the back of his ute, the top branch hanging over the windscreen of the cab and the glossy tip bent, just waiting for the angel. Kate wasn't an angel-loving person because of her middle name: Angelica. It wasn't the name so much, but the way she'd been given it. 'Are you getting one for the house?'

'Well of course we are. It's Christmas.'

'Mmm.' She stepped back to let him into the hall. 'Not fond of Christmas this year.'

'I can't chop one down for the house yet anyway. That whopper is taking up the whole tray-back on the ute.' He moved by her, not looking at her, and walked towards the kitchen. 'I can hear my paintwork screaming as the pine scratches it.'

Kate pulled a face as she closed the front door. Perhaps she wasn't the only one in a don't-know-what-to-do-with-myself mood. 'Where did you get it from?' she asked, following him into the kitchen and heading for the coffee pot.

'Ray Smyth's place. He farms the other side of the hill that shelters the town. Keeps a small patch of forest, just for Swallow's Fall Christmas trees.'

'Oh.' How accommodating of him, growing a forest for the town. And since Jamie had got the tree, maybe the feud was over. *Wonder who got the Santa suit.*

'Coffee?' she asked, pouring into his big workman-size white mug.

'Thanks.' He took the offered mug, still not looking at her.

'What are we doing today? Can I give you a hand with the wall down the road? Or the surgery, or something? I'll need to borrow gloves but I've got my own wellies.' She grinned, but he didn't see it.

'I'm taking a day off. Got to wait on the sparkies laying cable before I can continue the build at the surgery. What were you intending to do?' He glanced at the chalkboard, reminding her she was supposed to be making The Decision but she hadn't listed anything else on the board.

After talking to Jamie last night, this morning she'd awakened to a genuinely sad fact. She had nowhere she wanted to go, even if she made The Decision.

'It's day six, Jamie. And all I've done is sleep.'

'Perhaps you need it.'

'There's something weird going on.' She picked up her own coffee mug and sipped. 'I never sleep past six in the morning and now I'm lying in until eight or nine o'clock and then I need an afternoon nap. God. What's with me?'

Her mobile chirruped with birdcall. She pulled it out of the pocket of her flare-legged, navy polka-dot shorts. 'Kate Singleton,

Singleton's Sassy Sensation. Mm-mm. Uh-huh. No. Sorry. Bye.' She hit End Call and looked up at Jamie, her mouth curved in the same rueful manner her frame of mind had settled into. 'No decision. As if you hadn't guessed.'

'Why do you answer the calls when you obviously have no intention of helping out whoever is on the other end?' Jamie asked. 'Is it Fat Jacques?'

'It was his assistant, Sahra. And it's a ploy. I'm winding them up.'

The birdcall sounded once more. 'Kate Singleton, Singleton's...'

Jamie took the phone off her. How had he got to her side so quickly? He put it to his ear and spoke. 'She's busy. She's going to be busy for the next six days. Now go away.' He pressed the End Call button and then switched the mobile off.

'What are you doing?' Kate said, making a grab for her phone.

He held it up high. 'No phone calls to or from work.'

'What? I'm dangling them on a string, but not to the point where I don't know what's going on. I have email contact on that phone, you know. You can lose a model or a shoot or a design request like that!' She clicked her fingers. 'I'm working behind their backs.'

'This isn't getting any decision made, Katie. You've got to leave them to it and find your own way forwards. Or out of it. What are you going to do?'

'I don't know, alright? But I can't go without my phone.'

'No phone. Not for work. Only for if you need me.'

'Why would I need you?'

Jamie sighed and dropped his arm to his side. 'The way you're behaving at the moment, you're going to need me for something. Just don't make it everything. I don't need to know if you chip a nail or lose a shoe. I'm talking life or death moments.'

She gasped. 'You think I'm likely to have life or death moments?' She looked across at the chalkboard, eyes blinking. 'Should I chalk it up?'

Jamie shook his head. 'The country isn't ready for you, Katie.' He handed her the phone. 'Keep the phone switched off but keep it in your pocket.' He turned and walked towards the hall.

He stopped in the doorway. 'What *are* you doing today?'

She shrugged and strummed her nails on the bench top. 'No idea. What do you want me to do today? This is the bloody country. There's nothing to do!'

'Katie.'

Annoyance and frustration swelled. 'What?' she demanded.

'While I'm not keen to get my Bojangles mangled, might I risk an observation?'

She folded her arms. 'It's your house.'

'You're behaving like Contrary-Katie again. Sit down or something.'

'Sit down? I've been sitting down for days.' And what was it with the sudden temperamental manner? He'd gone all Excavator-man on her. Where had the generous landlord gone? The one who'd sat under the stars last night and offered her… Well, she wasn't sure if he'd actually offered the opportunity of, you know, sleeping with him. But it had sounded pretty close to an offer to Kate's ears.

She gave him a filthy look but it backfired when she got snagged in his penetrating brown gaze. His eyes held hers, piercing into her, and the frown on his brow deepened.

Kate trembled. She licked her lips and tried to take her eyes away from his but couldn't. He definitely had gritty, masterful sides to him. And they were a lot yummy.

'There's plenty to do, if you look for it,' he said. 'Or if you'd prefer to mope around here, go ahead. Be my guest.'

She was his guest. And she wasn't moping, she had nothing to do.

'Otherwise drive into town with me and help us decorate Main Street.'

Oh, God. Fun stuff. But she did want to know how Mrs Tam had got on with the strawberry-marshmallow ice cream recipe. And what Gemma might have drawn. Another chat with Grandy would help. And perhaps, if they were really lucky, they'd get to see Mr Tillman and Mr Penman draw swords and whip each other's backsides down Main Street. Or better yet, Mrs Tillman and Mrs Penman would have a tug of war with the Santa suit.

'Oh, alright then.' If he insisted.

'Hot tomatoes, everyone's here.' Kate cringed in the passenger seat of Jamie's ute, pressing her knees together as they entered the town.

'You mean hot potatoes,' Jamie said, slowing down and parking at the southern-most tip of Main Street, by the rundown Town Hall. 'Best park here for the moment.'

'Good idea. That way we have a quick getaway if we need one.' It looked like every town resident had turned out for the Christmas bunting party. The street was lined with parked cars with Go Slow signs and orange cones placed at either end of the street, warning unsuspecting tourists or passers-through that Swallow's Fall was in full Christmas swing.

'We'll be here all day, Kate,' Jamie said.

'Great.' Kate got out of the car and stood by the ute while Jamie got some gear out of the back seat. A huge metal tool box, rope and what looked like abseiling equipment. Holy snowman, was he going to get up on a roof to fix the tree in place?

'Have you had breakfast?' he asked as they sauntered past the petrol station and headed into the mix of people and children standing around the pioneer cemetery. 'We're in luck,' he said. 'Looks like there's a cookout happening.'

Bacon. The aroma wafted around Kate's nose.

'Ha ha — look at the horse!' Kate pointed to the oversized plastic neighing horse that sat to the right of the stock feeders' doorway. Someone had put a Santa hat on its head and made a red tinsel noseband and reins.

'Ted must be feeling some Christmas cheer,' Jamie said.

It was the first time today Kate had heard a smile in his voice. Funny how it made her feel safer. She was, after all, an outsider and she'd never liked large crowds. She couldn't drum up the glitz and glamour she used to swan into meetings and shoots. Not when everything around her was wholesome and countrified. Full of community spirit. The townspeople were in their comfort zone. Kate was as out of it as a gang gang parrot stuck in a cage without a door.

She sidestepped as they walked, getting a little closer to Jamie. 'Ted's the one having the feud with Mr Penman, right?'

'Right. Ted's our town committee chairman. He has a lot of ideas.' Jamie sounded sceptical, but the humour was still in his tone.

'He must be liked though, to be the chairman.'

Jamie laughed. 'It was Ted who set up the committee. I don't think the townspeople had much say in who they wanted for their chairman.'

They were coming up to the group now, and Jamie lowered his voice. 'He's not a bad sort… Good morning, Ted.'

'Ho hum.' Ted Tillman turned, belly first. '*There* you are.'

Kate hid her smile. He looked like a near-balding Santa even without the costume and the beard. And like Santa, there was no way Ted would get down a chimney.

'Been waiting on you,' Ted said to Jamie with a beady-eyed frown. 'Everything's in place. Everyone's here. What you need to remember, Jamie, is that we're all working to a deadline.'

'Thanks for the tip, Ted. I'll remember that. So who's getting the tree off the ute?'

Ted coughed up some remorse and Kate flicked her gaze off him in case she started laughing.

'Well now. I suppose I could lead a team, once I've formed one,' Ted said. 'Penman can't help though. He had to nip back into the shop to try for a you-know-what.' Ted rolled his eyes.

'He's been nipping in and out for the last hour,' Mrs Tam said, stepping to the fore, spatula in hand. 'Poor man. Hello Kate, have you met everyone? My, don't you look gorgeous.'

'Um. Thanks. Hello everyone.' Kate lifted a hand in greeting and smiled at the people who'd followed Mrs Tam, forming a semi-circle around Kate, Jamie and Ted. 'I'm Kate. Sammy's friend.'

'Jamie's girlfriend,' someone said, which inspired a lot of head turning Kate's way.

'No! Really, no. Just a mistake in holiday arrangements.'

'Are you hungry, dear?'

'No, thank you. Smells great though.'

'We like to make a day of it,' Mrs Tam said. 'Although this year we were hard-pressed,' she threw a penetrating look at Ted, 'to get the decorations up before Christmas Eve got to us.'

'Hurrumph,' Ted answered. 'If it wasn't for Penman…'

Jamie stepped forwards. 'How about I get a couple of the guys to help me take the tree off the ute and carry it down Main Street? Would that suit your plans, Ted?'

Kate wondered how Jamie had got it on the ute all by himself. Perhaps the farmer had helped.

'It would, Jamie. It would indeed. See?' Ted said to Mrs Tam, brushing the air with his plump, work roughened hand. 'Organisation, that's what was needed. Diligence. That's what I've been waiting for.'

'Organising?' Mrs Tam said, looking flabbergasted as she wiped her hands on a yellow pinny patterned with teacups and saucers that was tied around her middle. 'How much organising do you think it took to get all this underway?' She threw an arm behind her, indicating the cooking bacon on the grill and the women standing behind trestle tables, handing out hot sandwiches and...*ooh, were they croissants*? Kate's mouth watered.

'A sight more diligent than getting your Christmas tree put up, I'll bet,' Mrs Tam finished in what Kate recognised as a very huffy manner indeed.

'Where's the tree going?' Kate asked, butting in before it got too heated. The sun was already high in the morning sky, burning down on eighty-odd heads. Any further arguments or feuds might set the tinsel alight.

While Jamie and three guys off-loaded the four-metre tree and carried it down Main Street, Kate settled on the steps of the walkway opposite where she had a grand view of the open space between the stock feeders' and the pioneer cemetery. She alternated between munching on a slice of crispy bacon she'd pinched off the grill, and twirling strands of red and white tinsel together. She was making candy cane–striped lengths for the women who were decorating the walkway railings. All around her, Main Street looked like an industrious scene from Santa's grotto. The

Swallow's Fall elves were energised and lively with a happy temperament, working as though Christmas might pass them by if they didn't get a move on.

The shopkeepers had strung fairy lights around the windows and doorways of their businesses, and stuck fluffy fake snow and snowflake decals onto the windows. Kate had been right about them draping tinsel everywhere but had to admit they'd done it carefully and with some consideration. The shopkeepers didn't seem to be fighting over fancy window displays either. Each had the perfect little white lights and similar decals of snow scenes. The overall effect was cooling, which helped, in this heat.

There was a lot of hearty male humming going on too, Ted having told his committee choir to exercise their vocal chords while they worked.

Kate smiled, a sort of heartfelt contentment settling inside her as she worked alone, sitting on the steps. But she didn't feel outcast or snubbed. They'd thrust sacks of tinsel at her when she'd offered to help, and left her to get on with it. And anyway, sitting here she had a grand view of Jamie and his muscles as he hefted and levered the tree into position by the pioneer cemetery gate.

Kate scrunched her face as she considered her childhood. Christmas in Australia meant long summer holidays from school, the beach and vacations. They'd been in swimming gear as they stood next to Christmas trees for family photos, not woolly hats and muffs. Although she'd spent many Christmases in Paris, England, Milan and New York as an adult and had seen all the snow stuff, the roasted chestnuts and the *Ho Ho Ho* winter wonderland scenes, she preferred Australia's Christmas. Probably mostly because it was the one she recognised. A tableau of sunshine, melting ice cream, cold beer and steaks on the barbeque. Didn't mean there was no Christmas spirit, just because they were in a different hemisphere to the traditional winter Christmas. Just look at little ole Swallow's Fall.

Kate felt almost comforted by the knowledge she was helping them decorate their town. And the feuding was fun to watch too. She'd clocked Mrs Tillman and Mrs Penman earlier stuffing white sacks with wadding and making fake snowmen. Bickering over how to get the carrots to stick in the stuffed sack faces and how big the black felt patches for the eyes should be.

Ted's voice suddenly bellowed through the choir's humming and everyone's chattering, bringing the to-dos down Main Street to a momentary halt. 'Why are Christmas trees like bad knitters?' he asked. Nobody answered.

'Because they both drop their needles!' he bellowed, laughing.

Kate groaned, but a smile hovered.

'Nice one, Ted,' some accommodating man yelled. 'But no more, eh?'

'Just getting us into the spirit,' Ted said.

'Something we should have had two weeks ago!' called a woman.

Kate saw Mrs Penman throw a withering look at Mrs Tillman. The women on the walkway behind Kate sniggered, resumed their quiet chatting and began twirling their candy-cane tinsel around the railings once more. The male choir started humming 'In the Bleak Midwinter'.

Jamie hauled the tree into place with a lifting tackle. *Holy smoking gumboots, look at the muscles bulge in his arms!*

Kate chewed and swallowed the last of the grilled bacon, wiped her fingers on a paper serviette and got back to the task of tinselling.

✦

Two hours later and her hands were numb from braiding the tinsel and uncoiling forty metres of rope lights which would be used on the tree. It had been years since she'd used her fingers for dressmaking, when they'd had the nimbleness needed for picking up pins. Thinking back now, to those days when she'd started out as a designer, she missed the poverty. Strange thing to reflect on, let alone miss, but the youthful keenness and the constant hoping and working damned hard to find a way forwards had given her an edge. It was the edge she was missing now, because of Fat Jacques. Although, she couldn't put blame entirely on the scumbag.

What sort of woman built a successful business and lost herself on the way? How did that happen? How *could* that happen? Had she ignored clues while devoting herself to the things she loved most? The lively opinions, the style, the discussions. The thrill as one of her young designers punched through the window of opportunity and hit a high with his or her designs.

Had she ignored the greed, the gossip and the cruel spitefulness that had infiltrated her beautiful business over the last year? Yes, she had. How could she *not* have seen the hammer falling? Did she want to continue to be the woman she knew? The one who would fight, stilettos swinging.

If she didn't give in to his demands, Jacques would take the business off her and she wanted to let him. But she hadn't been quite convinced of her reasons for letting go. If she left her designer world what would she do? Travel. Great — by herself? Not so great. So she'd checked out of her business and the unwanted dilemma and escaped into the country.

'Nearly done?'

Kate looked up at Jamie who stood in front of her, a plastic coffee cup in his hand like the one she had on the step next to her, and a plate of…oh, boy. Talk about tickling a woman's fancy. And she didn't mean her landlord's muscles.

'What's that?' she asked, scrunching her eyes at the feast he held and counting the calories in her head.

'Mid-morning snack. Since you didn't eat breakfast.'

'I ate toast, know-it-all,' she said in a tone meant to provoke. 'And stop trying to make me eat more than I want to. What's wrong with you?' She took a pink-iced croissant though. And grinned at him. The sweet frosting melted in her mouth along with the soft, buttery pastry of the croissant. 'Who makes these?' she asked. 'She or he ought to be prime minister.'

Jamie laughed. 'I think Mrs J's daughter, Lily, made them.'

Mrs J! 'Where is Mrs J?' she asked. Mrs Johnson was the tall, sometimes unhappy-looking and sometimes quite ornery townswoman who kept a pig on a lead. A damned big pig. 'And where's Grandy?'

'They've driven into Cooma. Picking up the Christmas presents to go beneath the tree.'

'Prezzies for the children?' Kate asked.

'For everyone. I told you Ted wasn't a bad sort, once you get beneath the huff and the puff.' He looked at Kate. 'He organises this every Christmas, apparently. Gets each family in town to donate fifty cents per person per household a week. He conjures up over two grand by doing that.'

'Perhaps he'd like a shot at running my fashion house.' Although she'd need a lot more than two thousand dollars to keep it going. *If* she kept it going.

'Hey,' Jamie said, his voice soft and comfortable enough to make Kate's heart flutter.

'What?' she asked, forcing herself to look at him and trying not to let her breath catch in her throat as she bit into her raspberry-iced croissant.

'You've got tinsel bits all over you. You look like a cheerleader who's lost her pompoms.'

Kate laughed, happy to find him back to his comfortable and friendly frame of mind. She wiped her mouth, swallowed the second bite of her mid-morning snack and brushed the shiny strands of white and red off her polka-dot shorts and thin summer top.

'Are you having fun?' he asked, easing down to sit on the step next to her, his plastic cup of coffee in his big tanned workman's hand.

'You know what? I am. It's kind of restful, sitting back and watching everyone do their country community bit. Not so fond of Ted's jokes though.'

Jamie chuckled. 'Where do elves go to vote?' he asked, his grin cheeky.

Kate shook her head. 'Oh, that's bad. Real bad.'

'You don't know, do you?' He poked her in her side. 'Where do they go, Katie?'

She flicked his hand away before she laughed. 'The North *Poll*,' she told him pointedly, then looked away before she smiled.

By mid-afternoon the town glittered. The multiple colours of the buildings and the forest green of the tree stood out against the star-studded silver of the tinsel and the fairy lights. Difficult to see the twinkling effect the lights gave in the sunshine though. Maybe she could persuade Jamie to drive them into town tomorrow night, so she could see the efforts and work she'd had a hand in come to life in the dark.

The grill had been switched off, cleaned and put away. The tree was draped with the curl of the rope lights Kate had untwined. She made a note to suggest that someone put the lights back into the box in a more uniform manner when it came time to take all the decorations down. She sort of had a hankering to be around when that happened. It would be a shame not to help clean up and put away what she'd helped to produce.

Jamie made his way across the street, an ice cream in his hand. It looked vanilla white with curls of pink in it.

'We're having salad for dinner,' she said, taking the ice cream off him.

'Are we?'

'You're darn tootin'. I've been eating junk all day.'

'Hasn't done you any harm, from where I'm standing.'

'Huh, any more of this and I'll be twice the size of Ted.'

As though on cue, Ted's voice with its seemingly insatiable need for jollity rang out. 'Why is Christmas just like another day at the office?' he bellowed.

People paused in their tasks, looked around, perhaps waiting for someone else to offer an answer. Or perhaps they were just sick of his jokes. If you could call them jokes.

'Because,' the committee chairman said, looking chuffed that nobody knew the answer. 'You end up doing the work and the fat guy in the suit gets all the credit.'

Jamie guffawed. Kate shot him a look.

'Oh, come on,' he said. 'That was a good one.' He sank to the step next to her, leaning an elbow on the step above.

They sat peaceably in silence for a few minutes. He was obviously taking a break, and he deserved one with all the heave-ho-ing he'd been doing with the tree. Watching him work had reminded Kate of the possibly suggestive reference he'd made to her sleeping with her landlord. Which in turn reminded her of the framed photograph he kept in his bedside drawer.

'If you're a journeyman stonemason,' she said, making use of the calm, rest-awhile moment they were sharing, 'how come you chose to buy the house, and why Swallow's Fall? Did you have an epiphany or something?'

'I'm still a journeyman. I don't intend to live in the house full-time. If my work takes me anywhere in Australia, I'm following it.'

'Me too,' Kate said, licking her double scoop raspberry-ripple ice cream. 'Not that I think I'll end up living in the country, mind you. I don't think we understand each other.' Although she'd already got a mighty regard for Silver Bells House. But it wasn't hers and she doubted she'd find anything like it elsewhere in Australia. Not without a time-consuming search. 'But I'd hate to stop travelling.'

'Me too,' Jamie said.

'So how come this quaint ole place?' she asked again, indicating Main Street with her ice cream cone.

'Here.' Jamie handed her a paper serviette. 'You've got ripple on your chin.'

'Thanks.' She grinned at him. 'Raspberry anything is my favourite anything in the whole world.'

'That and pretzels, huh?'

'And Chardonnay. And stop changing the subject. Why did you settle down in Swallow's Fall?'

'You wouldn't believe me if I told you.'

'Let me guess.' She licked, rolled the ice cream in her mouth, and swallowed. 'Woman trouble.' Oops. Might be a bit close to the knuckle but she'd said it now and couldn't swallow it away.

'Sort of,' he said as casually as if he'd answered a question on why he'd chosen granite for the kitchen bench tops.

'Didn't mean to pry,' she said by way of an apology and opening the road for further discussion on the issue should he wish to take it.

'No problem,' he said. But didn't take her up on the invitation.

'So?' she asked, exasperation making her nudge his arm with her elbow. 'Why here?'

He looked at her and grinned. 'I saw a shooting star.'

'Ha! You're taking the Michael and it's not funny. It's rude to make fun of other people's dreams and aspirations.'

He just kept grinning. 'Okay then. I chose this town because…' He looked across the street at the tree and the scuffle going on between Mrs Tillman and Mrs Penman and the Santa suit. 'They make me smile.' He took a breath and sighed it out, crossing his arms over his 48-inch chest. 'And I needed some smiles around me.'

Kate quietened and concentrated on the bottom scoop of raspberry-ripple. So it was a woman.

'At least I think that's why I chose it. Come on.' He stood and held a hand out to her. 'Let's get the lights lit. And I did see a shooting star,' he added in a softer tone as she stepped down the walkway stairs behind him, her hand in his.

'He can't help his condition,' Mrs Penman was saying as they arrived at the base of the tree.

'Well, of course he can't,' Mrs Tillman said. 'But neither can he sit for more than ten minutes at a time.'

'Let's not argue,' Mr Penman said, hands raised, lanky legs crossed. 'I give in. Let Ted do it.'

'Now, now,' Ted said. 'We don't want to raise our voices and spoil the day.'

'Perhaps they could share the job?' Mrs Tillman said to Mrs Penman. 'Twenty minutes each.'

'But that isn't going to help my husband, is it?' Mrs Penman answered. 'What if he has to you know what in his twenty minutes?'

'If you've got any red material,' Kate said. 'I'll make you a second Santa suit. That way, there'd be two Santas available at all times, giving either the chance to nip off for a rest break.'

Every head in town swivelled Kate's way.

'Really,' she said. 'I'd need to borrow a sewing machine but I could knock it up tomorrow.'

'We can't have two Santas,' Ted said. 'The kids won't believe he's real if there's two of us.'

Kate agreed that Ted was the best choice for Santa, due to his belly but Mr Penman looked so drearily put out that Kate wanted to give him a runner-up medal. And anyway — what kid would believe either was the real Santa? 'How about we do a Laurel and Hardy Christmas,' she suggested, indicating Ted and Mr Penman. 'You two would look great as Laurel and Hardy. We could make it a movie thing. Have the kids dress up as their favourite cartoon character.'

'Laurel and Hardy?' Mrs Tam said. 'That's a splendid idea, what do you think, Ted? Mr Penman?'

'If there's another costume to be made, I can make it myself,' Mrs Tillman said, stepping closer to her husband.

'But you'll be busy making cartoon character costumes, Grace,' Mrs Penman told her. 'Because there's nobody in town who can sew.' She paused momentarily but the effect wasn't lost on Kate. 'Not like you can, Grace. And if we want out of this mess, we'd better be the ones to sort it.'

Kate managed to stop her eyebrows from shooting up.

Grace Tillman pulled herself upwards. 'You're so right, Mrs Penman, and in order to assist my townspeople, I'm happy to take on some costume sewing.'

A couple of the younger mothers clapped: Lily Johnson, who'd iced the croissants, with her two young kids standing next to her, and another woman with a baby in her arms and a toddler at her feet.

'Which means we'll kindly take you up on your offer, Kate,' Grace said. 'I can supply red cotton.'

'I've got red velveteen,' Mrs Penman said, a gentle hand on Grace's arm. 'So special. Plenty left to drape Ted.'

'That's very generous of you, Mrs Penman. Kate, dear…'

Dear? Holy snowflake.

'I'm sure Mrs Penman will lend you her sewing machine.'

'Delighted to.'

'Right,' Kate said. 'That's settled then. I'll whip up the costume. Have you got Ted's measurements?'

Kate shuddered as Jamie fixed the angel onto the top of the tree. Too many memories, and most of them on the ridiculous side.

'Come on then, we need someone to test it.'

'Test what?' Kate asked as Mrs Tam pulled her closer to the tree and to Jamie.

'The mistletoe.'

'We'll practise our Christmas Eve performances too,' Ted said, all buffed up in a pair of red corduroy trousers and a white wig. 'Mr Penman, would you accompany me on the recorder?'

'As long as we only do one verse and the chorus,' Mr Penman said, hobbling forwards, looking as though he was clenching his legs together…in case.

Ted cleared his throat, placed a hand on his chest and nodded at Mr Penman.

'Good King Wenceslas,' Ted began, trumpeting the words in a staccato manner, his chest heaving as he sang, 'last looked out, on the feast of…'

Poor Mr Penman's musical accompaniment almost got drowned out. Kate smiled, hoping her grin would be taken for enjoyment.

Two children joined in, playing recorders. Another stepped forwards, pushed by his mother, and started beating a drum in time to Ted's bouncing rendition. Two young girls began playing the violin and one boy played an acoustic guitar, plugged in, Kate noticed, to the lead and socket board used for lighting the tree lights.

She shuddered as a memory walked down her spine. Not exactly her memory, but one that had seen her born. 'Who did the electricity?' she asked Jamie as he stepped to her side.

'Mmm? Me,' he said.

'Thank God.' She'd hate to think she was about to witness the destruction of a whole town due to dodgy lights.

'Are you ready?' Jamie asked.

'What for?'

He smiled down at her, took her hand and pulled her gently to stand with him beneath the arched wooden gate to the pioneer cemetery. 'The kiss,' he said. He pointed up at the arch.

Kate looked up, saw a bunch of plastic mistletoe above them but before she had time to haul in a breath and get ready Jamie leaned down and kissed her mouth.

Holy bell-ringing Christmas. She grabbed his arms as illuminations ignited in her head and exploded. He pressed his mouth on hers as he put his hands onto her waist to hold her. 'Twas the brightest, most resounding halleluiah running through her body, making her glow like Rudolph. Jamie's electricity strummed through her, his radiating strength curling the tip of her ponytail.

Jamie stared down at her as the townspeople applauded and cheered and Ted's voice bellowed on about how brightly the moon shone and how cruel the frost was, to the accompaniment of the tinny-sounding band.

The first notion running through Jamie's head should have been why he'd kissed her so hard in front of everyone, but it wasn't. The kiss had been going to happen. He no longer cared about the where and the when. He'd wanted to do it all day anyway, watching her do her bit for the town. Wearing her flare-legged shorts and flat white pumps. Sitting on the steps, knees together, garlands of tinsel strewn around her as she laughed good-naturedly at Ted's jokes and the gentle bickering going on around her. His bad humour had backfired on him. His intent to stay clear of the homey feelings she wrenched from him had undone all the lessons he'd taught himself overnight. *Stay away from her. You'll get hurt.*

Now, thirty seconds after kissing her for the first time, questions were running amok in his head. Why had he bought Silver Bells House? Why here, Swallow's Fall? Why had he succumbed to the emotional compulsion of a shooting star? *What was wrong with him?*

He took hold of Kate's hand. She appeared to be teetering, eyes bright with shock. He'd told her he didn't want to know about the silly things that happened to her, like breaking a nail or losing a shoe, but he did. He wanted to know every little thing that affected her. Or hurt her. Or gave her pleasure.

God damn it, he wanted to know about every moment in her life. And most of all, he wanted to taste more of her. He hadn't opened her mouth with the kiss, not with everyone standing around watching them, but he'd wanted to. Desperately.

Kate ran the tip of her pink tongue over her lips as she stared up at him and Jamie wondered how much longer he could contain desperation. And if he couldn't — how much hurt he'd be dealing with.

Chapter Nine

'Cabling was done,' he'd said last night. 'Got to fill one of the ditches,' he'd said. 'I'll be up early and back late. Don't wait up.'

Kate had missed him at breakfast this morning. The air in the house didn't feel the same without his smile. Not that she'd had nothing to do. She'd cut out the velveteen for Ted's Santa suit. She'd chalked, pinned and tacked. She'd sewn it together using Mrs Penman's sewing machine and had got a buzz out of handling the 1940s dome-covered machine and its foot pedal.

The suit was finished; now she was working on the hat. She bent closer to the work, raised the needle from the velvet, lifted the presser foot and checked the feed-dog. The thread got tangled in the bobbin case every few minutes. She didn't blame Jamie for staying away from her, and that's what he was doing. His moods had been swinging like a pendulum for twenty-four hours now. First he'd been in a seemingly bad sulk. Then he'd become all relaxed and friendly at the Christmas decorating gig yesterday. Then he'd kissed her and gone all plumb moody again.

They'd hardly spoken on the way home. He'd made himself a beef and salad sandwich and gone to bed early. Kate had refused one, stuffed from all the delicious junk food she'd allowed herself to eat, and still ringing like a bell from his kiss. It had hardly been more than a mouth on a mouth, but it had lasted a good twenty seconds — that was a *long* kiss — and it wasn't the feel of his strong lips on hers that had got her all shook up. It was the zing, ping, pow that had resounded inside her as though she'd been turned into a mechanical doll on a music box by some sort of magic and Jamie had been the one to switch her on.

She jumped when he came in from the hall, and pricked her finger on the raised needle. Damn. She stood, sucking her fingertip. 'You're back,' she said, not quite managing to bring on a smile.

'Needed to pick something up. You hurt yourself?'

She held her index finger up. 'Just a Sleeping Beauty moment with the sewing machine.'

He walked across, a frown on his face, deeper than the one that naturally sat between his eyebrows. He touched her hand, lifted it to inspect the needle prick.

'Oh.' She pulled her hand out of his. 'Static shock.' She laughed it off but the room swam as the current zapped up her body and into her head, fogging her vision for a moment.

He wiped his hand on his trousers. 'Yeah. Must have been touching something conductive.' He looked around the room as though searching for the electrons. Or maybe not willing to meet Kate's eye.

He nodded. 'Okay. Well, I'll see you later.'

'You off to Burra Burra Lane again?'

'Yes.' He picked up his keys, halted and turned a shoulder her way. 'What are you doing this afternoon?'

Kate pointed to the work in front of her. 'Finishing off the Santa suit.' Which would be done in about ten minutes. Then what would she do?

He nodded. 'I'll run you into town tomorrow morning. You can drop it off.'

'Thanks.' Tomorrow. So he'd be gone all afternoon. 'What shall I cook for dinner?' she asked him, hoping he'd say he'd be home early and they'd maybe take a walk. Then perhaps he'd ask if she'd like to help him cook up a roast chicken or something. Then take a drive into town to see the fairy lights at night.

'Don't worry about me. I'll get something when I come in.'

Kate's shoulders sank as he left the room. Perhaps the kiss had reminded him of the beautiful young woman in the photo. The one he kept hidden. The one he really wanted to kiss.

The front door closed and after a couple of minutes, she heard the ute fire up. Gone. He'd gone.

She looked up from the sewing and glanced around the empty room. Maybe that's what she should be doing — going.

Kate folded the red denim shorts, aligning the waistband and the gusset. She rolled the linen trousers into a sausage shape and crimped the collar of her pyjama jacket until it sat neatly aligned with the crisply folded sleeves. She slipped the lot carefully into her suitcase. She'd dressed in a black-and-white herringbone patterned wrap-dress and her flat white pumps. She was almost sad to see the denim shorts go. In all likelihood she'd never wear them again. When would she find the time? She was better off in her work wear. *Or was she?*

She dated businessmen, when she dated at all. Men with drive and ambition. Had she already become the female equivalent? A scary thought. Although the herringbone-patterned dress felt flawless and smooth against her skin, wrapping around her body snuggly, was it simply covering the hurts and holding them in? Maybe an entire wardrobe overhaul was due. The last thing she wanted was to clock herself in the mirror of some elevator while riding to the executive penthouse and see a tight-arsed female diva with a hairdo so solid even sleep didn't disturb the permanent wave.

Her seven days hadn't been wasted though. Time to get a bit harsh with herself, that's all. She was at a crossroads. She was stuck at traffic lights. Felt like she'd reached a place of no return. A place of no decision. Like…nowhere to go. 'Got to head onwards, Katie,' she said aloud. 'Can't let this get to you.' It was, after all, just a kiss. And the woman in the photo frame was, after all… Who knew? Maybe someone so special that the memory of her and the shadow of her image would never leave Jamie free for any other woman. Not that Kate was putting herself out there as the owner of the *Hers* part of his bathroom vanity unit, but being kissed by Jamie, then ignored by him, had brought jealousy roaring back to her frontal lobe. Or whichever lobe part happened to hold the attraction-to-another bits.

She left her suitcase in the doorway to Jamie's bedroom, with a note on the top saying she'd send for it and thanking him for everything he'd done but something had come up and she had to leave. So polite. Professional courtesy. Nothing like the words in her head which she wanted to sing out loud to the accompaniment of the Swallow's Fall town band.

I'm sorry I'm not the woman in the photo.
I hope she comes back to you, wherever she went.
Because I think I like you. I think I like you more than I should.

She stepped back from the door, staring at her suitcase. She had the Santa suit and a pair of white ankle-strap stilettos in a plastic carrier bag tied to the handles of the carry-on. That's all she'd manage to carry. Seven kilos would undoubtedly feel like forty by the time she'd trudged the two hours to town. There'd be a bus once she got there. There *had* to be a bus.

'Going somewhere?'

Jamie's voice punctured her ruminations like another needle prick. But sharper and deeper this time. She spun around on the landing, the carry-on knocking against her leg.

He stood by the front door, keys in his hand. She must have been wallowing in her self-pity so deeply that she hadn't heard the door open let alone his ute pull up outside. Her breath wouldn't come to speak though it was there swirling in her lungs. She threw a hand behind her, indicating the rest of her luggage which he probably couldn't see, gathered her breath and let her worries out in a rush. 'I can't do Christmas, Jamie. It's not my scene this year.'

'Where are you going?'

'What are you doing back so early?' she asked.

He threw his keys onto the hall table and stepped to the bottom of the jarrah staircase. 'I've been a bit off with you, Katie. I'd like to apologise. And explain.'

'Oh, I didn't notice. Don't worry.' She looked away. 'I suppose I've been a bit irritable too, actually.'

'Were you going to walk into town?'

She nodded. 'I know how busy you are.'

'You haven't said why you're going.'

No. And neither did she want to. She pulled an excuse from the recesses of her brain. Not the real reason, but a semi-truthful reason and one she'd been contemplating for the last few days. 'It's my birthday.'

Jamie's gaze sharpened; he put a hand on the wrought-iron railing. 'Today?'

'No,' she shook her head. 'Christmas.'

'Your birthday is on Christmas day?'

She looked down at him. 'Sucks. I was born under a Christmas tree.' And she was wasting time by telling him this, but if she stopped talking now she might tell him the real reason she was leaving. And that she didn't *want* to leave. 'Dad was restringing the lights over the branches because they'd slipped off,' she said, 'and Mum was on a stepladder steadying the angel. Dad was never any good with anything electrical and hadn't noticed the worn cord, so when he plugged them in the fairy lights blew and my mum got an electric shock. Just a little one, but it was enough to make me jump too, and whoosh. Out I came. Under the tree.'

He smiled quickly, but blinked it away. 'Kate,' he said softly.

'It gets worse.' She held her carry-on up so that he could see the large lettered name plate. *K.A.S.* She always included her middle initial, even though she was ashamed of it. It wasn't as if anyone knew. 'A,' she said in a dead flat tone, 'is for...wait for it: Angelica.'

'Angel,' he said. 'What's wrong with that?'

'And,' she hurried on, 'I'm turning thirty.' Something else she'd been contemplating. For over a week now. Since New York, when the scumbag had suckered her life plans.

Jamie took his hand off the wrought iron and stepped back. 'Shit. That's bad.'

She looked at him. 'About being born under a Christmas tree due a fairy light malfunction?'

'No. About being that old.'

She gasped. 'You don't mean that. Do you?' *Did he?*

Jamie frowned. Was he pretending to think — or was he really evaluating her mighty age so negatively?

Oh stuff it. What was the point in trying to cover up the real problem? She let the carry-on fall from mid-air until it swung in her hand and knocked against her knee. 'It was the kiss, Jamie. That's why I'm leaving.'

Jamie nodded. 'That's why I came back,' he said, doing his damnedest to hold onto the worry in his chest. She'd hit the nail on its head with the hammer of reality.

He waited while she dithered at the top of stairs, clutching the handles of her leather bag, bobbing her head sideways and biting her lip as though she were in decision mode.

'The problem is,' she said at last, studying something on the wall. 'I liked kissing you.'

'I know,' he said. Time to put an end to the game-playing. 'I liked kissing you too.'

She tilted her face and studied him. 'You did?'

'I stayed away because I liked it so much I thought I might not be able to stop myself from doing it again, whether you wanted me to or not.'

She took a breath, eyes widening.

He smiled up at her. 'Want to do it again?' Anticipation prickled the back of his neck.

She furrowed her managerial brow and lowered her dainty, executive chin. 'Did my mouth feel really old?'

He smiled. She made him smile every time she spoke. 'No,' he said, 'but I'd like to test it again because I'm pretty sure an electric shock went from your mouth to mine and that's what interests me most.' Alongside simply wanting to nibble her, from the mouth down.

She was so seriously disturbed by her Angel name, the decision she'd made to leave — behind his back, he noted, although he couldn't blame her for that — and about what they were going to do next. 'So how about we start with another kiss? Before you turn thirty and give up on yourself.'

'Start?' she asked, ignoring his jibe.

Jamie nodded, put a hand on the bannister rail and stepped up one step. 'Stop flapping, Katie. We're going to kiss again.'

She hauled in a breath. 'I'm not flapping. I just wondered if you thought my mouth felt ancient.'

'Your lips tasted of raspberries. I only wish I'd opened your mouth and tasted the inside.'

She stared at him, her body stiffening, though he could see her somewhat trembling.

'Do you want to kiss me?' he asked. 'Or not.'

She nodded. She hadn't paused, not for a millisecond.

Jamie held both arms out. They'd been aching the entire day. Aching to hold her. No, damn it. Let's get to the truth. They'd been aching for seven long days.

She dropped the carry-on and skittered down the stairs with the grace of a Siamese cat.

Jamie caught her as she threw herself against him.

A split second later he'd steadied her, had his arms around her tight enough to hold her up and his mouth on hers before she had the chance to change her mind about the kiss.

Bingo. The shock trembled through them both as he opened her mouth and tasted her.

He deepened the kiss as her arms tightened around his neck. His sweet, executive lady had the name and the body of an angel. His lady. *His*. Jesus. He'd only met her a week ago and yet she sent shockwaves of adoration down his spine. 'Katie,' he said, releasing her from the kiss so he could speak. So he could tell her…

'Holy jalopy!' she said, breathless, eyes wide. 'You felt that? Yes? The tingle.'

He smiled, studied her face, and moved her fringe where a strand of her hair had caught on her eyelashes. 'Right down to my gumboots.'

'So what do we do now?'

'I think we need further tests.'

'To check the chemistry stuff before we sleep together?'

He loved the way she thought. No messing about. We've kissed, we liked it, next step is to go to bed with each other.

'I was never any good with sciences,' she told him. 'But I was good at maths.'

'So how long have we known each other?'

'A hundred and sixty-seven hours and—' She angled her head and glanced at the watch on his wrist. 'Thirty-two minutes.'

Jamie nodded. 'You're good. I could give you a job sizing up ditches if you want one.' She opened her mouth to speak but Jamie kissed it to stop her. He ran his hand down her spine until it landed on her right bottom cheek. He squeezed it.

'Am I getting fat?' she murmured through the kiss.

'You're getting sexier every day.'

'Because I'm putting on weight?'

'In here,' he said, pulling back and tapping her forehead with his index finger. 'You're getting sexier with every newfound discovery you make about how lovely you are. With every happy thought about yourself.'

'My mind is making me sexy?'

'You're damned right it is.'

'So are we going to sleep together because of my mind?'

'No. And we're not going to sleep until much later. We've got a few physical moves to get through first.'

Kate paused, holding her breath.

'Unless you've got something else to do...' His words trailed off.

She stared into his darkened brown eyes. Five minutes ago she'd been hoping for a bus. Now it looked like she'd be getting another fireman's lift from her rescuer.

'I didn't fancy the walk into town anyway.'

He didn't hesitate. He walked her up the stairs, backwards, holding on to her waist, a desperate look in his eye.

Her heart rate matched the sound of their footsteps on the stairs — wild. She clung onto his shoulders and let him lead her. 'I can't wait to get you out of your clothes, Jamie Knight.'

'Uh-uh,' he denied with a rasp in his voice as he pushed her through the doorway to the big main bedroom. 'Guests first.'

Chapter Ten

Undressing Jamie Knight was going to be better than undressing ten top-paid models. Better even than raspberry-ripple anything.

Kate was experiencing a wave of expectancy as, true to his promise, she was going to be the first to shed clothes. And she wanted to be naked when she undressed him, so that when she was done, there was nothing in their way.

Her fingers tangled with his. 'Just pull it out of the slot,' she told him as he fumbled with the wrap-belt of her stupid herringbone wraparound dress.

'I'm trying. Where the hell's the slot?'

She laughed, pausing them both by holding his waist and pressing her face to his chest. 'Oh, Jamie, I'm sorry.' She was tied up tighter in this dress than a trussed turkey in a baking tray.

He stepped away, letting her go. 'Okay, this is the way it's going to work.'

Kate's smile wavered with desire, her body tingling in all the unused places. The places that hadn't tingled for — who cared how long? They wouldn't be waiting much longer. 'How?' she asked.

'You undress yourself from that executive wraparound and I'll stand back and watch.'

His impertinent grin could untangle the belt on its own. But probably not quickly enough.

Kate unknotted the tie at her waist, ripped the belt apart and out of its side-slot and flung the dress back from her shoulders.

It landed on the floor at the exact same time as Jamie inhaled a hot-sounding ragged breath.

'Dear God, Katie. If I'd known you had those in your suitcase this would have been happening five days ago in the paddock.'

'Seven days,' she reminded him, slipping her white pumps off her feet while smoothing her hands over her hips and the string of her black lacy knickers. More of a tiny V-shape piece of nothing than an article of clothing.

'Or on the back seat of the digger.'

'There isn't a back seat,' she reminded him.

'Believe me, Kate, I'd have found the space.' He stepped towards her and Kate moved back. 'Uh-uh! You're watching, remember?'

'But I want to touch.'

'You said I had to get undressed before you did.'

'That was all of three minutes ago. I want my hands on your naked body, Katie. Now.' His gaze moved up her torso and rested on the matching lacy bra. The saucy, push-up half-cupped under-wire bra that she wore because she was a designer and was supposed to wear flibbertigibbet lingerie even though it was occasionally scratchy and not always the most comfortable. 'You want me to take this expensive old thing off first?' she asked, flicking the silky pencil-thin strap on her shoulder. 'Or these?' She snapped the straps of her lacy knickers.

'Shit. Just take it all off quick if you won't let me do it.' He toed off his boots and started undoing the buttons on his shirt.

'Hey!' Kate held up a warning hand. 'That's my job.' And she intended to enjoy every button-worth. But as he didn't look willing to wait, her striptease would have to happen another time. Please God let there be another time.

After *this* time…

She unhooked the bra and let the straps fall down to her elbows as she shimmied out of her knickers. By the time she'd stepped out of them, Jamie had his hands on her waist. He pulled her upright and kissed her as he slid the bra straps from her arms and off, his mouth hot and sweet-tasting on hers. His hands roamed her body, cupping and caressing, sliding and stroking.

'You're one damn fine piece of engineering, Kate.'

And she was happy to have him measure her and size her up. She was, after all, his next job.

He started on the buttons of his shirt again. Kate let him, the pads of her fingers prickling with pins and needles. She'd never deal with the small buttons. But she'd probably manage the khaki trousers.

She dealt with his belt buckle, then the buttons on his fly.

He growled like a bear as her fingers flicked against him.

He shrugged off his shirt. Kate tugged the trousers from his hips, then his boxer shorts. He stepped out of them and suddenly — Master of the Universe stood before her, naked.

He pulled her against 48-inches of muscle-bound He-Man chest.

She should be struggling to get her arms around the circumference. Fortunately, pressed so close to him, she managed. 'Hot Tamale.' He made her mouth feel all sizzly inside. 'You're so…so…'

'Desperate,' he said, looking down on her, clinging on to her.

'You could do the lot, Jamie.' She fluttered kisses onto his lime-scented chest then brought her hands from behind him to cup his handsome face. 'Nude. Photographic. Apparel.'

'I don't have time,' he said, taking hold of her bottom in his master-builder hands and yanking her against his pelvis. 'I'm going to be doing you.'

The man would hit the Top 50 Working list by bearing his left thigh on a billboard let alone the rest of his virile self. She'd dated now and then. She'd had sex — now and then — but Jamie was going to ruin her for all other men.

'I think I'm going to swoon.' Did women still swoon?

He moved with her still in his arms. Kate went with him, stuck to him, feeling like one big tropical heatwave. His skin was darkened from the sun. His muscles shaped from all the outdoor work.

As he pulled open the wardrobe door and grabbed something from the top shelf, she saw hot, humid summer nights, Pina Coladas, rum punch and Limbo dancing beneath flaming poles. All her unused places burned in the sultriness of this new climate. A girl could die of heatstroke in this place.

They were moving again.

They spent seconds, maybe minutes, in a tug of war. Limbs locking, mouths fighting. Each trying to get a better, closer hold of the other. Desire swelled within her with each caress from her master's hands. At last — she had a masterful man and a tropical beach where the waves in her head crashed to the shore of her body.

The best holiday she'd ever had.

'You are so beautiful, Kate.'

She was on the bed. How had that happened?

'Every part of you.' He pulled the pillows from beneath her head and flung them to the floor. He spent five seconds too long away from her as he dealt with a condom then pitched himself beside her. His weight dipped the mattress and Kate slid into the hollow and against his powerful chest.

Delirious shock flowed through her as he touched her.

His body was a furnace. All He-Man vigorous and muscle-packed dynamite.

She grabbed at the bedspread beneath her. The air got hotter. The light dimmed.

'Hold on to me,' he told her, moving his body over hers.

Kate grabbed his shoulder blades, attempting to pull him even closer to her.

'Oh, my God, I'm seeing stars!'

'Shooting?' he asked, his mouth nuzzling her ear.

'I'm not sure. They're all merging.'

'And so are we.'

'Jamie!' Her cry tailed off to a gasp as he nudged her legs apart and in one dynamic move — turned *then* into *now* and all her dormant bits to fizzing liquid pleasure.

Jamie studied the night sky outside the four windows in his bedroom. They hadn't drawn the curtains. No need. No-one to see in. And anyway, if either of them had found even a second of sense two hours ago, he wouldn't now be lying on his bed looking at the stars outside his windows while holding onto the woman he'd had sex with. Shared pleasure with. Made love with.

'You've been so kind to me,' she murmured.

'You're so welcome.' Jamie hooked an arm around her bare shoulders and brought her closer to his side, just managing to keep the smile out of his voice.

'I hope to God it wasn't pity, Jamie.'

'Was there a specific moment where I gave you some indication of my boredom with the situation?'

'Which time?' she asked.

'Second. There's no way I'd have let you know how bored I was the first time.'

'Testing the waters that first time, huh?'

'Yeah. And I can tell you, you got me. Big time.'

'Didn't I?' He felt her mouth move in a smile against him. She kissed his pectoral muscle, her lips soft on his skin.

'Both times were a whole lot satisfying,' he said, kissing the top of her head.

She snuggled into him but this time he saw her smile as she glanced up, before burying her face against his shoulder.

They rested awhile, Jamie stroking her hair and enjoying the feel of her breath, warm on his chest.

'I'll probably go back,' she said quietly. 'You know that, don't you?'

'I figured you would.' Pointless not answering her immediately and pointless flapping about it. Kate preferred things up front and equal. It would do him good to remember that. Before he got carried away with the smell of her. The sweet soft executive smell of her.

'Thing is, Jamie, I don't think I'm cut out for constant country living.' She levered up, resting on her elbows.

'I understand,' he said, and swiped the tips of her fringe from her eyelashes again.

'I think I have too much wanderlust in me. Or something.'

'Katie. When I've finished the contract for Ethan and Sammy, which won't be for another three months, I'll be taking jobs elsewhere too.'

She nodded. 'Australia?'

'Maybe.' He shifted until he had one arm on her back and the other behind his head. 'I've got the chance of two jobs overseas. One in England, in the Lake District, and the other in France, near Toulouse.'

'That's great. You're going to travel. And you'll always have Silver Bells House to come back to. I've loved it here. I found you and a few hours of passion.' She strummed her fingertips gently on his chest. 'My masterful man.' Her smile told him she was teasing, but the softness of her body, curling into him, told him she'd needed not only the release of sex but also that she'd wanted his protection for a little while. The comfort of his arms around her.

'But I can't stay,' she said. 'What would I do here?'

'You could start a Wellington boot factory.'

'In deepest remotest Australia?'

'Swallow's Fall isn't that bad!'

She laughed. 'No, it's not. But I'm not sure I want to start another business. I'm not sure I'd be very good at it anymore. I'm feeling really humble, Jamie.'

'Katie, you've got the guts to deal with anything. I'd put my last dollar on you.'

She sighed, settled herself — with her leg wrapped over his thighs — and snuggled into the crook of his arm again. 'You know, Mr Knight, I could fall in love with a man like you.'

He folded his arms around her, wrapping her up. 'Is that so?'

'Mmm. Quickly too.' Her voice sounded dreamy. All sleepy and rested. 'Like in a month.'

'That quick, eh?'

'A month is just weeks, really.'

'Uh-huh.'

'Just days, in fact.'

'Yeah?' *How about just hours?* Jamie thought. Like the moment her features had softened to acknowledgement of her situation, and how Jamie had felt overawed by her acceptance of him. Jamie Knight, the powerful protector. Or how about minutes? Like when he'd plucked her off the excavator and she'd nearly tripped, trying to figure out why she was at Jamie's house and not a holiday let. Or how about rewinding farther? Seeing her standing on the edge of her hire car. Waving madly at him over the stone wall, ponytail bouncing. 'Just seconds, really,' he said.

'What did you say?' she asked, her voice soft with almost-asleepiness.

Jamie didn't live life in a rash manner, he worked cautiously and carefully. He weighed up pros and cons. He left a situation if there were more cons than pros. And Katie Singleton had a suitcase full of cons — apart from her lingerie. Yet none of his mental negotiations with himself seemed to matter. Not anymore.

The sizzle of hot tamale desire still blazed through Kate's body. If this was waking up to the sexual aftermath of riding an impulsive decision made on a shooting star, she'd happily slide, slip and slither naked up and down it forevermore. Had Silver Bells House ever heard the sensual whispers, the seductive cooing or the downright X-rated vocal endeavours of two lovers before?

Oh, God. She had a lover! How so not like Kate.

Well... She sat up in bed. She'd *had* a lover.

She'd had sex with her landlord. It wasn't as though she'd get struck down for doing so. She might get thrown out though. If he hadn't really liked it like he said he had. Which he might not have. Because Jamie wasn't in the bed. Or the bedroom.

She listened hard and only heard the creak of the beams as they settled in for the start of the day when the sun shone on the tiled roof. He wasn't in the house. Or perhaps the State.

She flung the coverlet back and stepped out of bed. She padded to the window and peeked out between the curtains. His big He-Man Knights Works truck had gone.

No way could he have not liked what they'd done. Not after three goes at it. Three successful goes. Four for Kate. But she'd been a sexual time bomb, waiting to go off, so perhaps he hadn't had to put his all into it and that's why he'd decided she wasn't any good at it after go number three and had left.

'Now that's what I call a damned good morning.'

Kate spun to the door and to Jamie.

'A naked woman in my bedroom.'

Kate had trouble taking in everything about him at once. His jaw, covered in 8 am stubble. Designer-less and perfect. His height. His khaki trousers, the thick belt holding them up around his strong lean middle. The grey shirt tucked into the band of his trousers, opened at the neck. His neck. His bloody neck. Why did his neck send such peals of ringing wonder down her spine? Because it was the neck she'd nestled into and kissed. Getting all cosy before sleep.

'You don't feel at all shy standing there naked in front of me, do you?' he asked.

'I don't actually.' Was she supposed to?

'Yet when you're fully dressed in your Wellingtons, my socks and your straw hat, you blush like crazy.'

'It's your straw hat, not mine.' She looked down at her naked self and spread her arms. 'Do you mind?'

'Do I hell mind.'

She nodded at his hand. 'What's in the bag?' If her nasal cavities hadn't lost the sensory plot because of four incredible you-know-whats in one night, it was something sweet and delicious.

'Breakfast,' he said. 'Croissants. Only the shop-bought variety though. But I bought raspberry jam.'

'You went into town for those?' she glanced behind her and out the window. 'Where's your Knight Works truck?'

'I parked it around the back. I didn't want to wake you up.'

Her knees wobbled and weakened so quickly she had to press them together. He hadn't gone to work; he'd gone to town to buy her raspberry jam and had parked around the back on his sneaky return so as not to wake her. He *must* have enjoyed himself last night. 'What's behind your back?' she asked.

He pulled his arm from behind him and produced a bouquet of six pink roses. 'It's all Mr Penman had,' he said as two petals escaped from what was obviously yesterday's display, now wilted a bit, and fell to the floor.

Holy gumboots with tassels on. He'd bought her flowers!

'Thank you,' she said. 'Thank you so much. I've never… I mean nobody, that is no man has ever…' Given her a jar of her favourite jam and a droopy bunch of yesterday's flowers because it was all he could find.

He held the flowers up, another petal falling onto the steel caps of his size thirteen work boots. 'Before you say anything else, there's one condition for accepting my gifts.'

Her firstborn? Her entire collection of sling-backs? Her soul? She'd played Exasperation with the landlord, had received a foot massage from the gentleman, had been given a thoroughly marvellous seeing to by Excavator-man and was now on the receiving end of breakfast and flowers from the knight.

'Anything,' she said, emotion making her voice wobble.

'You stay naked.'

Chapter Eleven

Kate had said she could fall in love with a man like Jamie. She hadn't said she'd fallen in love with him. She hadn't professed anything about loving Jamie — only someone like him. That made sense, right?

She shook her head, gathered her hair in her hands, pulled it up into a ponytail then teased a thick strand out and wound it around to secure the knot.

He wouldn't have thought she meant Jamie, would he? Holy excavator. Two loving nights and one whole day in bed — mostly — and she'd toppled into the protection and warmth of his chest. Burying her head in that comfortable shoulder as though she had a right to be there.

Her emotions were riding a storm, had been since Jacques had pulled his fast one when she'd been in New York. That's why she'd crowed on about love; because of the lack of it around her. Maybe she should apologise to Jamie. Explain what she had meant.

'Ready?' he asked from the bathroom door.

Kate turned, with a smile and a hammering heartbeat. Look at him. Squeaky clean muscles from their mid-morning shower.

Plenty of room for both of them. Plenty of fun between them and seven jet sprays.

'Ready,' she said, her smile deepening as the memory of being close to him in the damp humid heat of the shower washed over her. 'How long will you be at the build?' she asked him, walking through the opened door he held for her and inhaling the fresh lime scent of him as she passed. 'Why don't we have a roast chicken and salad for dinner? I'll get one at the grocer's.'

'Why don't we?' he said, following her down the stairs, the sound of his work boots much heavier on the jarrah than her little white pumps. 'And tonight, we'll remember to eat.'

Kate laughed. 'Sustenance.'

He pulled on her ponytail as she hit the bottom step, bringing her to a halt. He turned her, wound his arms around her and kissed her mouth.

'You're going to need lots of sustenance, Katie,' he murmured when he released her.

Oh, boy.

'Okay. Thanks. I'll see you later.' Kate undid her seatbelt, opened the door of the Knight Works ute and picked up Ted's Santa suit in the bag at her feet. She'd been asked to help wrap some of the Christmas presents while Mrs Penman assisted Grace Tillman with the cartoon costume–making for the kids.

'I'll pick you up at five.' Jamie leaned over and took hold of her arm as she turned in her seat. 'Hey.'

Kate looked back at him and grinned wildly. His face looked darkly sexy, his thoughts vivid with the crease of a frown on his brow and the dangerous, gritty light in his eyes. 'I figure we'll get home, put the chicken on to roast and maybe have us a dandy time while it's cooking.'

Desire ran up and down Kate's body like a yoyo spinning fast on its thread. 'You're the landlord. Whatever it takes to pay the rent.'

His features lightened with his grin. 'Don't tempt me any more than you already do.'

She winked. 'I might need my stilettos then?'

He flushed, heat obviously creeping up his neck and into his eyes. 'They would definitely go a long way to paying all debts due.'

She slipped out of the seat and closed the ute door, smiling at him through the closed window.

'Later,' he mouthed, his smile now dark and hazy.

'Later,' Kate mouthed back and lifted her hand in a wave. Nine days in, three to go. Holy tabasco, she'd need a Bloody Mary soon to put out the fire inside the wicked bubble of her imagination. Shame the pub was closed.

She turned to the walkway stairs, a hand on the rail as she stepped up. Her knees quaked with so much desire for Jamie Knight, Master Builder, that she'd have toppled onto her bottom if she'd been wearing stilettos. But boy, was she going to wear them later.

'Afternoon, dear.'

Kate pulled her fantasies into line and pushed them to the back of her mind as she smiled at Mrs Tam. Wrapping Christmas presents with Mrs Tam, Ted and Mr Penman should go a long way to banishing sexy thoughts of any kind.

'I'm all yours,' she told the group outside the grocer's store. 'I've got the suit.' She gave the bag of Santa suit to Ted.

'Right,' said Ted, rolling his shoulders. 'There's four of us. We've got ninety presents to wrap. That's twenty-two-point-five each. And I'm not at all happy about the committee having to put in additional treasury monies for the last three presents.'

'Oh, go on with you, Ted. You'll recoup it next year.'

'Why ninety?' Kate asked. Weren't there only eighty-eight residents since Jamie moved in?

'The new guy who's bought Kookaburra's,' Ted said, 'Your Jamie.' He pointed a stubby finger at her. 'And you.'

'He's not my Jamie. And he's a resident, isn't he?' And Kate wasn't a resident, so shouldn't be counted as such but she didn't have time to say so.

'But he hasn't been putting his fifty cents into the kitty every week since last yuletide, has he?' Ted said. 'No. Just over a month's worth. And you.' Ted pointed his finger at her again. 'Can't go around disregarding guests, can we? Of course I had to figure you into the total tally.'

Kate ignored Ted's officiousness as happiness spread through her chest. They'd included her for the present-giving. 'I'll buy,' she said, digging into her pocket for her purse. 'I'll pay the committee for my present and for Jamie's and for the new guy too. The whole year's worth for all three of us.' She counted out fifty cents times fifty-two weeks times three recipients and handed over seventy-eight dollars cash. Cheapest and best presents she'd ever paid for. 'Right then,' she told Ted. 'Let's get wrapping.'

Jamie strummed his fingers on the steering wheel as he drove down All Seasons Road.

The hire car had gone. The tow truck had picked it up yesterday while he'd been busy with Kate. When he'd moved it from the field to the roadside a few days ago the mess to the front fender and the bonnet had sent shudders of worry down his spine. Thank God Katie had crashed through the gate and not the wall.

He was late getting to the surgery build. He'd received and missed three calls and two text messages from the plumbers yesterday. They'd done the job, waited a few hours for him to turn up, then headed back to Cooma. Jamie had missed the plumbers but hadn't missed a second of being with Kate and all that being with Kate involved. He'd almost asked her to put her bunny pyjamas on so he could take her out of them. Perhaps he'd do that tonight.

He smiled. So much serenity settled inside him that he wondered if maybe it was time to call Megan and demand she talk to him. He'd given her the eight weeks she'd asked for. Nearly nine now. He hadn't called, although keeping his thumb off her speed dial number on his mobile had been one of the hardest things he'd done in his life. But he had so much to tell her.

He pulled over to the verge on Burra Burra Lane, at the edge of the lower paddock where the foundations for the surgery and the partly built stone walls sat. An unusual nervousness poured through him as the ringing started. Would she answer?

'Hey, big brother. At last, you call me.'

Jamie smiled, sighed, and wanted to give the steering wheel a damn good thump. 'You didn't want me to call, remember?' he said, his smile blooming like a firecracker about to burst at the sound of his step-sister's voice. She sounded good. Whole. He nodded in contentment. 'I miss you,' he found himself saying.

She laughed. Oh, God. She laughed. He hadn't heard her laugh in a long, long time.

'I got your letters though,' she said.

He hadn't been able to let go of all contact with her over the last two months while she recovered herself, her strength and her willpower in the company of the dedicated family who'd taken her in. She hadn't answered his letters, but he'd known she'd got them because the lady she was staying with must have felt sorry for him. She'd left a message on his phone saying Megan had received the letters and all was well and it might be best not to rock the cradle by having an older brother breathing down her neck, regardless of his intention to help. That's all he'd known.

'Aren't you going to ask me?' she asked.

'No,' he said. He'd been asking how she was for nearly four years, and he knew she hated it because it had been so difficult for her to answer.

'Well, I'm okay. I'm doing good, Jamie. I'm doing so good.'

'Jesus, Megan, I love you, sweetheart.' Relief at her words and the laughter in her voice melted all resolve. 'I'm so glad for you. I'm so glad.'

'You wouldn't recognise me,' she said.

He scrunched his eyes as he recollected the bone-thin girl she'd been. Dying to ask her if she was eating, and how much weight she'd put on, he clamped his mouth shut.

'You want to know?' she asked. Again, laughter in her tone. She was messing him about, like she used to in the days before anorexia took hold and battered her.

'Not going to ask,' he said.

'Gained seven kilos.'

'Holy shit!' He thumped the steering wheel.

'And even better than that, Jamie — I think it doesn't look too bad.'

'Oh, baby. I'm so proud of you.' Tears stung his eyes.

'So what's with the sudden phone call, big bro?'

Jamie breathed in the wonder of everything he'd just heard. The wonder of what he'd discovered while holding Kate last night as she slept. Another second and the words popped out of his mouth. 'I've met someone.'

'I don't believe it! You're not talking business crap, are you? You mean a woman, right? Is it the real thing? Come on, give. I need info.'

Jamie's heart belted a beat not dissimilar to ten drummers drumming. His kid sister was getting better. He'd found a woman he was beginning to think he loved. But she wasn't going to stay in the country. And neither was he, for God's sake. He needed to travel in order to make a living, and so did Kate.

Now what the hell was he going to do?

'Okay,' he said to Megan. 'I don't think it's going to be easy.'

'Oh-oh.'

'I might need some feminine advice.'

'Double oh-oh, Jamie. Lucky for you I've got time on my hands.'

There was a smile in her tone and although Jamie didn't want to give Megan any worries, he had no-one else to talk to.

He'd found the essence of himself by being with a woman who was desperate to find hers. Sounded pretty fateful. The shooting stars. Buying Silver Bells House. Sammy's interference. Finding Kate.

'Okay,' he said again before his breath got stuck in his throat. 'Here's the lowdown, sis.'

Kate had been wrapping and rapping all day. She'd had a sneak preview of Ted and Mr Penman in their red suits attempting coordination of hand and feet dance moves to a rap version of 'Have Yourself a Merry Little Christmas' which had seen everyone in stitches of laughter, resulting in a breathless Mr Penman having to nip off pretty sharply to try for a you know what, and in Ted collapsing onto the steps of the stock feeders' in a sweating velveteen heap.

Kate had been surprised by the laughter and the egging-on, although unsure if the lead players had fully understood how funny they were in their efforts to be serious. She was impressed by the choice of presents too. Every person in town was getting one. Age only came into the equation with the kids, who each got a gift suitable for their grouping. Ted had done the right thing by his town too in purchasing the toys from Cuddly Bear Toy & Gift shop, which Gemma's mum ran. Babies were getting teddies, littlies were getting felt puzzles, pre-teenagers Rubik's cubes and teens — poor things — were getting crossword puzzle books.

Now she was waiting on the walkway outside Morelly's hardware store, sitting on the bench with young Gemma while she waited for Jamie to come pick her up. She wondered if Jamie's present would end up lost in his bedside drawer — the men were getting hand-carved, wooden ballpoint pens. Kate knew she'd never use her box of triple milled handmade soaps but she'd cherish them forever.

Holy pink trotters, there was Mrs J with her pig — on a lead. Kate lifted her hand in a wave. Mrs J studied Kate from across the street as she stopped to let the pig sniff at the feet of the plastic horse outside the stock feeders'. Eventually, Mrs J raised an arm in response, then carried on down the street towards the southern exit by the B&B. Probably heading home with the pig.

'What's the pig's name again?' Kate asked Gemma.

'Ruby.'

Kate slapped her knee as she laughed. 'Sammy sent me a photo of the painting Mrs J asked her to do of Ruby.'

Gemma grinned. 'The one of Ruby sitting on a red sofa wearing a straw hat?'

'That's the one.' And now she thought of it, the straw hat in Jamie's coat closet looked pretty similar to the one in the painting. Boy. She was sharing her wardrobe with a hundred-and-thirty-kilo pig. What would Fat Jacques make of that if he ever found out?

'What's *his* name again?' Kate whispered as a tall young man came out of the pub followed by Ted and Mrs Tam. The tall young man locked the doors behind them.

'Josh,' Gemma said quietly. 'He's going to be working for the new pub owner.'

Josh. Ethan was teaching him carpentry and building. He'd also had a part-time job in Cuddly Bear last time Kate was in town. 'He's going to be busy then,' Kate said.

'Yeah, but he's eighteen now. He can do anything.'

Turning eighteen, that golden age of *I'm free*. 'You're good buddies, eh?'

Gemma nodded, the flush on her thirteen-year-old face telling Kate there was a little bit of hero-worshipping going on. 'He's going to run the new craft centre that Sammy is setting up.'

Sammy had told Kate about the craft centre. Ethan had gifted his old veterinarian surgery and the house he used to live in to the town — lease-free. They planned on turning it into a showcase for local talent, of which there was surprisingly quite a bit — all the sewing, handmade gifts, Sammy's art, some carpentry pieces.

'He's saving up to leave town, that's why he's taking on so many jobs,' Gemma said a little softly. Then she perked up. 'He's got a motorbike. He takes me for a ride when he gets the chance. Not just me,' she said, holding up her hand, one of her coloured pencils between her fingers. 'All the kids. He's really good with children. For an adult.'

Kate smiled in response and kept her thoughts to herself. This kid was going get her heart burned one day if her worship of big, tall, lanky Josh turned into something painful for the heart to bear. Shame Kate wouldn't be around to help Gemma through. But Sammy would be here.

'That's it, then,' Ted said as Josh wandered down the steps to the street and made his way to a battered old car. Ted stepped towards Kate, Mrs Tam at his side. 'Shame the new man can't get here before Christmas Eve to open up the pub but we've got ourselves sorted without him.'

'How?' Kate asked, at the same time thinking *poor new guy* — did he know what he'd bought into?

'Well, he's said he'll have the bar running but no food. So a number of us residents will supply a plate of different foodstuffs.'

'You mean a number of us women,' Mrs Tam said, then turned to Kate. 'You see, there won't be time to get the kitchens going and the restaurant up and running.'

'More's the pity.'

Mrs Tam ignored Ted. 'So we'll have the present giving around the tree, then everyone can wander in and out of the pub to get a drink and some food.'

'We'll bring a plate of something too,' Kate said. Jamie would have an idea of what to make.

'Ninety residents,' Ted said with pride.

Kate re-did the calculations. Jamie eighty-eight, the new pub owner eighty-nine…'I'm not a resident,' she reminded Ted.

'Yet,' Mrs Tam said. 'But the committee likes to plan ahead.'

Yet? Did they expect her to return every Christmas?

'Kookaburra's will be open by late-afternoon on Christmas Eve,' Ted said. He checked his watch. 'Two days exactly.'

At midnight in two days' time Kate would be turning thirty and dang it, she hadn't thought about The Decision at all. She hadn't even organised another hire car to get out of town. She glanced to her left and at the sketchpad in Gemma's hands. She was drawing an autumn scene. A tree trunk in a purple sky, with yellow and gold leaves floating through the bare branches.

'What's that?' she asked Gemma.

'Freedom.'

'From what?'

Gemma shrugged. 'From whatever you don't want.'

Kate didn't mind not having made The Decision but she loathed the uncertainty surrounding her. The antidote might be to trust in something. But trust what? Or whom? She'd found consideration and kindness in Swallow's Fall. She'd been pulled into the community and had made friends but still felt she didn't belong. What had Grandy said? *Got to see yourself, Katie, before you can be seen by others.* She'd had some peace the last few days. Had been surrounded by honesty and hard work, but it hadn't settled inside her enough for her to find her own painting of freedom. Whatever that entailed for Kate Singleton.

She looked down the street, towards the sound of an engine she recognised. Her lift had arrived. Jamie Knight, master sex-machine and giver of comfort and strength was in town.

'Jamie's here,' she said, her heart lifting and a measure of courage returning.

Chapter Twelve

If he wasn't already the size of a bulldozer, Kate would have thought Jamie had grown even more. Something about his demeanour gave a proud, fulfilled look to the set of his shoulders and the tilt of his head.

'Okay, let's get this bird in the oven or we won't be eating. Again.' He picked up the baking dish with the prepped chicken in it, stuffed with a lemon and herbs and sprinkled with seasoning and dabs of butter. He leaned down and kissed the smile on Kate's mouth.

Tasty.

The seven-thirty news came on the quietly playing radio. What a homecoming Kate had received. The yummiest, sauciest quickie she'd ever participated in. And now she was starving.

Jamie put the chicken into the range and closed the door. Kate had prepared salads and had finely chopped vegetables for coleslaw — for which Jamie had made his own dressing.

'I'd like to talk to you, Kate,' he said as he took her hand and led her to the dining table where he'd placed her Chardonnay in an ice-bucket next to a bowl of peanuts. Turned out Mr Penman didn't stock pretzels.

'Sounds serious,' she said on a laugh, but her insides clenched. She took a peanut and crunched on it.

He smiled. 'It is. But of the good sort.' He left her at the table and stepped through the partly-pulled-down wall and opened the sideboard cupboard where he kept the boxed games. Kate hadn't wondered about the Exasperation and Monopolise games until now — who had he played them with? Why did he have them?

He returned to the table with a large photograph album. He sat opposite Kate, spun the album so its contents would be visible to both of them and put a hand on top, as though protecting it. 'Something wonderful happened today, Kate.'

Kate hoped her questioning smile was bright enough to hide the concern she felt gathering behind her eyes.

Jamie opened the album and skipped through four leaves. Kate caught a fast glimpse of family scenes, people outdoors, waving. Then he turned the album towards Kate.

Her heart seemed to stop beating. It was a photograph of the woman he kept in his bedside drawer. Whatever he was going to tell her, Kate was going to have to explain. But first, she needed to know who this woman was. And why Jamie felt so insistently that he had to show and tell. She put her hands beneath the table and crossed her fingers. *I've mostly been a good girl, Santa. Apart from the time I went looking for something that was none of my business. Please don't let me lose my present.*

'This is Megan, my step-sister.'

His *sister*! She pulled her hands from her knees, rapped her knuckles on the table as she lifted them to cover her face. 'Oh my God. This serves me right.'

'What's wrong?' he asked.

She lowered her hands, feeling her face burn with shame. 'I saw the photo you keep in your bedside table,' she told him in a rush before she chose not to tell him about her snooping. 'I thought it was some woman who'd left you with a broken heart or something.'

He smiled. 'And what did you feel about that decision?'

'Well, I was jealous, of course.'

'Of course?' He took her hand and held it on the tabletop. 'That makes me hopeful.'

'For what?' Kate asked.

'Later,' he said, stroking her fingers.

He breathed deeply, his smile settling to concentration again. 'I spoke to Megan today for the first time in two months.'

'Has she been away?'

Jamie nodded, his mouth pursed as he cast his eyes down at the photo album. 'She's not well.' He turned a page, then another, and a third.

'Oh,' Kate said, understanding and shock colliding.

'Yeah,' Jamie said. He put a finger on the edge of the photo showing Megan and her illness. 'This was the last photograph me and my dad took of her.' He paused for a beat and swallowed his obvious emotion. 'She'd been in the realms of this illness for a while, although we hadn't noticed at first…'

Kate put her hand over his.

'It's not just about food,' he said.

Kate nodded. 'I know. How old is she now?'

'Twenty-two.'

'And for how long?' she pressed, referring to the illness.

'Better than some. Two bad years to date. Two worrisome years previous to that.'

Kate gasped, wondering what Megan looked like now. 'And you spoke to her today?'

His smile warmed his eyes. 'She's getting better.'

'Thank God.' Kate had seen so many young models, as young as fourteen, starve themselves for what the controlling factors surrounding them wanted. Thin models. It was a mental illness, and often covered up by glossy *How to Avoid* magazine articles, or *How to Detect* health statements. And nobody seemed to care any more about this twentieth-century illness that had continued into the new millennium, unless something sensational happened — like a person dying, or the press posting photographs of those who…

Kate wiped a hand across her mouth, attempting to stay rational. She had two female business friends who'd witnessed this illness first-hand. One woman, coping with anorexia in her late twenties. Another woman whose sixteen-year-old daughter had been struck with the debilitating mental illness. One of the main charities Kate's business gave to was an Australian foundation for eating disorders.

Kate was reluctant to ask the next question but knew she had to in order to understand the whole story. She'd lead Jamie through this conversation as gently as she could. 'She doesn't look unhappy or uncomfortable with herself in the previous photographs.'

'She wasn't. She wasn't pushed into studying too hard, she wasn't forbidden to go out and do normal teenage things. She was loved, very much, but not cossetted.'

'What was she studying for?'

'A business degree. She wanted to come in with me on Knight Works and run the office. Do the bookkeeping, the promotion and marketing.'

'You would have let her?'

'Absolutely. Family business.'

'You said she's your step-sister.'

He nodded. 'My mother died when I was eight. Dad brought me up, then met Megan's mother. They married, had Megan, then she died when Megan was twelve.'

'I can tell from the way you talk of her that she's a real sister to you.'

'Of course. I helped bring her up — when I was around. We always got on well, we *are* a real brother and sister. More so now, since we lost Dad a year ago.'

'I'm so sorry.' Kate took a breath. 'Was there one event that might have tipped her over the edge?' she asked, cautiously, knowing how difficult it was for Jamie to discuss Megan, but also understanding that he'd been the one to open up and he therefore needed to talk a few things through.

'We don't know for sure. It could have been when her mother died although that was years before we got the first hint that something was wrong. It crept up on her and we didn't see it happening, then one day, it took over and ran us all down.'

'And you looked after her these last four years?'

'Me and Dad.' He shrugged and settled back into his chair, hands flat on the table top. 'Dad had retired but I had to work. I tried to keep the jobs close to home and short-term but often my work takes me Australia-wide.'

'You had medical bills?'

'Not so much medical bills, more the never-ending search for the best counselling. And she needed constant care — and watching over. Dad picked some additional work to begin with, writing articles for an agricultural magazine. He worked in forestry and environment before he retired. It helped. Then it was just me and Megan, so I stayed close to home. Always.'

'So where is Megan now?'

'In Victoria. She's staying with a woman who treats without treating. She and her husband live on a farm in the country. It's a big bustling family. Five children. Three dogs, a few horses, sheep, chickens, llamas. You name it. There's plenty of work for Megan, once she's up for it, which I think she must be now. It'll keep her occupied with something other than herself.' At last, he paused. 'Or at least, that's what's I've been told is happening.'

Kate reflected on his words. She was relieved about Megan being Jamie's sister, intrigued and saddened by what had happened to the Knight family, and worried for Megan. And for Jamie. What a hero Jamie was. A true knight. How often did an ordinary person come across one?

His family were lucky to have him. This town was lucky to have him. And Kate? She was lucky to have met him.

'Is that why you bought Silver Bells House?' she asked. It couldn't possibly have been because he'd seen a shooting star. She didn't believe that. 'Because of the country connection. Are you hoping Megan will come live with you?'

'I'm hoping you'll come live with me.'

Kate blinked. 'Me?'

'I've been wrangling with a decision too. And I've made it.' He put his hands onto the tabletop and straightened. 'I love you, Katie. I love you and adore you.'

Chapter Thirteen

Oh no. *No. No. No.* He couldn't love her. He *couldn't*.

'I can see I've shocked you.' He took his hands from the table and placed them somewhere beneath — on his thighs maybe. Or his knees. And why was Kate so completely concerned about where he'd put his bloody hands? It was her brain she should be considering. And any possible answer her brain might come up with.

'It's okay.' He nodded. 'I just had to tell you.' He pushed his chair from the table and walked to the fridge, opened the door and pulled out a beer. 'I wanted you to know.' He unscrewed the cap in the palm of his hand and took a quick slug. 'I don't want this to mess anything up for you, but you've been through a lot of crap and lies and it seems to me it's best to be truthful.'

Oh God. Did he want her to be truthful back?

'Aren't you going to chalk it up on the board?' he asked, with a smile, nodding at the forgotten lists on the chalk board.

'You're being awfully calm about what was a pretty big declaration.'

He shrugged. 'I can't do anything about what I feel, Kate. I love you.'

She held her hands up. 'Stop saying it!'

His smile deepened. 'This is going to eat at you, isn't it?' He leaned against the fridge and crossed his feet at the ankles. 'It's okay. You don't have to love me back — unless you want to.'

'I don't want to — I mean…' Holy missiles. 'That's not what I meant,' she said. She put her hands onto the table to steady herself. 'I'm sorry. I don't know what I mean.'

'That's okay too. I figure you'll work it out.'

'I can't believe you said it. I mean one minute we're discussing your sister and the next you're telling me you're in lo — You're in…affection-mode with me.' Craziness. Was it April Fool's Day or something?

'In love,' he said steadily.

'Don't you mean deep affection? Maybe a little adoration? Tenderness. That's what I feel for you.'

'No. I'm afraid I mean love.'

Damn that word.

'Why did you choose to tell me now?' she asked. And did he mean it? Had he thought this through?

'Well, Megan's doing well. She's getting better and she's happy. That makes me happy. You happen to make me happy too. And I can't help being in *adoration-mode* with you. Neither do I want to help it. I damn well love you.'

Kate put her hands over her ears and gave him a right royal managerial look of disapproval.

He uncrossed his feet and pushed from the fridge door where he'd been resting as though waiting for the next bus to love-town. 'Fancy a game of Exasperation?' he asked, putting his beer onto the table and sitting opposite Kate.

'You're joking, aren't you?'

He pulled the boxed game from the end of the table where they'd discarded it the other night. 'No,' he said, looking steadily into her eyes. 'I'm not joking. I'll be blue. You can be red.'

'Stop joking, Jamie.'

He looked up and grinned, the little frown between his brow sitting there, all patiently unconcerned. 'How come you haven't said anything with a country vernacular flavour?' he asked, pulling the bowl of peanuts closer to him. 'Thought you might have been holy-molying by now.'

Kate's mouth dropped open. 'Because I'm speechless!'

'Well that's a first.' He picked a peanut from the bowl, threw it into the air and caught it in his mouth. 'I might even win this game.'

'Come on,' Jamie said as he pulled her by the hand into the bedroom an hour later. 'It's late. You don't want to play a game. You don't want to eat my roast chicken — although I have to tell you, it was very good. So let's go to bed.'

'Jamie, you can't expect me to…'

'You don't want to deny me my boyfriend rights any more than I intend to deny you your girlfriend rights.'

'Jamie!'

He stopped in the doorway and Kate bumped into his back. He turned to her, his gaze twinkling down in humour. *Humour!* Where had he found humour? This was a dead serious situation. He wasn't playing the game. He was cheating, big time.

'Oh come on,' he said easily, with a shrug for emphasis. 'We haven't argued. This won't be make-up sex; it'll just be the same type of sex we had the day before yesterday, yesterday and this morning.'

The amazing type. But this time he'd be doing it with love on his mind.

'And anyway,' he said with another shrug — and a smile. *A goddamned smile!* 'There aren't any clean sheets on the spare room bed. Wouldn't want you to have to sleep on a bare mattress. What kind of loving boyfriend hoping for more would that make me?'

Huh. Right. Kate straightened her shoulders, looked him in the eye and with a contemptuous flick of her ponytail, breezed past him into the bedroom.

She'd never felt so nervous about undressing in her life. She slipped her shorts down her legs, but kept her knickers on. As she was taking her top off she caught sight of Jamie. He'd undressed. Totally. And didn't seem to be bothered by any shyness.

Kate undid her bra, dropped it onto his chest of drawers as Jamie wandered — naked — over to the bed and pulled the coverlet back. He plumped up the pillows.

Well. If Jamie could do it, so could Kate. She slipped her knickers off, dropped them on top of her bra and walked to the bed.

He pulled the cover back, her side, but didn't look at her.

Kate slipped in the bed and lay there. She desperately wanted him to hug her and tell her he'd been joking. That he had an overwhelming fondness for her, but of course he didn't love her. It was too soon to fall in love. Nine days. What madness.

'Actually, Katie,' he said on a yawn. 'How about we just sleep, eh? It's been a pretty tiring couple of days.'

Tiring? Tired didn't come into the equation of Jamie saying he *loved* her. She'd never get to sleep.

'Are you going to blame me for not fulfilling my *lover* duties?' she asked, feeling suddenly affronted and disappointed all at once.

'Lover, huh?' he asked. He closed his eyes, settling his big workman's head on the pillow. 'That's a nice thought.'

He had his eyes closed? When she was naked next to him? And what about the term *nice*? What sort of word was *nice*? Surely he meant wonderful, amazing…even *fine* would be better than *nice*.

'Of course I'm not going to blame you,' he said, opening his eyes and aiming his gaze right at her. 'Not for anything. Anyway. Turns out I've run out of condoms.' He flipped onto his back, hooking her with his arm and snuggling her into his shoulder. 'So let's just cuddle.'

Run out? Kate tried to settle against him. She took a big, muddled-thought breath and sighed it out as though about to fall asleep. As though her mind wasn't racing. As though her mouth wasn't itching to open and tell him she had two emergency condoms in her suitcase. Emergency as in — in case it happened. Which it hadn't since she'd placed them into the elasticated side pocket of her suitcase some six, seven or ten months ago.

He sighed deeply, as though settling in nicely for a good night's sleep.

'Jamie,' Kate whispered.

'Mmm?'

Her mind played war games. Missiles fired in her brain. Tell him. Don't tell him. Go to sleep.

'I've got two,' she said quietly. 'In my suitcase.'

He turned from his back to his side and hauled her in against him, both arms around her naked, suddenly-warmed body. 'Well,' he said softly, kissing her lips with his toothpaste-tasting opened mouth. 'Isn't that just finger-lickin' lucky?'

Goddamn him — he'd got her.

Kate shoved the top right-hand drawer back into its chest. He had a whole box of condoms. A whole box of forty!

Forty? Holy smokin', devious, summer air and lime-smelling.... *man*! Typical. Just wait until she got him in front of that Exasperation board again. She'd pop him into oblivion.

Or would she? The thought of forty nights with Jamie sent shivers down her spine.

She felt so many things for him. Masses of...*adoration*. Heaps of tenderness. Bucket loads of friendship. Almost...almost... She shook her head. Not quite love. Not quite. It was too soon.

'You still up here?' he asked from behind her.

'Yes,' Kate answered, and opened the curtains on one of the windows. 'I was just tidying up.' She moved the next window and flung the curtains apart.

'Are you hiding?'

He was right behind her. He'd crept up on her. He turned her to face him and tilted her chin up. He bent and kissed her mouth softly then brushed the fringe from her forehead. 'I don't want you to make the wrong decision.'

'I can't even think straight after last night.'

'That's why I want you to take your time. Think about you, Kate, not me. I want you to read yourself properly, from the inside out. All you've done so far is skim the surface. You think you've found yourself but there's more.'

'I don't think I want to talk to you about it.' She still felt too raw and confused.

'That's fine too. Now stop moping and come on downstairs. We've got to make up a plate of food for tomorrow's festivities.' He released her and moved to the door.

Kate yanked the top drawer of the chest open, pulled out a pair of rolled up workman's socks and lobbed them at his back. 'I don't want to go anymore.'

The socks bounced off his shoulder and onto the floor but he ignored them and continued out of the door and down the hallway. 'Come on, Contrary-Katie,' he called. 'Come give me a hand.'

Kate crossed her arms and leaned a hip against the chest of drawers. 'I like you a lot,' she yelled after him. 'But you can't expect me to *you know what* this quickly.'

No response. Kate slammed the drawer closed and stomped after him.

Kate walked cautiously towards the landline telephone in the kitchen. She didn't recognise the number on the ID... Dang! Of course she didn't. It wasn't her phone. Wasn't her house.

She punched the caller ID number into her mobile in case it was business and Jamie needed to call them back. He had taken a few business calls on his mobile, but nobody had rung on the landline. Not since Kate had arrived. And he'd gone into town for foodstuffs for tomorrow's Christmas Eve present-giving gig.

She picked up the telephone and pressed the answer button. 'Hello, Knight Works. Jamie Knight's residence.'

'Oh — you sound lovely.'

She did? So did the young female voice on the other end of the phone.

'I'm afraid Jamie isn't here,' Kate said. 'Can I take a message?'

'I know he's not there, that's why I'm calling you. It's Kate, right?'

'Right.'

'I'm Megan.'

Oh, my goodness! Kate clutched at the bench top.

'Jamie's sister.'

'Yes, hello. How are you?' Damn. Kate winced. Perhaps she wasn't supposed to ask that question.

'I'm fine. Pretty good. Jamie told me he's fallen in love with you.'

'Um...' There it was again — the *love* word. 'Yes,' Kate said softly. 'He told me too.'

'I just called him now, on his mobile, so I knew he wasn't at home.'

'You're calling to talk to me,' Kate said, worry at the upcoming conversation gnawing at her stomach. Was she going to have to admit to Jamie's sister that she didn't love Jamie enough? That love was there, bobbing around deep inside her somewhere. But that she felt so much pressure to get everything troubling her right that her emotions had crashed into a brick wall and were currently sinking in knee-high mud and getting showered in all sorts of parrot poop.

'Can I be open with you?' Megan asked. 'Since we might — you know — be sisters soon.'

Oh dang. Kate squeezed her eyes closed. 'Of course.' Here it came. *Do you love my brother? Will you cherish him forever?*

'I bet Jamie's told you all about me,' Megan said. 'And my illness.'

Kate forgot her own fears and straightened her spine. 'Yes, he told me, Megan.'

'What I've got is a mental illness, you see. I realise it although I've only just managed to say so.'

'You're the bravest,' Kate said softly.

'There's more to the world than I thought, Kate. I'm beginning to see other people. Those around me, you know? The family I'm staying with. I bet Jamie's told you where I am.'

Kate said, 'Yes, he did.' Megan didn't seem to mind. Truthfulness, Kate reminded herself. So long as it didn't harm.

'Well, you see — these people I'm staying with, I'm finding out that they have tough things to deal with too. Like ordinary things which are tough. Hard work — you have to get up early on a farm.'

'I know.' Kate didn't know what happened on a farm other than what she'd read about it being a twenty-four-seven job. A struggle. A hardship that somehow every farmer and his or her family loved and endeavoured for. *And where was this conversation heading?*

'I've missed out on so much over the last four or five years,' Megan said. 'And I don't want to miss the next decade. Know what I mean?'

'I do.' Kate thought of her business and her lost *raison d'être*.

'I look back now…' Megan paused, the silence filled with what were obviously challenging thoughts for the young woman. 'I realise how well I did. At school, at college. I got good grades even while feeling desperate about myself.'

Oh, you poor darling. To be so alone with this illness.

'I didn't think I was good enough.'

'You are good enough. For anything you want to do.'

Another silence. Kate held her breath.

'Jamie missed out too.'

Kate swallowed.

'My brother missed out because he was helping me.'

'He wouldn't have had it any other way, Megan.'

'I know that. That's why I love him the extra special bit. That's why I don't want him to miss out on anything else. You…'

'Me?' Kate asked, almost breathless with panic now.

'He loves you.'

Kate clutched the phone, blinking through a cloud of confusion. What was love? A condition of the heart, supposedly. Nobody had ever said anything about bells ringing and snowflakes falling, making your skin tingle in a cascading ripple of pleasure. Like when you came in from out of the cold and sat barefoot in front a roaring fire, wiggling your toes and getting all warm and content. Or about wanting to help decorate and do up a stone house with a sloping roof and a paddock for a back garden. Or learn how to roast a chicken. That wasn't love. Love was supposed to hurt so bad you couldn't think straight, not sit around choosing colour schemes in your mind for bedrooms or think about how many cushions the Chesterfield would hold. Or whether or not tarragon and lemon peel would be a tasty topping for a roast chicken.

'Kate,' Megan said, breaking into Kate's condition of the heart. 'It's none of my business,' she said, 'but I do hope you love him right back. That would be great.'

'It's not always easy, Megan... I mean—'

'Oh, I'm not pressuring you, Kate. Honestly. But he's never been in love before — that I know of.'

Please stop saying the love *word.* 'I have a lot of business problems at the moment.' Sounded worse than pathetic. Look what this young girl had gone through and Kate was blathering on about business problems? 'But I do like Jamie. So very much.' So much it hurt. The pressure was building inside her now. To get something right. What did Fat Jacques matter? It was Jamie she should be gunning for. 'He's the best man I've ever met,' she told Megan. 'He loves you very much.'

Megan laughed. 'Sometimes too much.'

There was no way on earth Jamie Knight could love too much. To be under the spell of his eternal love would be magical.

'Thanks for talking to me,' Megan said. 'I've got to go, I have pig feeding duties to attend to.' She laughed, as though the remark was some personal joke.

'It was lovely to talk to you, Megan. Thank you for calling me. I know how much Jamie means to you.'

'Bye, Kate. Hopefully I'll get to talk to you again. Maybe see you one day.'

Maybe. 'I hope so too. Bye, Megan.'

As she ended the call Kate's mobile rang. She checked the ID on the vibrating, lit-up rectangular face. Fat Jacques.

Perfect. *And you know what, Jacques Burch?* Kate said to herself as she picked up her phone. *You can have it. You can have the lot. I've made my decision.*

She pressed the Answer key. 'Kate Singleton.'

Jamie closed the front door and paused. The atmosphere in the house was as sharp as a razor. The walls felt all shook up. Any second now he imagined the roof might cave in.

He looked up to the landing at the sound of a door slamming, then a chair or something being scraped across the floorboards, then the rollers of…a suitcase?

He took the stairs two at a time. From the racket going on, he half expected to see the fourteen-tonner fired up in the bedroom. Instead, he found Kate.

'What's happened?' he asked.

'Fat Jacques,' she said, and threw her white pumps into the open suitcase on the bed.

'What's he done now?'

'He's thrown me a hard ball.'

'You mean curve ball.'

'Whatever. His aim is pretty good.' She moved around the bedroom like a bullet. Whipping clothes from a bedside chair, scrunching them up, folding them haphazardly and slamming them into the suitcase.

Jamie held his hands up. 'Slow down, Kate. What's happened?'

'I have to get back to Sydney.'

That razor blade pierced Jamie's heart. 'Now?'

'I rang a car hire company in Cooma. They're sending a car down for me tomorrow morning. They said they'd leave it in town because it's Christmas Eve and they have to...whatever. So I asked them to leave it with Mrs Tam at the petrol station.'

Jesus.

'I'll drive to Canberra and catch a flight to Sydney. I've booked that too.' She paused in her whirling dervish activities. 'This is costing me a fortune.' She slammed the suitcase lid down and zipped it closed.

'Kate.'

She looked across at him, and straightened. 'I have to go, Jamie. I built this business with my heart. I can't let someone walk all over me and take it from me. I mean... They can have the business — but not my reputation. *Never* that. Do you know how hard I worked?' she asked, poking herself in the chest with her finger. 'For how long I worked to get to where I am today?' She shrugged in some sort of despair and turned, heaving the suitcase off the bed.

Jamie stepped forwards and took it off her, putting it on the floor.

'My *reputation*!' she said. 'I won't let him take that from me.'

'How has he ruined your goddamned reputation?'

'Don't swear at me,' she yelled. 'I'm teetering on the edge here.'

'Alright. Alright,' he said again, calmer. 'What's the bastard done?'

She sniffed. 'He brokered that deal, remember? The one that would take Sensations into the big time.'

'Yeah, and you had a choice. Let him take it and go along with it, or pull out. That's what this time in the country was all about. Making your choice. The choice you want.'

'Well, the scumbag has gone one better and razed all my choices. Apparently, the only way the deal will go through now is if I resign.' Her eyes widened in bitter fury. 'Resign! Give up everything I worked for. Because…' She threw her arms up. 'The new financiers have been told that I'm not to be trusted.' She thumped her chest with her fist. 'Me! Not trusted! Can you bloody believe that?'

No, he couldn't. 'You're feeling torn apart, Kate. Why don't you stay here with me until after Christmas?' He was getting desperate and he knew it. But he didn't have a choice. 'We can figure things out. Chalk up the lot on the board downstairs.'

'No time. I have to go tomorrow. If I could get into Cooma tonight I'd go now.' She looked at him, blinked. 'You wouldn't take me, would you?'

He shook his head. 'No.' He walked across to her and took hold of her shoulders. 'Are you sure you want this business? From what I've learned of you, you don't. You're making a snap decision.'

'About time. I've been dawdling for days.' She broke from him and walked to the windows.

'Pretty good days though, weren't they?'

She stopped her edgy pacing. 'Jamie.' She came to him and put her arms around his waist and her cheek on his chest. 'I've had a fantastic time here with you.' She looked up. 'You do understand? Don't you?'

About why she was going? *No.*

'Will you come back?' he asked.

'I don't know.'

So here he was again, not wanted. What was the point in giving your heart if duty of care didn't matter to the recipient of your love? This wasn't the same as giving Megan her space, this was losing. There was every chance Kate wouldn't return.

'You're scared, Katie. That's all it is.'

'Maybe,' she said softly. 'But we both know that if I stay in the city, this thing between us wouldn't work.'

Now it was a thing?

'You travel, I travel.' She stepped back from him, took his hands in hers and tilted her head in what appeared to be bewildering exasperation. 'We'd be travelling all the time. We'd never see each other.'

He smiled, released her hand although it was the hardest thing he'd ever done. Worse even than letting Megan go off without him to her country farm. But he had to let Kate go. She had to find her own way through this, and he had to force himself to make it easy for her. 'Jumpin' jackfish, Katie,' he said, forcing the smile into his eyes and into his voice. 'You gone broke my heart, girl.'

She shot back, covering her face with her hands. 'Don't say that. Don't joke about it.'

He stepped forwards and wrapped her in his arms. 'It's alright. Hush now.' All he could do was let her go and hope she'd come back.

Where were the magic stars when you needed them?

Chapter Fourteen

Jamie stopped on the walkway outside Cuddly Bear Toy & Gift shop. He peered through the fake snow and snowflake decals stuck on the glass and ran an eye over the window display behind. This was the only shop in town that sold gifts and he wanted one for Kate. He didn't have time to drive into Cooma. Leaving Kate on her own yesterday while he shopped for groceries had been difficult enough. He'd thought she might scarper behind his back because he'd told her he loved her. She was ready to hear it in her heart, but not her mind. And the two hadn't gelled yet. He'd half expected her to get into the excavator and drive that out of town. But he'd had no idea what trouble he'd really be going home to.

Now here he was in town again, this time to check that her hire car had been delivered.

It had. Thank God, because there was no way he was going to drive her anywhere. She was going to have to get used to hearing him say he loved her because he did love her. Adored her. And he was used to playing mind games although he hadn't thought he'd have to use them to this extent. This time, it was Jamie who was cheating.

It didn't feel like Christmas Eve, it felt like hell.

'Morning, Jamie. What are you doing in a toy shop? Where's Kate?'

Jamie smiled at Mrs Tam who stood at the counter next to Ted and Mary Munroe, Gemma's mother, who owned the shop.

'I could say the same to you both,' Jamie said, indicating Ted with a nod.

'We ran out of teddies,' Ted said. 'Mary here ordered two more. Just got time to wrap them before this afternoon's extravaganza.'

'What can I do for you, Jamie?' Mary asked, pushing her short blonde hair behind ears that somehow held up gold hoop earrings so big a dog could jump through them. A small dog, anyway.

'I'm buying a present for Kate. I saw something in the window I think might be perfect.'

Ted huffed. 'Love in the air, is it?' he asked. 'I've only just changed the population sign for you. I've got to change it again for the new guy, so if your woman is staying too, let me know soon, would you? Save me two trips up the ladder with a paintbrush in my hand.'

His woman. Sounded good. 'I'll let you know when I know, Ted.'

'Like that, is it?' Mrs Tam asked with a motherly frown of concern.

'I'm afraid so, Mrs Tam. But don't worry. I've got a plan.' And maybe the townspeople could help. 'Actually, folks, I couldn't have a confidential quick word with you all, could I?'

They hadn't made love last night but Jamie had held her. All night. Kate thought she must have dozed on and off. He'd been awake each time she stirred. Each time her eyelids flickered open. Perhaps he hadn't slept.

She reviewed her appearance in the bathroom mirror. Smart. Professional.

He appeared in the bathroom doorway, a hand on the frame. 'Okay. The car hire people have dropped off your car. It's parked next to the petrol station.'

She looked at him in the mirror. 'Thank you.' She blinked at him. 'How do I look? Fighting fit?'

'You look just fine. Five minutes, and we'll go. I've put your luggage in the ute.'

He disappeared from the doorway.

Kate plucked the lid off her lipstick, angled her face to the mirror and applied the dusky-rose colour to her lips.

This is the best thing to do, she told her reflection. She straightened the jacket of her raspberry-red suit and shuffled the slim-line skirt over her hips. Yes. Fighting fit.

Kate's heartbeat had been racing the whole fifteen-minute silent drive into town. She'd concentrated on remembering everything, like a montage in her mind. The No Through Road driveway from Silver Bells House, and the towering gum trees lining her way out of the country. The wildflowers on the verges of All Seasons Road. The endless road into town.

The road out of town.

Jamie parked the ute next to the hire car and handed her the vehicle keys before getting out of the ute and walking to the tray-back where all her belongings sat.

He heaved them off and put them onto the ground behind the car.

'My, my. What a surprise to find you leaving, Kate,' Mrs Tam said as she came out of the petrol station's office.

'Something came up,' Kate said with a forced smile. 'I have to leave earlier than expected.'

Mrs Tam tutted and looked up at Jamie.

'She's made a decision,' he told Mrs Tam. 'That's why she was in town, to make a decision. And she's made it. Sort of.'

Sort of? Kate looked up at Jamie. She had made The Decision.

'I see,' Mrs Tam said, and patted Jamie's arm.

What did Mrs Tam see?

'What a gentleman, Jamie. A true gentleman. Bringing your lovely girlfriend into town and letting her leave.'

'Thank you, Mrs Tam. I'm hoping this will work.'

Hoping *what* would work?

'Well, bye, dear,' Mrs Tam said, lifting a hand in farewell before turning and sauntering off towards the stock feeders' where she stopped to chat with Grace Tillman and Mrs Penman who were standing beside the plastic neighing horse.

'Bye,' Kate said, her voice soft. She frowned at Jamie. 'She didn't seem too sorry to see me go.'

'She didn't, did she?'

Kate raised her hand and waved at the women. 'Bye,' she called out. 'Thank you so much for letting me help out. I had a great time.'

All three ladies smiled, lifted a hand in response and returned to their conversation. A door closed on the walkway opposite. Kate looked over the street as Ted and Mr Penman came down the walkway stairs, chatting effusively about something. Ted's arms were waving. Mr Penman's legs were crooked. Poor man. Must still be struggling with his condition.

'Ted,' Kate called. 'Did the suit fit?'

'Thank you, it did.'

'Bye then,' Kate said. 'I'm leaving now. Hope you have a wonderful afternoon.'

'Everything's organised,' Ted said. 'Everything's arranged with precision. Why shouldn't we have a wonderful afternoon?'

Kate shrugged. 'I was just saying...'

Ted and Mr Penman walked on by, heading to the ladies outside the stock feeders'.

'That's weird,' Kate said. This was no ordinary day for Swallow's Fall, she reminded herself. It was Christmas Eve and they had the party and present-giving this afternoon. Why should they care what the visitor from the city thought or did?

'What about your wine?' Jamie asked. 'You've got six bottles left. Want me to post them?'

'You keep them.'

He smiled. 'Thanks. I will. Your Chardonnay will go nicely with my roast turkey tomorrow.' He walked past her and put her suitcase and her carry-on into the boot of the hire car.

A man who cooked his own Christmas turkey. Kate felt like she'd cooked her goose to smithereens and shared the charred bones with Scrooge. God, what was this nonsense going on inside her head?

She ran both hands over her head, smoothing her hair back and checking the knot of her ponytail.

All secure.

Right then. This was it.

Holy tear ducts. She was crying.

Jamie slammed the boot and walked to her side. He dug into the pocket of his khaki trousers and produced a clean white handkerchief. 'Here,' he said, handing it to her. 'I had a feeling you might need it.'

She took it and pressed the folded square of cotton beneath each eye. 'Don't be nice to me,' she said, her voice catching. 'I done gone broke your heart, remember?'

He opened the driver's door. 'Don't worry. I'll forget about you in around sixty years.'

A sob caught in her throat. She'd be looking at her ninetieth birthday in sixty years. What would she have to look back on? What trials would she be most proud of? Not this one, that was for sure. She was nothing short of varmint — or vermin — whichever it was. A rat deserting the sinking love boat.

'Keep it,' he said when she offered him the handkerchief. 'Oh, oh.'

'What?' Kate asked as he peered into the car.

'Manual shift.' He looked down at her red stilettos. 'You going to manage?'

Kate swallowed. 'Of course.' She got into the car, settled herself in the seat, checked the controls and pulled at the seatbelt. She'd stop outside town and take her stilettos off. But she wasn't going to do that now. That would make her look incapable. Flappy. Undecided.

Kate turned the key in the ignition. Jamie closed the door. Kate pressed the window button. The country air, so fresh and warm blew into the car as did Jamie's essence. Lime-scented fragrance. Strength.

Kate put the shift into first gear.

Jamie slapped the roof with his hand. 'Okay. Drive safe.' He stepped back from the car.

Was that it? Drive safe? No last use of the *love* word? No final declarations of adoration? No swearing to never forget her, even after sixty years?

'Well if you're going to take it *that* way!' What was wrong with this town today?

'See you, Kate.' Jamie turned and walked away.

Kate twisted in her seat to watch him. He stopped by the group outside the stock feeders', slipped his hands into his khaki trouser pockets and started up a conversation with the ladies. They smiled up at him. Ted laughed. Even Mr Penman had a grin on his face. Had Jamie told them a joke or something?

Holy mackerel. They'd slapped her in the face. Why had they done this? Because she didn't belong, that's why.

Right. *Sassy*, she told herself silently. *Sensational*. She shot around in her seat, checked the street for traffic, did a fast U-turn and drove off, heading south. Heading homewards. Heading towards a big fight. And boy, was she in the mood for it.

Jamie sat at the bar in Kookaburra's nursing his beer, his misery and his hope. The new guy seemed like a decent sort. Resident number eighty-nine. While Jamie's perfect, pretty, executive number ninety was... Where? What was Katie doing? Was she thinking hard about everything, or still stuck inside her snap decision to leave and fight the world on her own? The former, hopefully. That's what he was betting his heart on. And he hoped to God she'd had the good sense to stop the car after careering out of town the way she had, and change out of those damned four-inch heels. She'd practically left rubber marks on the bitumen.

'Not long now, Jamie. I'm sure of it,' Mrs Tam said, coming up to the bar and offering him a party pie from the platter in her hand.

'No thanks, not hungry.'

She patted his arm and Jamie was tempted to hug her. Or bury his head in her motherly shoulder.

'Hang in there, Jamie.'

'I am.' He checked his watch.

Kate sat in the hire car, fingertips resting on the bottom of the steering wheel as the warm summer breeze flew through all four opened windows.

She'd pulled over and parked next to a school playing field when the pictures in her head began to make her vision swim. She hadn't meant them to plunge full steam ahead into her mind while she was driving. She'd thought she'd be using the pictures in the future. Basking in the memory of her time in Swallow's Fall with a soft-hearted fond recollection of Ted's stupid jokes and Mrs Tam's ice creams. She glanced at the clock on her mobile which sat on the dashboard. They'd be handing out the presents in town about now. Wonder if Mr Penman would manage to get through the twenty-minute stint?

Oh, to see the faces of the littlies as they opened their felt-puzzles. And the babies, snuggling up to their teddies. Dang. Hope the toy shop managed to get those two missing teddies or there'd be two babies crying.

And Jamie. Wonder what he thought of his pen? And would he have picked up her soaps? No. Sammy had probably done that. Sammy and Ethan should have arrived home from their honeymoon by now. Jamie had fixed up their property. Hot water and electricity all sorted.

Why hadn't Kate left town a bit later? She could have stayed another two hours, couldn't she? To see her best friend. To say, welcome home, best friend, and boy what a home town you have. She could have stayed with them at their homestead and spent Christmas with — somebody.

Her eyes prickled with tears. Good job she was wearing waterproof mascara. She blinked, and felt her eyelashes stick together. Great.

She pulled a paper tissue from her handbag, dabbed her eyes dry. Well, dry-ish, and picked up her mobile. She hit the speed dial for Sammy and waited.

'Where are you?' Sammy asked, sounding tetchy.

'I left.'

'I know that. I'm home and you're gone.'

Kate winced. 'Did you have lovely honeymoon?'

'Beautiful. Why did you leave? What about Jamie and the shooting stars?'

'Yes, Sammy,' Kate said, getting all agitated, which was much better than sitting around in an empty car getting all sorry for herself. 'What about them? What did you do?'

Kate listened to the silence.

'I thought you'd fall in love with him,' Sammy said at last. 'I thought you'd fall so madly in love you'd stay and I'd have my best friend in town.' Sammy sighed, possibly accepting the truth. 'Where are you?' she asked.

'Sitting in my hire car. I'm just south of Cooma.'

'What? You left hours ago. You should be at Canberra airport by now. In fact, you should be halfway to Sydney. You've missed your flight.'

'I know. I stopped outside Cooma for an ice cream and couldn't go any further.'

'Why?'

'I left my Wellington boots behind.'

Silence. 'Want me to post them to you?'

'No thanks. Thought I might nip back and get them.'

'Okay. Jamie's in Kookaburra's. We're all here. The new guy opened up.'

'But my wellies will be up at the house.'

'Yeah, but you're not coming back for your wellies, are you?'

'You okay, Jamie?' Sammy asked him as she slipped onto the bar stool next to him.

Jamie swiped a hand over his mouth and attempted to remove the frown from his forehead but it wouldn't budge. He checked his watch. 'Getting a little nervous,' he said.

'Have you heard from her?'

'No. Have you?'

Sammy nodded, and hope and dread partied hard in Jamie's chest.

'She said she'd forgotten something,' Sammy told him. 'Left something at your house.'

'Right.' Relief poured through his veins. 'Okay. So that's how it's going to go. I was wondering.'

'Weren't you going to go after her?'

'I was hoping there'd be no need.' He picked up his beer, saw that his hand was shaking and put the bottle back onto the bar. 'Although, I swear to God, when I see her, I might just pick her up and shake her for putting me through this.' Torture. Agony. His shoulders were so tense he doubted he'd feel the pain if he was run over by a twenty-four-tonner.

Sammy's shoulders relaxed as she leaned an elbow on the bar. 'Ah-ha,' she said pointedly. 'Starting to make sense.' She grinned. 'You got the whole town involved in this tough love program?'

Jamie nodded. 'Some of them. And let's hope there is an *ah-ha* moment, Sammy. Otherwise I'm about five hours late.'

She grinned wickedly and Jamie reached out and put a hand on her shoulder. 'Thank you,' he said. 'For finding Kate for me.'

She clapped her hands. 'Oh, this is going to be *so* good!'

Jamie grimaced. *Let's hope so.* He checked his watch.

Okay so here she was, back in town. Fine. She could cope with whatever came her way. Kate Singleton was an ex-executive with experience and panache. She could breeze her way into Kookaburra's and find Sammy and — anyone else —with a smile and a debonair, breezy attitude. It's what she'd been doing all her life. Gliding into powerful situations, grabbing them, running with them and getting on with it.

So why was she shaking?

She got out of the car and looked down at her white pumps. No, she wouldn't change them. She looked up and down the street. The fairy lights were lit. So this is what Swallow's Fall looked like on the evening of Christmas Eve. Someone had set up tall spotlights around the Christmas tree — Jamie, probably — and a group of young people were gathering around, sorting out their musical instruments. Oh, good. She hadn't missed all the Christmas cheer. Maybe the choir were going to do a candlelight session. She hoped so. She wanted to cheer them on. She even knew all the words, after hearing them practise that day she'd helped decorate the town.

She made her way across the street, walked up the steps to the walkway and pushed her way through the swing door of Kookaburra's and into the bustling, friendly, excited atmosphere.

Hot potatoes. Everyone was here.

'Hello, Kate,' Mrs Tam called from a crowd of townspeople. 'Are you hungry, dear?'

'No thanks. I'm fine.' Kate smiled and looked around for Sammy and Ethan. And — anyone else.

She made her way through the families. Everyone wore cracker hats — yellow, blue and red paper crowns. Dang. She'd missed the Christmas cracker pulling.

Funny how everyone was just nodding and saying, *Hi, Kate*. Funny that they were behaving as though she'd just popped out of town for a spot of shopping and nothing more. Funny how Jamie was marching across the bar towards her…frowning. Oh, boy. How was she going to handle this? He looked gritty. A bit peeved. And so muscly.

'Hello,' she said as he came up to her.

'You came back,' he said, taking hold of her arm, turning her and leading her to the door.

She tripped. Holy flat white pumps. She never tripped!

He led her outside onto the walkway. The music, laughter and chatter filtered out from the pub and straight onto the balmy, Christmassy night-time scene outside.

'You came back.' he said again, stopping them both by the walkway railing.

'I forgot something.'

'Ah-ha.' He nodded, looking wise suddenly. 'How far did you get?'

Kate took a breath. 'Cooma.'

He checked his watch. 'You must have been sitting there for close to four hours.'

'I left something behind.'

'You came back.'

'My wellies. And I think I left a lipstick in your bathroom.'

'You could have sent me a text message,' he said. 'I would have posted them to you.'

'Well, I figured that might be too much to ask.' Kate cleared her throat. 'Did you pick up my Santa present?'

He jutted a chin towards the pub. 'I left it on the bar. I think it's a box of soap or something.'

Kate nodded. 'It is. Twelve soaps. Did you like your pen?'

Jamie nodded. 'Yeah. It's a good pen. I got you something else, actually.' He reached into the back pocket of his trousers and produced a tiny, tiny present wrapped in silver gift paper, with a pompom-type silver bow on the top. The type that showered ribbons over the present.

'Oh, golly gosh.' She took it off him. 'You got me a present?'

'Open it.'

'I didn't get you anything.'

'Yes you did.'

'Did I?'

'Open it.'

She ripped at the ribbon and the paper. Holy snow globe. Except this tiny snow globe didn't have snow. She shook it and a million silver stars flew around the watery interior and fell around and over a little model of a cottage. 'It's beautiful.'

'I got lucky,' he said. 'Found it in the toy shop.'

She blinked up at him. 'What did I get you?'

'You gave me one hell of a scare, Katie.'

'When?'

'I thought it'd only take two hours. Three maximum. You had me on tenterhooks for nearly six damned hours.'

'That was my present to you?'

He took the star globe off her and put it onto the walkway railing. 'You came back, Kate. That's my present.' He tilted his head, narrowed his eyes and frowned at her. 'Oh-oh. Is that a nearly-thirty-year-old's tear I see glistening in your right eye?'

She sniffed, and let the tear roll down her cheek — as though she'd be able to stop it. Then one rolled out of her left eye. She nodded as it drifted down her other cheek.

'How often are you going to cry?' he asked. 'Like — every Christmas birthday?'

'What's it to you?'

'Just wondering how often I'm going to have to deal with it over the next sixty years.'

'Oh, Jamie.' Kate flung herself at him, her heart almost bouncing out of her chest. He caught her, and held her. And held her. Tight. So tightly she felt like she was magic in a bottle, all shook up and ready to explode.

'Do I love you?' she asked. Her vocal chords must have got twisted when she lunged at him because her voice broke on the *love* word.

'Well I hope you don't intend to throw yourself at the next new man who walks into town, or I'm going to think you don't.'

The band started playing 'It's Beginning to Look a Lot Like Christmas'. Kate winced. 'The band's playing.' She untwined herself from his arms. 'They're not very good.'

'Terrible,' Jamie agreed. 'But there's hope. They can only get better.'

'Not sure if I'll get better at this…'

'This what, Kate?'

She took a little breath. 'I spoke to Fat Jacques. I told him to stuff it.'

He raised one eyebrow. 'How much stuffing did you give him?'

She licked her lip. 'The lot. I've sold him my half of the business.'

'And what about your reputation?'

'I'm going to build it again. Different this time, though. I'm going to go back to drawing the designs, like Sammy used to do. But I'm also going to start up another business. I was thinking of an online fashion house. That way — I could work from anywhere.'

'Good for you, Kate. I told you I'd put my last dollar on you.'

'Did you hear what I said?' Kate asked. 'Anywhere. I could work from anywhere.'

'Why would that be so important?'

She hung her head, staring down at the wooden planks of the walkway. 'Because I love you so much my heart hurts without you for even six hours,' she whispered. 'I love you so much I couldn't drive any further than Cooma. I sat in the car for over four hours, eating ice cream that is no way as good as Mrs Tam's while hurting and hurting because I wasn't with you.' She looked up and down the street to the Christmas tree, all lit up. 'Is that true love, Jamie?'

'Well, darling Katie. It's certainly looking that way.'

She turned to him and hooked her arms around his neck. 'That's what I thought too. That's why I came back.'

'I would have come after you,' he whispered against her ear. 'Another ten minutes and I'd have got in the ute and come after you.'

'You're so good to me.'

'I am, aren't I?' he said with a slow comforting smile.

She clung on tighter still, her arms wound around his neck, her smile hurting. 'So. Decision made. I love you.'

He bent his head and kissed her cheek. 'I knew you did.'

'Before I did?'

'Yeah. You talk in your sleep. You say my name. You say it softly. And when you look at me, your eyes spill softness all over me.'

Jamie, Jamie. Hold me tight. Don't let me go.

'You say my name as though you're trying to catch something through a flurrying wind,' he said. 'As though you want to hold on to that something.'

'I never thought I'd find it, let alone catch it.'

'I love you, Kate.'

'I love you too, Jamie. I feel part of something bigger just standing next to you.' She turned her head to look over her shoulder, down Main Street. 'Look at this. It's wonderful. It's joyful, and I want to be townsperson number ninety. Do you think they'll let me?'

'They will if you start paying up your fifty cents a week.'

Kate smiled at him, love glowing within her.' We can make this work, can't we?'

He nodded. 'Yes. We can.'

'We can live here. We can travel together. I'll go wherever you go.'

'You can work from wherever we go. And I'll be with you when you need to go to London, or Paris, or New York. And we'll always call Silver Bells House home.'

'Always,' Kate affirmed. 'I want to be at your side for the next sixty years. Until we find everything that makes us happy.' Together. Whatever. Always together. 'I want to live my life with you. Every second.'

He pulled her in so tight to his chest, Kate lost her breath and her heartbeat bumped with his.

'Okay, Katie,' he said softly. 'Let's go build our dream.'

Her Christmas Kisses

SUSANNE BELLAMY

For my parents,
who celebrated their wedding anniversary
every Christmas Day and shaped my ideas of love and family.

Chapter One

Flick Ardmore unlocked the back door and turned on the lights in the kitchen of Pecorino. Stainless steel gleamed and light glinted off her baking tools hanging on the rack her father had installed in her corner of the family kitchen. Her kingdom. Her gaze landed on the German mixing machine in pride of place on the counter. A little burst of pride blossomed in her chest like the spray of flowers on the engagement cake she'd delivered yesterday. The mixer had cost a week's wages, but it was a marker of her progress towards achieving her dream.

Flick's savings were nowhere near enough to buy her parents out yet, but Dad had estimated five years before they were ready to retire. Then the best family-run restaurant in Brisbane's east side would become her top-end patisserie. Would her parents be happy helping out part time, or would they do the grey nomad thing for a while?

No. She could imagine Mum's response to that suggestion: *Felicity, why on earth would you think I have any desire to eat dust with every meal?*

After washing her hands and donning her apron, Flick checked the running list for the day. Leading up to Halloween, she needed to bake more orange and dark chocolate cakes for Pecorino and she had an order to fill for one of Brisbane's upmarket Southbank restaurants.

Through the kitchen window the glow of pre-dawn intensified into a band of gold that lit a bank of low clouds. The sight lifted her spirits and she turned optimistically back to her morning routine. *Better get the ovens on and the cakes in before Dad arrives.*

She bit her bottom lip. Dad would arrive in his vintage VW with a cheery toot of the horn, and Mum would follow thirty minutes later in the delivery van. Her mother's first words would probably be: *Felicity, why haven't you finished those biscuits. Really, must I do everything for this business?* She'd follow that with a lingering look at Dad. A look full of censure and anger and disappointment. A look that had become more common over the past couple of months.

Flick wrapped her arms around her waist, hating the burn like bad indigestion racing from her stomach to her throat. Lately when her parents were together, Flick could cut the tension with a boning knife.

She headed into the cold room and assembled the ingredients for the special order, including a light, blood-red paste she'd prepared last night to create a spider-web pattern through the layers of vanilla cake. Focusing her mind on the design for the special order, she returned to the kitchen and set the first cake layer on a board.

Hinges creaked as the back door opened, and she glanced up. Her father stood in the doorway. Still, silent, sad. He didn't enter the kitchen.

'The ovens are heating, Dad, and I've started the special order—' Her words died, along with her voice.

Her father leaned against the doorjamb as though, if he moved an inch, the building would collapse. His head shook like a bobble-head toy in slow motion, up-and-down, side-to-side, useless, winding down, drained of energy, hope, joy.

Dad's face was pale beneath his stubble and his hollow eyes, and he looked older than his fifty-five years. Older than Yoda and as weak as Benjamin Button at either end of his life. But it was the expression in his eyes that would haunt her dreams.

Lost, lonely and unloved.

Flick set the thin-bladed knife on the counter and gripped the squared edge. She tightened her grip until her fingers turned white and the metal dug a ridge in her palm.

Only something wrong with her mother could put that expression on her father's face.

'What's happened? Is it Mum?' Her parents' love affair was the stuff of Flick's other dreams. Dreams that had taken a battering when her jerk of an ex-boyfriend Jason had dumped her. She aspired to a love like theirs. One day. Swallowing against bile rising in her throat, she forced herself to stay upright. 'Has something happened to Mum?'

He shook his head again. A muscle jumped in his cheek. Slowly, as though he was the Tin Man working oil into his rusted jaw, he opened, closed, opened his mouth. Words dropped like pebbles, pinging like hail on a tin roof.

'Your mother is divorcing me. And she's served me with a court order. I'm not allowed to enter Pecorino.'

They faced each other across the picnic table at the rear of the restaurant, neither one able to meet the other's eyes. The folded beach umbrella cast a long shadow across her father's chest.

Divorce. D-I-V-O-R-C-E. The act of breaking apart a marriage.

Flick's brain froze around the word. 'How, Dad? Why? This happens to other people, not to you and Mum.'

'Apparently, it does. I knew she wasn't happy, but ...' Dad looked up at last, and his hands made a vague gesture. He looked helpless, hopeless—

Lost.

The pain in her strong and dependable father's expression hit Flick like a kick in the guts. 'I thought you were happy, in love. It's your thirtieth wedding anniversary next month.' She had planned a cake shaped like an oyster for their pearl celebration.

Her father dropped his head into his hands. 'She said she needs to *find herself*, whatever the hell that means. Probably that she's bored by our life together, all that we've achieved.' He turned towards the building and exhaled a shaky breath. 'I'm barred from entering the restaurant in any capacity. Flick, I don't know what I'll do without the restaurant.'

'And home—has she kicked you out of the house too?'

'Yes. I've asked Charlie down at the bay if I can stay in his fishing hut for the time being.'

The sound of tyres crunching over the gravel drive gave Flick brief warning before the delivery van pulled up behind Ruby, her small, ancient, but freshly painted red sedan. Her mother got out of the car and strode towards them.

'Felicity, why aren't you inside baking today's orders? And you—' She turned eyes like chips of granite on her husband. 'You're barred from the premises. You need to leave now or I'll call for the police to escort you off.'

Her father lifted his head as though weighed down by an anchor and looked at her mother.

Without hope. Without care. Without passion.

'I didn't set foot inside the restaurant.'

Oh God, his voice ... emotionless. Flick stared at his blank expression, seeking a trace of her passionate, caring father.

'The court order includes the outside area. You aren't allowed on the property at all.' Her mother folded her arms and glared.

At last Flick understood. The love between her parents had died, and at this moment, she hated her mother for turning her father into a broken man.

Flick stood, untied her apron and dragged it over her head. 'Pecorino is us, all three of us, and I can't work here if Dad isn't welcome.'

Essie Ardmore folded her arms and pinned Flick with a look that told her more than words ever could. Her mother was miffed at most. Not sad or angry or surprised or any of a dozen emotions that suggested a connection between mother and daughter.

Miffed negated every sense of security, of belonging that Flick had ever believed in. 'I'll collect my utensils and leave too. If Dad isn't welcome here, neither am I.' She might not be welcome, but her heart wrenched at the thought of leaving the restaurant.

'Do as you wish. You've always been your father's daughter. You might as well pack your gear from home too. Both the house and restaurant are going on the market today. They're both in my name.' Flick froze. For a heartbeat that expanded, pounded and filled her ears with a rush of blood that made her dizzy. All that Flick thought she knew of her mother vanished with those words. This woman with the outward appearance of Flick's mother was a stranger.

'You're selling Pecorino?' Her voice was flat, disconnected from emotion, distanced from pain.

'Of course. I need my share of money from both sales to get away from here.'

Flick struggled to keep a note of pleading out of her voice. 'If you'll give me a little more time to save the deposit, I'd like to buy the business. Will you do that for me?'

Her mother shrugged, the action uncaring. 'Do what you want. If it hasn't sold by then, I'll sell it to you. I don't care who I sell it to. Frankly, I don't know why you'd want such a damned millstone around your neck, but you're more like your father every day. He likes being tied down to one place too.' Without a goodbye, her mother climbed into the van and backed out of the driveway. Out of Flick's life.

'Sweetheart, I'm sorry about …'

'You have nothing to be sorry for, Dad.'

'But I have. Now you've got no home and no job. I should have tried harder, done more, though God knows what.' He hugged her, rocking a little as she held him close.

Dragging in a deep breath, Flick eased out of his arms. 'Since you're heading to the Bay, I might head south for a break. Maybe go to Newcastle for a bit. If I can save enough for a deposit, we can reopen Pecorino. Dad? We'll keep Pecorino going—together.'

Chapter Two

Xander McIntyre had the door of the taxi open before it came to a complete stop at the western entrance to the Rainbow Cove shopping centre. He handed over two fifty-dollar notes. 'Keep the change.'

'Thanks.' The taxi driver's eyes lit up as he tucked the notes into a tatty, faded-black wallet. 'Thanks a lot, mate.'

Xander nodded, slammed the door and strode around the back of the vehicle towards the far lane of the car park. He'd have known where to find the accident, even without the police information. A crowd had gathered midway down the lane, shoppers returning to their cars, passers-by drawn like vultures to a carcass. Overhead, a police helicopter veered away, and a news chopper edged into the air space above the crowd.

Xander shouldered through the onlookers, lifted the fluttering yellow tape and ducked under it, bypassing a uniformed constable.

'Stay back please, sir.' The constable, young enough to pass for a school student, thrust a hand in front of Xander in a futile effort to stop him.

Fuelled by adrenaline and anger, Zander ignored him and pushed past until he reached his target. 'That's my car.' He stab-pointed in the direction of the silver vehicle now meshed with a small, red, parked sedan. 'It was stolen two hours ago from my hotel and—'

'Mr McIntyre?' A plain-clothes officer held up his ID, stepped between Xander and his car, and waved off the rookie uniform.

'Yes. And you are?'

'Detective John Wilkins. The PolAir helicopter located your vehicle when it was spotted speeding down the highway and followed it here. Could I have a few words with you now?'

Xander inhaled a calming breath. The detective's intervention was smooth and low-key. He took another deep breath and tunnelled irritated fingers through his hair.

There was a process to follow, but the wasted time grated. Tamping down his impatience, he turned from his car to the detective. 'What do you need to know?'

The time? Two hours ago.

Where the car was parked? In the secure parking of my resort hotel.

Your hotel? Yes, I own it.

Long minutes passed as Xander answered the detective's questions, and passed on details supplied by his security team.

A forensics team worked methodically, taking every item from the vehicle and dusting the car and its contents for fingerprints before setting each item in a row on a drop sheet.

'How long have you owned Rainbow Cove Resort?'

'About twelve months. Renovations are ongoing. The secure car park where my car was taken from is yet to be upgraded.'

Somebody has a lot of explaining to do when I get back to the resort.

'Something is always last in a project that size.' Detective Wilkins jotted a note in his book.

Xander glanced at his watch. He was cutting it fine to arrange for another vehicle before his sister's plane landed. 'How long will you need my car?'

'It will be towed to the police lock-up yard for further examination. Your insurer will most likely have a hire car option available in the interim, but, say, a week. Yours is repairable. Can't say the same for the other vehicle.' The detective scanned the bystanders and the wider view of the parking lot.

Xander glanced at the red car, sparing a pitying thought for its unknowing owner. He extracted a business card from his wallet. 'Losing my car is a damned nuisance, but the other car's copped the worst of it.'

'Extra annoying, I guess, since your car was taken from your own premises.'

Xander handed over his card. 'Do you have a card in case I need to contact you?'

'Sure.' Wilkins handed one over and tucked Xander's into his wallet.

'I'll be launching a full investigation into how this occurred.'

Thank God it was my car and not one of my guests'.

How would his sister react when he showed up in an unfamiliar car? According to their mother, Jenny was less inclined to become agitated by change since her operation, but Xander remained sceptical. Until he saw her for himself, he'd do whatever he could to avoid a repeat of his sister's nerve-wracking tantrums.

The detective turned to the second uniform. 'Any news on the other car's owner?'

'Yes, sir.' A female senior constable stepped forwards, flipped open a notebook and thumbed over a few pages and read the details. 'Felicity Ardmore. Last known address is in Brisbane, Queensland.'

Wilkins bent down and peered at the car's crumpled front assembly. 'So, Queensland plates could mean the owner is here on holiday.' He beckoned the young constable over. 'Go into the shopping centre and get them to put a call over the speaker system for the owner to come to her car.'

'Yes, sir.' The constable lifted the tape and ducked under it, shouldering through the crowd in the direction of the shopping centre.

A young woman with auburn hair and an armful of groceries emerged from behind an elderly couple holding a trolley with a giant assemble-it-yourself inflatable castle. She slipped under the tape and came to an abrupt halt. Glossy pink lips formed an O shape as she stared at the red car. For several heartbeats her gaze was glued to the point of impact before she turned a dark blue gaze on Xander.

'You. What the hell have you done to my car?'

Gritty-eyed and tired, Flick blinked, desperate to make sense of the scene in front of her. A silver Beamer's grill was meshed with Ruby's caved-in front in a twisted mechanical embrace. Her faithful, fifteen-year-old car had brought her from Queensland, across the border into New South Wales to Rainbow Cove. And now it appeared the northern resort town would be its final resting place. Her stomach lurched, and she gulped her next breath through her mouth.

What the hell was she going to do? A deep-bellied, primal cry sounded a great option. Homeless, jobless, and as bereft as an orphaned child, everything she owned was in the boot and back seat of Ruby.

Why, oh why had she pulled in here to buy groceries?

Palm trees lining the border of the car park swayed in the breeze.

A tall, dark-haired, grey-suited man with an annoyed frown and a BMW keychain dangling from his hand turned his head and looked her way. His gaze flicked from her face over the rest of her.

'You. What the hell have you done to my car?'

His gaze snapped back to her face. 'Ah, you're the other owner. Ms—Ardmore, is it?'

'How do you know my name?'

'The police checked your rego plates. They're probably looking for you inside the centre as we speak.'

Of course they had checked. She was the only one still out of the loop, as always.

Bitterness at the blows life kept pegging at her fed Flick's anger. She stormed across to where he stood between two police officers. Setting her bags of groceries on the bitumen, she glared at him 'You—you're the incompetent driver of this vehicle, I take it? How the hell did you manage to hit Ruby?'

'Ruby?'

'My car. You hit my vehicle, though God knows how you—'

'You've—named your car?' The man looked at her as though she was missing a few marbles.

She stiffened her shoulders and glared at him. 'Doesn't everyone?'

'Guess I missed that class at driving school.'

'Humph. That and a few others by the looks of this effort. How did you crash—'

'I didn't. My vehicle was stolen this morning.' He sketched a hand at the mangled wrecks. 'This is the result.'

A man held out a business card, smoothly inserting himself into the conversation. 'Ms Ardmore, I'm Detective Wilkins. Mr McIntyre's stolen car was being followed by our helicopter and ended up here when the thieves attempted to evade arrest. We have apprehended the three occupants of the vehicle and ascertained who was driving at the time.'

Heat ran up Flick's face and she closed her eyes and groaned before looking at Grey-suit. 'Sorry, I'm sorry. You didn't drive into me. I get it.'

'We're both victims of those hoodlums, Ms Ardmore.' He gestured at Ruby. 'Your car is more damaged than mine. You won't be able to drive it once they're separated, let alone open your boot.'

Flick looked down the side of her car and her insides curled. The impact had pushed Ruby into the light pole behind her car. Even from the front she could see the crumpled boot.

The detective glanced from her to the man.

McIntyre, was it? The reality of her situation hit home. Did his name matter? The mangled mess was a visual metaphor for her life.

Destination—going nowhere; employment prospects—nil; finances—desperate.

'We'll be a couple of hours here at least. Perhaps you could go for a coffee and a bite of lunch. I can phone you when we're ready to tow both cars.' The detective's tone was businesslike, but his eyes conveyed sympathy.

'Excuse me?' An older couple with a trolley signalled for the police officer's attention and pointed at a station wagon two down from Ruby. 'Do you think we could get our car out now? We're on our way to our granddaughter's birthday party with her present.' The man tapped the box in their trolley.

'Certainly, sir. Come through.' Wilkins turned back to Flick. 'Can you give your details to the constable first, and then you might find it more comfortable inside out of the heat.'

'Sure.' There was nothing for it. Given Flick hadn't been present at the accident, the constable's questions were few and her answers were short and to the point. 'I was gone about thirty-five, maybe forty minutes in total, I guess.'

'Thanks, Ms Ardmore. We'll let you know when we're done with your vehicle. If you need a tow truck, I can give you the names of a couple of reputable local operators.' The constable closed her notebook and handed her card to Flick. 'If you have any questions you can call me on this number. I'll ring you with the accident report number later today for you to give to your insurer.'

'Okay, thanks.' Flick bit her lip—there would be little insurance payout on poor, ancient Ruby. She bent to retrieve her groceries, only to find Mr Grey-suit had beaten her to it. He stood with her two hessian shopping bags dangling from one tanned hand. They looked incongruous against his tailored suit.

'Give me those—I can carry my shopping.' The waspish tone wasn't Flick, not normally. But her life was spiralling out of control. She had to hang on to whatever she could, even if it was only the handles of her grocery bags.

'It's the least I can do.' He lifted the police tape and followed her away from their crashed cars. Inside the shopping centre, he indicated a trendy café on the right of the main doors. 'This place does a good coffee.'

At the entrance to the café there was a cut-out Santa and sleigh piled high with glittery fake presents; inside, Christmas decorations and tinsel had replaced the Halloween theme still evident in a few shops while soft smoky-jazz replaced the canned carols piping through the shopping centre's sound system. With fewer than eight weeks until the holiday, Flick was grateful to be spared chirpy Christmas carols. Her frazzled nerves couldn't handle *goodwill to all men*. Not towards the thieves who had stolen her companion's car and totalled poor Ruby.

The café was busier than when she'd glanced into it on her way back to the car. The scent of ginger slice fresh from the oven had tempted her then, but now food was the last thing on her mind. She headed for a table near the back and sat.

He set her shopping on the bench seat and extended a hand. 'I'm Xander McIntyre. I live out on the cove.'

'Flick—Felicity Ardmore. I am—was—just passing through. Guess I'll have to find somewhere to camp. Any recommendations for caravan parks or camping grounds close by?'

A frown flickered across his forehead and he shook his head. 'The caravan park closed last year and there's no camping allowed along the foreshore. But there is the resort if you fancy a few days of relaxation.'

A *resort*? She probably couldn't afford a meal there let alone a single night. Not when every cent she had was destined for a deposit on Pecorino. Mr Fancy BMW-driving Grey-suit probably never had to practise economies like she did. She doubted he'd ever struggled with making ends meet or choosing between eating for a day and buying a work tool. She grimaced at the memory—her fancy French whisk had cost her an arm and a leg.

Poor Ruby. What am I going to do without her?

'If Rainbow Cove isn't your destination, where are you heading?'

'Oh, I was aiming for Newcastle, I guess.' Distracted by the scent of ginger and subtle spice, and worry over her car and immediate prospects, Flick realised too late how slack this sounded when Xander frowned again.

Judgemental, pompous ...

She fiddled with the fringed bottom of her Balinese shoulder bag. What business was it of his anyway?

'You're on holiday?' He unbuttoned his jacket and set one arm along the top of the booth.

'Kind of.'

'How can you be *kind of on holiday*? Either you are, or you aren't.'

Her head snapped up and she clenched her hands on her lap. Right now, she needed Xander poking and prodding into her personal life like she needed a hole in the head. 'I needed a change from my old job, okay? Can we leave it at that?'

Xander raised both hands before folding his arms on the table. Grey eyes met hers. 'Not my business. What would you like to drink? My shout.'

Embarrassment curled through Flick. She wasn't the only one whose day had been ruined. Xander, at least, was trying to be pleasant while she was behaving like a total bitch. She closed her eyes and took a deep breath before meeting his gaze. 'I'm sorry. I shouldn't allow shock to overwhelm my good manners. Do they have berry smoothies here?'

'A good choice. That's their speciality.' His smile tipped up one side of his mouth as he stood.

It softened the harsh planes of his cheeks, and turned Flick's first impression of corporate pomposity on its head. *Maybe if he lost the tie* …

'Don't worry. I'd be surprised if you weren't still in shock. I've had a little more time than you to process what's happened.' He moved to the counter and joined a short queue, pulling out his phone and tapping out a message while he waited to order.

Flick ran her hands over her jeans-clad thighs and tipped her head to one side. Xander was being decent about it all, in spite of being just as inconvenienced, and through no fault of his own. She needed to calm down, to take a moment to regroup and appreciate his thoughtfulness and consideration.

There was more to him than the suit. His dark hair, neatly trimmed but shorter than she liked, was more dark brown than black beneath the café's downlights. His smart suit and clean-shaven jaw placed him firmly in the corporate sector, at least in her mind, but his lean body was more along the lines of an Aussie Rules player. Did the suit make the man? Would he look as good in boardies and T-shirt?

As if I don't have more pressing concerns than a chance acquaintance's good looks.

At fifteen years old, Ruby was insured at the minimum level. Given the extensive damage, Flick considered her insurer unlikely to offer to repair her little car.

There had been a television helicopter filming. What if her parents saw her car on the news?

She took out her phone and texted two quick messages that she was unharmed, but Ruby was probably a write-off, and hit send on the second message before Xander returned. Dad would be frantic if he saw her car on the news. *Mum probably wouldn't notice.*

Xander set a metal stand on the edge of their table and her eye was drawn to the artwork; their table number blazed on the side of a cartoonish cappuccino cut-out. It was kind of quirky in the sophisticated setting of black tiles and stainless steel café. 'So, back to your problem, Felicity.'

'Please—can you call me Flick? Only my mother calls me Felicity.' And that was punishment for daring to be her father's daughter. Flick sighed softly and slipped the phone back into her bag.

'I see.'

His keen appraisal suggested that he did indeed see. Far more than she was comfortable revealing, far more than she was willing to share.

'You know what, forget it. Felicity is fine.'

A dull headache began building behind her eyes. Lack of sleep and emotional emptiness did that to her. She'd reached breaking point. Her eyes pricked with angry tears and if she didn't get out now, she'd have no dignity left to preserve.

Grabbing her shoulder bag, she opened her mouth to tell him she'd changed her mind about waiting with him.

The waitress, carrying a tray with an espresso shot, a glass of water, a light purple smoothie, and two plates, one bearing a chocolate brownie and the other a piece of ginger slice, stopped at the end of their table, effectively blocking Flick's escape. The scent of ginger—her favourite comfort food—curled under her nose.

'Who's having the brownie?' The waitress held the plate and glanced from Flick to Xander.

Flick turned her head and eyed off the ginger slice. Her nose may have twitched at the heavenly aroma of fresh, good-quality baking.

'Your choice, Felic—Flick. They both look good.'

Flick. He called me Flick.

It highlighted how tightly wound she'd become that she placed so much store on a name. With her emotions all over the place, sitting down for a drink with Xander offered a brief respite.

Her stomach gurgled—loudly. She pressed a hand against it. 'I skipped breakfast.'

'In that case, would you like something more than a slice? Toasted sandwiches, maybe?' Xander grinned, a full-on, disarming smile that made him look—less corporate executive and all too human.

Appealingly human. Distraction of the best kind.

'Just the slice. Are you sure you don't mind which you have?'

Xander nodded, giving no indication of a preference either way.

'The ginger for me then, thanks.'

Plates and drinks sorted, the waitress left them alone. Flick cut her slice into four and raised a piece to her mouth. The scent of ginger offered rare comfort, a reminder of her first cooking attempts with her father. Closing her eyes, she breathed in flavours and memories.

Her tongue touched the corner of her mouth, remembering the taste, texture, scent—security.

Opening her eyes she looked across the table.

Xander hadn't moved. His gaze appeared riveted on her hand, or the slice—or maybe her mouth—before his eyes flicked up and met hers. On another man she'd interpret it as interest, but on him …

One brief, revealing glance. Awkward, uncomfortable … distracting.

She was mistaken. They'd only just met. Shock had skewed her view.

Lips a hair's breadth from the slice, she tried to gather her scattered thoughts.

Think, Flick, why else would he be looking—there?

'Um, would you like to taste this one?'

He shrugged. 'It doesn't matter. It's just food.'

'Of course it matters. My father taught me to tell quality cooking by its aroma across any room. This slice will be amazing.'

She set her piece of slice down, balanced an untouched quarter on the knife and lifted it onto his plate. 'Good cooking creates so much more than *just food*. It's made with love and should be bliss in each bite. Taste that and then tell me it's *just food*.'

Xander tipped his head to one side. 'You sound as passionate as my friend, Christophe. He has the restaurant at the resort.' Xander picked up his knife and cut the brownie into two neat pieces, balancing one half on the knife and lifting it onto Flick's plate before wiping his fingers on the paper serviette.

Regretting the impulse that had lost her some of the ginger slice, Flick eyed the brittle-edged brownie with resignation. 'Where's this resort?'

The espresso cup looked ridiculously small in Xander's hand as he watched her over the rim. 'As the crow flies, just the other side of the headland. By road, about five kilometres. Why? Are you interested in taking a room there?'

'I—maybe.' Telling Xander she couldn't afford to stay in a resort was too personal, but if this Christophe shared her passion for food and if—a big if, and she wasn't about to get her hopes up yet—there might be a chance of finding work with him, she was interested. If her hopes were dashed after the morning she'd had, the breakdown that had threatened when she'd looked at Ruby's caved-in front and rear might still happen.

'There's a taxi rank on the eastern side of the centre. Everyone knows the resort, and I'm certain there are vacancies at this time of year.'

'Great—wonderful. Okay then.' She bit into her slice and closed her eyes, concentrating on the flavours melting on her tongue. Living in the moment and focusing on the simple pleasure of good food and a tentative contact at the resort would get her through the rest of the morning. After that ...

A five-kilometre walk to the resort would be a breeze compared to the three hundred kilometres she'd planned on driving before she stopped for the night. It would be good to stretch her muscles and give her time to plan her approach to Xander's friend, the chef.

A tiny nugget of ginger released a delicate hit of flavour on her tongue. *Ha, the best laid plans ...*

Apparently Rainbow Cove had other plans for her.

Chapter Three

Jenny's plane touched down and taxied to the front of the terminal while Xander tapped his credit card and looked for a free space. He parked the hire car, a metallic midnight-blue MG, in the short-term parking area and raced into the building. With seconds to spare he managed to be positioned at the gate where his little sister could see him as she disembarked.

A splash of daffodil yellow—her favourite colour—caught his eye beside a summery green dress. His mother held her daughter's hand as they descended the steps of the Dash-8 and stepped onto the tarmac. In the six months since his last visit home Jenny had grown so that, now, the fourteen-year-old's nose was on a level with her mother's shoulder.

Born with Down syndrome years after his parents had given up hope of another child, they had almost lost her in last winter's flu season. He watched them follow the diagonal yellow markings towards the terminal. Time spent with his sister was a precious gift.

Consultation with her doctor had reassured Xander that swimming and horseriding along the beach would be good therapy, especially since she'd begun riding lessons. This visit to Rainbow

Cove, her first trip since corrective heart surgery, would also be her first visit without their mother staying.

How will it go?

Xander checked the departure time for his mother's plane. Besides the full-time care of his sister, he had to ensure the resort's renovations remained on schedule.

Jenny saw him, her arm waved wildly, and her smile beamed.

'Xander! Hi, Xander!' Like a tugboat leading a cruise ship, Jenny towed her mother through the doors into the terminal. Releasing her mother's hand, Jenny threw herself into his arms. 'It was bumpy in the clouds and the man across the aisle from Mum spilled his drink down his shirt.'

The passenger who followed his mother through the door sported a red wine stain down his shirt. Jenny caught sight of him and pointed. 'That's the man. See.'

'I see, Jenny, but don't point, remember.' Xander wrapped an arm around each of Jenny's and his mother's shoulders and kissed her cheek. 'Hi, Mum, do you have time for a coffee before your return flight?'

Green suited his mother, or perhaps it was the prospect of a whole carefree week with her husband that brightened her eyes. Dearly as they all loved Jenny, Xander knew his offer to have his sister stay with him was appreciated.

Why wouldn't my parents appreciate a little one-on-one-time after fourteen years?

'That would be nice, thanks, darling. Your father and I are planning an early night before we fly out to Fiji tomorrow and I've a few things to tell you.'

'Problems?'

They sat at a corner table in the café and his mother reached over and touched his arm. 'No, and you don't have to try to fix everyone else's life, Xander. Relax. Jenny's doing much better now and—'

'Xander, can we go swimming at your hotel?' Jenny gazed up at him, her blue eyes hopeful and happy.

'Would you like to swim?'

'Mum bought me yellow swimmers.'

'Great. And what will Mum say if I tell her Christophe is making a special surprise dinner tonight?' Well aware that he needed to not only keep an eye on what Jenny ate, but on her exercise, he smiled at their mother over the top of his sister's head. 'I'm really looking forward to this week with Jenny, Mum.'

His mother tucked a strand of hair behind Jenny's ear and took her hand. 'I know, darling, and I'd say Jenny's a very lucky girl to stay with her brother while Dad and I go on our anniversary trip. Now, where's that coffee? I've got a list of contact numbers for you and twenty minutes to chat before I have to board again.'

Flick's backpack bulged and the handles of the hessian carrier bags bit into her fingers as she trudged along the road to Rainbow Cove Resort. Buried somewhere at the bottom of her pack there was a hat, but she was too hot and tired to stop and unpack on the side of the winding bitumen road.

Five kilometres. It's only five kilometres.

Heat bounced off the road and sweat ran into her eyes as she trudged on, head down and trying not to count off her steps. It wasn't that she didn't enjoy walking—she did. Just preferably without a backpack stuffed, rather than properly packed, with whichever of her belongings had been on the back seat of Ruby. The boot would have to be cut open before she could retrieve everything else.

The angle of the road ahead changed, levelling out. A few more paces brought her to the highest point of the road before it curved gently downhill towards the resort and the blue Pacific Ocean beyond. Lifting her head from contemplation of her white sandals against the black road surface, she wiped an arm across her sweaty brow and drank in a vista of blue and green edged in white sand that opened before her.

Beckoning like an oasis, the main resort building rose gracefully above an irregular circle of palms. Four storeys high, it appeared to float on a carpet of green. Dotted here and there between lush plantings of palm trees and glossy green bushes, the steeply sloping roofs of low-set buildings hinted at hideaway cabins. Blue water glimmered through the trees as fronds danced in the sea breeze. Flick imagined sliding into the cool depths, and the salty tang of the sea on her lips.

Funny how the sight of blue water—coupled with the ease of a downhill walk—lifted her spirits. Hoisting the backpack into a more comfortable position, she set off along the downward curve of road.

A hundred metres or so further on, an open-top metallic blue MG with two passengers passed her. The driver pulled up on a narrow shoulder a little way ahead. His arm rose, pointing towards the resort and his companion sat up on the back of the seat.

One advantage of having an open-top car, Flick thought as she drew nearer.

The spot the driver had chosen to look at the view was the only place on this stretch of road where one could safely stop, and even then, it wasn't ideal. But Flick understood the attraction. Her eyes were drawn to the changing perspective as she descended, and a kernel of hope sprouted, the first positive sign in weeks. Fate, karma, kismet—call it whatever. Sometimes, it was as if bad stuff had to happen to be able to appreciate the good when it arrived. She looked out towards the resort.

Rainbow Cove—even its name was a promise of better times.

As she approached the vehicle, the driver's door opened and Xander McIntyre stepped out. He'd removed his suit coat, but his navy-blue tie was still as neat as when he'd sat across from her in the café.

Flick stopped and tipped her head to one side. 'I see you managed to get a new set of wheels. Nice.' Suddenly self-conscious of how dishevelled she must look, she pushed a sweaty lock of hair off her forehead.

He, on the other hand, appeared as fresh as when she'd first met him. If she discounted his windblown hair. The open-top MG had mussed the neatly combed style–cut; the look suited him and surprised her.

Usually she preferred longer hair on guys, but Xander rocked the short look.

He rested a hand on the open door. 'It was the only vehicle available at five minutes' notice. So—no taxis at the taxi rank, hey? Are you heading to the resort?'

Flick lowered her carrier bags of groceries and shrugged off her backpack. The straps had bitten into her shoulders and, as she set the pack beside her, relief all but made her groan. 'The sign to the resort pointed this way and yes to both questions. Besides, I enjoy walking.'

'Great. Look, I'd offer you a ride if I could but—'

'It's a two-seater and I don't fancy being a bonnet decoration, but thanks.'

'I can take your gear for you. At least you can enjoy the walk without that weight on your back.'

'Xander?' The passenger was a young teenage girl in a daffodil-yellow dress kneeling on her seat, her hands gripping the headrest. Her fair hair many shades lighter than Xander's framed classic features indicative of Down Syndrome. 'Is she your friend?'

'This lady is called Flick.' His gaze turned from the girl and settled on Flick. 'And this is my sister, Jenny.'

For the second time that day Xander surprised her. The softening of his expression as he looked at his sister, and his offer to transport Flick's belongings showed thoughtfulness and a sensitivity she'd missed earlier. Beneath his suit and his corporate mask, there lurked a hidden empathy.

Flick smiled at his sister. 'Hi, Jenny. That's a pretty dress you're wearing. I love bright yellow.'

'But you're not wearing yellow. If you like it, why aren't you wearing yellow clothes?'

'I have a yellow hat in my bag. It just seemed too much effort to unpack it on the side of the road.'

Xander closed his door and came towards her. He reached for her bags and backpack. 'How about I stow these in the boot, and you can look for your hat without having to spread your gear in the dirt?'

'Thanks. That would be nice. And I can show Jenny my hat, so she knows I'm telling the truth.'

The boot of the MG was deeper than Flick expected and contained only a yellow carry-on case and matching suitcase that barely filled one half of the available space. She unbuckled the clips of her backpack and pulled out random belongings until she was able to slip her hand down the side. Right near the bottom, beneath a plastic bag containing her work shoes, her fingers touched brushed cotton. She shook out the soft hat and set it on her head. 'See?'

Jenny clapped her hands. 'It's pretty. Xander, can I get a hat like Flick's?'

Flick glanced at Xander. 'Oops, sorry. Unintended consequence there.'

'Hmm, maybe you can let me know where you got it, or I'll go looking online for something similar.' He waited while she quickly shoved her possessions back into the backpack and retrieved her water bottle from the side pocket before closing the boot. It shut with a soft hiss that oozed expense and quality design.

'Well, thanks for carting my stuff the rest of the way.'

'No problem. I'll leave it with the concierge. We might see you around, although I think Jenny has a busy few days planned for us.'

'Are you staying at the resort?'

'Yes. Jenny's on holiday with me for a week.'

'I'm going swimming and horseriding and—'

'And we'd better go and get Jenny settled in and let you get down to the resort. The main pool has a shaded swim-up bar. I recommend a chilled mineral water followed by a pina colada. You'll forget all this morning's bad stuff once you're settled into the pool. Bye, Flick.' His gaze lingered for a moment before he got into the car.

Flick waved and, moments later, she was alone again on the road to Rainbow Cove and thinking about her second encounter with Xander McIntyre rather than her litany of woes. Welcoming the distraction, she conjured up an image of him, of the kindness in his eyes and the gentle redirection of his sister's attention. If she were to get a job at the resort, it would be pleasant to see a familiar face, even if only for the first few days.

She ignored the flutter of attraction, told herself it was only gratitude for his help, and set off downhill.

Minus the weight of her luggage, the walk to the resort was easy, and she arrived at a pair of wrought-iron gates, open and inviting, in a better frame of mind than she'd managed in several weeks. Now, if only she could convince the chef to hire her, she might yet land on her feet and find that breathing space she so desperately needed.

Chapter Four

Xander hung his jacket over a chair and slipped off his tie, dropping it on top of his jacket. He took a bottle of mineral water out onto the balcony of his penthouse apartment. The sound of Jenny's off-key singing from the shower melted into the sound of waves shushing into the sandy cove and the controlled hum of the air-conditioning.

He pulled the door closed behind him and strolled across, leaning on the rolled and polished railing as he drank. A sea breeze cooled his face and the tang of salt mingled with the scent of sun-warmed flowers. A lush carpet of subtropical planting surrounded the main complex, but his gaze was drawn to the ocean. Deep blue stretched from the horizon to the rocky headland that separated the resort from farmland and the town of Rainbow Cove, gradually shading into a lighter blue before running up onto the sand of the cove.

Breathing deeply, he unbuttoned his shirt and pulled it out of his trousers, allowing himself a few moments to relax and enjoy the prospect of time with his sister.

He needed to be near the sea, smelling the salt. Sea and sand and salt-laden air invigorated him, almost as much as successfully concluding another renovation. If negotiations went well, his next resort purchase would add another dimension to his work, another challenge. A jewel in his property portfolio and the crown in his business.

A flash of yellow caught his eye. Down by the pool Flick Ardmore took off her hat and spoke to one of the poolside staff. She'd made good time over the last kilometre, but even from four floors up he could see her face and arms had caught the sun. At least he'd been able to transport her gear for her, which reminded him ...

He went inside, sat at his desk and rang down to reception. 'Phil, has Ms Ardmore checked in yet?'

'No, sir. She asked if we could store her luggage for a couple of hours, but she didn't request accommodation.'

'Well, when she does—'

'Mr McIntyre, I don't think she plans to take a room. She mentioned something about how lovely it would be to have a holiday here and then asked me if there were camping facilities within walking distance.'

Camping? Flick had asked him about camping this morning, but he'd put it down to her not knowing his resort existed.

And she walked from the shopping centre. Sure, it's only five kilometres, but ...

Three taxis had been waiting at the rank when he crossed the road to the car rental business and Flick had left the café with him, headed for a meeting with the tow truck.

An image of her small, elderly car with its crumpled front and rear came to mind. Perhaps it was a question of money and camping was all she could afford. But if that were the case, why had she made the effort to walk out to the resort with her gear?

'When she returns for her luggage, don't let her leave before you let me know. I need to speak with her.'

He hung up as Jenny perched on a breakfast stool between the kitchen bench and the satinwood desk. A loose yellow and orange and hot pink dress covered something yellow.

'Are those your new swimmers under your dress? You look like sunshine.'

Jenny nodded and ran her hands over the dress, stroking it and smiling the wide smile Xander had hoped to see during their holiday. Was this the next step her doctor had spoken about? After waving goodbye to their mother as she boarded the plane home, he'd been psyching himself up for a bad reaction when she saw the hire car instead of his silver Beamer. There'd been none, and now Jenny appeared to have settled into the apartment.

Come to that, he hadn't expected her to chat freely with Flick either.

Maybe there's something in the power of bright yellow and an optimistic outlook.

'Can we go for a swim now, Xander? I want to swim.'

'Can you wait for me to get changed?'

'If you don't take long.'

Xander pulled a small bottle of water from the fridge, opened it and handed it to his sister. 'By the time you finish drinking that I'll be ready. Okay?'

Ten minutes later, Xander led Jenny to a pool lounge in the shade of the building. He set the plunger bottle of sunscreen on the table and squirted a generous dollop onto his hand. 'Put your towel over the back of the lounger where you can see it when you get out of the pool. I'll put sunscreen on your back while you do your—'

He turned his hand to apply the sunscreen and met—empty air. A blob of cream hit the pavers. Jenny waved as she headed with her rolling sailor walk towards a lounger half-hidden from his view by a giant leafy plant in an oversized planter box. 'Flick. See my yellow swimmers? I'm going swimming. Are you swimming too?'

A pair of tanned legs swung over the edge of the lounger and next thing, Flick was standing beside the plant and smiling as Jenny made a beeline for her. 'Hi. No, I haven't brought my bathers but I thought I'd sit in the shade and cool off. Hi, Xander.'

He strolled over and joined Flick, taking the opportunity to apply the sunscreen to Jenny's back and shoulders. 'Glad to see you arrived safely. Have you ordered a drink yet?'

If he'd blinked he'd have missed the shuttered look that flitted across Flick's face before she shook her head. What that look meant was still unclear as he wiped his hands on his board shorts.

'I'm good. I had a drink of water.'

'That's a start, but that was only the first half of my recommendation. Now for the second part.' He caught the waiter's eye and beckoned him over. Jenny reached over and picked up Flick's yellow hat from the sunlounge. She set it on her head and laughed as she caught her reflection in the plate-glass window. 'Jenny, it isn't polite to take other people's belongings.'

Jenny's face fell, and she thrust her chin forwards, usually a precursor to a meltdown.

But Flick adjusted the sun hat on Jenny's head and turned her to look at her reflection again. 'It's not a problem. Besides, Jenny needs to know if she likes it before she gets one of her own. What do you think, Jenny? Would you like a hat like mine?'

Breathing a sigh of relief, Xander made a mental note to go online at the earliest opportunity and find Jenny a hat like Flick's. 'Thanks. That was quick thinking.'

The waiter arrived and raised a mini iPad to record their order.

Xander turned to Flick. 'I'll get you that pina colada now, unless you'd prefer a different drink.'

'Oh, no thanks. I'm sure it's delicious but—'

'On me.'

'I couldn't. You shouted me morning tea. If anything, I should really buy you a drink.' There it was again; that odd fleeting expression, as though she didn't want to offend him, but was uncomfortable about him buying her a drink.

Why was he pushing it?

His analytical brain couldn't let it rest. He ticked off a mental list. *Old car—sidestepped my question about no taxis—and there's the mystery of why she bothered to walk five Ks to a resort she probably can't afford.*

Spreading his hands, he kept his tone gentle, undemanding, pleasant. 'Flick, it's no big deal. I'm getting drinks for Jenny and for me, and I'd like it if you'd join us. And since this was my suggestion ...' He ordered the cocktail, a juice for Jenny and a light beer.

'Can I swim now, Xander?'

'Sure, but leave Flick's hat with her. She won't want it to get wet. Look what Rob's brought out for you.'

The hot pink inflatable flamingo ring drew a squeal of delight from Jenny. She stuck her head and arms through the opening and walked down the wide, pebbledash steps into the shallow end of the pool. Xander kept an eye on her as he led Flick to the table beside his sister's lounger.

Flick gripped the strap of her Balinese bag and looked less than happy—with him? Jenny splashed in the pool as Flick perched on the edge of the cushioned seat. 'Look, about that cocktail—'

'I invited you to join us. It's just a drink, Flick. Please don't read anything more into it than that.'

She frowned briefly before fixing a smile on her face. 'Thanks. That's kind of you.'

'So, what are your plans while you wait to hear about your car? Will you book into a room here for a few days?' It wasn't his business, but beneath the outward confidence and can-do attitude he glimpsed vulnerability. Not that Flick was a project, but if he could do something to help—

It's just that my car rammed hers and I feel partially responsible for her loss.

If his hotel security had been properly in place, the theft and accident wouldn't have happened.

'I—can't afford to stay in a place like this, but you mentioned your friend, the chef. I thought I would see if he's hiring and if he might have a vacancy.' Beneath the light sunburn, her cheeks turned a darker shade of pink. 'Not that I want you to ask him for me.'

Xander remembered what it was like to make every dollar count. 'I appreciate that, but I'd be happy to take you to the kitchens and introduce you to Christophe when Jenny's had enough of the pool.'

She bent her head and blinked several times before meeting his gaze. Blue eyes glistened. 'Thank you. That's very kind of you.'

The waiter arrived with a bowl of assorted nuts and three drinks, which he set on coasters. 'Will there be anything else?'

'Nothing more for now thanks, Rob.' Xander picked up his beer glass and tapped it against Flick's cocktail glass. 'Here's to landing a job with Christophe.'

She sipped the pina colada and set the glass on a cardboard coaster. 'I'm a pastry chef, but I'll take anything if he offers.'

'Desserts, hey? No wonder you could tell a good slice at ten paces.'

'Xander.' Jenny splashed water at him. Most landed on his bare feet and a few drops splashed up Flick's legs. 'Come in the pool, Xander. Come and swim with me.'

He glanced at Flick's legs. 'Sorry about that. She may be in there for a while. Sit back and enjoy your drink and—thanks for understanding Jenny's fascination with all things yellow.'

Xander led the way into the kitchens at the rear of the resort. He strode, hoping Flick understood his need to fulfil his promise to her as quickly as possible and get his sister back to their apartment. Jenny was tuckered out and becoming grumpy and he didn't dare leave her at the retro milk bar with Mel for more than a couple of minutes.

Please let Christophe be in the kitchen and happy to take on a potential new chef.

'This way, Flick.' Xander held one half of the swing doors open and ushered her into the resort's main kitchen. Christophe's tall figure and bare forearms were nowhere in sight, but he could be in the cold room or any one of half a dozen places. That's what being *hands on* meant to his friend. 'It's organised chaos at its finest. Christophe is a perfectionist in culinary art.'

Flick's gaze ran across the white and stainless-steel scene before them. 'It looks efficient and smells wonderful.'

'Chris runs it like a military operation, but the food that comes out of his kitchen is world-class.' Guests shouldn't be here, but, given the circumstances, Xander trusted Christophe would excuse him bringing Flick into the heart of the kitchen instead of the office to meet him. He breathed deeply, savouring the flavours of another of Christophe's French-focused menus. Despite what his friend thought of Xander's taste, he appreciated good food.

'So it's not *just food* in his hands?' Flick grinned. 'Your words this morning.'

'You got me. But Chris definitely has a love affair with each dish he creates. What was your comment? It's never *just food* when made with love. *Bliss in every bite?*'

'You remember that?' Flick's astonished expression drew a grin from him, a grin he tried to hide as Andy, the resort manager, approached. His smart black suit and name badge with the resort logo were out of place in the kitchen. A twinge of unease ran with spider-light legs down Xander's spine.

'Andy, has Christophe come in yet?'

Andy shook his head and steepled his fingers beneath his chin. 'He was here, but there was a problem with the seafood delivery. He's gone to sort it out.'

'Because he trusts nobody else when it's about his beloved bouillabaisse. I get it.'

'Can I help?' Andy rounded the counter. His gaze landed on Flick and his eyes widened in appreciation, just for a moment, before his professional training took over.

Only one moment, but it was like a light switch turned on in Xander's brain. In the car park at the shopping centre, his emotions had been riding a tide of anger over his car and angst over his sister's arrival. Flick had been little more than a fellow driver he'd felt sorry for. But in the café, he'd noticed her. Noticed a pair of sad blue eyes, a lush mouth, and vulnerability beneath her snarky responses.

His gaze was drawn back to her mouth, to lips pink with the last of her lipstick and tilted up at the corners like they were used to smiling. He'd noticed her ... And so had every male staffer in the kitchen.

A proprietary sense had him raising an arm to her waist, but at the last moment, he dropped it on the counter beside her hip.

Windblown hair and a flush of sunburn added to her appeal; Flick was an attractive woman. Auburn hair fell past her shoulders and framed a heart-shaped face. Dark blue eyes were bright with energy as she watched Christophe's team move in well-oiled synchronicity. He held few doubts this was her domain too.

He scanned the kitchen for signs of Chris. How the hell was he going to handle the coincidence of showing up with a slim, attractive stranger just days after avowing he had no time for a relationship? And if he protested too much, Chris would be sure to take it the wrong way.

But was it the wrong way? A strange reluctance to hand her over to Andy made a mockery of Xander's protestations. He checked the time on his watch. Jenny needed him and he couldn't wait any longer.

He turned to Andy. 'This is Felicity Ardmore—Flick. She's a pastry chef looking for short-term work and I wanted to introduce her to Christophe, but my sister is out at the milk bar—alone—and very tired.'

'I can make the introductions and I'll let Christophe know Miss Jenny will love a special dessert for this evening. Something to welcome your sister to Rainbow Cove.'

'Good call, thanks, Andy.' It was the sensible thing to do. He slapped a lid on the spark of reluctance to leave Flick with Andy and turned to her. 'Do you mind if I leave Andy to introduce you to Chris when he gets back?'

Flick lightly touched his arm. 'I'll be fine. Thanks so much for doing as much as you have for a complete stranger. I really appreciate your help.' Her eyes were bright and her smile more genuine than the forced one she'd given him in the café and by the pool.

It was a smile that—as much as he loved his sister—would have tempted him to spend the evening getting to know this woman better. But Jenny was waiting. His sister needed him, and he needed to put aside the odd reaction Flick elicited in him.

'Perhaps you can find a room in the staff quarters for Ms Ardmore and arrange for the delivery of her luggage when the police retrieve it from her car.'

'With pleasure.'

'But what if Christophe doesn't hire me?'

'You need somewhere to stay tonight, but I doubt you'll have anything to worry about.' If Flick's skills and résumé matched her passion for food, Chris would want her for his restaurant. 'I have to get back to Jenny.'

'Of course. Thank you.'

As Xander walked away, Andy led Flick in the other direction. And now Xander would have to get a move on. Leaving Jenny when she needed a rest was a recipe for disaster.

Andy's phone rang, a subtle chirp like a cicada in summer. 'Excuse me, Flick.'

'Of course.' Flick itched to get in and start baking alongside the kitchen staff. It wasn't just her parents' impending divorce and her voluntary disbarment from Pecorino. She needed to create delicate desserts. Talking about her passion to Andy while Christophe's kitchen hummed like a beautiful, well-oiled machine triggered a need to get in and create.

Andy closed his phone and banged a ladle on the stainless-steel counter, waiting until all the staff looked at him. 'Everyone, we have a problem. Christophe is stuck on the highway with a shredded tyre and his spare is flat. He's waiting for the roadside assist service, but apparently it will be a long wait. We have the Truman engagement party booked in this evening. Where are we at in preparation for it?'

The sous-chef handed Andy a menu. 'Entrées and mains are under control, but Chris had planned to make that dessert tower for them.'

'Thanks, Jake.' Andy checked off the menu before looking at Flick. 'Christophe won't be getting in any time soon. Sorry, Flick, but I doubt you'll get a chance to talk with him tonight.'

'As in he'll be flat out catching up when he does get back? No problem. I understand.' It was all very well for Xander to assume his friend would be happy to hire her, but how could she accept lodgings for the night if she didn't get a chance to speak to the chef? If she wasn't employed at the resort, she had no right to a room in the staff accommodation.

Jake frowned and pointed at the item at the bottom of the engagement menu. 'Andy, what are we going to do about the cake?'

Flick took a step away. 'Look, maybe I should head back into town and—'

Andy's eyes narrowed, his gaze settled on her and his manner switched into manager mode. 'Look, this might be a bit unusual, but Xander said you want to work here and … Xander said you're a pastry chef. I'm thinking your specialty might just save the day.'

Flick's hopes rose, poised like a rollercoaster ready to fly into the biggest loop of the ride. 'What do you need?'

Andy took her elbow, turned on his heel and led her into a changing room. 'Spare jackets et cetera in that cupboard. Do you have appropriate shoes with you or are they still in your vehicle?'

'They're in my backpack, but—what are you doing?'

'The engagement party booked into the restaurant this evening specially requested a—' Andy scrolled through the calendar on his phone, enlarged an image and turned the screen so Flick could see.

'A croquembouche.' She'd made one just like it for her final exam.

'Can you make one of those before eight o'clock tonight?'

Flick added tiny, edible purple flowers around her towering croquembouche and stepped back to admire the result. The fine netting of angel hair toffee glistened around the profiterole tower. She rolled her shoulders and relaxed tense muscles, happy with what she'd produced, hopeful it would win over Christophe—who still hadn't returned.

A flicker of white moved into the edge of her vision and a man in a chef's jacket bent towards her creation, turning the platter around slowly until he'd seen it from all sides. 'Like Lady Liberty—perfect from every angle.'

He crossed his arms and the sleeves of his chef's jacket crept up, revealing strong forearms and big hands with neat fingernails. His French accent and proprietorial attitude gave Flick hope.

'Are you Christophe?'

'I am. And who are you, little queen of cakes?' His accent reminded Flick of the pastry chef she'd studied under.

'Flick Ardmore. I was waiting to meet you when Andy got your call to say you had broken down.'

'And why did you want to meet me?'

'Xander commented this morning that my philosophy about food was very similar to yours. I'm—looking for work and I came to ask if you were hiring.'

'Xander said that? Interesting. Perhaps beneath his suit and workaholism, he is a romantic after all.'

Had Xander made comments to Christophe similar to his 'It's just food' in the café this morning?

She rushed on, keen to explain how she came to be cooking in his kitchen. 'I was talking to Andy before you called him. Andy asked me to make this for tonight's booking ... the engagement party? He said it was an opportunity to show you what I can do as well as not disappoint the bride-to-be and her family.'

'That was very clever of him.' Christophe's gaze narrowed, and Flick held her breath, hoping that she hadn't annoyed him by taking over this small corner of his busy kitchen. 'And very—lucky for me.'

Lucky? Did that mean—

'I have my résumé in my backpack. I'm hoping this—' she indicated the profiterole tower '—demonstrates what you'll be getting if you take me on.' Despite knowing her creation was well-executed, her heart thudded. Was it what the master chef had intended? What if—

Christophe broke apart one of the unused puffs and tasted a morsel before breaking off a second piece and scooping leftover cream filling from the bowl. He ate it, nodding as he chewed and swallowed. '*Parfait*—it tastes as good as it looks. I could not have done better myself. It is as if my good friend Xander saw my need and brought you here. You have—what is it that Andy says? *Oui*, you have saved my bacon. Consider yourself hired.'

Chapter Five

Xander stared through the plate-glass window into the twilight beyond the softly lit balcony. From the bedroom, Jenny's crooning was soft, but his gut clenched at her need to self-soothe. Was it just first-night blues, being away from home and her mother? What could he do to make her happy again? The long, muted buzzing of the house phone intruded on his thoughts. Welcoming the distraction of work, he snatched up the phone before it rang a third time. 'Xander here.'

'Xander, *mon pauvre ami*, you do not sound like a man whose sister is visiting him—a man who is now on holidays and relaxing.'

'Chris, did you sort out the seafood problem? Is your car okay?' He lifted the phone away as a disdainful snort erupted beside his right ear.

'With you it is always work first. Work, work, work … my restaurant, it runs like clockwork. Your resort …'

'What about my resort?' He wasn't in the mood for Chris's joshing about the theft of his car from his own secure parking. Not with Jenny's crooning rising in pitch.

Perhaps some of his frustration leached into his voice, but the response was unexpected. 'What can I say? It runs like my kitchen.

Speaking of which ... when I learned you had sent your girlfriend to me, I feared it was some misguided attempt to keep her happy, but you have found me a kitchen goddess.'

'You've met Flick then? Great.' In the back of his mind Xander dimly registered the girlfriend comment. It worried him less when Chris said it than when Andy had revealed his appreciation of Flick's looks. If Chris thought he and Flick were together, well ... he'd made enough comments about Xander's bachelor state and lack of female company that he'd probably encourage any perceived relationship, mythical as it was.

He focused on Chris's last comment. 'So, if she's some kitchen goddess, can you make a place for her in your restaurant? Does that mean her résumé stacks up?'

'Pfft. Mere paperwork! I've seen and tasted one of her creations already.'

Flick's success put one of Xander's worries to rest. He opened the door and stepped out onto the balcony. She was staying around for now and the job meant she had somewhere safe to stay. A tiny voice whispered in his mind—*and I'll see her each day.* 'I haven't tasted her cooking, but chatting with her after our cars crashed, it seemed to me she has the same attitude to food as you do.'

'That's half the battle right there. I've sent her up to your apartment with a sample of her cooking. Little Jenny will like it. You—*you* may be a philistine when it comes to appreciating good food, but you are a genius when it comes to hiring the right people. And who knows? Your Flick may educate your taste buds where I have failed.'

Your Flick. From what he'd seen, Felicity Ardmore wasn't anybody's Flick. She was independent and resourceful. Rising to the challenge of losing her car in an unfamiliar town, her *Ruby*—he chuckled at the memory of her *'Doesn't everyone?'*—she'd trudged out to the resort and found herself a job.

Phone pressed to his ear, he leaned on the railing and breathed deeply. Chris liked Flick, and Jenny, who had an uncanny knack of reacting to good people, liked Flick too. All in all, after a pretty lousy morning, the day had delivered positives for all of them. 'If that happens I may have to put her in charge of the restaurant.'

'Yeah, yeah, and pigs may fly. Don't forget, I own this restaurant. You just encourage your guests to dine here. Hey, you're outside, aren't you? I can hear the night birds calling. Go inside and open your door. Flick will be there shortly.'

Xander chuckled. Chris's dry humour usually put him in a good mood, even on the bleakest of days. As he strolled back into the apartment, the doorbell chimed. 'That must be Flick now. I'll bring Jenny down to see you tomorrow. Thanks, Chris.' He put the phone on the desk and headed to the door.

Flick balanced the plate of profiteroles on one hand and tucked a loose strand of freshly washed hair behind her ear with the other as she waited outside the penthouse apartment. Her croquembouche had passed Christophe's intense inspection and met with glowing approval from the bride-to-be's mother, so why was she nervous about offering the leftover profiteroles to Xander and Jenny?

She adjusted the position of a pair of yellow nasturtiums chosen, in place of the tiny purple flowers gracing the engagement cake, to suit Jenny's colour preference, and held her breath as the door swung open.

Xander wore a navy polo shirt, casual trousers and a distracted welcoming smile. 'Flick. Come in. Nice timing.'

As she stepped inside, Jenny's high-pitched crooning stopped her in her tracks. Her gaze sought Xander's. 'Is that—'

'Yes. She's tired from the trip and it's her first time visiting without Mum.'

'I don't know if this will help. I've been cooking.' She held out an oval platter. 'I brought profiteroles for Jenny and you.'

'That's kind of you, Flick. I'll see if I can entice her out with—'

A door across the room flew open and Jenny appeared, hands clasped to her chest. 'Flick! What did you bring me?' Dressed in a white nightie printed with yellow flowers and ducks, Jenny was smiling broadly as she joined them.

Xander's hesitation was brief, surprised, before he wrapped an arm around his sister's shoulders and drew her across to where Flick stood, still holding the platter. 'Come and see what Flick cooked for you. They're called profiteroles.'

Jenny skipped as she crossed the room and pointed at the nasturtiums. 'There're flowers on the plate. You can't eat flowers.'

It seemed Jenny had gone from anxious to excited in ten seconds.

With no experience to guide her, Flick relied on instinct. Jenny's obvious pleasure at seeing her and turning up with dessert might help the teen's homesickness, if that was what she'd heard when Xander opened the door. 'If it's okay with your brother, and if it isn't too late for dessert—' She looked at Xander.

He nodded in approval and Jenny clapped her hands.

Flick deposited the platter on the dining table. 'You can eat these flowers if you like, although they might taste a little bit peppery.'

Xander moved into the kitchen. 'I'll get some plates. Jenny, have you washed your hands?'

'I will.' Jenny ran through the doorway and the sound of water splashing into a sink carried into the sitting room.

'Have a seat. Would you like a drink? Coffee, tea, wine?' Xander moved around the kitchen with the ease of long familiarity. Even for a resort penthouse, the cupboards appeared to be well stocked.

'Coffee please, black and no sugar. This is a pretty amazing apartment. Have you stayed here before?'

Xander tipped his head and met her gaze as he set two mugs and a pile of small plates on the bench. 'I live here. I told you I lived out on the cove.'

Flick looked around. 'You didn't say you lived *at* the resort. Lucky you. I kind of assumed you had a house out this way or something.'

She added what she thought might be an Italian suit and classy BMW to the evidence surrounding her and wondered if he owned the whole place. 'It's very nice. Bet it feels like you're on holiday all the time.'

Xander's gaze flicked to the door where his sister had disappeared and back to her. 'I live where I work. This resort is my current project. I'm not on holiday.'

Had she just made the dumbest comment ever or was the concept of holiday unfamiliar to him?

'But ... I thought you were taking a holiday with Jenny? So this apartment is one of the perks of your work?' She glanced at him, saw him frown and backed away from the conversation. 'Sorry, it's none of my business. I misunderstood.'

'I find it's easier to oversee the resort renovations when I'm on site all the time.' Xander switched on the electric jug before setting the plates and three forks on the table. 'Anyway, I hope I can do both, although I admit it will be a challenge keeping Jenny amused and active while keeping an eye on the work here.'

'Why don't you hand over control to a supervisor while you have a proper break?'

'I don't need a break. I enjoy my work. Besides, I've usually found it quicker to do away with the middleman in renovations like this. I employ the right people and let them get on with their jobs, but when it comes to creating the right tone, there's nothing like being hands on. Aren't you the same with your cooking?'

'Yes, but I also appreciate some down time to just chill. You might benefit from an actual holiday, Xander. You know, the kind where you take a few days completely off work and have fun and relax.'

'What gives you the idea I don't have fun?'

Flick opened her mouth to tell him how buttoned-up he'd been this morning, but quickly closed it. They'd both been on edge about their cars.

And I only met him this morning! Who am I to tell a virtual stranger to chill?

Jenny joined them at the table, her gaze drifting from Flick to the profiteroles beneath a glistening topping of leftover toffee shards.

Xander set two mugs of coffee on the coasters and reached for a glass of milk that he set down in front of his sister. She pinned him with a hopeful gleam in her eyes. 'Can we eat now, Xander?'

'Absolutely. Flick, would you be kind enough to serve?'

'With pleasure. Here, Jenny, try a piece of toffee while I serve everyone.'

Jenny took a small piece of spun-gold topping and popped it into her mouth. A long-drawn-out 'Mmm' was all they heard from her until her plate was empty.

When the last profiterole had been eaten, Xander glanced at his watch and then gently spoke to his sister. 'Thank Flick and then it's time for bed, Jenny.'

'Thank you, Flick. Will you make the profit dessert again tomorrow?'

Xander answered before Flick had time to consider how to respond. 'No, Jenny. Profiteroles are a special treat, not for every day.'

'I could help her.'

Xander shook his head. 'Maybe next time. Don't forget to brush your teeth.'

Jenny's face fell, but she headed off into her bedroom and closed the door.

Xander's eyes closed briefly and he sighed—the sound so soft Flick almost missed it. In repose, his face was sharp planes and the aquiline angle of his nose. When he opened his eyes, grey with reflections of toffee-gold from the outdoor lights, their gazes connected. 'Would you like a glass of wine or a port?'

Tired as Flick was, Xander's offer seemed more of a request for company than that of a host doing the right thing. He seemed—lonely.

An odd idea, but one Flick couldn't shake.

'Half a glass of white wine please. I'm delighted to say I'm working tomorrow.' Landing a place in Christophe's kitchen felt like the first thing that had gone right for her in months.

She glanced at Xander opening a bottle of wine.

Second thing. If Ruby had to be crashed into by anyone's car, she was grateful it had been Xander's.

'I'll bring it out onto the balcony. There's usually a breeze off the sea at night. Leave the door open. I need to hear if Jenny calls out.'

Flick wandered out and leaned over the railing. Below, the pool activity was quietening down and several al fresco tables were filled with couples drinking coffee or wine. Tiki torches lined the path leading off to Balinese-style cabins she'd learned were advertised as honeymoon retreats. She raised her gaze and looked out over the treetops. Beyond the palms, waves ran onto the shore of the cove and crashed onto the rocks of the headland.

'It's peaceful, isn't it?' Xander handed her a glass of wine and touched it with his. 'How's the staff accommodation?'

The glasses chinked, the sound cheerful and reminiscent of holidays with friends. A sense of peace and hope filled her, that here in Rainbow Cove her life was finally turning around. 'Fabulous. I wasn't expecting a mini-suite all to myself.'

'Good. Thanks for bringing dessert up.' Out here, his voice had an intimate quality. Or maybe it was only that the night was close around them and the sounds of the sea were linked in her mind with better times—happier days.

'My pleasure. Jenny enjoyed it. It must be lovely to have your sister visiting you.' She sipped the wine, pleased to find it was a light Frascati.

'You have no idea how much. My last project was closer to the family home. Since I moved up here I don't see her as often as I'd like to. She's used to staying with me, but before now Mum's always come with her. I think her crooning was just first night separation anxiety.'

'Was she upset before I arrived? I don't mean to pry only …'

'You heard her crooning? She does that to soothe herself, but it's hard for me to listen to. I want her to be happy.'

'From where I'm sitting I'd say she's happy to be here. How will you look after her though? I mean, you said you're not taking time off so how will that work?'

Xander raked a hand through his hair and leaned back in his chair. 'Our parents are flying to Fiji for their anniversary. It's been a while since Jenny's last visit and I guess I forgot how closely she needs to be supervised, but I'll make it work. I have to make it work. The most important thing to me is that she has a good time.'

'Isn't there anyone you trust enough to oversee renovations for a few days?'

'My car was stolen from our supposedly secure parking lot. It's one of the last areas to be renovated, but given the theft, I need to prioritise the upgrade. No, I'll manage.'

Flick sipped her wine and looked out at the distant sky. Moonlight highlighted low clouds over the sea and made a path that shimmered in the gently rolling waves. 'There are only twenty-four hours in a day, Xander. Even you can't make it longer, no matter how much you want to.'

'Maybe not, but I can make every one of them count.'

Chapter Six

Flick was shaping chocolate quills to decorate a torte now cooling in the cold room when Xander and Jenny entered the work zone. Christophe set aside his notebook, stood and hugged Jenny. 'How's my favourite girl?'

'Good.' Jenny ducked her head and then looked up sideways at him. 'Have you cooked biscuits today?'

'Well, Flick has been baking. Why don't you go and see what she's made?'

Jenny looked around, spotted Flick waving, and made her way around the workbench towards her. 'Hi, Flick. What are you making?'

'Chocolate decorations to go on a special cake.' Flick allowed the broad knife blade to turn up too soon and grinned at the small, fat roll of chocolate. Beside the elegant scrolls she'd already made, it was out of place. 'Oops, I made a mess of that quill. If your brother agrees, would you like to taste it?'

Xander gave her one of his distracted smiles, the kind that showed his mind was on things other than chocolate swirls and social niceties; it set her wondering how he was managing his first morning of juggling work and family.

Jenny's eyes feasted on the treat as she took the small plate Flick offered.

In the middle of talking with Christophe, Xander's phone gave a two-note peep. He frowned and looked at his screen. 'Jenny, you'll have to come with me. I'm needed on site.'

Jenny looked up; chocolate smeared one corner of her mouth and the remains of the stubby roll of chocolate melted on her fingers. 'I don't want to go. I want to stay with Flick and help her.'

'Flick's working. You can't stay with her.'

'But—'

'No buts, Jenny. Remember I told you that I might still have to do some work things while you were here?'

Jenny's mouth turned down, a mutinous expression boding ill for Xander. Flick glanced at Christophe. The chef shrugged as if to say, *What can we do, it isn't our business.*

Not usually one to intrude in other people's affairs, something about Xander's frazzled edge and Jenny's yearning look at the chocolate spread across the marble board led Flick to speak up. 'Xander, if it's okay with you—and with Christophe—I'd love to have Jenny stay and help me. I have to make cupcakes for the staff's morning tea and they'll need icing and decorating.'

Xander's gaze narrowed and his frown suggested an internal battle. Was it so difficult for him to accept help?

Jenny clapped her hands and then clasped them in front of her. 'Please, Xander, can I stay and cook with Flick?'

His gaze pinned Flick's, conveying a silent question. *Are you sure about this?*

'If you trust me, I promise I'll look after her until you get back.'

'Chris?'

Christophe's hands spread, palms up, and he smiled. 'It will be our pleasure to have Jenny cook with Flick. She will be no bother.'

'Thank you. Jenny, you do what Flick tells you, and no more than two cupcakes, okay? Remember you're making them to share with everyone.' Xander turned to Chris. 'Sorry, mate. Bad timing getting the call just when we got here.'

Christophe waved away any obligation. 'It will be our pleasure to have Jenny join us for morning tea.' He slung an arm over Xander's shoulders as they walked towards the door and the rest of their conversation was lost to Flick.

'Come on, Jenny. We need to get you a jacket and an apron.' When Jenny was dressed for work, Flick led her to the sink. 'I want you to wash your hands thoroughly, twice, okay? Then use those paper towels to dry your hands and come back to me.'

'Yes, Flick.'

While she finished the decorations and retrieved the torte, working the chocolate back to a pliable state, Flick kept an eye on Jenny. 'Would you like to watch how I finish off this cake for Christophe? After that, we'll make those cupcakes.'

Chatting while she built up a deceptively simple pile of chocolate quills, Flick finished off the torte and stepped back. 'That's done. Now, we'll put it in the cold room and get the ingredients for our cupcakes. What colour icing do you think we should put on them?'

'Yellow ... and can we do some pink ones?'

'Sure.'

Some time later, Jenny watched as Flick dripped several drops of rose-pink colouring into a bowl of icing, and then mixed it, round and round and round.

'Can I taste it now, Flick?' She held up a finger.

Flick handed her a spoon. 'We only ever use a clean spoon to taste, never fingers, and only use the spoon once, okay?'

'Okay.' Jenny dug the spoon into the icing and lifted a loaded spoonful. She popped it into her mouth. 'Mmm, s'good.' She set the bowl on the bench, looked away and froze, pointing at the corner.

Flick spun around.

A white gecko clung to the cornice.

Flick set the bowl of yellow icing down and moved towards the corner.

Jenny was quicker. She climbed onto the chair and then mounted the table, reaching for the gecko. 'Here, gecko. Come here.' Muffled by the spoon in her mouth, Christophe heard her.

He rushed over with the kitchen hand, Nico, hard on his heels. 'Jenny, come down. You'll hurt yourself.'

'I want to pet the gecko.' She stretched up, trying to catch the little creature. It ran.

Jenny edged along the table, stretched.

'Stop, Jenny. Wait there.' Flick's voice was sharp with fear, but Jenny teetered on the edge of the table. It rocked.

'Wait, gecko. Wait for me.'

Christophe moved in and caught her as she stepped off the table. He lowered her to the floor. 'Ah, *ma petite*, falling is not fun. We will catch the little gecko and let him go outside. A kitchen is no place for such a creature.'

'But—'

Christophe led her to a seat and hunkered down so he was at her eye level. 'Imagine how bad it would be if he fell into one of my saucepans.'

Jenny's eyes rounded, and then she giggled. 'He can't swim in your saucepan.'

'Shall I put up a sign: No swimming allowed in saucepans.'

'I'll make a sign for you, Chris. When we finish icing the cakes, I'll make a sign.'

'*Merci, ma petite.*'

Xander headed to the kitchen, aware he'd probably used up all his favours with Chris for the next year. Leaving Jenny with anyone hadn't been on his radar, but Flick's offer out of the blue left him torn. It had always been family first with him, no question. But Jenny had looked so disappointed; he knew she'd see him as an ogre if he tried to take her away and Flick had seemed comfortable with having his little sister stay.

Still …

He opened the kitchen door, surprised that the regular clatter and clang was missing. A flicker of apprehension skated through his mind. A group of kitchen staff had gathered around the counter where Flick had been working. Xander's gut took a dive. He drew in a deep breath and strode over to see what was going on.

In the middle of the group, and the focus of everyone's attention, Jenny held an icing bag and was decorating a cupcake. She finished with a flourish and set the bag on the benchtop. A streak of pink icing ran across one cheek, and her eyes were bright.

Catching sight of him, she laughed and clapped. 'I've made you a special cupcake, Xander. Come see it.'

A pathway cleared in front of him and he passed between the staff and joined Jenny.

Flick stood to one side, a grin on her face. 'Ta-dah! See what Jenny's made for you.'

He looked from Flick to Jenny to the cupcake. Bright yellow icing—he'd expected that—but there was a hot pink cartoon face with a wonky smile that ran off the edge of the cake. A drop of pink icing fell on the stainless-steel counter.

'This is for you.' Jenny giggled and passed the cake to him. 'See, it's you. You're in pink icing.'

He swallowed a lump that was part pleasure in Jenny's joy and part remnant of his concern. 'I look great in pink. Thank you.'

'Now can we have our cupcakes please, Jenny?' Nico leaned on the bench.

Jenny looked at Flick for guidance and, when she nodded, turned and picked up a tray of yellow and pink iced cupcakes and offered them around.

Flick leaned close and lowered her voice. 'She's had a ball, and she's done everything really carefully. Has she done much cooking before?'

Jenny's confidence among strangers stunned Xander. Stunned and pleased him. The doctor had been right about her post-operative progress.

He shook his head. 'Not that I know of. Thanks for offering to look after her. It won't happen again though, I promise.'

Flick tipped her head to one side. 'That would be a shame. We both enjoyed ourselves. Why don't you ask her if she'd enjoy doing some more cooking? I'm happy to spend time with her like we did today if Christophe approves—and if you're okay with me stealing her away for an hour or two?'

'Stealing her …'

'I know you want to spend time with her, but look at her … She's really enjoying herself and learning a skill. And I loved working with her.'

Jenny's new air of confidence and a surprising maturity as she carried the tray of cupcakes among the staff brought a lump to his throat, along with pride in his little sister. He hadn't considered when he'd offered to look after her that she might find an activity that developed life skills such as those she was demonstrating now.

He shook his head. 'Seeing her like this—so happy and confident—well, it kind of puts this morning into perspective.'

'What does that mean?'

It meant his little sister was growing up and that, maybe, she didn't need him by her side all the time. The thought was bittersweet, pitting his need to protect her against his need to give her every opportunity to develop life skills. 'Letting go just a little. It means I'm really proud of her. If Chris is agreeable, I'm sure Jenny would love that, but I'll let you invite her. It's only fair.'

'Great. Shall we say ten o'clock tomorrow morning?'

Chapter Seven

'So the secure parking will be complete by the first of December, including all surveillance cameras?' Xander signed the last of the contracts for the final stage of renovations and capped his pen. Blind spots in the car park security system had been identified, and removal of the old wire fencing had begun.

'Guaranteed.' Rob Carter rolled up the plans and slid them into a canister.

Xander shook Carter's hand. 'I'm glad you took over the company when your father stepped down as managing director. Thanks, Rob.'

Rob raised his hard hat and wiped an arm across his forehead. The temperature in the resort was a balmy twenty-eight degrees, but here on the expanse of bitumen, it was several degrees hotter. 'Now all we need is—'

Xander watched the digger reverse.

Waited for Terry to move.

Watched.

'No beeps. There's no bloody reversing …' He sprinted towards the unwitting workman.

It unrolled in slow motion. Xander had never believed people who'd told him that ... until now.

He yelled, Terry turned, fell.

The machine rolled towards him.

Frantically, Xander waved at the driver to stop.

Brakes squealed and Xander slid down the small slope. Dimly aware he'd lost his hard hat, Xander kneeled beside the fallen workman. The wire fence, partially removed, had stopped the workman's slide.

'Terry, mate, are you okay?' Xander looked at his scrunched-up face, ran his gaze down Terry's body. Blood spurted from his thigh, spurted over twisted wires, stained the ground below. He yelled over his shoulder. 'Get an ambulance. I think he's nicked an artery.'

Xander grabbed the fencing, lifted it away and tried to clamp a hand over the wound at the same time. Slippery with Terry's blood and his own sweat, the panel slid in Xander's grasp, gashing his hand. A pole fell, clipping his head and shoulder.

Rob scrambled down the other side of Terry's body and lifted the panel off Xander's hand. More hands reached in, helping, dragging, lifting the injured man.

Xander kept his hand clamped over Terry's thigh. Bright red blood welled between his fingers. 'It's okay, Terry. Ambulance is on its way.'

Xander slumped against the wall outside the kitchen. His head reeled and his body ached like he'd battled a giant octopus—and come off second best. Three days of dropping Jenny at the kitchen to spend time with Flick had quickly become routine, for which he was profoundly thankful.

Thank God Jenny hadn't been with him this morning.

Clanging and the clatter of a busy kitchen aggravated the throbbing in his head, but he dredged deep for a smile—or something that passed for one before Jenny saw him—and pushed the door wide with his shoulder.

Seated at a small table in the corner behind where Flick was working, Jenny caught sight of him and grinned. 'We made pikelets today, Xander. I kept some for you.'

'Great.' Damn it. His voice sounded gravelly. He had to do better or risk Jenny noticing. Hand throbbing in time with the headache pounding behind his eyes, he focused on the chocolate cake taking shape beneath Flick's skilled hands. Lemon icing looped between delicate pink flowers. With her next loop he breathed in, held his breath for the second and third loops, and released his breath on the next two.

Repeat.

Repeat.

Mastering the pain, he raised his eyes.

Flick's gaze skimmed over him, caught on the tear in his jacket sleeve, stalled on blood streaking his cuff. Her eyes widened in wordless question.

He shook his head and slid a glance towards Jenny. Flick nodded once.

He was a mess, but in the toss-up between going to shower and changing and reaching Jenny before word of the accident got back to the resort, reassuring Jenny won. Mud streaked his dark drill trousers and his right hand was hidden in his pocket. The shirt-sleeve button was undone and the loose cuff was streaked in mud and blood.

Some of it mine.

'Xander?' Jenny's smile faltered.

Had he answered her? What had she said?

The room was at a strange angle, and the edge of his vision was blurred.

Flick set down her spatula and wiped her hands on the cloth hanging from her waistband. 'You'd better sit down and get into those pikelets fast. Jenny's been guarding them for you. The guys scarfed the rest.'

He felt the tug of Flick's hand on his elbow, the press of a hand on his back, the wood of the seat against his knee, and sat.

Jenny's small corner table was away from the workflow area. She put the pencil she'd been writing with on the notebook in front of her and picked up the plate of pikelets. Four remained.

'All the rest were eaten because they're so good.'

He eyed the odd shapes blobbed with strawberry jam and cream. A sweet, buttery smell rose from the plate and his stomach roiled at the thought of eating. He leaned away from the plate Jenny had shoved almost under his nose and sat well back in his seat. The curved wooden back held him prisoner. Looking from the pikelets into Jenny's excited eyes, he swallowed, refusing to give in to his heaving stomach. 'They look delicious. Tell me what else you've been doing. What are you writing in that notebook?'

While Jenny told him about her morning and showed off the notebook Christophe had given her to write down all the recipes she made, he felt Flick's surreptitious glances, assessing, checking. He'd trusted her not to exclaim over his injuries and make a fuss, but, trying to focus on Jenny's chatter, he felt awkward and off-balance. The doctor had given him a local anaesthetic before he clipped the edges of the jagged cut, but Xander's right hand throbbed.

'Coffee, Xander?' Flick leaned on the table and nudged the untouched plate of pikelets closer to his left hand.

Right, pikelets. He needed to take a pikelet to keep up appearances. 'Thanks.'

'Aren't you going to eat your pikelets? See, this one is an X shape. X for Xander.'

'Then that's the one I should have first, although that one looks like a J. Would that be for Jenny?' He pointed at one with his left hand. Streaks of dried blood showed on his fingers and he quickly lowered his hand before Jenny noticed it.

Certain that Xander had had an accident but was trying not to frighten Jenny with the sight of blood, Flick touched Jenny's shoulder, drawing her attention. 'Jenny, would you go and ask Christophe if he has some brandy please? Tell him it's for a special coffee for your brother.'

'Okay.' Jenny wandered off in the direction of Christophe's corner office.

'What have you done?' Flick had probably bought them a minute or two at best before Jenny returned. 'I'll help you clean the blood off without worrying Jenny, but tell me before she comes back.'

Gingerly, he eased his right hand from his pocket and rested his elbow on the table. His hand was heavily bandaged, and the movement seemed to drain colour from his face. 'I got the worse end of an encounter with a fence and a machine on the car park fence line. Doc wanted to send me to the hospital.'

'And of course, you said no.'

'You know I can't go. Jenny would freak out. Anyway, the doc gave me a tetanus shot and I've got painkillers in my pocket.'

'And you'll soldier on as though nothing has happened.' She checked over her shoulder to be sure Jenny wasn't scurrying back.

Through Christophe's office window, the chef made eye contact with her. She pointed to Xander's bandaged hand and Chris nodded. He'd keep Jenny occupied while Flick cleaned the blood off Xander's hand. As for his clothes ... she just hoped Jenny wouldn't notice the streaks of blood.

With a hand under Xander's elbow, she led him past where Jake was making sauce for a chicken roulade. 'Jake, do something with those pikelets, will you? Jenny will notice if that plate isn't empty by the time she comes back.'

Jake glanced at her and then at Xander's injury. 'Hey, man, not cool. What happened?'

'Jake? The pikelets.'

'Sure.' Jake turned down the gas below his pan of sauce and made a beeline for Jenny's plate of pikelets.

Flick led Xander into the change room. He sat on the hard bench beside the sink and she took down a first-aid box from the cupboard before turning on the tap. Antiseptic wipes at the ready, she removed blood from the back of his uninjured fingers, looking for cuts before turning his hand over. His palm was red-sticky, and dark lines of dried blood marked his hand like trails on a map.

'Not much of it's mine. I clamped my hand over the other guy's leg until someone managed to get a tourniquet on it. The accident must have nicked an artery because there was so much blood.'

Her stomach did a flip at the metallic whiff of blood.

Moving gently, she eased his hand under the tap. Clear water flowed over his palm and ran towards the plughole in a turbulent path of red. A few spots of red-tinged water splashed onto his cuff, adding a lighter pattern of red to the dried streaks of blood. 'How did this happen?'

'A lapse in safety protocols. There'll be an inquiry, but I don't recall the beeper sounding when the digger began reversing. One of the site workers was knocked out and his leg was cut open.'

'Were you standing next to him?' She stepped back from the sink. Her leg brushed Xander's bandaged hand and he winced. 'Sorry.'

'It's okay.' He exhaled even more slowly before pressing his lips together and drawing in a slow breath. 'No. I just happened to look in his direction and saw him fall. It was lucky, or the digger would have crushed him.'

'So how did your injury happen?' She pulled several paper towels from the dispenser and patted his hand dry.

'Terry—the worker who was knocked out—slipped on a mound of newly turned dirt and fell under a section of old fence that's scheduled for removal. His leg was ripped open on the exposed wire. The same wires cut my hand when we were lifting the fence off him and dragging him free.'

'Will he be okay?' She balled the used paper towels and tossed them into the rubbish bin.

'I think so, but he lost a fair bit of blood. Doc said the hospital had an operating theatre ready to go as soon as the ambulance arrived. Flick—' He gripped her hand with his uninjured left. 'Not a word to Jenny, please.'

'I figured that out, but I hope you've worked out a good answer, because she'll want to know why your hand is bandaged.'

'I know. I wanted to get clean clothes and wash off the blood, but I couldn't let the news of the accident reach her before she saw me.'

'No one here would have told her.'

He shook his head. 'I had to be sure. She had to see I'm fine. The bandage will be less worrying now she knows I'm okay.'

'True. Christophe won't be able to keep her in his office for long. We'd better get back out there.'

'Right.' Xander rose and staggered, bumping into Flick. His left hand, unfettered by the bulky bandage, gripped her hip, and his head tipped onto her shoulder. 'Dizzy. Sorry.'

She gripped his shoulders, holding him upright, but he was heavy against her. She leaned in, bracing her legs and supporting him.

She heard the door open behind her and then Jenny's voice, loud enough for the whole kitchen to hear.

'Xander, why are you kissing Flick?'

Chapter Eight

Xander's dizzy spell slowly faded, but his eyelids were heavy. If he could keep them closed and rest—just for a few moments …

The scent of chocolate and cherries and warm woman soothed the aches in his body, eclipsing the memories of blood spurting and calming the remembered surge of adrenaline that had fuelled his sprint to the injured man. He wanted to lock those moments down and not think about them, or the sharp pain of wire ripping his hand when he wrestled the fence panel back to staunch the blood.

But there was something … someone who needed him. Jenny. What was it he had to do for his sister?

'Are you okay?' Warm breath skated over his neck. *Flick?*

His right hand throbbed. Pain relief rested in tablet form in his jacket pocket, if he could find the will to hold his head up and take it. Realising he'd missed several vital seconds, he exerted what felt like superhuman power and lifted his head from her shoulder. 'What?'

'Don't say *what*; say pardon.'

Xander blinked and focused past Flick's ear. His sister stood in the open doorway. Arms folded across her chest, she watched them with keen interest. A quickly muffled giggle from Flick brought him to his senses, to awareness of where he was.

And what he was doing.

His one good hand gripped Flick's hip, and the scent of baking—of berries and rich cream frosting—wafted beneath his nose. Loose strands of her hair clung to his sweaty skin. Beneath his good hand, the curve of her hip was warm, enticing … intimate in an odd way that had little to do with his spinning head.

He forced himself to stand straight, but his hand wouldn't release his hold of the woman who had prevented him from taking a fall and likely cracking his head on the tiled floor. If anything, his grip tightened as she swayed.

Or he swayed.

Blue eyes scanned his face, peered into his eyes. 'Maybe you should sit down. Did you hit your head?' she said very quietly.

'I'll be okay.'

Chris appeared behind Jenny, easing past her into the change room. 'Xander, you okay, mate?'

'Don't fuss. I'm fine.'

'Are you going to get married?' Jenny's question dropped into the quiet room and carried through the open door into the work place, quiet except for the hiss of gas and the squeak of rubber-soled shoes in the kitchen beyond.

There was a sense of waiting, a quality of listening with bated breath as the room and the kitchen and his sister and Chris waited for his answer. And Flick? Amusement brightened her blue eyes. Why did the question amuse her?

Xander looked at his sister. 'Of course I am. One day.'

'You were kissing Flick. Mum says when people kiss they're married, or they're going to get married.'

Chris let out a sharp and quickly cut-off laugh, but his eyes crinkled above the smile he couldn't quite wipe off his face. '*Oui*, that is often the case, Jenny. People kiss then *wham*! They get married and have babies.'

'Shut it, Chris. You're not helping.'

Flick grinned, took a breath. Her lips parted and, in a lucid moment, Xander knew he needed to stop her denying they'd been kissing. Kissing was far less of a problem than admitting to his sister he'd almost fainted. She would worry if she thought he was sick, and fret over what would happen. Jenny needed strength and stability from him, not the weakness he'd just exhibited. Jenny needed what she thought she'd seen to be true because the reality was scary.

He dipped his head and touched his lips to Flick's. There—now he had kissed her. Now she couldn't say they weren't kissing because … because … Why had Jenny thought they were kissing?

Had he in fact kissed Flick and forgotten the moment?

Startled, wide eyes looked at him and she lifted a hand to her lips.

'Xander and Flick are getting married. Yay!' Jenny clapped, and a wide smile settled on her face.

Chris took Jenny's elbow and led her out of the change room.

'Why are we leaving, Chris?'

'Because if they are getting married, then they will want to be alone, *ma petite*.'

Flick looked up at Xander. Her gaze was no longer deep blue but stormy-grey. Hands on hips, the look in her eyes threatened emasculation. 'Did you hit your head as well as rip your hand?'

'You were going to tell Jenny the truth. She won't cope if she thinks I'm injured.'

'So you kissed me to—' She frowned and tipped her head to the side.

The throbbing in his hand was sharper. With an indrawn breath, he reached awkwardly with his left hand into his right pocket for the small bottle of painkillers the doc had given him. The bottle caught on something.

'Here, let me get that.' Flick slipped her hand into the pocket and took the bottle out. She looked at the label. 'How many do you need?'

'One for now. I've got to take Jenny back to the apartment.'

Without a word Flick half-filled a glass with water and set it beside him before shaking out one tablet into the lid and offering it to him. He tossed the tablet into his mouth, following it with a long mouthful of water and a heavy sigh.

Flick pressed her lips together. 'We're going to talk about what happened later. Go and rest.'

Without another word, she opened the door and held it, waiting for him to leave.

Chapter Nine

Xander and his sister and their relationship weren't Flick's business, but there were things that he'd made her business because of that kiss … Setting him straight on that kiss was going to happen right now.

She smoothed the fabric of her dress and knocked on his apartment door. Clearly Xander hadn't been in his right mind at the time and that was the reason—*the only reason*—she hadn't challenged him in the change room.

Her life had gone pear-shaped and the only man who'd kissed her in over eighteen months had done so because he was out of his head.

But it was Jenny's delighted *Xander and Flick are getting married* that preyed on Flick's mind. In the days they'd spent cooking together, it was clear Jenny adored her much older brother. It had also become obvious that once she fixated on an idea, shaking it was very difficult. Disabusing Jenny of that notion was Xander's job, and Flick wanted it made clear now. She knocked again.

'I'm not allowed to open the door.' Jenny's voice sounded close against the other side of the door. Close and—strangely flat.

Why wasn't Xander coming to the door? A sick feeling of dread did backflips in Flick's stomach. Was he lying comatose from some other unsuspected injury? Common sense kicked in. The doctor who had stitched his hand would surely have checked him over thoroughly, but—there was still that odd kiss, distant and disconnected. She needed to be sure. 'Jenny? It's Flick. Is your brother okay?'

'He's asleep. I'm not allowed to open the door if I don't know who it is, but I know you. Can I open the door, Flick?'

'If Xander is asleep, maybe you'd better not.' Asleep sounded deliberate, not suspicious. Her immediate concern allayed, Flick considered Jenny's lacklustre response. Jenny didn't like being alone and Xander sleeping in the middle of the day was probably odd in her world. As much as Flick wanted to get things straight with Xander, he *had* been injured and painkillers would knock him out for an hour or two. 'How about I pop back later.'

'Flick? Please will you come in? I'm lonely.'

Torn between respecting Xander's privacy, his need to sleep, and Jenny's plea, Flick compromised. 'How about I go to the main kitchen and get a few things to bring up here and I'll show you how to make a simple meal for Xander. He'll probably be hungry when he wakes up.'

'Don't be long, Flick.'

'I won't, I promise.'

When Flick returned with a large stainless-steel bowl filled with the makings of a simple salad, Jenny had put on the apron Xander had bought after her first cooking adventure. It was a clear plastic and patterned with oversized yellow flowers. 'I washed my hands. See.' She held out both hands.

Flick saw. 'Maybe you should wipe off the bubbles at your elbow before we start.' She set the bowl on the kitchen bench and pulled a bib apron over her head, wrapping the strings around her waist and tying it in a front bow.

'I've brought ingredients to make a salad, and a few slices of cold meat to go with it so it won't matter when Xander gets up. Ready?'

Jenny was mixing salad dressing in a container as though it was a maraca when Xander lurched out of his bedroom. He wore navy boxers and clutched a grey T-shirt in one hand while his injured hand was raised across his bare chest. His hair stuck out on one side and lay flat on the other.

He frowned and his eyes, heavy from a drugged sleep, seemed to have trouble focusing on her. The idea of telling him what she thought of his high-handed kiss vanished when he leaned heavily against the doorjamb.

'Flick, what are you doing here? Did I sleep through the night?' He lifted the hand holding the T-shirt and rubbed at his eyes, blinking rapidly, and so obviously not properly awake as he stared at his hand and his bare chest. Moving awkwardly, he put his injured hand into the T-shirt and manoeuvred the bulky bandage through an armhole with a soft, hissing, indrawn breath.

'You don't need to bother dressing on my account. I'll go and—'

'S'fine, just give me a minute.' He shoved his left arm through the other armhole and pulled the shirt on. His head emerged, and he tugged the material over his abdomen before his gaze fixed on his sister. 'Jenny, what are you shaking there?'

Jenny held the plastic container aloft. 'Salad dressing. Flick helped me make a salad for you. She said you'd be hungry when you woke up. Are you hungry, Xander?'

'Thirsty and hungry.'

'I'll get you a drink.' Jenny set the shaker on the bench and took a bottle of water out of the fridge. 'Here.'

Xander took the bottle. His attempts to open it were hampered by the bulky bandage on his right hand and a lack of co-ordination, unusual in a man always rigidly in control.

Flick held out a hand. 'Like some help?'

He looked at her, bemusement and frustration clear. He shook his head and handed the bottle to her. 'Helpless as a bl— ahem, as a baby. Thanks.'

He sat at the table and drank half its contents in one go. As he set the bottle down, he pinned her with a look accentuated by the raised eyebrow above. 'Just curious but—why are you in my apartment in the middle of the day? It is still today, isn't it, or have I slept through the night?' He raked a hand through bed-hair and glanced through the sliding doors.

Flick's gaze followed his. Mid-afternoon sun cast the shadow of the resort building across the closest trees and the white light of noon had softened into a warmer gold. The day was hot and the sea enticing, and suddenly she felt wrong-footed and out of place. Why hadn't she listened to her instincts instead of letting annoyance gain the upper hand?

'It's still today and I'm on a split shift.'

She wasn't going to have a conversation about that kiss with him now; not with Jenny listening in. 'I wanted to talk to you about something, but when Jenny said you were asleep and she was lonely, I offered to show her how to make a light lunch. I had no intention of intruding.'

'I'm grateful to you—again. Would you like to join us, or have you eaten?'

'No, to both. Maybe we can talk later. It's—private.' She glanced at Jenny who was balancing cutlery on top of three plates as she walked slowly to the table. That niggling sense of frustration at not getting a chance to talk to Xander had dissipated as she taught Jenny the basics of salad making. Xander didn't act like a man who'd kissed her. What if he didn't even remember doing it? Maybe she should forget it before—

'Fine. How about you come here when you finish work tonight?'

Once the thought had lodged in her mind, it wouldn't let go. What if she was making a big deal out of nothing? She clattered around in the kitchen, gathering containers to return to the kitchen and hedging for time. 'It might not be until ten-ish. That's probably too late.' It had always been too late for her ex-boyfriend.

'Suits me. I'll see you then. And thanks again for lunch.'

Her ex, Jason, had dumped her, claiming her working hours didn't suit his lifestyle, but Xander was more realistic. She took a moment to appreciate the differences between them before nerves overtook her again. Second-guessing herself wasn't helpful. As she headed back to her quarters to change her clothes before the second half of her split shift, she resolved to save herself any embarrassment and cancel their meeting.

Had he kissed Flick? Stretched out on the lounger on the balcony, Xander sipped mineral water. A mosquito droned past on a current of humid night air, circled back and drifted lazily across his vision. He waved it away.

Hazy memories of the morning intruded, but no matter how hard he tried, he couldn't recall anything with clarity, other than the sickening pain in his hand and the driving need to reassure Jenny.

And the rest? *Pure imagination.*

Yet he couldn't shake the memory of Flick's lips against his, a fleeting, soft, sweet brush of mouth upon mouth. Xander did *not* like the sensation of being out of control, of not having perfect recall, but the haziness of details and the circumstances under which he might have kissed Flick were too crazy to be real.

But those two words—*it's private*—taunted him. And the memory of holding her hip. That, he hadn't imagined. His palm curved, remembering the shape and feel of her.

Jenny was asleep, and he was due for another painkiller, but Flick was due any minute. He checked the time on his phone. Ten-fifteen. Tossing up whether to take the tablet and risk feeling drowsy, he wandered back into the apartment. Two knocks sounded on the door, so soft he wouldn't have heard them if he'd been out on the balcony.

He crossed to the door and opened it to find Flick bending down, a slip of paper in her hand.

'Oh—you're awake. I thought—' She stood suddenly, her fingers running along the crease in the note and her gaze darting between his and into the room beyond his shoulder.

'I was expecting you so, yes, I'm still awake. You knocked so softly I almost missed it.'

'I … didn't want to disturb Jenny. Or you, if you were asleep.'

Watching Flick's strangely nervous behaviour, an odd thought hit him. 'If it hadn't been that you asked for a private meeting, right about now I'd be thinking you're trying to avoid talking to me.'

'That would be crazy.'

It was hard to tell in the subdued lighting of the foyer, but he thought a hint of pink flared in her cheeks. 'It would. Come in. Would you like a wine or—'

'Nothing, thanks. Look—' She stopped just inside the front door and took a deep breath. 'No, it's too weird. I'm sorry for disturbing you. I should go.'

Xander touched her shoulder. 'Did I kiss you? Is that what this is about?'

'You don't remember?' Her eyes widened. The hint of pink flared into full-blown embarrassment in her cheeks and he had his answer.

'So I did kiss you. Sorry, I wasn't sure if I dreamed it. It wasn't much of a kiss, was it?'

'It wasn't, but it was enough to potentially cause a problem.'

'Jenny. Right—I thought that was part of a dream too. That's why you're here now, isn't it?'

'Yes. I can't think of a single good reason for that kiss.'

'Come out to the balcony. It's clear we need to talk about what happened this morning.' Xander grabbed another bottle of water from the fridge on the way through and set it on the outdoor table before sliding the glass door most of the way shut.

He wasn't proud of his behaviour; even knowing he'd done it for the best of reasons, he hadn't factored in how Flick would feel. He hadn't thought at all. And now she was here, wanting to discuss the whys and wherefores of his actions.

Flick sat on the edge of her chair and opened her bottle.

Xander picked up a half-empty bottle from beside the lounger and took a seat to her right, where the outdoor lighting fell on her face and allowed him to watch her reaction. 'First, I need to apologise. Please—put it down to being out of it for a few minutes.'

She nodded and toyed with the label on the plastic bottle. 'I'm willing to accept you weren't in a normal state of mind at the time. You mumbled Jenny's name, which made no sense. Can you tell me—why did you do it? I mean, you can't even remember kissing me.' In spite of the jokey tone and a passable attempt at a smile, her gaze searched his face.

Kissing Flick and forgetting the kiss had been wrong on so many levels and he felt lousy for hurting her. Hurting—and disappointing her. With an effort, he tried to recall the sequence of the morning's events. 'Forgive me. I'm hazy about it, but I think it was when Jenny opened the change-room door. I am truly sorry for dragging you into the situation. I reacted on blind instinct, in the moment, but I didn't mean to hurt you. But you see, if Jenny thinks we were kissing rather than that her brother, who she looks up to and who keeps her safe, all but passed out, she won't worry about me disappearing into hospital. She spent several weeks in the children's ward last year. We came close to losing her and now, any mention of hospital freaks her out.'

'She nearly died? I'm sorry.'

Xander lifted the bottle and sipped. Even now, the thought of how close they'd come to losing Jenny brought a lump to his throat. 'It doesn't excuse that kiss, but I hope it explains how and why it happened.'

'It's not a problem. I didn't want to make a big deal out of it—just to understand what motivated it. I mean it was just a kiss.'

'Hardly even a proper kiss.'

'And clearly it was forgettable. I'm sorry I mentioned it.'

She made a move to get up.

Xander put his hand on her arm and stopped her. 'I hope you will forget it. You have a right to expect nothing less than the real thing.'

A kiss should mean something, not be dropped into a conversation like a bad one-liner.

'Both parties should be wholly present in the moment and I wasn't. You deserve proper kisses and I failed to deliver. I'm sorry.'

Flick sank back into her seat and tipped her head, looking at him as though seeing him for the first time. Perhaps she was. Maybe he had suffered a knock on the head when he raced in to save Terry from the digger. Either that, or he was growing philosophical with age.

When had he ever thought deeply about kissing a woman? It had never seemed more than the prelude to a pleasant encounter before, but tonight it mattered. The thought that he may have let Flick down didn't sit comfortably with him. She was caring, and kind, and she mattered. Their first kiss should have been memorable.

'Wow. You really do mean that, don't you? Honestly, Xander, it's no big deal. I'm sorry I mentioned it.'

'I'm not. I'm glad we talked about it and I'd like a chance to make it up to you.'

Her lips parted, and she stared at him, her disbelief plain to see. And something more. Rising up beneath her disbelief was—dare he hope?—curiosity and a desire to find out what their kisses might be like. Her gaze flickered down to his lips and back up to meet his. 'You can't mean ...'

'I want to kiss you—properly.'

Chapter Ten

'Of course, that's only if you want to, but I have to say I do. Want to, that is.' Reciprocated attraction simmered between them on the humid air of almost-summer.

Xander's voice was pitched low in deference to the lateness of the hour and the fact they were out on the balcony. Combined with the velvety night and the perfumes drifting up from the tropical flowers, it seduced and tempted Flick. Until this moment, she hadn't known she wanted to kiss Xander. Now, the idea of not kissing him, of not knowing what a *proper* kiss from him would be like, was impossible to ignore. Of its own volition, her body leaned towards him. But the instinctive need to protect herself made her jump in first and keep things light.

'Well, if you think you can do better than this morning, I guess I could give you another chance.' She set her bottle of water on the table and took a deep breath. She was really going to do this.

The idea of kissing him sent little tingles of anticipation fluttering in her stomach. No man had even vaguely tempted her since Jason. But there was something about Xander. His dark gaze focused on her was an aphrodisiac. And there was no chance he wouldn't remember this time. He wanted to kiss her.

His gaze dropped to her mouth before he cradled her neck with his left hand. 'That's very generous of you. I promise to be fully present this time.'

She edged forwards on her seat. His thumb brushed her cheek. She caught a reflection of outdoor lighting in his eyes, but the balcony wall lights affected her ability to see his expression clearly. Why hadn't she thought to sit where the light would fall on his face? 'Me too.'

'Ready?'

She nodded and met him halfway.

His kiss was gentle, a slow exploration of her lips that teased her with possibilities and hinted at leashed restraint. He was as into it as she was and when she finally came up for air, she was surprised to find they were standing and wrapped in each other's arms. Or rather she had both arms around Xander's waist. His bandaged hand rested on her shoulder, but his left arm held her as though he wasn't ready to let her go.

Relaxing a little, she leaned back, her breathing ragged as she looked at him with a dawning sense of wonder. How could a simple kiss make her feel so special?

Simple? She squelched a nervous giggle.

'Wow.' Her insides were jittery with sensation and she couldn't recall feeling this way before, ever. 'You lived up to your promise.'

He smiled, a smile that softened his stern lips, and his arm tightened as he whispered, 'I aim to give full satisfaction. And if you liked it, I'm looking forward to your repeat business.'

Her insides curled, and she lifted her face in silent invitation.

His kiss was another slow, soft exploration of her lips, the corner of her mouth. 'Can I tempt you to come back for more?'

'I could become addicted to your kisses—' Then the sane, cold voice of reason kicked in. 'But, regretfully, no.'

Not when Xander owned the resort, which included the restaurant. Technically, that must make him her boss, and dating the boss was fraught. *Pity I didn't think this through before I discovered what I was missing.*

'No? Why not?' Genuine disappointment coloured his voice and his good hand tightened on her waist.

Did she really mean that? As the rational part of her brain came fully awake and processed what she'd done—where it could lead—she shook her head. 'It's not sensible to get involved with my boss.'

His eyes narrowed, and the silence grew tense, but Flick knew she'd made the right decision, despite her regret.

'Is that your only reason for refusing a repeat performance? I thought you were enjoying yourself.'

'Hmm, you were there this time, weren't you? Did those kisses strike you as disinterested?'

'Definitely interested. And yes, I was fully invested in kissing you this time. I want to kiss you again—lots of times. So, my question remains—is that the only reason you don't want to kiss me now?' His disappointment seemed to have morphed into a note of teasing optimism that made her want to mesh mouths again. If only there was some way around it, but not dating her boss was a hard rule.

She'd seen how bad things could get when her best friend had got entangled in a similar situation. Were a few kisses, no matter how head-spinningly good, worth the long-term pain? Better not to set off on that path. She shook her head again. 'I won't date my boss. I can't.'

'That's excellent news for me. I'm not your boss—Chris is. He owns the restaurant, not me.'

Joy bubbled up within her, and anticipation of more kisses with Xander fizzed in her veins. 'Christophe is my boss? You're sure about that?' Her heartbeat sped up as desire for a repeat performance arrowed through her body.

'Positive.'

'In that case—' She pulled his head down, raised her lips and kissed him again.

When they finally drew apart, he rested his forehead against hers. 'So—dare I ask again? Does this mean you'll be back for more?'

'I'm a very *loyal* customer.'

'And I take pride in delivering only top-quality products.' He kissed her forehead before, with obvious reluctance, stepping away from her. 'I'll do better when I have both hands free to hold you.'

Better?

'Seriously? Much more than that and you'll blow my mind. When you focus on something, you really do focus.' Her hands slid down his arms as she stepped back towards the doorway. 'I can't wait until next time, but I should go. It's getting late and I have an early start in the morning.'

His gaze held hers as he tucked a strand of hair behind her ear. 'See you tomorrow? How about I pick you up when you finish work and we can—'

Work! The four-letter word slammed through her happy daze and smashed the bubble his kisses had wrapped her in. Work meant people watching, listening ... judging her.

She stepped in front of him and slapped one hand over his mouth and the other on his chest. Even if he wasn't her boss, he owned the resort. *Management and an employee? No way under the sun.*

Her gut clenched at the potential fallout. 'Stop right there—please.'

If Xander arrived in the kitchen with kisses and claims on her time, she might as well pack up and leave now. Picking her up from the kitchen would isolate her from her co-workers, mark her as a woman who thought too little of her ability to get ahead on her own merits.

Xander's not my boss. I'm not his employee. But still her stomach roiled. People saw what they expected to see.

'Flick, now what's wrong?'

When she opened her eyes, Xander was frowning.

'I need to make one thing clear. I know you said you're not my boss, but you own the resort. Can we just keep things private, kind of low-key for now?'

He took hold of her hand and raised it to his lips. 'If that's what you want, of course we can. I won't complain about keeping you all to myself.'

'I'm serious, Xander. No kissing or holding hands or anything that remotely suggests a connection. Especially not when Jenny is around. Oh—'

He nodded, as though her thought had seamlessly transferred into his mind. 'About that. I'll think of something to tell her. God knows what, but I'll work it out.'

'Thank you. I never quite figured out how kisses equal getting married in her mind.'

'I suspect that was Mum's way of teaching her about personal safety around boys.'

'Ah, that makes a kind of sense.' And it meant, even in the apartment, they would have to be careful not to repeat this morning's mistake in front of her. 'How much longer is she staying with you?'

'We have a couple more days. I promised to take her horseriding tomorrow afternoon.' His gaze held hers and brightened. 'Would you like to come with us if you're not working then?'

'You don't think she might want you all to herself, do you? I mean, if she's only got her big brother for a couple more days, she might not want me tagging along too.'

'Jenny likes you, Flick—a lot. I'm pretty sure she'll love it if you come too. When do you finish work?'

'At two.'

'Great. See you at the stables at three, if that's enough time for you to change?'

'Three is fine. I'll see you there.'

He slipped one hand into her hair and tipped her head up to meet his lips. If she didn't dream about him for the rest of the night, she'd be surprised. As goodnight kisses went, his were very satisfying.

Chapter Eleven

Xander held the reins in his left hand and mounted the roan gelding with a little less grace than usual. His right hand throbbed, and it was his own damned fault for choosing to miss a scheduled painkiller, but as he watched Jenny settle on the most docile mare in the resort's stables, he knew he'd put up with a lot more pain to give her this treat. 'Ready?'

Beneath her brand-new yellow sunhat sticking out beneath the riding helmet, a wide smile lit Jenny's face. She had flatly refused to wear the helmet until Flick had come up with that suggestion. 'I'm ready. Are you ready?' She looked to her right.

Mounted on a bay mare, Flick wore a faded pair of jeans that hugged her behind in a way that would keep Xander's mind off the pain in his hand—if she took the lead. Last night's kisses had sealed his fascination with her. The promise of more stolen kisses later tonight would help him to put up with any pain during the ride.

'I'm all set.'

'After you, Flick.'

'You'd better lead the way. It will be safer if I bring up the rear; I don't know the trails around here.'

'Sure. Jenny's already learned to trot so we'll try out that skill now.' He knew a momentary deflation of spirit as he lightly touched his mount's sides. The gelding sprang forwards and, following his command, turned at the end of the practice yard before moving into an easy trot. Bouncing along on horseback jarred his injury more than he'd expected. The decision not to take a painkiller had had more to do with not wanting to feel drowsy, but he was regretting that choice even more by the time they reached the lookout on the rocky headland.

'Let's stop here and check out the view, and Jenny, it's time we had a drink of water.' He pulled up and, with a sigh of relief, dismounted and awkwardly tied the reins to the highest rail of the post-and-rail fence. His hand throbbed.

Is dismounting up here a bad decision?

Jenny's riding lessons had gone well, but mounting was still a bit hit and miss for her. Getting her back in the saddle might be a challenge with only one hand. He looked around for a largish stone she could stand on before turning to assist her down.

Flick was quicker and had already helped Jenny to dismount. Jenny patted her horse's neck while Flick tied the reins beside Xander's mount. 'I've got the water.' She opened her saddlebag and handed Jenny a bottle.

'Have a drink now before you go walking.' Xander leaned against the fence, watching as Jenny dutifully drank. She wandered towards the far end of the lookout with her bottle and he called to her. 'And don't go past the bush with the red flowers.'

'I won't, Xander.'

Flick tucked two bottles of water in the crook of her arm as she closed her saddle pack. She glanced at him and then loosened one cap before offering the bottle to him. 'You don't look very comfortable. Is your hand hurting?'

Aware that he was cradling his right elbow in his left hand, he straightened up and rested his injured hand on the top rail.

He hated being injured, hated the feeling of lack of control.

The bulky cream bandage was a nuisance, but it reminded him how quickly accidents could happen. And that he wasn't bullet-proof, even if he tried to maintain the image for his little sister. 'It's nothing.'

'If you say so.' Flick turned to the view, but not before he caught a glint in her eye.

So much for his show of stoicism. She knew his hand was caning him but let him have his white lie and the illusion of dignity. 'I'm glad you could come with us. Jenny was excited when I told her this morning.'

Glad didn't really explain how he felt. Having Flick join them gave him hope that last night was the first of many they would spend together. And her ban on going public suited him. Less fuss and fewer people to tell when his work on Rainbow Cove Resort ended, as it would in less than two months. New Year was the time limit on the relationship they'd embarked on last night.

If not for work, he would have been tempted to leave it open-ended. There was something about Flick …

'I'm enjoying myself. It's been a while since I've had the chance to ride. My parents used to—' She bit her bottom lip and turned away again.

Whatever the issue with her parents, it was a biggie, and recent if he didn't miss his guess. Gently, he steered the conversation back to less contentious topics. 'Your parents used to what? Own a horse?'

A soft sigh escaped, and she sipped her water before she answered. 'We used to live in the Redlands area of Brisbane, out where the strawberry farms were. I had a horse when I was in my early teens, back before we moved in closer to the city.'

'What happened to your horse when you moved? Were you able to keep him?' Did she know her expression softened when she talked about her childhood? Her shifting expressions fascinated him. Flick fascinated him.

She shook her head. 'We went from several acres of bushland to a suburban backyard. Before we moved, Karen, our neighbour, bought Dusty for her two boys to learn to ride on. And we opened our restaurant while I was in high school. Pecorino was small, but we made it one of the best family-owned and run restaurants on the east side of Brisbane.' A definite note of pride coloured her voice. Here was her passion for creating food he'd sensed the day they met, the passion that had led him to mention Christophe.

If not for his idle comment about their similarities, Flick wouldn't be standing here with him now. 'Is that how you came to be a pastry chef?'

'Partly, I guess. Dad encouraged me to pursue my dreams, but Mum—'

She broke off and drew an audible breath that sounded somehow fragile.

'You don't get on well with your mother? Is that why she's the only person who calls you *Felicity*?'

She stared at him, her mouth open. 'Why do you remember random things I've said?'

Because you fascinate me. Because I want to kiss you right now.

He glanced at the horses and shrugged, reluctant to share words that would lead to kisses she didn't want. Not in daylight. Not where people or—heaven forbid—Jenny might see. 'The idea seemed to fit what you told me. Am I wrong?'

'No.'

Regardless of her family problems, it sounded like she was close to her father. He hoped so. He couldn't imagine life without his parents and his sister.

Without meeting his gaze, she pointed to the north with her free hand. 'What's that peak way off in the distance?'

'The one closest to the coast? That's—'

'Xander, come quick.' Jenny's cry was high and urgent. He pushed off the railing and raced to where he'd last seen his sister, calling as he ran. How could he have lost sight of her? How could he have taken his eyes off her long enough that she had disappeared? Fear and desperation tightened his throat while he scanned the bushes for a flash of bright yellow.

'Where are you, Jenny?'

'Here. Come see what I found.' Her voice was high, and her tone didn't indicate she was in pain, but his gut clenched with worry. Fear gave his feet wings. Dry-mouthed, he prayed she hadn't found a snake.

He spied her yellow hat and helmet through the branches of a bush and pushed his way through. Concern for her safety lessened, but his anger grew that he'd taken his eyes off her for even one moment.

Beyond the bush, Jenny sat in the dirt, her legs straight out and in her lap sat …

It took him a moment to realise she was petting a young wombat lying on its back in her lap.

'She's cute. Don't you think she's cute, Xander?'

Behind him, Flick pushed through the bushes and came to a halt beside him. 'Wow. I've never seen a wombat this small.' She dropped into the dirt beside Jenny and stroked the broad head. 'Where did you find her?'

'Under the bush.' Jenny waved vaguely to her right. 'Can I take her home with me?'

Xander moved closer, his heartbeat still elevated. Trust his little sister to find a baby animal in the bush. Her menagerie back home occupied a lot of his parents' energy and most of Jenny's free time. But this native animal wasn't about to go home with her. 'You have to put her back where you found her. Her mother will probably be looking for her.'

Jenny turned her head in that way he knew all too well. She was ignoring him. Sometimes he wondered if it was more like an unconscious choice on her part, her way of making the world suit what she wanted. Catching his sigh before it released, he kneeled beside his sister.

'Do you think she's run away from home?' Jenny looked down at the baby animal and kept stroking the broad head. 'Did you run away from Mummy? You want to come home with me, don't you?'

'Come on. Let's get her back where she belongs.' Xander went to lift the wombat from his sister's lap. Jenny hunched her shoulder and moved an arm to prevent him taking what he rapidly realised she had decided was her newest pet.

Flick put a hand on his arm. 'Do you have any idea how much a baby wombat weighs—even a small one? You'll pull your stitches if you try to lift it. Let me.'

It galled letting Flick deal with returning the wombat to where he could see what looked like its burrow, but she was right. Even if he'd taken a painkiller, he'd do more damage if he insisted. 'Okay. Thanks.'

She hunkered down in front of Jenny and resumed stroking the animal's head. Keeping her voice gentle, she appealed to his sister's good nature. 'Jenny, this little wombat is too small to stay with you. It needs its mother, and I think it needs to sleep. It will be sad without its mummy. Is it okay if I put it back in its burrow now?'

Jenny's eyes watered, and her bottom lip quivered and when she drew her knees up a little way, Xander was certain she was heading into tantrum territory. Tears ran down her cheeks, but when Flick set a hand on her shoulder and their gazes met, Jenny sniffed and nodded. 'Okay. Bye, baby wombat.'

Carefully, Flick scooped up the young animal and carried it to its burrow. Jenny kneeled up in the dirt and watched avidly as Flick set the animal down at the burrow entrance. It stood still for several heartbeats before slowly disappearing into the hole. Flick dusted off her hands, reached for Jenny's and pulled her up before resting a hand on her shoulder. 'It's hard saying goodbye, but you did the right thing. Baby Wombat would have been too sad without its mother. Come on, let's see if there are some biscuits in my saddlebag.'

Jenny groped for Xander's hand and turned her face into his chest, which became damp with tears and snot. 'I miss the wombat. I wanted to take her home to live with me and Mum and Dad.'

'I know, sweetheart, but think how sad the wombat mummy would be without her baby. Are you hungry for some of Flick's biscuits? I wonder what sort she's brought?' Over the top of Jenny's head, his gaze connected with Flick's.

Compassion filled her eyes, and a small wedge of regret flickered through him. If only they'd met when he first arrived in Rainbow Cove instead of two months before he was leaving. Two months felt like too short a time to enjoy one another's company, but that was all they had before he moved on to his next project.

They strolled together back to the horses and Xander gave Jenny his handkerchief to wipe her face while Flick unpacked a container of biscuits from her saddlebag.

'I thought you might like Smarties on the biscuits. See, Jenny, they're green Christmas trees with yellow decorations. And I made some with other colours too.' She offered the container to Jenny and his sister's tears dried as she took two biscuits, both decorated with all yellow Smarties. One final noisy sucked-in breath later, she bit into a biscuit before wandering over to the fence. Leaning on the top rail, her face turned towards the coast, she seemed settled and happy again.

Xander breathed a relieved sigh and took a biscuit from the container. 'Thank you. The biscuits were a smart idea.'

'Smart-ie idea.' She grinned and bit into a Christmas tree biscuit topped with mixed colours. Her tongue touched the corner of her mouth, catching an errant crumb.

Memories of their tongues tangling last night blasted through his mind. All he had to do was lower his head and …

Eyes riveted on her mouth, he must have made a move towards her, drawn like iron filings to a magnet. Her eyes widened, her gaze flicked across to Jenny, and she shook her head. She stepped away just as Jenny skipped towards them.

'Can I have another biscuit please?'

Flick glanced at him for approval before opening the container again. 'Here you are; one more and then I'd better pack the rest away.'

'Will you teach me how to make these, Flick? I need to write the recipe in my book.'

'If your brother can spare you for an hour or so tomorrow?'

His sister's second-last full day—he needed to make it special. 'Of course.' Flick had given a lot of thought to what Jenny liked and was attuned to her needs in ways that, as much as he loved his sister, just didn't register on his radar. 'Jenny's interest in cooking has grown thanks to you. I'll bet Mum will be delighted she's learning new skills.'

'Jenny's a great student. *And* she gets to enjoy the end result. I'd call that a win-win situation.'

'I'd have to agree. You've certainly made my life easier this week.'

He'd been concerned all week about the amount of time Flick was putting into cooking with his sister, but now it struck Xander that genuine fondness motivated her.

Jenny smiled up at Flick and rested her head on Flick's shoulder. Xander blinked at the sight. All her life Jenny had been wary of strangers, but with Flick, it had been different from the beginning. Was it the same kindness and genuine interest in others that had drawn him to her as well? He prided himself on being a good judge of character and in Flick he'd found a strong and positive and caring woman.

'You say that even after how we met?' She grinned and put the biscuit container back in her saddlebag. 'That morning, I needed serious de-stressing. All I wanted to do was get into a kitchen and bake.' She buckled the strap and turned to Jenny. 'How about you climb onto that lowest fence railing and I'll bring your horse to you?'

Xander shook his head. He'd been looking for a freestanding rock. 'If you help Jenny, I'll bring her horse alongside.'

When Jenny went home, Xander was going to make the most of the time he and Flick had. There were lots of private places they could go if Flick didn't want to be out in public with him.

She might have put an embargo on hand holding and public kisses, but privacy had its compensations. He'd promised Flick his full and undivided attention and he was a man of his word. Yes, he would make the most of the time they had.

Chapter Twelve

Xander was drained and drowsy as he sat with a cup of coffee at his desk in the penthouse. Jenny had talked incessantly about the wombat and her animals at home until she went to bed. As much as he loved his sister, he wondered how his parents managed all day, every day, with only occasional respite. Feeling guilty that his tired brain had thrown up such disloyal thoughts, he decided he would offer to have her visit him more often. Shorter stays than this one, maybe, but he could set aside three days every month or two, give his parents a break and enjoy some quality time with his sister.

Operating on automatic, he reached for a pen to sign off on another completed job. His injured hand knocked the desk lamp and he bit off a low-voiced oath, aware that Jenny hadn't long stopped crooning.

How the hell was he supposed to sign off on anything when he could barely hold a pen? Glaring at the heavy bandaging, he picked up the pen in his left hand. Signing his name was such a basic action, but changing hands required him to rethink the process. He changed the angle of the paper, hunched his shoulder and rested his right hand on top of the page to hold it still. Laboriously, he wrote his name, and when he finished and looked at the signature, he tossed the pen down in disgust. He couldn't hold a pen and write his name or even hold Flick properly, not in the way he wanted to.

No sooner had his thoughts turned to her than frustrated desire called up the image of her eating that damned biscuit this afternoon. But for Jenny's presence, he would have taken her in his arms and kissed her and eased the need that had taken up permanent residence in him since last night. Before he knew he was doing it, he'd picked up the phone and pressed her number in his contacts.

The phone rang several times before he glanced at the time display on the microwave. It was after ten o'clock and disappointment filled him. Maybe she was on a split shift or maybe she was already in bed or—

'Hello.' Her voice curled around his frustration and disappointment and blew them away. But she sounded a little distracted.

'Flick, hi. I didn't wake you, did I?'

'No. I was researching lavender for a new recipe. What's up? Is Jenny okay?'

He wasn't sure why he'd called her; only that the desire to talk to her was strong. If he was honest, he needed to hold her and indulge in some serious kissing before his brain exploded with the memory of her taste and the feel of her pressed against his chest. 'A bout of crooning herself to sleep, probably because I said no about the wombat, but all good now. Fancy a late-night coffee or something?'

'Sure. I'll be there in ten minutes.'

Slipping into the resort via the kitchen was easy with her security pass. Flick made her way up to the penthouse apartment, pleased when she reached it without meeting anyone. Staying off everyone's radar was important to her. Xander had been agreeable, but she wondered just how easy discretion was going to be to maintain.

As the lift doors opened, he was waiting in the open doorway of his apartment. 'Hi.'

'Hi, yourself.' She crossed the tiled foyer and stretched up to give him a quick kiss.

Clearly 'quick' wasn't in Xander's vocabulary—not when it came to kissing her. He drew her into a one-armed hug and kissed her. His lips covered hers, his tongue teasing her to open to him. The sense of urgency, of need, of desire sent seismic tremors rippling in her belly. She gripped his shoulders before sliding her arms around his neck. One hand tunnelled into his hair, holding his head as she lost herself in a world of sensory overload.

When he lifted his mouth from hers, they were both breathing harder than usual. Her eyes opened slowly. Desire burned brightly in his gaze as she took a slow breath. 'Wow, where did that come from? Not that I'm complaining, but that was some hello.'

'I'm glad to see you. I wanted to kiss you today up at the lookout.' He tugged gently on her hand and drew her into the apartment, closing the door behind with a push from his foot.

'That would have been counterproductive with Jenny looking on. She'd have had us married and with a family ...'

He glanced towards a closed door.

Jenny's bedroom?

Flick sensed tension in the frown that appeared on his brow. Why had she opened her mouth and let the elephant into the room? 'Is that why you wanted to see me? Did you have trouble explaining to her why you kissed me yesterday?'

'No, that's not it. I just—wanted to kiss you.'

'You sounded a bit stressed on the phone. Can I do anything to help?'

'You already have.'

'How?'

His gaze dropped to her lips before he pulled her close and laid a trail of kisses from one ear to her mouth. 'Kissing, baking—we each have our forms of stress relief.'

Distracted by his warm breath on her skin, she tipped her head, offering him better access to the sensitive spot below her ear. 'Are you saying you're using me—as a distraction?'

'Not using you. You are a distraction, in the best possible way. I think I'm only just realising how challenging not touching you is going to be.'

'You're touching me now.'

'Ah yes, but remember that neat little proviso you set? The anticipation when we're in public will likely kill me.'

'Or sharpen your appetite.' She hadn't intended to drive them both to distraction, but it seemed that was an unintended consequence of her relationship rule. 'Is that a bad thing?'

He groaned and pointed at some papers on his desk. 'I was trying to work, but all I could think about was you.'

She looked at the topmost paper and drew it closer. 'Is this meant to be your signature? It looks like chicken scratchings.'

'I'm wounded to the core. That's my best attempt with my left hand.' He sighed and leaned his forehead against hers. 'Until you lose something you don't realise how much you take it for granted.'

That was true about what she'd lost—family, home, certainty. Not that she'd taken them for granted; only the fact that they'd always be there for her …

Until they weren't.

Easing out of his arms, she slipped around the island bench. 'I'll put the kettle on, unless you prefer something stronger?'

'I'd better not. Coffee please.'

She busied herself in the kitchen, trying to turn her thoughts back to just how good Xander's kisses were instead of brooding over what she had lost. Learning to live in the present was a skill she hadn't mastered. She wondered if she ever would. 'How was Jenny tonight?'

'Finding the wombat and then having to leave it set her off. She crooned herself to sleep in the end.'

'That must have been distressing for both of you. Does it happen often?'

'Not as often as it used to. She seems to have grown up since I was home last time. The day we met—'

'When your car wiped out Ruby—'

'Yes. I was worried Jenny would have a meltdown when I turned up in the hire car because she had been fixating on my silver BMW. I suspect it was the cup holder, or maybe the display screen that fascinated her. But she was excited about going for a drive in a car with no roof.'

'Is she keen to get home to her parents?'

'I think she will be, even though she's done lots of fun things here. Going for a short trek on a horse was the biggie on her wish list, but now I think cooking with you may be the highlight of her holiday. Thanks for being so generous. I appreciate it, more than I can say.'

'I've enjoyed teaching her. She's a lovely young woman. You must be very proud of her.' Flick poured boiling water into two mugs, added milk and carried them out onto the balcony. She set the mugs on the white cane coffee table and then sat beside Xander on the two-seater sofa. 'When do you take Jenny to the airport?'

'The day after tomorrow at eleven o'clock. It will be her first flight alone. Mum will be at the gate waiting for her at the other end.'

'So, what have you planned for her tomorrow? Will there be time for one more cooking lesson?'

'I'm taking her on the catamaran cruise along the coast in the morning. Maybe she could pop into the kitchen in the afternoon, between packing and a swim in the pool. I don't want her to be too tired before the flight home.' He sipped his coffee before setting the mug on the table. With his good hand, he covered her free one. 'I'd like to take you out sailing one day soon. Would you like that, Flick?'

'On a catamaran—yeah. I grew up near the water, remember?'

'Does that mean you know how to handle a boat?'

'Sails, motor—if it floats, I'll love it.'

'Excellent. Once Jenny's gone home and I can hold more than a toothbrush in my hand, I'll take you sailing up the coast. I know several secluded spots where the water's clear and the swimming is pretty safe.'

'Secluded sounds—promising. You know, if it wasn't for your car being stolen, we'd never have met.' It was the first time in her life she'd understood the meaning of a silver lining to every cloud.

'I thank my lucky stars for cosmic coincidence.' Xander smiled and began kissing her again, slow, drugging kisses full of promise and intent. Kisses that she dared hope would be on tap for a very long time. Was she wishing on a star, thinking of staying in Rainbow Cove beyond the insurance payout for Ruby?

By the time Xander released her, she was fairly certain she didn't want to move on again. Working for Christophe and perhaps one day being confident enough to move in with Xander felt possible. She reached for her coffee and drank a mouthful of the now-tepid brew. 'Why did you really invite me over tonight?'

He quirked an eyebrow and a wry smile tugged up one corner of his mouth. Tucking a strand of hair behind her ear, his hand lingered on her cheek. 'If I tell you, I'll be handing over a powerful secret.'

'I'm very good as a keeper of secrets, you know.'

'In that case—I couldn't go another hour without kissing you. If you hadn't come, it would have been almost forty-eight hours. I couldn't survive until tomorrow night.'

Her qualms about a relationship with Xander, sensible or not, disappeared with his admission. Xander was proving to be wonderfully good for her self-confidence but his kisses were both motivation to be with him and the biggest test of her decision to avoid going out in public.

Public. So long as they kept their relationship out of the spotlight, so long as no one knew about *them*, maybe she could relax and just enjoy time with Xander. Time ... And kisses that made her crazy world make sense.

'I'm glad you called.'

'Shall we reduce the waiting time until tomorrow night a bit more?'

She moved into his arms and tilted her face to his. 'Let's.'

Chapter Thirteen

Flick turned the Egyptian torte around on the turntable as she spread the top layer of hazelnut. Light and crunchy, and one of the simpler recipes in her repertoire, the alternating layers of biscuit, custard filling and crunchy hazelnut topping made it the perfect dessert as temperatures increased day by day.

She wiped her forehead on her sleeve and stepped back to assess the overall appearance of her torte. All around her, familiar sounds rose from a kitchen preparing for another busy Saturday. Most staff were on duty and a long day stretched ahead of all of them. She thought longingly of cooling breezes and the slap of waves against a double hull. If only she could have been out on the catamaran trip with Xander and Jenny.

As Christophe took a turn around the various workstations, she stopped him, her spatula raised above the torte. 'Christophe, do you want the pavlovas cooked as individual serves, or as a single large dessert?'

'We usually make them as a single big one, but—what's your reasoning for small ones? They don't look as impressive.'

'True, but they hold their shape through to the last serving, whereas you only need one clumsy cut to mess up the entire large plate. I know how busy the restaurant is going to be tonight. Can I make them small this time?'

Christophe pursed his lips and frowned slightly, a look she had come to recognise meant he was giving the idea serious consideration. Finally, he nodded. 'Let's do mini pavlovas surrounding a large, lightly-flamed meringue. Make the large meringue the centrepiece with mounded topping, peaked like a mountain, and the small ones like those who have come to adore.'

'Yes, chef. I'm on it.' She visualised a snowy Mt Blanc shape with clusters of free-form meringues topped with locally sourced kiwifruit, and indigenous red berries. They would be enhanced by a subtle lavender colour if Christophe agreed. Before she could second-guess herself, she called after him. 'Do you mind if I try out a lavender-flavoured cream to complement them? I've done the research and I arranged for a small quantity of lavender to be delivered from one of the local farms.'

'Let me taste the cream first. If it's as good as the idea sounds, and if there are enough flowers, you could create a lavender field at the base of the meringue mountain.' He smiled before turning on his heel and striding into his office.

A field of lavender on a snowy meringue mountain …

Christophe's ideas for presentation were often quirky, but always visually appealing. Almost every day Flick found yet one more reason to be grateful her car accident had happened here at Rainbow Cove. Without it, she wouldn't have had the great experience of working with the Frenchman—fate had well and truly landed her on her feet.

And I wouldn't be sneaking out to meet Xander and wanting more than moonlit kisses.

She sighed as she separated eggs, sourced locally like almost everything Christophe used in his restaurant, and tipped the whites into a shiny silver mixing bowl, giving thanks for this particular detour in her life. Christophe had taken a chance on her when she'd been at her lowest point. Now she was baking again, her world had settled into a comfortable rhythm. Watching how he ran Chez Christophe was feeding her dream of one day owning her own restaurant. That, and putting away money towards a deposit. Chez Christophe might not be her parents' Pecorino, but the dream would be hers, and she would stay there forever.

Nobody would take that dream from her.

Xander took Jenny's hand and helped her step from the backboard of the catamaran onto the dock. Her cheeks were flushed with excitement and her eyes were bright. 'Did you enjoy net surfing?'

'It was fun. But I like cooking with Flick better.' Jenny skipped a few steps along the dock. Her towel slid off her shoulder and was caught by a couple who were following them.

'Here you go.'

Jenny took the towel from the young man, her gaze sliding away as she remembered her manners. 'Thank you.'

A burst of pride filled Xander. For so long, Jenny had been shy and unwilling to interact with strangers, but this visit had changed so much for her, and meeting Flick had been the catalyst.

'You're welcome. My wife caught it.' The man pulled the woman close—surely honeymooners by the way they were all but joined at the hip—and kissed her cheek.

'Are you married?' Jenny's gaze fixed unblinkingly on the couple.

Both grinned. 'Yeah, why? Does it show?'

'Mum says people who kiss are married—or getting married.' She glanced up sideways at Xander and giggled. 'Xander's going to marry Flick. He kissed her in the kitchen.'

Damn it. He'd meant to talk to Jenny about that, but the right time never seemed to eventuate.

Suppressing a groan, Xander nodded to the couple and dropped an arm over Jenny's shoulders. 'Thanks again, folks, and glad you enjoyed the cruise. Come on, Jenny. We'll have lunch and a swim, and then we'll pack your suitcase ready for tomorrow.'

Her face fell as it had when he'd mentioned packing earlier.

'You want to see Mum and Dad, don't you? They're certainly missing you.'

'Course I do only …'

'Only what?'

'Can I be a bridesmaid when you and Flick get married?'

Enough already.

Xander led her into a shaded part of the pool surrounds and sat her at a table before taking the seat beside her.

'Are we going to have lunch here, Xander? Can I have chips please?'

He took hold of her shoulders and waited until she was looking at him. 'Maybe. Listen, Jenny, we need to have a talk about Flick and me. We're not getting married.'

'But Mum said …'

'I know what Mum said, but not everyone who kisses does it because they plan to get married. Sometimes grown-ups like to kiss just because they like each other.'

Jenny frowned. 'So, you and Flick aren't going to make babies?'

Xander's breath whooshed out in disbelief. Where had Jenny got that idea? Did she even know how babies were made? If their mother had had *the talk* with Jenny, why hadn't she mentioned it to him? 'We are not going to make babies. All we did was share a kiss.'

'Because you like Flick and she likes you.'

'That's right. I kissed Flick because I like her.'

'You liked Eve on the catamaran too, but you didn't kiss her. Why not?'

Xander thought about his very pregnant employee who was about to go on maternity leave. Jenny hadn't commented on Eve's pregnancy bump and he hadn't mentioned the baby in Jenny's hearing. 'Um, because I like Flick in a different way. I like kissing Flick.'

'Would you like kissing Eve too?'

'Eve is married. But you don't kiss everyone just because you like them.' *How do I get out of this now?* He could see this discussion would never end unless he found a definitive answer.

'Do you like Flick more than Eve? I like Flick best.'

'I like Flick in a different way to how I like Eve, or Christophe, or Mum. Or even you.'

'But you kiss my cheek.'

'That's the kiss for a friend or family member.'

'You kissed Flick on the mouth.'

'I like kissing Flick on the mouth. It's different, but it's not a kiss you give to anyone unless they are really important to you.' The sense of uttering a truth flitted through his mind. Flick *was* important to him. As pleasurable as the feel of winter sun on his skin, or a long, cold drink on a hot summer's day. He needed her, needed to kiss her ... Every day.

Jenny ploughed on. Unless he could distract her, she would keep on until she got an answer that satisfied her, and Xander didn't have one.

'Flick's important to you, but you're not getting married to her? How come?'

'I like Flick in the way that for some people *might*—and that's a big *might*—lead to marriage when they know one another really well. But we don't know one another very well yet. Does that answer your question?'

'So you *might* marry Flick one day?'

Xander huffed out a quickly cut-off sigh. 'It's possible. But I won't know until I've kissed her lots of times. Now, you asked for chips. Since this is your last full day here, let's have a treat.'

'Thank you, Xander.' She sat with her hands in her lap while he ordered a bowl to share and two hamburgers from the pool bar. 'And Xander?'

He looked into his sister's eyes, surprised to see she looked happy in spite of being told he wasn't about to marry Flick. *The power of 'might'*, he thought. *Such a useful word.*

'Can I be a bridesmaid when you decide you're going to marry Flick?'

Flick glanced up at the clock. Another hour until her extended shift ended. The whimsy of the clock—a chef crying over chopped onions that Christophe had installed in the kitchen just for fun— made her smile, even as her neck muscles tightened. She tipped her head back and rolled her head from side to side.

'Okay, Flick? Thanks for staying to cover for Jake.'

'No problem. I hope Jake hasn't got that summer flu I read about.'

'Me too. We're coming into the busiest time of year, not the best time to be a staff member down.'

She gave the sauce a final stir and raised the spoon, examining the viscosity. 'Does this taste right to you?'

Christophe picked up a spoon and dipped it into the pan. He tasted the sauce and reached for a shaker of lemon thyme. 'Just a dash *et voilà!*' He stirred the sauce and handed her a clean spoon. 'Try it. See what I mean? A dash of the right herb lifts any dish.'

She held one hand beneath the spoon and sipped, closing her eyes to concentrate on the subtle flavour. 'You're right. It has a similar depth of flavour to my lavender cream—'

Eyes opening, she found herself staring into Xander's. A flicker of annoyance buzzed through her. They had agreed he wouldn't turn up at the kitchen to meet her, to avoid any hint of a relationship. She'd even texted him to say she was staying on to cover for a sick colleague, so he knew to expect her late for Jenny's final dinner.

Something was off. His body was tense and a permanent frown seemed to have indented itself on his forehead. And his eyes … they were dark and some emotion had scrunched the corners until tight lines radiated from them.

Her throat constricted. The only thing she could imagine causing him to look like this was … 'What's wrong?'

'Have you seen Jenny since lunch?'

She shook her head, glanced at Christophe and back to Xander. 'No. She hasn't been in here all day. We weren't expecting her yet. Didn't you have that cruise on the catamaran?'

'Yes, and we had lunch and a swim at the pool and then went to the apartment so she could pack her suitcase. She said she wanted to do it by herself so I let her.'

Christophe gripped his shoulder. 'Did you leave the apartment at any time?'

'No. I never leave her alone. I took a couple of calls out on the balcony, but—' His eyes widened. 'One was business, but the other was with my mother. I told her about Jenny's week and her activities, including cooking with you. I hoped maybe she'd slipped down here early to visit you.'

'I'm sorry, Xander. If she'd shown up here without you, I'd have called you.'

'I'm at my wit's end where to look. I've got to go look for her.'

Breath tightening in her chest, Flick took a step towards him, but Christophe caught her shoulder. 'There will be plenty of staff to help him look. They will find her happily playing with a puppy or something similar.'

She pressed her lips together and sucked in a deep breath. 'Of course they will. Jenny wouldn't go far, but she does get distracted by animals ... and pretty yellow things.' She turned back to her sauce and set it on the warmer. If she hadn't been so worried about Jenny going missing, she'd have enjoyed learning more about the Australian ingredients in this part of Christophe's local-themed menu, but her mind buzzed with possibilities.

From what she'd learned over the past week, Jenny could be single-minded and stubborn, but she was caring and—.

A nebulous thought, swirling since Xander had mentioned telling his mother about Jenny's activities, crystallised into an image of Jenny at the lookout, cradling the baby wombat.

She gripped the edge of the workbench.

Was that where Jenny had gone?

Turning off the gas, she hurried to where Christophe was cooking a kangaroo steak. 'I've got to call Xander right away. Give me five minutes.'

Christophe's gaze narrowed before he nodded. 'You've thought of something? Go, ring him.'

She bolted through the doors to the back dock, quiet at this time of day, and fumbled for her phone. It rang and rang, and she clenched her hand tightly around it, willing Xander to pick up.

'Have you found her?' His voice was tight, rough with emotion held on the tightest of leashes; it grated over her taut nerves.

'No, sorry, but I just thought … you were telling your mother about Jenny's week. We went riding. Yesterday we rode up to the lookout—the wombat—remember? She wanted to take it home. Is it possible she might try to find the baby wombat?'

'Shit. Why didn't I think of that? I'm on my way.' The call ended abruptly, and Flick's heart thudded so hard, she leaned on the wall as a wave of dizziness crashed through her.

What if she was wrong? What if she'd sent Xander on a wild-goose chase?

Chapter Fourteen

Slanting rays from the setting sun blinded Xander as he turned the corner of the horse trail and emerged into the open area of the lookout. Holding a hand to shade his eyes, he spied the gentle mare Jenny had ridden yesterday grazing on long clumps of grass, loose reins trailing dangerously. The mare whickered a welcome to his gelding and ambled towards them and the stone-like lump in his gut shrank. Flick had been right after all.

He called Jenny's name before he touched the roan's flanks and brought it up beside the mare. Speaking soothingly to the little horse, he caught her reins before dismounting and tying the reins of both horses to the top railing.

Jenny was here somewhere. Heart thudding with hope, he stepped away, calling again as he pushed through the bushes to where she'd found the wombat. Deep shadows filled the spaces between the long fingers of sunlight. Desperate for a glimpse of Jenny's yellow sunhat, his first sighting filled him with dread. Snagged on thorns, it hung from a spiky bush. He pulled it free and shoved it into his pocket. Narrowing his eyes against the blinding sunlight, he searched for the wombat burrow. Footprints—*from*

Jenny's shoes?—led to a hole beneath a bush, but of Jenny, there was no sign.

'Jenny, where are you, sweetheart?'

She had been here; her horse and her hat were indisputable evidence of that, but she was missing.

'Jenny.'

Birds called overhead while nearby, soft slithering sounds reminded him of the life beneath his feet. His breathing sounded harsh, desperate, deafening him to the little sounds of the bush. He sucked in a deep breath and held it, straining to hear over the blood rush pounding in his ears. A twig cracked off to his right. He spun around, seeking a flash of movement, and followed the sound. Carefully stepping between two bushes, he crouched down and lifted an overhanging branch.

From the shadowy depths, Jenny stared up at him, cuddling the baby wombat close to her chest. She looked fine. Seemed unhurt.

Relief surged through him, smashing the stone wall of fear that had built within him with each passing hour of her absence. Ruthlessly he held back his need to hold her close, kept a tight rein on his desire to demand answers. Neither would go down well with his sister. In the gentlest voice he could manage, he held out a hand. 'Come out, Jenny.'

She shuffled forwards, clutching the wombat over her shoulder and took Xander's hand. 'Baby wombat came out to play. Look.'

'I see, but now it's time for him—'

'Her.'

'For her to go back to her mummy and go to bed. And it's nearly dinnertime. Flick's coming over for dinner with us. You don't want to miss seeing her, do you?'

'No, I want to see Flick.' Jenny hugged the wombat, kissed its nose and set it down at the entrance to the burrow. 'Bye, baby. See you later.'

Giddy with relief, Xander set his arm over Jenny's shoulders and drew her out of the clearing towards the horses. It would be fully dark before they made it back along the trail to the resort, but the route along the road was twice the distance. He led Jenny to the fence and brought the mare to her as Flick had done. 'Come on, Jen. Up you go.' So thankful was he to have found his sister unharmed that he couldn't even be cross she'd forgotten to wear a riding helmet. Unbuckling his helmet, he held it out to her. 'Put this on, Jen.'

She dropped the reins and her hands smacked onto her head. 'My hat! Where's my hat?'

He pulled it out of his pocket and handed it to her. 'Here. I've got it.'

She settled it on her head and added the helmet on top of her sunhat. Xander gathered the reins and held them out to her. Then he mounted, took up the leading rein, and her little mare followed his gelding back to the trail.

'I've got to make a phone call. Can you follow me and stay close?'

'Course I can.'

'Good girl.' He pulled the phone from his shirt pocket and pressed the speed dial for Flick.

She picked up on the second ring. 'Have you found her?'

'Yes, you were right. She's safe. We're riding back now, but can you let Andy know please. He can contact the search party and give them the good news.'

'He's found her and she's fine.' Flick's voice was muffled. In the background he heard Chris's voice before Flick spoke again. 'Christophe said he'll have dinner ready in an hour or so. If you text me when you're back, I'll meet you at the apartment with the food.'

'Thanks. See you soon.' Xander tucked the phone back in his pocket and turned to Jenny. 'Okay back there?'

'I don't like the dark, Xander.'

Thank God I found her when I did. Jenny alone in the dark would have been her worst nightmare come true. And none of this would have happened if he hadn't been distracted by those phone calls, if he had just stayed in the apartment instead of heading out onto the balcony. The lesson was salutary, and his parents would need to know just how adventurous Jenny had become.

'Stick close to me, sweetheart. We'll be home soon.'

Jenny's eyelids were drooping as Flick helped pack her suitcase. 'Why don't you clean your teeth and I'll finish the last of your packing?'

'Okay, Flick.'

Flick set out the dress and shoes Jenny had chosen to wear on the plane tomorrow. A twinge of sadness at the departure of Xander's sister caught her unawares. No more baking cupcakes or worrying if Jenny had found her pet of the day in Chris's kitchen.

Like the albino gecko.

Flick slipped a pair of sandals into the case and set the yellow sunhat on top of the folded clothes. Touching the material, she smiled.

Memories. They'd made plenty of them to treasure, and the teenager had touched her in ways she imagined she would have felt if she'd had a younger sister.

When Jenny emerged from the ensuite, she surprised Flick by giving her a quick hug. 'I'll miss you, Flick.'

'I'll miss you too, Jenny. But each time you bake something, think of me, and how we made the recipe here. Will you do that?'

Jenny nodded. 'I've got my recipe book in my carry-on case. Mum told Xander we'll make one of the recipes when I get home.

I'll think about you then.' She turned and climbed into bed. Her eyes closed as she mumbled, 'Night, Flick.'

Flick turned off the light and quietly closed the door behind her. Xander was still on the phone to his mother as she moved into the kitchen and began stacking the dishes in the dishwasher. He ended the call and tossed the phone on the desk.

'Leave it, Flick. I'll see to it later. Come outside.' He sounded weary, but the strain that had marked his expression this afternoon had disappeared.

'Do you want coffee or anything?' She wiped her hands on the hand towel and hung it on its hook.

He held out a hand. 'Just your company, unless you want a drink?'

She shook her head and, taking his hand, followed him onto the balcony. A gusty sea breeze tugged at her messy bun and strands of hair blew across her eyes before the wind died away. 'Is your mother still happy to let Jenny fly by herself after this afternoon's adventure?'

'She wants to try. I'll get Jenny settled in the plane at this end, and Mum will be waiting at the gate at the other end. She's still keen to give Jenny a little more independence.' Xander drew Flick down beside him on the plump-cushioned two-seater and dropped an arm around her shoulders. Half-expecting him to kiss her once they were settled, she was a little disappointed when he didn't. His strange mood seemed to have shifted their relationship to a different level, one that sought her company for its own sake.

He relaxed against the cushions and Flick dropped her head onto his shoulder. 'She certainly showed initiative this afternoon.'

'Initiative?' He snorted and shook his head. 'It was pure coincidence the horse she rode yesterday was saddled and waiting at the stables. The staff down there each thought someone else had attended to the booking when they discovered the horse was gone. But yes, heaven help us, I guess that's showing initiative.'

He pulled her closer and rested his cheek on her head. 'Thanks for your help.'

'Help? I couldn't even leave because we were a couple of staff down in the kitchen. How was that helping?' But how she had wanted to race out of the kitchen and search alongside Xander. The memory of his desperation and drawn face would likely haunt her dreams.

'You were the only one who thought of the wombat. I had a dozen people looking around the resort and down on the beach and not one of them suggested that.'

'Another lucky coincidence is all it was. To be fair, we were the only ones who saw her with the wombat yesterday, and you'd just mentioned that you'd told your mother about Jenny's adventures. That one was my most recent memory.'

'And still I didn't think of the wombat.' He cupped her cheek and met her gaze. 'I let Jenny down.'

She sat up and held his face between her hands. The balcony lighting revealed a degree of self-recrimination that concerned her. 'Xander, *you* found her. As for my suggestion, well, as much as I care about Jenny, I'm not her family. Without the emotions of close family ties distracting me, it was probably easier for me to think than for you. I know if I had a younger sibling who'd disappeared, I'd have been off my head with worry. But you—you organised a full-scale search and made sure you succeeded. In my book, that's the opposite of letting anyone down.'

His gaze pinned her, intense, dark and searching. Flutters of anticipation started in her belly, increasing when he dipped his head. Before she drew another breath, his mouth claimed hers with a fierceness that spoke more of need than desire. Xander needed her at this moment and she was more than willing to distract him from dark thoughts of what might have happened if he hadn't found his sister before dark.

And then she stopped thinking and sank into a kiss that demanded her full participation.

He lifted her onto his lap and she slid her arms around his neck, wriggling closer, holding his head still so she could dive into the kiss like a woman drowning. A whisper of thought floated through her mind that having banned public displays of affection had sharpened her need for him.

Breathing heavily, they finally drew apart and rested their foreheads against each other. As she sat back, Xander grunted.

'Sorry, did I hurt you?' The second the words were out of her mouth, she recognised the source of his discomfort. Her hip was pressed against the bulge in his trousers.

A rueful grin touched his mouth. 'Not intentionally. I was thinking, tomorrow night when Jenny's not here, will you stay over?'

Even while her logical mind rejected the idea—she wanted to keep their relationship secret, not shout it out—her body knew what it wanted ... Flick wanted Xander in her arms, in her bed, and moving to the next level. She wanted to let loose and find out just how good they would be together.

He nuzzled her ear, his breath warm on her skin despite the gusting wind. 'No one will see us. Jenny will have gone home and we'll have the whole apartment to ourselves. Please, Flick? Stay?'

Chapter Fifteen

All day Flick's mind ran on dual tracks, but, try as she might, anticipation about spending the night with Xander caught her at odd moments. His invitation to stay had come out of the blue. Did it have more to do with the emotional rollercoaster he'd been riding yesterday, or was it a reaction to suppressing outward demonstrations of affection in public?

The wooden spoon slowed and stopped in the middle of the saucepan as she replayed last night's kisses. Yes—he'd needed her, but need didn't explain the heat and passion zapping between them. Her fingers rose to touch her lips.

'Flick, your sauce has caught.' Christophe raised an eyebrow. 'Is everything okay?'

Her gaze flew to the contents of the saucepan. The sauce should have been pale lemon; a mid-brown goop silently accused her. 'Sorry, chef. I'll start over.'

'*Bien.*' With no further comment, he set a bowl of fresh butter beside the burner and took down a clean saucepan for her before continuing his rounds. Unlike the tortes she could almost make in her sleep, they were so familiar to her, helping out with some of Jake's work while he was on sick leave required a more conscious awareness. She made damned sure to keep an eye on the new sauce the second time around and moved the saucepan off the gas burner as soon as the colour was achieved before moving on to the next task.

By the time the crying chef clock showed it was the end of her shift, she barely had time to wash her hair for her date with Xander. As she dried her hair with the towel, her phone vibrated on the table. Xander's name appeared on the screen and she grabbed the phone.

'I had a thought. Would you like to have dinner on the beach? I can order fish and chips from the café and we can find ourselves a slice of sand. What do you think?'

Flick looked through the window. The sun had set and muted tones of pink and purple above the trees were fading as she stood there, phone pressed to her ear. She hesitated a moment, but the chance of being seen was slight.

'Okay, I'll meet you at the beach.'

'Great. How about up near the northern arm of the headland in half an hour?'

'See you there.' She pressed the end call button and stood by the window, tapping the phone against her hand. Meeting Xander without Jenny and outside his apartment felt just a little bit dangerous.

Dangerous and delicious.

Jenny's holiday had been the reason for their horse ride, and Flick's presence unremarkable. Most staff knew of Jenny's daily cooking lessons with Flick, but now, anyone seeing them together would guess they were on a date.

A drop of water ran down her back and she shivered in the air-conditioned cool of her quarters. Meeting Xander on the beach was pushing the rules she'd laid down to the limit. Was she a fool to risk being seen with him?

The sand retained some warmth from the day as Flick stepped from the cover of the trees towards a carefully controlled spill of light. A shadowy figure leaned back on his arms on a picnic blanket, legs stretched towards the water. There was no way she'd have known who was sitting on the beach if she hadn't been meeting Xander. His choice of location and lighting were well thought out and quashed her fears of being recognised.

Her footsteps squeaked with each step through the sand. Xander looked around at the sound and jumped to his feet as she approached. 'Hi. They were quicker than I expected cooking the fish and chips. I hope they aren't cold.'

'I'm sure they'll be fine.' She looked around before sitting and tugging his hand to join her. The thick bandage had gone, replaced by a heavy-duty material waterproof plaster. 'You picked a nice spot. And I like your choice of lighting.'

Now she was next to it she could see the light came from an old-fashioned shutter lantern. 'Where on earth did you find this? It's wonderful.'

'In an antique store in Coffs Harbour. I had it converted to run off a small gas cylinder. I thought you might like the atmosphere it creates.' He reached for a cardboard box containing a white paper-wrapped package. A grease patch showed on the bottom as he unwrapped their dinner and set it on the blanket in front of the light. 'Dinner is served.'

'Thanks.'

The fish was barramundi, and the chips weren't quite hot, but Flick licked her fingers when she finished. She wrapped the scraps and followed Xander to the water's edge to wash her hands.

'It's lovely down here away from the rest of humanity.' She flicked water from her hands and patted them dry on her jeans.

Threading his fingers through hers, Xander settled his other hand on her hip. His touch set off a bone-deep desire that fluttered and trembled between her thighs. She stepped closer, pressing her body against his, her lips against his mouth. A salty kiss, a sea-kiss, the sort that could lead to sand in her shorts and fresh-washed hair.

She didn't care about either.

Xander drew in a deep breath and held her shoulders. 'Would you like to walk along the beach before we head back to the apartment? I need a few minutes before we head back.'

She tipped her head back. Stars shone brightly in the sky and the gentle whoosh of waves on the sand soothed her soul as she tried to read his expression in the darkness. Feeling for Xander's hand on her hip, she took hold of it and walked backwards, pulling him along. 'I'd like that.'

The tide was on the turn and waves lapped her ankles as they reached the nearest rocks on the headland. Xander set both hands on her waist and steadied her as she climbed onto the largest rock before climbing up beside her. She edged closer until their thighs touched and he dropped an arm around her shoulders. It wasn't that she was nervous about returning to his apartment. All day she'd been looking forward to the night with him.

There was something very appealing about conducting a clandestine affair with Xander. Skirting on the edge of doing something daring gave her a sense of control and choice. And knowing what lay ahead, drawing out the anticipation …

Control and choice were her new addictions.

Xander's apartment was different without Jenny's presence. The door to the second bedroom stood wide open, the lounge lights were dimmed, and Xander took her in his arms as soon as the front door closed behind them.

Their previous kisses had been on the balcony, when his sister was asleep. Flick turned her face up and wrapped her arms around his neck. 'What are you waiting for?'

He looked into her eyes. 'Just appreciating how powerful an aphrodisiac anticipation can be.' His words vibrated through her chest, his breath skated over her cheek.

'It's torture of a kind, a sort of pleasure-pain.' She felt it too, the kick of desire, the certainty she was about to leap from the highest cliff into the sea below. Taking their relationship to the next level felt natural—and momentous. 'Do you have a cure?'

'Definitely. Let me kiss it better.' He trailed a line of kisses from her ear to her mouth, lightly nipped her lower lip.

She nipped him back and then soothed his lip with a slide of her tongue.

His hands slid under her T-shirt, lifted it over her head, nudging her backwards towards the master bedroom.

She pulled his shirt out of his jeans, ran her hands over the warm skin of his abdomen, undid the buttons. A trail of clothes lay behind him, leading to his bed. They fell onto it.

He tucked her hair behind her ear, his touch tender and determined at the same time. 'Now let me see what I can do to turn your pain into pleasure.'

In the early light of dawn, Xander woke and reached for Flick. Feeling nothing but faint lingering warmth on the other side of the bed, he sat up. 'Flick, where are you?'

A thin line of light showed beneath the door of the ensuite and he leaned back against the headboard. Moments later the light went out and he heard the soft click of the door opening.

'I thought you'd left while I was asleep.' He reached for the switch of the bed lamp and turned on the soft light.

Flick gasped and froze, one hand on her throat. 'Sheesh, you know how to startle a woman.'

Dressed in the outfit she'd worn last night, her sandals dangled from one hand. Her eyes met his and quickly dropped.

Disappointment creased his forehead, curled in his stomach. 'You *were* going to slip away, weren't you?'

'Yes. It's easier this way.'

'I'd hoped to have breakfast with you.'

She edged towards the door. 'Maybe next time. I should get back to my room before—'

'Before anyone is around to see you.' He threw the sheet back and swung his legs over the side of the bed. 'Let me at least make you coffee before you go.'

She held up a hand, the one with the sandals hooked over her thumb. They swung as she opened the door. 'Don't get up. I'm fine, really. Thank you for a lovely night. I enjoyed—everything.' She stepped into the living area and closed the bedroom door behind her.

Xander rounded the bed and pulled the door open in time to hear the front door clicking closed. He could catch her before the lift arrived, but to what end? Accepting her condition they gave no public indication of being together meant agreeing to clandestine dates.

Meeting on the beach last night had been fun and had given him an excuse to use the shutter lantern. It had been romantic and mysterious. He'd enjoyed it. And she'd stayed and shared his bed as he'd hoped.

He ran a hand through his hair and headed into the kitchen. There was no point going back to bed. He looked through the balcony doors at the silhouettes of nodding palm trees against the early dawn sky. Sleep had vanished, along with Flick.

For the first time, the consequences of his lifestyle hit him smack in the face, full force.

Did the women he'd made love to in casual hook-ups and brief affairs feel this sense of disappointment when they woke to find him gone?

I don't like this feeling—this emotion or whatever the hell it is—at all.

He made coffee, black and strong, and carried it out onto the balcony. He took his first sip; it was strong enough to sear the hairs in his nostrils but nowhere near strong enough to still his confusion.

Self-reflection wasn't something he usually contemplated. *Navel gazing*, he'd called it when his mother suggested it wouldn't do him any harm. Give him a column of figures and a set of business scenarios and he could analyse them to a sound conclusion.

But Flick's abrupt departure threw him. It wasn't just because he had always been the one to leave, the one in control of the situation, although if he were honest, it felt a bit like being dumped. He leaned on the railing and sipped the coffee. A wash of pale light hung above the dark water, growing brighter by the minute.

Last night he'd fallen asleep expecting to wake beside Flick, to sit across from her at breakfast and watch the day dawn. He'd looked forward to sharing plans for the day and more than half expected another round of bed play.

His phone pinged. He almost ignored the incoming message, but thinking it might be Flick he hurried indoors, grabbed the phone and turned it on.

Negotiations progressing well. On early flight north to assess prospect on the ground. Bob.

His disappointment was searing, and damned unfamiliar.

Normally, such an update from his second in charge would have him whooping. In Bob-speak, *progressing well* meant he was on track to nail the deal. If Bob stitched it up quickly, they wouldn't need much down time after New Year. Xander dropped the phone on the desk and walked back onto the balcony—*I am happy, dammit.*

Everything he'd worked towards, every goal he ticked off, everything was coming to fruition. So why did he have this nagging sense of missing the mark with Flick?

Chapter Sixteen

Christophe sat opposite Flick and set a mug of coffee on the table in front of her. The aroma teased her nose before she picked it up and drank. Christophe opened a notebook on his desk and picked up his own mug of coffee. 'So, we are going to review your work today and consider where we go from here.'

Something in the way he said 'where we go from here' worried her and her hastily consumed breakfast croissant roiled in her stomach.

'Is there something in my work you aren't happy with?' Aside from burning the sauce when she was covering Jake's shift, her desserts had been triumphs of taste and artistry. It wasn't arrogance on her part: she knew her work was good.

He sat back, resting an arm along the desk, and sipped his coffee before he answered. His dark eyes crinkled at the corners and a smile broke through his serious expression. 'For all of two minutes after I was told Xander's girlfriend wanted a job in my kitchen—until I tasted your croquembouche. Then, ah *ma petite*, then I knew you were a treasure.'

Relief made her shoulders sag, freed from a palpable weight. Huffing out an audible breath, she smiled back. 'So everything's good?'

Christophe nodded, but his smile faded. 'To be honest, I don't want to lose you. I don't wish to pry, but—you and Xander—where do you see yourself going from here?'

A lump of fear settled in her throat. One brief question and her pleasure in Christophe's compliment was shot to bits. *You and Xander ...*

'We're not—there is no me and Xander. We're friends, that's all.' She slipped her hands between her knees and pressed them together, trying to still the crazy tremors. 'Why would you think that?'

Christophe frowned and spread his hands. 'Forgive me. Perhaps it is that I saw you often helping him with Jenny, but if you say there is nothing in it, then I will not give it another thought. Although I think you would suit one another.'

Her stomach flipped and her breath sounded harsh in her ears. 'Please—don't say things like that.'

'I meant no offence. Forget I said it, please. Now, back to your work here at Chez Christophe.'

She nodded and huffed a relieved sigh, but the turmoil in her stomach swirled like a river in flood.

One misstep—that's all it will take.

'If you're happy with my work, I'd really like to stay on indefinitely.'

'I am overjoyed to hear this.' He nodded, picked up his mug and raised it in an airy toast. His response was all Flick had hoped for, but a frown reappeared on his brow.

She raised hers and sipped, but any desire for coffee had disappeared at mention of a perceived relationship. He'd let that go, but ... 'What is it, Christophe?'

'At some point, won't you want to start your own restaurant—maybe a patisserie?'

An image of her parents' small restaurant in Brisbane flashed through her mind. She could almost smell the herbs in her father's signature dish; the spices in the biscuits and slices her mother baked for the café side of their business. And her corner of the kitchen with the hooks her father had mounted to hold her baking tools.

The weight of loss and crushing sorrow caught her unawares.

Pecorino was meant to be mine one day.

It hit her then. Her feelings about her parents' divorce were about so much more than their separation; more than the loss of her family unit; her home.

'I've dreamed of owning my own business since before I graduated.' There was little substance to her voice. Would he believe the wisp of sound belonged to someone with enough determination to set up a successful venture? In her heart of hearts, she hoped Pecorino would still be on the market by the time she saved a deposit. The sale of businesses slowed down over Christmas and New Year, so the real estate agent had told her. Surely if she was careful with her salary and forgot about buying a car to replace poor Ruby, she'd have enough saved for a deposit in five or six months.

She sipped her coffee before setting it on a corner of the desk and meeting his eyes. 'I have a long way to go before I have enough for a deposit on my own place. I'd love to work for you until then.'

'*Bien*. That suits me very well. And we will discuss any questions you have about setting up and running your business.' He extended a hand and, in a daze, she shook it.

'Thank you. I can't tell you what that means to me.'

Xander glanced down below the edge of the table at his phone and checked his messages for the third time since his meeting had begun. Nothing from Flick. So much for his reputedly great business sense. He'd been certain she'd get in touch after last night, but when it came to personal relationships, it seemed he was as clueless as any other bloke.

'... and the projections are well within acceptable parameters. What do you think, Xander?'

His gaze snapped back to Zoe, his company's chief accountant. 'Excellent. Tell Phil to go ahead with the informal offer and get legal onto the contracts. I'd like the preliminaries wrapped up by Christmas. Pass on my thanks to the rest of the team.' He pushed his chair back from the table, stood and offered his hand.

Zoe shook hands and a smile appeared briefly. 'You've achieved beyond the expectations of the board on each project.'

'Thanks. Being on site makes a big difference.'

'Everyone's looking forward to the next one. This eco approach—it's another step up again, but you won't be able to stay on site.'

'I couldn't take on a project and not be around for the day-to-day decisions. That's not my style.' Nothing would change his mind on that score, not even Flick, although it was going to be a wrench leaving her. He glanced at the determinedly blank screen of his phone. But would she find it as difficult when he left?

Zoe closed her briefcase with a snap of locks and lifted it off the table. 'Except with this next one starting from the ground up, you'll have to find somewhere else to live.'

'Bob will start looking for me now we have agreement in principle. I'll see you at the full board meeting in a fortnight.'

As Xander headed towards the lift, he caught himself checking again for a message from Flick.

Enough. Either call her, or call it off.

Chapter Seventeen

Flick emerged from the bathroom, drying her hair with a fluffy white resort towel. She felt wrung out, like the proverbial dishrag, and an early night sounded like bliss. Long days working in the kitchen didn't usually drain her. But then today hadn't been *normal*. Heat crept up her neck at the memory of Xander catching her early morning escape; the careful shuttering of his expression as she fumbled through pathetic excuses to leave.

I didn't mean to hurt him.

Their evening had been romantic, and sex with Xander had made her forget her own name—her body tingled at the memory of his lips on various parts of her body. And then …

'I'd hoped to have breakfast with you.'

'Maybe next time.'

Replaying their conversation in her mind, Flick sat with a thump. No wonder she hadn't heard from him. Wrapped in her own insecurities, the idea only now occurred to her. 'I'll bet he thought I was dumping him.' Saying the words out loud gave them weight and shape and an awful reality she didn't want to acknowledge.

Was it too late to make amends? She checked her messages.

Nothing.

Before she could second-guess herself, she scrolled through to his number and pressed the button to connect. As the ring tone continued unanswered, butterflies began a chaotic dance in her stomach.

What would she say to him? What did she want to happen between them?

Nothing.

His voicemail asked her to leave her name and number and a short message ...

She disconnected the call. No answer *was* his answer. He'd interpreted her running away as lack of interest and she had only her paranoid, scared self to blame. Closing her eyes, she fell against the cushion at her back. Wallowing in a sea of regret was ridiculous and she would give herself no more than one minute to indulge. One minute to think about Xander and what her fear had lost her and then she'd pack it away alongside other recent losses.

Xander picked up the empty beer bottle and looked over his balcony at the buzz of a busy resort approaching peak holiday season.

My resort.

Pride in his achievement seemed cold comfort tonight. Before she'd fled this morning, he'd imagined spending most nights with Flick. Looked forward to fun times and good company before he headed north to his next project.

He looked at the empty bottle in his hand. *What the hell—a second bottle with dinner won't hurt.* Picking up the internal phone to order room service, his eye fell on his mobile. As he waited for the connection to the kitchen, his thumb brushed the on button. He didn't mean to, but it was as though his subconscious refused to let go of hope. The screen showed a notification and he raised the phone to read what it said.

A missed call.

He put down the receiver, cutting off a 'good evening' on the other end. Flick had called not ten minutes ago while he was outside.

Staring at the notification, optimism opened like a chink of light through curtains. He checked the time.

Should he phone, visit, or ignore the contact? Do it now, or wait?

Damn it, he wanted to see her, wanted to talk and find out why she'd run out on him this morning. Phone in hand, he walked back onto the balcony and glanced to the right. Over there, out of sight beyond the trees, were the staff quarters. He imagined Flick in one of the rooms, tried to imagine walking up to her door and knocking; the shock on her face when she saw him standing outside. *Not a good idea.*

Hitting the reply button, he held the phone to his ear and waited.

'Hello?' She sounded sleepy.

'Hi. I hope I didn't wake you?'

'I may have dozed off. It's not a problem. Um, is everything okay?'

He paused. 'You called me. I missed your call earlier.'

A soft intake of breath, a rustle of material as though she was getting out of bed, a sigh. 'Of course I did. Sorry, long day. I— wondered if we could maybe talk? About this morning.'

'Have you had dinner?'

'No. I meant to but— You guessed right. I fell asleep.'

'I'll order something from room service if you want to come over to my place. Unless you prefer—'

'I'll come to you.'

Xander opened the door. 'Come in. You've beaten room service.' Shadows lurked in her eyes.

Tired, or wary, or both?

'Would you like a glass of wine while we wait for dinner?'

'Lime and mineral water please. I don't think I'll be able to stay awake if I have wine.' Interlaced fingers pressed against her stomach and she moved to the sliding door. One hand reached for the handle before she turned and asked, 'Can we sit outside?'

'Fine by me. Go on ahead, I'll bring the drinks out.' He set a beer and the bottle of mineral water on the bench, and then watched as she slipped through a narrow opening and stood, a hand on each of two chairs as though the decision of where to sit was too hard.

He sensed Flick had more emotional baggage than simply not wanting to go public. He wasn't looking for complicated in a relationship. But she was kind and talented and sexy, and he wanted to know more about her. A day spent analysing his reaction and thinking about her had shown him theirs was a relationship worth pursuing. He picked up the drinks and carried them out to the balcony.

Flick was seated with her back to the door and the lights. She jumped and gasped when he set her drink in front of her. 'Oh, thanks.'

'Are you okay?'

She nodded, her gaze fixed on the glass in her hand as she turned it around and around on the table. At last, she looked up. 'I want to apologise for the way I behaved this morning. Last night was wonderful.'

'It was, right up until you walked out. What happened?' He kept his voice calm, but the fact they were talking gave him hope they were still going to be okay.

'Waking in your bed spooked me for some reason. It probably sounds hypocritical, but I couldn't face the idea of anyone knowing about us. I'm—a very private person.'

'I understand that. If there's one thing I've had to get used to running my own company, it's the intrusive interest the media has in my private life. Flick, I don't have a problem with staying off the radar, but I'd prefer it if you'd tell me when something is wrong.'

She sipped her mineral water before setting the glass down in the middle of a circle of condensation. One finger trailed through the puddle. 'Some crappy things happened and then another crappy thing happened and I let my feelings of betrayal leach into other parts of my life. You got caught up in the ripples. I'm sorry. I can't promise you I won't feel like that again, but I'll try not to let it affect us if—'

Even in the soft lighting, he saw the ripple of her throat as she swallowed whatever doubt she was feeling. 'Can we call this morning a hiccup and leave it at that for now?'

She nodded. 'I'd like that.'

'And if you want to share any of the crappy stuff any time, I'm a good listener, but no pressure.'

The door chimes sounded, and Xander rose from the table. 'That will be dinner.'

She put a hand on his arm and looked up. 'Xander, thank you.'

He dropped a kiss on her forehead. A spicy scent, subtle but unforgettable, clung to his lips as he walked to the door. Dinner had arrived, and afterwards, if Flick stayed, he'd share his remedy for crappy days and happy nights.

Chapter Eighteen

Flick took all of two minutes to make her bed and tidy her tiny sitting room. That was a benefit of living in a mini-suite. No photos or knick-knacks or other people's detritus cluttering every surface like at home.

Home. She flopped into the armchair and looked at the sparse furnishings, white walls, limited edition decorator picture. It was clean and neat and felt nothing like home used to. It lacked warmth. It lacked identity.

It lacked the illusion of loving parents.

'Get over yourself and get a move on.' She rarely talked to herself, but after another night in Xander's bed, in his arms, her sterile room reminded her how tenuous relationships were.

She turned on the shower, waiting for the water to run hot before stepping under it and washing her hair, a quick wash. She hated running late, missing time with Xander.

The lyrics of an old Rod Stewart song—the tune she'd assigned to Xander—blared from her phone where it lay on the bathroom vanity.

She flung a towel around her body and grabbed her phone. 'Hi, nearly ready. I'll be there in—' The week before Christmas was as busy in Rainbow Cove as in Pecorino and she was running late.

'New plan, if it's okay with you. Meet me down by the boatshed. We're going for a short sail on the catamaran. I've packed a picnic.'

'*You've* packed ...' She couldn't imagine Xander doing the actual packing of food, but the idea of a picnic was tempting. Most evenings since Jenny's departure, they'd met for dinner in his apartment. And each morning, she'd tiptoed out early, trying not to wake Xander. She rarely succeeded, and it had become a game. But a *frisson* of excitement ran down her spine at the idea of an evening on a catamaran.

'Okay, see you there in ten minutes.' Tossing the towel over the railing, she grabbed the hairdryer and gave her hair a quick blast. Then she dressed quickly, slipped her key card into her shoulder bag alongside her toothbrush and a change of underwear and pulled the door closed.

Hawaiian-style tiki torches lit the way to the beach, but she turned off onto a less well-lit path and followed it to the boatshed. Early evening light faded beneath the cover of palm trees lining the path and she passed no one. Most activities had pulled back to the confines of the resort with the setting of the sun.

Xander was waiting at the land end of the jetty, one hand in his pocket, his heavy bandage long gone, replaced by a waterproof plaster, his white shirt untucked and pale against the darkening sky. 'There you are. Hi.' He held her shoulders and dropped a light kiss on her lips. She stepped back quickly and looked around.

'It's safe, Flick. There's nobody down here at this time of night.'

She swallowed the quick skip of embarrassment and the lick of regret that took the edge off her pleasure at seeing Xander outdoors. 'Sorry. I know you think I'm over the top wanting to stay off everyone's radar.'

'I respect your wish for privacy. It's not a problem. In fact, it inspired tonight's idea.' He picked up the handle of a large rolling esky and set his hand on her waist as they walked to a catamaran moored at the end of the jetty. '*Moonglow* is ready for departure.'

Moonglow's furled sails appeared to be hot pink, and a warm light emanated from the cabin.

'I haven't seen *Moonglow* before, or any others like her. I thought all the resort watercraft were much smaller?'

'That's because she's mine, not the resort's.' He stepped onto the backboard, set the esky down and turned to take her hand as she joined him. 'Welcome aboard.'

He stowed the esky before starting the engine. Flick slipped off her sandals and put them beneath the starboard bench seat and then headed for the bollards. 'Would you like me to untie the mooring ropes?'

'Yes, please. We're not going far. Help yourself to a drink once we're underway.'

'I'm fine. Happy to wait until we've reached our destination.' As soon as she'd coiled the ropes, Flick sat in the seat on the port bow and watched the light change as they left the resort behind. Tipping her face to the sky, a silly desire rose to do a Kate Winslet in *Titanic* pose. She giggled and slapped a hand over her mouth.

It had been too long since she'd known this degree of freedom. But one-on-one time with Xander away from prying eyes combined with being out on the water was all it took for her to relax.

Not far proved to be the next bay to the north. Isolated by a near-vertical rocky headland, one of two arms that defined the bay that lapped the resort, *Moonglow* was the only vessel to drop anchor there. As the anchor caught, the boat rode a tiny swell until the chain took up the slack. Gentle rocking and the slap of an incoming tide muffled the faint sounds of music and people coming from the resort.

Together they set out plates of antipasto and a bottle of French champagne.

'I'll leave the main course in the esky for now. I've got prawns and oysters on ice.'

'Can't wait.'

He poured champagne into a flute and handed it to her before filling his glass and setting the bottle back inside the esky. 'Cheers.'

'Cheers. To starry skies and quiet bays away from the madding crowd.' She tapped her glass against his and sipped. 'Oh, that's wonderful.'

'Chris calls me a philistine with food, but when it comes to wine—'

'Did Christophe pack this for you?' Her heart sank a little. Weeks ago, she'd worried when she thought that Christophe had known why she'd burned the sauce. If he'd packed the picnic for them, he'd know now for sure. A ball of embarrassed heat raced along her veins. Keeping her relationship with Xander private was hard, but how much harder would it be if her boss knew she was dating his best friend?

A plop in the water off the stern was a welcome distraction. She turned away, raising her glass and taking a too-big mouthful. Xander's plans for the evening were thoughtful and romantic and she fought the snarky desire to tell him his choice might have blown their cover.

His fingers trailed softly over her cheek before tucking her hair behind her ear. 'Relax. When I said I'd packed a picnic? I literally meant I had packed it. I picked everything up in town after my meeting today. Including the antipasto platter.'

'Really?'

'Yes. I figured Chris would get suspicious if I appeared in his kitchen asking for a picnic basket. I knew you wouldn't like that.'

Surprised he knew her so well, and pleased with his thoughtfulness, she murmured, 'Thank you.' Words failed her for several heartbeats and she breathed in the salty tang of air before meeting his gaze. 'I'm impressed, and delighted. Let's try some of that antipasto. With luck, there'll be Sicilian olives in the mix.'

'Like them, do you?' He set his glass down and removed the clear cover from the mix before offering the plate to her.

'I do, especially in a lemon and herb marinade.' She selected a plump green olive and popped it into her mouth. Zesty citrus hit her tongue.

Xander's gaze was fixed on her mouth as he picked blindly from the plate and bit into a cube of feta.

The kernel of an idea blossomed and she examined the food before choosing a pitted Kalamata olive. Picking it up between two fingers, she gave Xander a sideways glance before facing him.

Holding his gaze, she raised the olive to his lips. He leaned forwards, opened his mouth and took the olive, holding one of her fingers with gentle pressure between his lips. His tongue touched her finger, the contact fleeting—shockingly intimate and suddenly not enough.

He released her finger, chewed and swallowed before he caught her hand and took her thumb in his mouth. His tongue swirled around her thumb while her blood fizzed with desire to replace her digit with her mouth, her tongue—any part of her he wanted to set his lips on.

'Flick—' He released his hold and set both champagne flutes on the table. Drawing her into his arms as though he'd read her thoughts, his lips claimed hers. Hunger for food fled, replaced by a need for Xander—his taste, the feel of his bare skin beneath her palms—that burned brighter than any sun.

'Yes—'

'Are you sure you don't want to eat before—'

'Now, Xander. Don't you know it's not polite to keep a guest waiting?'

'Never let it be said my hospitality was called into question. Allow me to show you to your room.' He grabbed a couple of cushions from the starboard bench before leading the way along the port side to the trampoline. Tossing the cushions down, he turned to her. 'Is madam happy with the water view, or would she prefer a more *private* room?'

Flick sank onto the trampoline and tugged his hand until he knelt beside her. 'Madam loves the view. And the company she's in. And she'll be perfectly happy if said company finds a silent occupation for his lips right now.'

A wicked grin flashed before she found herself on her back, her head on one of the cushions and the stars beginning to peep through the darkening sky before Xander lowered his head. Kisses more drugging than champagne sent goose bumps down her arms, pebbled her nipples and set light to an ache between her thighs that nothing would satisfy until Xander …

She gasped as his hand cupped her, warm and firm, ratcheting her need in a tight spiral of desire before she lost herself in his arms.

Xander rolled over and lay flat on his back. A sea breeze cooled skin dewed with sweat as strands of Flick's hair blew across his face and chest. He moved a strand that tickled his lips before pulling her closer to his side. Lying on his back under the starry night with the catamaran rocking gently beneath them, a sense of contentment filled him. Right here, right now, he could claim he was happy and mean it.

'Hungry?' He nuzzled her ear.

'I don't know about you, but I've worked up an appetite.'

He sat up, took her hand and pulled her to her feet. The cat rocked on the top of the tide and she slapped both hands against his chest. 'Oops, sorry.'

'Feeling a little weak in the legs, are you?' He tried not to grin, but it was a point of honour that he made each evening memorable for Flick.

'Hmm, probably that French champagne has gone to my head.' Her lips pressed together.

He was sure she was teasing, even before her lips twitched and laughter erupted.

'I'd like to say *You rock my world*, but that's so cheesy when we're on my boat.'

'Even for you.' Grinning, she straightened her skirt and took his hand for the walk back to their abandoned feast.

Their champagne had lost its chill. Xander emptied both glasses over the side, poured fresh glasses and handed her one.

He offered the platter of antipasto to her. 'Sounds like you need more fuel before round two.'

Twin points of light shone in her eyes as she looked at him. 'Sounds like you've got plans for the night.'

'*Big plans*. I want to discover more of what you like and what else tips you over the edge. And then I want to see how many times we can make that jump.'

One fingertip slowly circled the rim of her glass before she sipped and set it down. 'You're on two and counting.' Selecting a slice of pastrami, she wrapped it around a green olive and bit the whole neatly in two.

He watched Flick as she ate, saw the slick of olive oil on her lips, and her tongue as it touched the corners of her mouth. His imagination ran free. What he might do with more of that oil later was the stuff of fantasy.

She created another olive pastrami sandwich and offered it to him. 'Of course, if you're talking about simultaneous jumps, we're at one. But I'm happy to practise all night ...' She paused and grinned, gesturing vaguely towards the cabin, 'But it depends how much you're up for.'

He tipped his head and looked down his nose at her. This was what he'd missed in the long, slow months of focusing on nothing but renovating Rainbow Cove; this light-hearted ribbing that bubbled along the surface of a deeper connection with someone.

Not just anyone—Flick. 'I'll be *up* for it as often as you want. Now eat up and enjoy. That seafood is still waiting.'

Bantering with Flick was fun. Sexy bantering was a turn-on. Not that he needed another reason to want Flick, but a week of watching her interact with his sister and waiting to steal a kiss or three had sharpened his need to know her in a physical sense until the idea of a medieval rack seemed almost kinder. The past few weeks had cemented that need until he knew.

Change was coming and he needed to find a way around the distance between the new project at Airlie Beach and Rainbow Cove.

Their first time making love outside—under starry skies, with soft sea breezes cooling heated skin—had a surreal quality he planned to repeat—often. There wasn't much time before he went north to his next project, but he would find a solution.

There has to be time enough to find one.

Chapter Nineteen

Sunlight batted against Flick's closed eyelids. She raised a hand to shield her eyes and turned her head away from the light. Her nose discovered a sprinkling of chest hair on warm skin with an underlying scent of sex, and memory returned with wakefulness. Opening her eyes, she looked into Xander's.

'Good morning.'

'Morning.' She blinked at the unexpected close-up of his grey eyes, silvered in the early light of day and drew the sheet across her breasts and under her arm. With a wriggle and a grin, she sat up and leaned against the headboard of the double bed. Usually she was up and dressed before he was fully awake, and on her way back to her quarters. This waking up beside him with sunlight streaming in through the window was deliciously new. Exciting. Probably addictive.

The catamaran rose and fell gently on a full tide as Flick pushed her hair back behind her ears.

Dark stubble outlined Xander's chin and cheeks, and his hair, usually so neat, was messy in a way that made her want to smooth her fingers through it just for the pleasure of messing it up again.

He rolled onto his side, one arm crooked beneath his head, and raised a hand to trace her mouth. 'Do you want breakfast before we head back to the resort, or can I interest you in—'

'Round four?' Gently she bit his finger as it traced the seam of her lips. 'How long have we got?'

He rolled away and picked up his watch from the bedside table. 'It's five-thirty. Plenty of time before we have to pull up anchor.'

'My shift starts at seven.' Part of her regretted agreeing to do an extra half shift. If not for that, they could have stayed in the cove on Xander's catamaran all morning. The temptation to call in sick was strong, but Flick wouldn't do that to Christophe.

Xander set his watch down and leaned up on his elbow. One finger traced the swell of her breast above the sheet. When her nipples reacted to his touch, he traced them through the fine cotton of the sheet. 'How long do you need to get ready?'

Her eyes closed as a familiar, needy ache for Xander radiated from her core. 'Thirty minutes to shower, eat, dress and get to the kitchen.'

'And thirty minutes to weigh anchor and motor back to the jetty. So we have thirty minutes.'

'Make it forty. Eating is overrated.'

Slipping her arms around his neck, she rolled—he rolled—until she sprawled on top of him like his own personal blanket. Mouths meshed, limbs entwined, they made every one of their forty minutes memorable.

Xander brought the *Moonglow* alongside the jetty and Flick nimbly tied off the bow and stern lines. Grabbing her sandals and handbag, she caught Xander leaning on the helm and just watching her.

A flash of daring mixed with a need to touch him one last time before she left. Pressing herself against him, she wrapped one arm around his neck and kissed him.

Intensely. Passionately. An I-don't-want-to-let-you-go kind of kiss he returned in full.

When they surfaced, her lips tingled. 'Wow.' She rested her forehead against his chin, eyes closed against the brilliance of a new day picking out the tips of waves in the cove.

'Yeah, wow.' Gently he held her shoulders. 'Any chance you'd be free tonight for a repeat performance?'

'For sure. I'll bring dinner this time.'

'My place? Or do you want to go out on *Moonglow* again?'

'Your apartment. I'll drop a few things up there ready to cook dinner tonight, if that's okay?'

'That's fine, except I'll be away all day in a meeting. How about I call into the kitchen on my way out and give you a key?'

She frowned, already shaking her head at the idea of the gossip that would spring from such a visit. Her stomach took a dive and a little of the shine rubbed off the idea of tonight. 'I'd rather you didn't.'

'I'm not going to march up to you and hold the key card up and say "Here's the key to my apartment, Flick." Nobody will know; I'll put it in an envelope and mark it *From Jenny* if that makes it easier.'

From the depths of her bag, the phone trilled a reminder: *Shift starts in 15 mins.* Shuffling from foot to foot, she realised she'd run out of time. 'Fine, an envelope from Jenny. Got to run. Later.'

Stepping off the backboard onto the jetty without looking back took every ounce of self-discipline she had. The desire to run back and kiss him or argue a case for him not to turn up in her workspace was almost too strong.

She was never going to be the woman who dated her boss, no matter how wrong anyone who thought that would be.

Slinging her bag over her shoulder, she sprinted down the path away from the boatshed and temptation.

Respecting Flick's wishes went without saying for Xander. But her *I'd rather you didn't* felt like a roadblock that defined and limited their relationship.

In the beginning, he'd been glad—delighted he had an exit strategy for when he moved north.

But now the thought of leaving Flick behind left him feeling empty.

Even if he flew back once a week, where did that leave them?

Checking everything was shipshape, Xander pocketed the key before he hefted the esky onto the jetty. He picked up the handle and wheeled it along the jetty.

As he stepped onto terra firma, Eve approached. At eight months pregnant, she was about to go on maternity leave, and she still had a lot to do before handing over responsibility to Marta, who would be taking over her job.

Eve tucked a loose strand of blonde hair behind her ear and resettled a peaked cap on her head. Standing in the small patch of shade cast by a nearby palm tree, her hands went to the now familiar position in the small of her back as she chatted. 'Hi, Xander, I know it's my day off but I arranged to come in to answer some of Marta's questions. Even though she grew up here, she's been away for a while and was worried she might be a bit rusty on local stuff.'

'Thanks, Eve.'

'Will you be wanting *Moonglow* again?'

'I won't need it tonight, but would you mind getting one of the boys to drive it back to its mooring for me? I'm running a little late.'

'Sure.' She glanced at the path down which Flick had disappeared and bit her bottom lip. 'Um, will you be wanting a service on the interior as well as refuelling?' Her gaze skittered across his, not quite making contact, and he knew.

Careful as he and Flick had been, they were busted.

'Yes, please, Eve.' He fished in his shirt pocket and pulled out the key of the catamaran. 'You'll need this.'

'No problem.'

He nodded and headed back to the main resort building. The wheels of the esky crunched through a stretch of gravel, rumbled on the brick pavers, and squeaked on the foyer tiles. As he passed the giant Christmas tree, he knocked a glittery bauble off a branch. It hit the floor with a tinkling crash and rolled towards the front desk. Everywhere he walked, it felt as though the esky announced his presence, revealing Flick's secret assignation with him.

Had it been stupid on his part to imagine they could fly under everyone's radar? Noting the interested looks from staff on reception—quickly disguised by raised papers or sudden telephone conversations—he acknowledged staying in his apartment would have been far less obvious. Going out on the boat with Flick, coming back to the resort wearing yesterday's clothes and stubble, and pulling an esky at seven in the morning—he might as well have taken out a paid advertisement.

And yet there was nothing wrong in the scenario. He wasn't Flick's boss.

He stabbed the call button on the lift and pulled the esky in behind him. With a quick wave of his key card across the reader, the doors closed, and the lift rose. Christmas carols—bright and light and full of joy to all mankind—accompanied his ascent to the penthouse. He'd felt joyful after the night with Flick, right up until Eve had asked him about servicing the interior of the catamaran. Flick would hate that news.

There was nothing wrong with dating Flick, and everything right. So why did he feel as though he'd failed her?

Chapter Twenty

'What do you mean, you think Eve knows about us? How could she?' Flick turned abruptly and leaned on the railing. Warm night air carried scents of subtropical flowers and laughter up to Xander's balcony, but his news shattered her pleasure in the evening. Running her hands over her bare arms, her mind raced through damage control options. Their choices seemed limited to going public—her stomach clenched at that thought—or breaking it off. Neither option appealed.

'I guess she saw us leaving the jetty last night, or maybe she saw you leaving the boat this morning. Not that she asked outright, but I got the impression she'd put two and two together. But I doubt she'll say anything. Eve's discreet and—'

'Jeez, Xander, we don't need *discreet*. All I wanted was for no one to know we were going out. Honestly, I didn't think that was too much to ask.'

'It wasn't—it's not. Look, I'll speak to Eve and ask her not to mention us to anyone.'

'Like that ever worked.' Hunching her shoulders, she stared off into the distance. Over the treetops, beyond the headland, the vast darkness of a moonless night beckoned. The spectre of her highly publicised break-up with Jason loomed in her mind. Why hadn't she told Xander about that? Would it have made a difference to the choices they'd made?

It will be impossible to go on as we have been.

'Flick, look at me.' He leaned an elbow on the railing beside her, not quite touching, but close enough that she felt the warmth of him, breathed in the scent of his skin and aftershave.

The first night in his bed was all it had taken before she knew she didn't want to walk away from him. In less than two months he'd got under her skin.

And seeing him with Jenny—his love and care for her—had got past Flick's careful guard. The last few weeks, private and intense, meant that now she couldn't pull back. Wanting their relationship to develop, she needed to find out if she could have a different path with him than her parents had followed. But what if she was doomed to repeat the mistakes of her parents?

I have to put a stop to this now.

She didn't want to meet his gaze. He wanted her to believe it didn't matter if people knew about them, and if she looked into his beautiful grey eyes, she knew she'd see compassion and desire, and lose herself. Common sense would flee in the face of that desire.

'Flick? We can solve this.'

'Solve it?' Her gaze darted to meet his and clung. She'd been right to be wary of it, of the gentle concern she read there. Already her body softened and melted towards him. 'If you have any bright ideas, I'd love to hear them because I really don't want to become food for the rumour mill.'

'As I see it, we can ignore the possibility that word will spread and go on as before. I know Eve and I trust she won't say anything, but I understand you might not feel sure about someone you don't know.'

She nodded. 'Okay. I might be wrong about her, but there's a lot riding on that chance as far as I'm concerned. She has no reason to care what I think; she doesn't know me at all.'

'She knows me and she knows I value my privacy. But there is another option.'

'I can think of two more.' She wrapped her arms across her waist.

'Want to share them with me?'

She knew which option she didn't want. Hated the idea of. But it was still an option and she put it out there first. 'We end this now.'

He was silent for several heartbeats and she could have sworn his eyes became a dark stormy-grey. A muscle spasmed in his jaw. 'Is that what you want?'

Her traitorous body wouldn't countenance the idea. She didn't mean to, but her head shook from side to side even as she tried to force out words that would be the death of them. 'I should want that, but I don't.'

'And neither do I.'

She gazed helplessly up at him. Was she brave enough to voice it, let alone do it? The spectre of her parents' loving but ultimately doomed relationship hovered at the edge of her mind. Just because theirs had failed, did it mean she would follow the same path? Was she a fool to give up the chance that she had found a man she might build her future with?

'You said there was another alternative. It's the one I prefer.' He waited, giving her the chance to suggest it.

Her throat worked, opening—closing—wanting to release the words. They wouldn't come. *Coward.*

She was all knots and tense muscles and fear fluttering in her belly, and her voice, when she found it, was little more than a whisper. 'Maybe it's the one I want too.'

'Move in with me.'

Words of invitation spilled from his mouth as though he had no more control than a teenager. Xander had had no intention of asking Flick to move in with him when their conversation began. And yet, once he'd spoken the words, they felt right.

Flick's eyes opened wide and her lips parted. For a single moment, he saw joy flash through her eyes before she lowered her gaze. 'I know I said there was another alternative, but how does that solve anything?'

'It's open and honest. It tells people we don't have anything to hide.' And now the invitation was out, he realised he wanted her to accept. He wanted her to accept now and come with him when he moved on to his next project. With her baking skills, she could work anywhere. Cupping her face, he stroked his thumb over her cheek. 'It says we think we're good together.'

'We are good together.' Flick leaned into his touch.

'Tell me, why don't you want people to know about us?'

'I told you, the boss–employee thing.' Her shoulders hunched and her gaze slid away.

Classic denial. What's lurking behind that?

From the beginning he'd suspected their work situation wasn't the whole reason for her reluctance. Now, he was certain it was no more than a quick let-out. He pressed on, gentle but implacable in his need to understand her. 'But that's not the case with us. Not even close. What's beneath that, Flick? The real reason you don't want people to know?'

Huffing out a cross between a sigh and a gasp, she turned her back on him. Her hands gripped the railing.

He set a hand on each side of hers, cutting off escape. 'Not this time, Flick. Whatever the problem is, talk to me. Together we might be able to work it out.'

She remained stubbornly silent, until he wrapped his arms around her waist and rested his head against hers. 'Trust me, Flick. I won't let you down.'

A barely-there nod, the slick of her tongue across her top lip, a release of breath that could have been a sigh … Her body relaxed against his. He hadn't let her down; not once since the drama of their meeting.

'The day we met, I was running away.'

'Running? From what, or who?' His arms tightened. Within his embrace he could protect her from self-centred, feuding parents, if the hints he'd picked up were accurate.

'Myself as much as anyone else.' Her voice took on a narrative quality and she looked towards the sea, as though the only way she could reveal her worries was at a distance; as though she was telling someone else's story. 'My parents are getting a divorce, our home is to be sold and our business is on the market. My mother got a court order restraining my father from entering the premises. I couldn't desert him and do what he wasn't allowed to, but my whole working life had been in Pecorino. Without being able to bake for our restaurant, my parents not speaking to each other, and with no home, I had to get away.' She turned in his arms and leaned back on her elbows, looking up at him.

'I can see how the situation would have been distressing for you, but I don't understand—'

'You're right, there is more to it. Call me leery of getting involved, but what frightens me is how easily relationships can break down. My parents passed from love to intense dislike. At least that's how it is with my mother. Dad seems lost and confused. The thought of getting into a relationship only for it to disintegrate scares me, and I threw out my one-line stop sign. You found a detour around it.'

'So you're saying you didn't want to get into a relationship because you were worried how it would end?'

Her gaze dropped to his lips before reconnecting with his. 'It might sound silly to anyone who hasn't been collateral damage in the fallout of a relationship, but it's devastating. With my parents I tried not to take sides, but somewhere along the way, I was forced to. And then chunks of my life—my identity—fell away until I didn't know what to do. But I'm saving all I can to put a deposit down on Pecorino. Then Dad can come home and work in the restaurant he built up from nothing.'

'That's great. Well done.' That right there—the core of Flick was strong and solid and so sexy. He admitted it: he found Flick's pursuit of her dream sexy.

'Thanks. But you know there's one more miserable part to this sorry story.'

'Tell me now so I know the worst. And then I'll find a way to make you forget.' He moved into her space and she was left in no doubt how he planned to help her leave behind the pain of her family.

She slid her hands up over his chest and around his neck. 'My ex-boyfriend was a celebrity on the Brisbane music scene. Associating with him was great for our business.'

Xander's eyebrow arched above an enquiring gaze and she shook her head. 'That wasn't why I went out with him. I wanted what my parents had. I thought I'd found it with him. When we broke up, it was a very public and embarrassing split. I got hammered in the press, labelled a gold-digger. Bookings fell away at the restaurant and, for a while, I couldn't go out, couldn't do anything, without cameras flashing in my face.'

Lights flashing, blinding, accusing. And the press of bodies surrounding, trapping her, stealing the air from her starving lungs ... Her stomach clenched at the memory, still crystal-clear after more than a year.

She dragged in a shuddery breath, feeling the warmth of Xander beneath her fingers. 'You wonder why I don't want to be seen with you in public. You have a high business profile and I couldn't face another media frenzy like what hit me after Jason dumped me. Between that and what's happened with my parents ...'

'I get it, believe me. My sympathy. The press can be like sharks scenting blood in the water.' He'd told her how much he hated the often-intrusive media attention, and how the women he'd dated had basked in reflected glory.

Flick preferred to shun the spotlight.

'Jason claimed we were breaking up because he didn't like the hours I worked. It took me a long time to realise that was just an excuse. We really weren't that compatible. He just saw it before I did.'

'He's a fool if he couldn't see what he was losing.' Xander kissed her forehead and slid his hands up to her shoulders. 'I happen to think you're amazing.'

She tipped her head and leaned close, invitation in her eyes, on her lips. He was going to kiss her until they both forgot how they'd started arguing in the first place.

'But first I need your answer.'

'To what?'

'To my question. Will you move in with me?'

Chapter Twenty-one

'I'm home.' Flick pushed the front door closed with her foot and hurried towards the dining table with an armload of paper shopping bags.

Xander rose from his desk to help. Tinsel spilled from one paper bag and a tinkling sound aroused his suspicions about her secret project for the evening.

He slipped both arms around her. 'Two of my favourite words when you say them.' Then he pulled her into a kiss aimed at distracting her from her mission. Three nights since Flick had begun *coming home* to the penthouse and Xander was sure he wouldn't tire of listening for the ding of the lift arriving on his floor, or the squeaking sound of her work shoes crossing the tiled foyer.

Or her voice as she called a greeting to him. He loved her voice. He especially loved the sound of her pleasure when he kissed her—a soft, low hum that filled him with joy. Like now.

When he finally broke the kiss, her eyes opened slowly, soft-focused and sensual. 'If I say *I'm home* again, will I get the same reaction?'

'Every time.' He dipped his head, suiting action to words. Kissing Flick anywhere, anytime, was little short of a miracle. The staff on reception hadn't tried to hide their smiles the first morning he'd exited the lift hand in hand with Flick. And yesterday, when he'd walked into the kitchen and kissed her, Chris had grinned, but refrained from comment. It would come—the knowing *I told you so.*

Xander looked forward to the moment, and to nudging Chris to look for a woman.

Xander kissed his way down Flick's neck to the place he knew melted her tiredness and made her cling to him as though she'd never let him go. Being open about their relationship outside the apartment was liberating. He'd not understood what a gift that could be. But the best kisses, his favourite kisses, were still those they shared in the privacy of the penthouse.

'Are you hungry?' He nuzzled her ear before leaning back so he could watch her eyes, her expression. 'I know I am, and not just for food.'

She stood on tiptoes and nipped his lower lip. 'I'm starving.'

'In that case—' Reluctantly he let her go and headed into the kitchen. He removed the alfoil covering a plate and the plastic wrap over onions he'd already chopped.

She lifted her head and sniffed. 'Is that—'

'Dinner? Yes. I marinated a couple of steaks and made a salad.'

'*You* did?' Her surprise was gratifying. And a reminder that Flick had cooked every time they'd dined together.

He pulled out a chair and gently eased her onto the seat. 'Did you think I couldn't cook? Just because I ordered fish and chips, or picked up an antipasto platter and seafood one time, doesn't mean I'm incapable.'

'I hadn't thought about it, other than that you probably don't have much time to cook. Can we eat now?'

'Sure. I'll turn on the barbecue. Is fifteen minutes soon enough to eat?'

'Great. I'll have a quick shower and come and help you.'

'You can have a lazy shower if you like and then relax—or talk to me while I cook.' Flick's workdays were longer as they raced towards Christmas, and he'd adjusted his work hours around hers so they had time together no matter which shift she worked.

She dropped a quick kiss on his mouth and avoided his hands before he could pull her in for another deep kiss. 'Back in ten.'

He carried the dish of steak and onions onto the balcony and turned on the gas to the barbecue. While it was heating, he set the outside table with plates and cutlery. Before Flick had erupted into his life, the idea of a night at home would have meant working late and falling into bed after midnight, his mind buzzing with problems to be solved and deadlines to be met.

He set the steaks on the grill, stepping back from the hiss and steam and spatter of red wine marinade hitting heat.

A night in with Flick meant comfort and excitement all rolled together—in their bodies joining, and conversation and falling asleep with his arms around her.

He added the onions to the grill. Waking beside her was his ideal of how every day should begin. Her sleepy smile, a finger trailing down his chest ... Running late for work because he couldn't get enough of her.

Flick's arms slid around his waist and she laid her cheek against his shoulder. 'I know what your smile means, Mr McIntyre, and no, I need feeding before we get to *that*.'

'Spoilsport.' He dropped a kiss onto her head.

Yes, life was damned near perfect.

Flick was about to finish her shift when Christophe called her into his office and closed the door against the clamour of lunch service in full swing.

'Flick, I'd like to invite you to Christmas Day lunch at my home. I cannot return to my family in France this year so I'm hosting an orphans' party. I mentioned it to Xander earlier. He thought you'd both be free, but suggested I check with you.'

'You've given everyone two days off and closed the restaurant, so yes, I'm—we're free.' Less than a week had passed since she'd moved in with Xander. Her stomach still fluttered and flipped each time she publicly acknowledged their relationship. Would she ever give her complete trust to Xander, or would her parents' ravaged relationship, and the media frenzy following her break-up with Jason, continue to shadow her? 'What can we bring?'

'Nothing. I've planned the menu already, but if you would help Nico clear and stack after each course, that would help on the day.'

'Sure. It's the least I can do. Thanks, Christophe.' She headed to the door, her thoughts swinging back to how she planned to decorate the final torte for the evening dessert display.

'Before you go, I want to tell you one more thing.'

She stopped, her hand on the doorhandle. Christophe's voice held an unfamiliar tone. Forget butterflies. Giant bogong moths battered the walls of her stomach. What he thought about her relationship with Xander was no one's business but theirs. Still, her lover and her boss were good mates. Her grip tightened on the handle. 'Yes?'

'Don't look like you're heading for the guillotine, Flick. I just want to say I'm very happy you and Xander have got together. It is a good thing.'

She released a quick huff of relief and blinked to clear her eyes of unexpected tears. 'Thank you.'

'I hope it works out. But Flick, don't lose sight of your dream because you're with Xander.'

'I'm home.' Flick pushed the door closed, her attention diverted by the gaily decorated walls. Tinsel hung in garlands, draped the light fittings, and in one corner a small Christmas tree stood, half-adorned in purple and gold decorations. A half-empty box of glass baubles sat on the side table next to the tree.

Xander appeared in the doorway to the main bedroom wearing a grin, and a towel around his hips. Water dripped from his hair and ran down his chest.

'Hmm, something's changed, but I can't put my finger on why the room looks different. Maybe I've walked into the wrong apartment.'

He leaned against the doorjamb and crossed his arms over his chest. 'Since I diverted your energy from decorating last night, I thought it was the least I could do to make it up to you. Is this okay?'

A breeze came through the open balcony doors and set the tinsel garlands swaying. They fluttered, catching the wall lights. 'It's wonderful. Can I help you finish the tree?'

'Yes, but first ...' He reached for something in the bedroom. When he stepped into the room, his hands remained behind his back. 'I've got something special I need your help with.'

Flick slipped her shoes off and Xander stopped in front of her. The wall lights were reflected in his eyes and the corner of his mouth tipped up, as though he suppressed a smile.

'It's maybe *the* most important Christmas tradition.' His arm rose above her head.

She tipped her head up to see what he held. His mouth settled on hers in a kiss that scattered all thoughts of decorations and tinsel and Christmas trees. She wrapped her arms around his neck and stood on tiptoes, relishing the heat of his bare chest against her cheesecloth top.

Xander lowered the arm he'd held above her head and slid both hands down her back, pulling her closer. 'I'm glad to see it works.'

'What works?' She tugged on his arm. 'I thought that was my *I'm-glad-you're-home* kiss.'

'Mistletoe.' He raised his hand and slowly twirled a sprig of fake mistletoe between thumb and fingers. 'I couldn't decide on the best place to hang it.'

'It's perfect right where it is, but if you get tired of holding it up, you could try nestling it in the tinsel above our bedroom door.'

He let her go and set the mistletoe in a couple of twists of tinsel, and then stood there looking up.

Flick joined him in the doorway. 'What are you doing? It's fine there.'

He looked at her and then up at the green leaves and red berries. 'I don't think it's working.'

She nudged him until he stood right beneath the decoration. 'You have to be standing underneath for it to work.' She slid her hands up his chest and kissed him again before stepping back. 'See, it's working just fine.'

'I may not move from here.'

'Or—you could wear a hat with mistletoe attached.'

'Now there's an idea.' He slid an arm around her waist and laughed, a wickedly sexy chuckle.

'We might not get any work done if you do that though. Speaking of work, Christophe has given us all time off for Christmas, and he's invited us to his place for lunch.'

Xander dropped his towel on the bed.

Flick's gaze followed the play of muscles as he reached for a slim-line pair of green boxers and pulled them up. Dammit, she didn't need mistletoe. Xander was kissable at any time—all the time.

'His orphans' party—yes. He mentioned it this morning. I thought you might like to go since neither of us have our families nearby.' He tugged on a plain black T-shirt and a pair of boardies.

Mention of family hit Flick like a bucket of cold water. What was there to celebrate back in Brisbane? A day spent trudging between her depressed father and her angry mother—was there a worse way to spend Christmas Day? 'I'd love to go. And we can have a sleep-in. No early shift or—'

'I like your thinking—a Christmas Day sleep-in!' He picked her up, swung her in a circle and kissed her again before leading her onto the balcony. 'I set dinner out here again. I hope that's okay. The breeze is cooler tonight off the sea.' He busied himself pouring drinks and serving a lasagne with salad onto each plate.

Flick sat, her heart doing a little stumble and catch-up run. Jason had just whinged about her hours, but Xander …

She sniffed and swallowed a lump of emotion. Twice this last week he'd prepared dinner when she was on a late shift. Busy as his work was, he'd rearranged his schedule around her. He'd rearranged his apartment, his drawers, and his life.

A woman can't ask for more.

Chapter Twenty-two

Xander knocked on Christophe's open front door and called a greeting as he stepped into the cool interior. Voices rising and falling in conversation emanated from the kitchen, along with a clatter of pans. Xander's nose detected the rich smell of roasting turkey before Chris poked his head around the corner.

'Xander, glad you made it. *Joyeux Noël, mon ami.*' He grinned and ambled down the hall, wiping his hands on a tea towel. Extending one hand, he wrapped the other around Xander's back and thumped him in a very Aussie man-hug.

Glad that Chris didn't feel the need to kiss him on both cheeks as he did to other friends, Xander eased out of the hug. 'Same to you. Here.' He held out a bottle of Grange, aware it was too much for a simple Christmas gift.

Chris looked at the label and held the bottle up to the light falling through the window beside them. 'Thank you. You shouldn't have, but I will enjoy every drop.'

'I wanted to say thanks for hiring Flick. I should have said it weeks ago, but mate, I'm grateful.'

'She has become important to you. I see a different man standing before me today to the one who had no idea how to relax and enjoy living in paradise.'

'That's true. And I hope you won't mind if I steal her away from your restaurant.'

Chris frowned and half-turned towards the kitchen. 'Steal her ... what are you planning? Tell me while I check on my sauce.'

'I'll tell you later, after I've talked with Flick. You didn't think you were going to keep her forever, did you?'

'Perhaps I did.' Chris led the way into the kitchen and set the bottle of wine in a corner away from the work area. He picked up a wooden spoon, but turned to ask, 'Er, why doesn't Flick know about your plans if they're as big as they sound?'

'She will soon, but things only fell into place last night.' His hand touched the breast pocket of his shirt where a red envelope held Flick's Christmas present. One of them at least. The other present was wrapped in dove-grey tissue paper with a silver bow. 'Do you have a Christmas tree?'

'Of course. It's in the family room.'

'Do you mind if I put Flick's present under the tree? I was going to give it to her before we came, but we—ran out of time.' *In the best possible way.* Waking with Flick spooned against him was the best Christmas morning ever. In a euphoric daze, he'd almost forgotten to collect her gift from beneath their Christmas tree as they were leaving.

A grin pulled up one side of Chris's mouth. 'Hmm, never known you to run late, except for the day thieves stole your car. I think Flick is a bad influence on you—in the best possible way.'

'I think you're right.' He didn't try to stop the grin that spread across his face. Today was shaping up to be the best Christmas ever.

'There's wine and beer in eskies. Help yourself. What time is Flick arriving?'

'She's out in the car talking to her father. He rang just as we pulled up outside. Can I get you a drink?'

'I've got one. Go and get a beer for yourself. I'll be out in a couple of minutes.'

After Xander set Flick's present beneath the Christmas tree, he went through the sliding glass doors onto the covered patio. The heat of the day was less intense here, but a beer would go down well. Two eskies stood side by side in the corner. Small rings of water puddled beside one, about the size of a beer bottle. He tipped up the lid and helped himself to a bottle of light beer.

As he twisted the top off the bottle he spotted Joe and strolled over to join the farmer and Marta, Eve's relief events co-ordinator at the resort. 'Joe, Marta, season's greetings.'

Undercurrents swirled between them. Marta stood rigidly at Joe's side, but Joe shook his hand. 'I thought Flick would be with you?'

Marta smiled, a brittle-edged socially-polite smile with a dash of dislike Xander didn't understand.

His internal radar detected negative vibes pulsing between Joe and Marta. Was Marta's apparent dislike simply spillover because he'd interrupted an argument? 'She'll be along soon; she's taking a call from her father.'

Wondering if he should give Joe and Marta space to sort out whatever was bothering them, he looked back towards the house.

Flick stepped through the sliding glass doors and looked around the small group of Chris's Christmas orphans. Xander waved.

She made her way across to him and kissed him on the lips. It still delighted him that she had finally become comfortable with publicly acknowledging their relationship. Stolen kisses were all very well, but not touching her, not even holding her hand when others were around, had been killing him.

'Everything okay at home?'

'Fine.' A quaver in her voice, a break in the single syllable, a sniff. He looked more closely.

Her eyes were slightly red-rimmed and his stomach dropped at the evidence of her sadness. Wanting to wrap her in his arms and kiss away her hurt, he reached for her before realising that social niceties demanded he introduce her, if she hadn't already met Joe and Marta. He slung an arm casually over her shoulder. 'You know Flick?'

Joe greeted her warmly. Marta's greeting was less enthusiastic. She moved slightly forwards, putting herself between Flick and Joe. Xander could almost see the cat claws unsheathing before Chris appeared with a tray of hors d'oeuvres, and asked Joe to pass them around.

Relieved to escape from the thick tension zapping between the couple, Xander took Flick's hand and they wandered out into the large garden.

'That felt uncomfortable.' Flick wound the chain strap of her small handbag around one finger.

'Something's going on with them. Hope they sort it out and don't let it spill over into Chris's lunch. Are you okay? You seemed a bit—' He stopped as he caught sight of movement beside him. Turning, it took him a moment to switch back into party mode. 'Hi, Kiet.'

'Happy Christmas.' The oyster farmer raised his bottle, tapping it against Xander's. 'I didn't expect to see you at an orphans' Christmas party. Don't you usually spend the holidays with your parents and sister?'

'Yeah, but Jenny was up for a visit just last month. She's doing so much better that Mum and Dad decided to take her down to Phillip Island to see the penguins as a special treat. So it's just me and—' He pulled Flick close to his side. 'Kiet—have you met Flick?'

'We met when Kiet delivered some of the best oysters I've seen outside of Sydney. Nice to see you again.' She extended a hand and Kiet shook it.

'Yeah, likewise.' Kiet's gaze seemed to linger on where Xander rested his arm on Flick's shoulder. He lifted his chin to indicate Chris, who was carrying a tray of hors d'oeuvres between small groups of guests. 'Chris is excited about having you working at his restaurant.'

'I enjoy working there. He's a great boss and I'm learning lots from him about running a restaurant.'

'Do you want to run your own some day?' There was a snide tone Xander had never heard Kiet use before.

What the hell was in the water? First Joe and Marta had acted strangely, and now Kiet was behaving like a man with a massive chip on his shoulder.

He almost missed Flick's tiny gasp. He didn't miss her wide eyes and parted lips, or the way she pushed back, away from Kiet and his simple question. This was raw nerve territory and Xander had no idea why, only that something must have happened between him leaving her in the car talking to her father, and her red-eyed appearance at his side.

She dragged in an audible breath before answering. 'I do, but it will be years before I have enough money to buy my own.'

Xander pulled her closer and kissed her temple. 'You never know.' The urge to tell her his news tugged at him, but he planned to save it until they were alone. Until they could celebrate what his news meant for them. Maybe he should wait until they were back in his apartment. But he was getting ahead of himself. 'Can I get you a drink, darling?'

Her gaze snapped back to his, sharp and intelligent and—suspicious. Eyes pinning him with a *what-the-hell-was-that* look, she nodded slowly. 'White wine, please.'

He grinned, knowing that his *'darling'* had caught her attention. If she didn't like *darling*, he'd try other names on her later, but whichever pet name they settled on, it was long overdue in his book. 'A glass of white coming right up.'

'Darling'? What is Xander up to? Flick pressed both hands over her stomach and wondered why she couldn't settle into this newly acknowledged relationship with him. Was it as simple as the spectre of her parents' divorce continuing to haunt her, or did it have more to do with the fact that Kiet was smirking at her?

He quirked an eyebrow as their gazes met. 'Going out with the boss, hey? I reckon you've got it made then.' Kiet seemed angry, or maybe annoyed, and a muscle ticked in his jaw.

'What do you mean?' The question fell from her lips. Stupid, really, because she knew what Kiet meant.

'He'll look after you is what I mean. You won't have to bust a gut trying to make it on your own. Not like everyone else.' He tipped the last of his beer into his mouth and gave her a less than friendly look.

Anger vibrated through her, unsettling and building on the back of her dad's unwelcome news. 'I don't want or expect favours because I just happen to be going out with Xander. Whatever I achieve, I'll do it for myself and by myself. Excuse me.' She moved away from Kiet, away from anyone she'd have to make polite conversation with until she got her emotions under control.

Great, just great. What a fabulous Christmas Day this is turning into. First, Dad's call and now this jerk needling me.

Xander approached with a glass of wine for her and a bottle of light beer for himself. They met halfway across the yard. 'Here you are, Flick.' She accepted the drink and he tapped his bottle against her glass. 'Merry Christmas.'

Still fuming over the assumption she was sleeping with Xander for whatever she could get out of him, words were beyond her. She lifted her glass in sarcastic acknowledgement of his toast before gulping a mouthful. As her gaze darted over the group, anywhere but at Xander, she caught sight of Kiet watching them. Deliberately turning her back, she stepped around Xander. Coming to Chris's place had seemed like a nice idea to forget her broken family today of all days. If only she hadn't received that call from Dad before they came in.

'Flick, what's wrong? You looked like you'd been crying when you came in, and you're as tense as fence wire. Has something happened at home?'

There was no home for her. Nothing to return to. Not anymore. Dad's news about the sale of the restaurant couldn't have come at a worse time.

She shook her head. 'It's nothing. Leave it be.'

Wordlessly, he took her elbow and headed into the back corner of the large block. When they were out of sight behind a row of buddleia bushes, he took her glass and set it beside his bottle on the raised wooden edge of Chris's herb garden. Scents of sun-warmed basil and mint rose around them, joined by lavender as her dress brushed a heavily flowering bush.

Xander took hold of her hips and pulled her close. She wanted to bury her nose in the open V of his shirt and drink in his scent. In his arms, she could forget what Kiet had said, forget that there would be plenty of others who would think the same way as him, forget her own fears that what she and Xander shared couldn't last.

When had she turned into this insecure woman?

Since Dad's news had rung a death knell on … everything.

Xander's lips brushed her forehead before he leaned his against hers. Maybe he could make her forget she had no home. No dream. Finally, she allowed her gaze to connect with his.

'Tell me what's wrong, darling.'

Just like the night of their first kiss—their first *proper* kiss—Xander's touch briefly diverted her from melancholy thoughts of what she'd lost. If only she could stay in his arms forever and never have to think about the past.

'Our restaurant's been sold. Dad told me. The papers were signed yesterday. I had this vain hope of being able to save enough for a deposit to buy it myself before that happened, but now …' She shrugged as though it was no big deal.

'Is that why you're sad?'

Did sad explain the black hole in her heart where her dream had died?

'It's like a death in the family. The sale of Pecorino means it's all over. Dad and Mum will never get back together now.' The enormity of the loss probably didn't make sense to Xander. To her, it meant her family was broken. For good. The loss of the restaurant was the loss of her hopes and dreams. She gasped and buried her face in his shoulder.

He wrapped her in his arms and held her while she cried and cried until, finally, she had no tears left. He stroked her back and rocked her gently. 'Feel better?'

'Like a wrung-out rag.' She leaned back and wiped her cheeks. 'How bad do I look?'

'Well—you rock the raccoon eyes, but it looks more Corpse Bride than Christmas.'

She wiped her hands across her cheeks. 'Corpse Bride? Oh my— How do you even know that?'

He lifted an eyebrow. 'Jenny. I watched it with her a dozen or more times when she was in hospital. If you want I can probably quote chunks of it?'

Flick sniffed and tossed her hair out of her eyes. Xander's dry humour was the best antidote for her Christmas blues. 'I'll leave that pleasure for another time, but I should get more festive looking before Chris announces lunch, don't you think?'

He put a finger beneath her chin, tipped her face up and kissed her lips. 'You'll feel better if you do. Come on. We can sneak down the side of the house and back in through the front door and no one will notice.'

By the time she'd washed her face and reapplied her makeup, her emotions were back under control. But the intensity of the morning's news had left her feeling exhausted. She opened the door of the guest bathroom. Xander was leaning against the wall, an empty bottle of beer in his hand. In her fractured world he was the only certainty she had. Grateful he hadn't disappeared on her too, she smiled at him. 'I should warn you, I plan to drink a little too much wine, and tell a lot of corny Christmas cracker jokes.'

'No problem. I'll drive. One glass of champers for a Christmas toast and that will be it for me.'

'Thank you. It sucks when things go wrong, but it feels so much worse at Christmas.'

'Worse than any other time of year. But there won't be any more dramas from now on. Only good things.'

Chapter Twenty-three

Xander touched the red envelope burning a hole in his shirt pocket. If only he hadn't decided to leave giving it to her until they were alone. But maybe Chris's lunch would be a good time to make the announcement, if Chris was agreeable. Xander could share the news and then give Flick her gift. Anything to make her happy again.

After the lousy timing of her family selling up their restaurant, this might be just the pick-me-up she needed. *Off with the old and all that.* He grinned. That sounded more like a New Year's resolution, but he couldn't bear to wait that long.

From the patio Chris's voice encouraged everyone to take their seats. A minute or two passed before Flick opened the door and stepped out of the guest bathroom. She gave him a quick smile. Aside from a sadness he was determined to erase from her eyes, no one would guess she wasn't her usual optimistic self.

'Come on, Flick. Lunch is about to start.' Grasping her hand, they strolled out to join everyone. Most seats were occupied down both sides of a long table covered in overlapping white tablecloths, but there were vacant chairs at both ends. Guessing Chris would take the spot at the head of the table, nearest the kitchen, Xander led her to the far end. He held Flick's chair as she sat and then edged his closer. 'Chris has done an amazing job. Look at all this food.'

She picked up a silver-painted gumnut decoration and rolled it between her fingers. 'I love how he's embraced Aussie ways, but still manages to keep his French heritage. Look at that pastry dish!'

Chris stood at the other end of the table and spread his arms, welcoming everyone to his home. 'Nobody should spend today alone, and I am happy you are all here, together.'

Then he began serving until someone told him his work was done and to sit down and enjoy the fun. 'Just serve yourselves and pass the plates along.' A chorus of voices urged Chris to join them.

'We might be your orphans, but that doesn't mean we're incapable of helping ourselves,' Xander told him, as he passed a plate to Flick before spooning an extra serving of glazed carrots from the bowl for himself.

The party rolled on with rising levels of chatter as the pile of empty bottles rose in the recycling box. Flick was quieter than usual, but she rose to help clear and stack dishes after the entrée.

Gradually the wine and easy company did the trick. She smiled and blinked slowly as she met his gaze. 'It's a lovely party.' Her hand moved a little wildly as she gestured at the gathering with her glass and wine sloshed over the table and his arm. 'Oops, sorry.'

'It's okay. No harm done.' He wiped his arm and tossed the crumpled napkin onto his empty plate. Flick was keeping her promise to drink a little too much. Maybe giving her the special present now wasn't the best move. He checked the time on his watch. It was almost time to call his parents and sister. 'Maybe someone else can help with the dishes after the mains?'

She was dabbing at the spilt wine as he took hold of her free hand and kissed it before pushing his chair away from the table and standing. 'I promised I'd call my family.'

'Don't be too long. Chris will be serving his *bûche de Noël* soon.'

'His what?'

'The Christmas log dessert.'

He leaned down and kissed her, just because he could. 'Save me a piece.'

Feeling hazy and more than a little ready for sleep, Flick was only half listening to the conversation of her neighbours across the table, sisters who seemed to have their own family issues from the little she'd picked up. The afternoon heat shimmered across the surface of the swimming pool, and she closed her eyes against the blinding sparkles of light. Somewhere down the back of Chris's block, Xander was on the phone to his family. His loving, still-living-together-and-happy-for-it family. No amount of wine could dull the knowledge that she wouldn't ever have that love and security and closeness again.

A hand landed on her shoulder. Surprised to realise her eyes were closed and that she'd—possibly—nodded off, Flick forced her eyelids up. *God, I hope I wasn't snoring.*

Chris looked down at her, a frown furrowing his brow. 'Hey, Flick, are you okay?'

She drew in a deep breath and widened her eyes before blinking. How embarrassing to be caught napping at her host's table. 'Yep. I may have had more of your wonderful wine than I should have.'

Chris picked up a jug of water and poured a glass. He set it in front of her and smiled. 'Your summer heat doesn't combine well with wine, but I'm relieved. I thought you looked sad.'

'As opposed to drifting off to sleep? I'm not sure which is worse.'

'Sad, definitely. Nobody should be sad at Christmas. But if you were, I was hoping it was because of the thought of leaving me.'

'What are you talking about? I'm not leaving you. At least not until I save enough to open my own restaurant. Or maybe I'll start with a patisserie. What do you think, Christophe?'

'Change is supposed to be good for personal development and growth, but I prefer stability. After Xander said he was stealing you away I thought that maybe … It doesn't matter. I'm happy to know I was wrong.'

'You can keep your change. I'm happy working for you.'

'*Bien*. And I don't want to lose you either. Happy Christmas, *ma petite*.'

'Happy Christmas, Chris. Boy, that's hard to say after a few wines.' She grinned as she pushed up from the table. 'I'm just going in to the little girls' room.' Weaving her way past chairs, Flick headed inside.

Her head was spinning. Aware she should have eaten more and drunk less, she diverted into the kitchen and took a bread roll from the almost empty basket on the bench. Nibbling on it, she replayed her conversation with Chris. Where had that strange idea come from?

Xander said he was stealing you away.

It made no sense. A mere week had passed since they had gone public, since she'd moved out of the staff quarters and into the penthouse. But Xander's work on the renovations was winding up and a grand party was happening on New Year's Eve to celebrate the completion. Was that it? Was Xander finally planning a real holiday, one they could share?

Excited at the prospect, Flick dumped the uneaten half of bread roll on top of mounds of vegetable peelings in the compost bucket and slipped out of the house. Her father's phone call had blindsided her and she needed some good news. If Xander was taking her away for a few days, she wanted to know now.

He was strolling backwards and forwards at the bottom of the yard in a stretch of shade cast by trees along the western boundary. As she approached, he turned and saw her.

'Here's Flick now, Jenny. You can wish her a Happy Christmas. Wait a moment and I'll put you on speaker.' He took the phone away from his ear and tapped a button.

'Flick?' Jenny's voice rose in an excited squeal.

'Merry Christmas, Jenny. Have you seen the penguins yet?'

'Merry Christmas. We saw the penguins last night. They're tiny, Flick. You'd like them. Mum and Dad gave me a yellow bedspread and a soft toy penguin.' Jenny's words rushed out in a torrent, as though she had to fit all her news into a six-second sound bite.

'Wow, that's wonderful. I hope I get to see them one day.'

'What did you get, Flick? What did Xander give you?'

Her gaze meshed with his. Heat filled her cheeks and she covered her mouth.

Waking early, their lovemaking had been languorous before it became—very artistic. Crinkles formed at the corners of Xander's eyes as though he could see the image in her mind. Probably he could. Cream in a can had only one reason for existing in her world.

'I—haven't given Flick her present yet, but maybe she can call you back tomorrow and tell you what she got. How about that, little one?'

'Okay. Bye, Flick; bye, Xander.'

The home screen appeared and Xander chuckled. 'Jenny must have ended the call. Some days I forget she's so literal.' He slipped the phone into his pocket and looked at Flick. 'So—were you thinking of other ways to use whipped cream too?'

'Maybe. Hey, I didn't mean to intrude on your call.'

'You didn't. Jenny wanted to talk to you and next thing, there you were. Perfect timing, I'd say.'

Flick slipped into his arms, draping hers around his neck. 'She asked what you had given me for Christmas, but I didn't think I should mention this morning's—*gift*.' Or how long he'd taken to deliver it. Her core clenched at the remembered pleasure.

He chuckled. 'A bit too X-rated for my sister's ears. On the other hand, you seemed to enjoy *unwrapping* my present.'

'Ha! The gift that keeps giving.'

'Speaking of which …' He took a red envelope from his shirt pocket and looked at it for a moment. 'There's a wrapped present inside under Chris's tree, but there is also—this.'

Certain it contained plane tickets or a hotel booking, Flick wanted to clap as she eyed the envelope. Tickets would work perfectly with the present she'd bought for him. She reached for the envelope, but he moved his hand just out of range.

'You know my work in Rainbow Cove is almost finished?'

She nodded.

'Which means I'll be moving on to my next project after New Year.'

I'll be moving on …

Xander had referred to the coming change in the singular. An inkling of something missing dropped like a stone in her belly. 'You're leaving?'

'That's what I do. I move on to a new project and I live on site. You know that.'

She knew it all too well, having made the mistake of assuming he was on holidays because he was in the penthouse at Rainbow Cove. But this— She pulled away and stared at him. Shock was the worst way to sober up, but now her mind grasped the implications.

'We've only just started to let people know we're going out and now you're leaving?'

And she was about to be dumped again.

He frowned and pinned her with a surprised gaze. What did he expect? That she'd be happy about him leaving?

Bile rose in her throat. She wrapped her arms around her waist and backed away. 'Thanks for making this the shittiest Christmas ever.'

'Flick, I'm not leaving *you*. Oh my God, that's not what I'm saying!' He reached for her, took her by the elbows and pulled her back to him.

'You're not?'

'*We* are leaving—*together*. The contract for the new project was accepted last night. How do you feel about heading up to Queensland, near Airlie Beach?'

Sucking in a breath, the constriction around her lungs eased. 'Honestly? Right now, I can't think past the shock.'

'I am so sorry. That came out totally the wrong way. But babe, you can't think I'd let you go now I've finally got you to hold my hand in public?' His grin carried the promise of making it up to her.

'If I was thinking clearly, maybe I wouldn't have. So, what's in the envelope?'

'Okay, let me start again. After New Year, *we* will have a short holiday together up near Airlie Beach.' He wiggled the envelope before handing it to her. 'Happy Christmas.'

The back flap was stuck down. She slipped a finger under a loose end and ripped it open. Before she removed the folded paper, she looked at him. 'So this is what Chris meant by you stealing me away?'

'He doesn't know what I've planned. I only said I was stealing you, but not why.'

'He was worried I was going away for good. It's kind of nice to feel like I belong in his restaurant.' She pulled out the paper and opened it, her eyes widening as she saw where they were going. 'Isn't this the island where celebrities go to escape from public view?'

'Yes. They call it exclusive. It caters for the top end of the market.'

'Wow. So this one is operational, but weren't many of the resorts flattened two or three years ago?'

'They were. In fact, my company has just signed a contract on a small island resort not far from where we're going. It was severely damaged when Cyclone Debbie hit. I'll be working with a new architect to rebuild it from the ground up. Seb Winslow specialises in environmentally friendly, natural disaster–resistant design. It will be exciting to be on a cutting-edge build rather than the makeovers I've been involved with so far.'

'A new project. Where will you live?'

He tucked her hair behind her ear and grinned. 'On the mainland. I'm looking at property in the area of Shute Harbour.'

She'd seen pictures of the Whitsundays and knew the area had wonderful scenery, but few places had more stunning views than Shute Harbour. It was beautiful—and it was a long way from Rainbow Cove. Even if Xander flew down to visit her each weekend, she doubted even her work would be enough to overcome missing him. 'That sounds nice. But it won't be the same here without you.'

'About that.' He linked his fingers through hers. 'Come with me, Flick. I don't mean just for the holiday. Move up there with me. We can oversee the build together.'

It sounded idyllic and wonderful even if she had to leave Christophe. 'I can start looking around for somewhere to start my business once I've saved the deposit and ...'

Pieces fell into place with startling speed and clarity, but she had to ask … just to be absolutely certain this time. 'And when that build is finished?'

'We'll move on to the next project, wherever that may be.' He was smiling as though he hadn't just carved a huge chunk out of her fragile optimism.

Was it possible, after several discussions they'd had, that he could still have no idea what she wanted? *What she needed.*

'And after that, I suppose we'd just move again.'

'That's how this business works.'

She closed her eyes and pressed her lips together. How stupid of her not to have taken that into account before she lost her heart to Xander. 'This is your life, isn't it, moving every year or two?'

'Is that a problem?'

'It is for me. I can't set up a restaurant or a patisserie and then twelve or twenty-something months later pull up roots and transplant it somewhere else. A business takes time and nurturing to grow, to develop connections with customers and become part of a community.'

'What if you set up your restaurant in my resort? We could sell it as a going concern to the new owners and there wouldn't be a problem.' There he went again, solving her problems in a neatly tied package, gift-wrapped with a tag saying *this is how we stay together.*

Except real life wasn't neatly gift-wrapped, and his solution shattered her dream. Despite the heat of the day, a chill filled her. Had this been his proposal all along? Work together, build something special, sell it and move on?

She pressed her hands over her stomach, trying to subdue the jitters building with seismic intensity. 'Except that every year or so I'd have to cut ties with what I'd created. Don't you understand?

Losing Pecorino is terrible. I put so much of myself into our family business and I won't—I can't—go through that pain again.'

His expression had become bleak. 'You want your own business, more than you want to be with me.'

'I need my own business and I need to put down roots. I—I can't go with you, Xander. Not when it means leaving part of myself behind with each move. And I can't give up my dream.'

Chapter Twenty-four

A long walk to the headland hadn't lessened his sense of loss. By the time Xander returned to the penthouse, it was dark and Flick had packed up her things and disappeared. Not that she'd had a lot of gear, but her warmth and vibrant curiosity, the aroma of her cooking wafting through the apartment, all the evidence of her presence in his life had gone. It was too late to wish he'd thought through his surprise from her perspective. He knew how insecure she felt—when she'd finally opened up about how her break-up and her parents' divorce had impacted on her relationship with him, he'd understood.

But not well enough. He hadn't considered her dream. Just thought being with him would compensate. *If it had only been about her parents, we might have made it.*

He had built his business empire by continually being on the move, conquering new territory—changing location was part and parcel of his world. It wasn't part of Flick's. The truth was Flick knew it took time and personal interactions to build a business. To become part of a community. She needed stability and security as much as she needed to know he would be there for her.

He sat at the desk, one finger tapping as he tried to work out a way around their conflicting needs.

Because the one thing he was certain of was that he didn't want to lose Flick.

Flick walked and scrambled over rocks until she reached the quiet inlet south of the resort. Nobody would come this way tonight of all nights. Away from the festivities and Christmas cheer, she sat on the warm sand and tucked her arms around her knees. Her insides felt as hollow as a conch on a coffee table. The lingering heat of the day was blown away by a fresh north-easterly off the water. Would she ever feel warm again?

How could Xander have thought she'd be okay with setting up her business and selling it each time his work necessitated another move, another change of address? A mere week ago—seven days and seven nights of living openly with him—she'd thought they were finally on the same page. He had won her heart, and she'd given him her trust. Now, everything was broken, in pieces like driftwood on the beach.

The only good thing she could see coming out of Xander's move north was that she could continue to work with Christophe and keep learning the business side of managing her own place. Eventually she would have saved enough for a deposit.

Where she bought was the question. Somewhere small and coastal, so she could get back to sailing on her days off. Sailing with Xander on his catamaran had reignited her desire to be near the ocean, and a smaller tourist location might be within her price range within the next couple of years.

The ease of that decision felt odd, but she refused to consider the missing link. Xander would never be a part of her future. What each of them wanted was too far apart to ever reconcile.

She turned her face to the breeze. Feeling twin lines of cool she raised her hands to her cheeks. They were damp with tears. She drew in a couple of ragged breaths before scrubbing away her tears. There was no point adding her tiny bit of sadness to the ocean of salty water that lay before her.

No more. She had a plan and a goal and the will to achieve it. Now all she had to do was survive the next week by avoiding Xander and she could get on with her life.

Chapter Twenty-five

New Year's Eve parties were in full swing in every public area of the resort. The private function room Xander had selected to celebrate wrapping up the renovations was equally as noisy as contractors mingled with company staff.

Christophe had promised a triumph of a cake to suit the end of work on the resort, and to farewell Xander and his core company staff.

The double doors opened, and Chris and another white-jacketed figure wheeled in a trolley with a four-tiered cake in a realistic facsimile of the resort. Blue icing and miniature palm trees completed the image. As they positioned the cart for the official photos, the person beside Chris turned around. Beneath the chef's hat, Xander got his first glimpse of Flick since Christmas Day.

Shadows underlined her eyes and she seemed slimmer—too slim. Her chef's outfit hung loose and an air of fragility clung to her. Until their eyes met and he saw steely resolve glinting in hers. He nodded in greeting, receiving the barest nod in return before she turned away.

Chris looked from one to the other before putting a hand on her shoulder and leaning close to speak to her. Flick nodded in response to whatever he said and slid away behind the serving cart as Xander approached.

Chris turned to him. 'I have somewhere else I need to be, *mon ami*. Flick has agreed to stay on and oversee the cake cutting and distribution. But—' he gripped Xander's arm '—be nice to my pastry chef.'

'I have every intention of being nice, but I should warn you—I still plan to try and win her away from you.'

Chris tutted. 'It won't be easy. Be very sure what you offer her is what you both want, not just what you would like to be true.'

'Wish me luck.'

Chris held out his hand. 'Even though it will lose me the best pastry chef I've ever had, I wish you *bonne chance, mon ami*.' He pulled Xander in for a man-hug and then, with a glint in his eyes, kissed both his cheeks. 'Happy New Year.'

At the other end of the cake cart, Flick stood unmoving, her hands folded in front of her. Her casual stance didn't fool Xander. She was as highly strung as on Christmas Day, after receiving her father's news about Pecorino.

Once the speeches had been made and the cake had been cut, they were going to talk.

Properly and openly about *them*.

As various representatives spoke, congratulated one another and Xander and his company for bringing so much employment to Rainbow Cove over the past couple of years, Xander could barely contain his need for it to be over. When finally it was his turn, he kept his thanks and congratulations brief. 'Now let's cut this stunning cake.'

Flick handed him the handle of a heavy kitchen knife. He allowed his fingers to brush hers, pleased when she reacted with a soft gasp. A hint of pink coloured her cheeks and for a few brief moments, their gazes held and the noise and sway of bodies faded.

Slow clapping reminded Xander … he had one more duty to perform and then he could begin his exit strategy. Looking around at the assembly, he smiled before plunging the knife into the top layer. Flashes erupted from a multitude of phone cameras. Flick edged away.

As the number of flashes dwindled, he turned to Flick. 'This is where you take over.'

All week he'd wondered how to breach the wall between them. Nothing had felt right, but those words were perfect. He would remind her of them as soon as they were alone.

Flick couldn't ignore how much Xander's reaction to her work meant. She had needed to make the last thing she ever did for him something special, and the cake had turned out brilliantly.

And now it was over.

Quietly she stacked used plates on the lower shelf and pulled the trolley cover across to hide them. She sliced a few more pieces of cake and set them out neatly on the serving platter. Then, checking there was nothing more to be done, she edged past several groups and slipped through the door.

Her phone vibrated. She pulled it from her pocket and opened a New Year greeting from Dad. He'd attached a photo taken somewhere on Southbank. But it wasn't the fizzing fireworks that caught her attention. Dad's arm was around a woman a little younger than him. A woman who was vaguely familiar …

Flick looked more closely. *That's Karen.* The neighbour who, with her two sons, had taken in Flick's horse, Dusty, the year after her divorce. Now her father was living at the Bay again, it looked as though he'd reconnected with Karen. *The best possible timing.*

Flick zoomed in. Dad's smile was like the one he used to wear when she was little, back when their family had been happy and complete and her parents had still been in love.

His message simply read: *Happy New Year. Ours got off to a great start. Dad xx.*

Leaning against a palm tree Flick closed her eyes. *Well done, Dad.*

She was happy for him. He deserved to be happy. Deserved someone who would make him laugh. Someone he might one day find a new love with.

Like I thought I'd found with Xander.

She pressed a hand over her aching heart. She'd made it through the evening, got through seeing Xander one last time and stayed strong. And now she was going to …

'Flick, I hoped to catch up with you tonight.'

Grey eyes met hers and the intensity of his scrutiny hit her like a sledgehammer. She hadn't planned for this. Christophe had assured her when he asked for her assistance there would be no need to talk to Xander. Gathering the remnants of her pride close, she raised her chin. 'Mr McIntyre, Happy New Year to you. I wish I could stay but I still have work to do.'

'Chris told me you were off duty once the cake had been handed out.' He took her hand. His thumb brushed her skin.

Tingles that were both a delight and torture ran through her and she couldn't stop herself leaning towards him.

'Please, Flick, come for a walk with me. There are things you need to hear, things you—'

She wouldn't call him uncertain; Xander was never indecisive. It was more like he was opening himself up to her and giving her a choice.

Which made no sense, because there were no more choices left to make.

But she couldn't help herself. 'What do I need to hear?'

'Can we walk down to the beach? Please?'

She pressed her lips together, wanting—needing—to turn down his request. But curiosity, always her strength but now her weakness, won out. She *needed* to know what he had to say. 'Okay.'

They walked through a side entrance and into the humid air. She pulled off her chef's hat and unbuttoned her jacket.

'Feel better?' Xander took her hand in his again.

She knew he meant losing her work clothes, but holding his hand made her feel better too. 'Yes.'

He waited until they reached *their* stretch of beach, the more distant northern end. It was quieter up here away from the beach bonfire and the dancing, although bass notes from the music carried on the breeze. They sat on the sand side by side before he spoke again. 'I've always prided myself on getting all the details and making informed decisions in my business activities, but I forgot that real life is more than just facts. It's also hopes and dreams and messy emotions, intangible things, but they cloud our thinking. I'm sorry I forgot that and hurt you. I have no excuse to offer, but I promise I'll do my best to never hurt you again.'

Momentarily stunned, she shook her head. 'Loving me isn't enough, not when we want different things. I can love you with every fibre of my body and still we'll end up hating each another when our dreams and goals are so different. You need to move. I need to stay, develop friends, become part of a community. Dammit Xander, I need stability.'

'You're right. I understand that now. In my defence, I was excited at the idea of us working and travelling together, but I overlooked the key part of your dream. I won't do that again.'

'Xander, I—'

'Please, hear me out, that's all I ask. Then, the choice is yours. It's always been yours, but I want to make it easy for you to choose me. So ... when you know where you want to set up your business, together, we can look for a house or an apartment nearby. I'll do most of my work from home, with occasional overnight stays wherever my current project is. What do you think?'

She'd sworn she was done with crying, but the bonfire blurred and wavered as she looked at Xander. 'But you've always said your way of working was hands on, managing every detail; that that's why your projects work so well. If you aren't there all the time, maybe you'll come to resent me keeping you from your work.'

'I am hands on, and that's in every part of my life. I can happily work if I'm on site for a couple of days each week. I can't live without being hands on with you. Flick, I love you. I want to fall asleep each night with you in my arms and wake each morning with you beside me. If I can't have that, what's the point in working so damned hard?'

Wonder, happiness, the reality of her dreams—all of them—there for the taking ... She drew in a deep breath, daring to hope. 'You'd really do that for me?'

'Yes. You're my dream, what I want my life to be. What do you say?'

'I'm happy here in Rainbow Cove for now.'

'Then we can live here until you decide where you want to build or buy your patisserie.' Gently he drew her to her feet.

'But your project—it's in the Whitsundays.'

'It is, but it's just work. All that makes life worth living is wherever you are. I don't care what our address is, so long as you're there to say *I'm home* every night.'

She turned to look around the cove. It was beautiful and welcoming, but it was just a place. The scenery didn't matter. The address was irrelevant. All that mattered was the man who stood in front of her, his hands resting on her hips. Wherever he was, she would be. Together they made any place home.

She slipped a hand around his neck and pulled him close. 'I say Happy New Year, Xander. Now kiss me.'

'Always, darling.'

In the distance voices rose in unison counting down to a bright new beginning. '... four, three, two, one—Happy New Year!' Fireworks lit the sky, sparkling over the water in bursts of colour.

They were the colour of her dreams—their dreams.

Together.

NAUGHTY OR *Nice*

LAUREN K. McKELLAR

For my spirit animals:
those people who love Christmas just as much as I do.
May your Christmas reads and
your Hallmark movies fill your heart with joy.

Chapter One

Hamish

Nice is my specialty.

Got a kitty needing rescuing from a tree? I do it more often—and looking better—than a fireman.

Have an old lady who needs a hand across the road? Sign me up to your local senior citizens' club, because I am the guy you'll need.

Got a free coffee because the person ahead of you paid it forward? That guy was probably me—and don't worry, you can thank me later.

That niceness doesn't stop in the public eye. I also enjoy being extra nice to the ladies in my life. Call me a traditionalist, but I am a big believer in women going first—through doorways, when speaking, and into orgasm.

That was why I didn't understand Claire Roberts.

I studied the woman at the desk across from me, the jet-black hair that framed her face even blacker than her heart. Ever since I came to work at this firm, she'd made it abundantly clear that she had neither the time nor the inclination to get to know me, despite my many attempts. How could she resist my extreme level of niceness when if you looked the word up in the dictionary, you wouldn't just find a picture of me, but a link to a bible-length appendix citing my virtues?

'Quit staring.' She didn't even look up from her computer screen. How did she do that?

'I'm not staring,' I replied, my eyes still on the evil temptress tap, tap, tapping away at her keyboard. 'I'm admiring your beauty.'

'Can you please admire my beauty from a distance? We have a meeting in'—her eyes flicked from her computer screen down to the phone beside her—'five minutes, and I'm trying to prepare.'

'I could help you with that. I'm very good at preparing. Doing my research.' I paused, staring at her full pink lips. 'I like to give my undivided attention to the project at hand.'

Finally, she met my gaze. Cool green eyes glared at me over the top of the silver rim of her laptop. 'So do I. Which is why I need you to take those bedroom eyes away from my desk.'

'So you think my eyes belong in the bedroom.'

'Yes. *Your own.*' She sighed, but was that a smile lurking at the corner of her lips? 'Can I please just have four-and-a-half more minutes of peace to get this done?'

'Of course.' I pushed back in my chair and took the file from the corner of my desk. As I passed her, I glanced at her screen. A long list of names ran down one side of it. 'Deciding who's been naughty and who's been nice?'

The screen blinked off in an instant. She swivelled in her chair to glare at me, and this time it wasn't just your average glare—it was next-level, all-out murder. 'Yes. And guess what? You made the cut.'

'Let me guess—you'd like to punish me for my naughty staring ways.' I wiggled my eyebrows, hoping to make her laugh.

'Can you stop being such a sleaze for just one minute?'

'I'm hurt.'

She smiled sweetly, then took her phone and tablet from the desk, standing. The scent of flowers and coffee teased at my nostrils, and damn, that was sweet. 'Yes. You're a sleaze. And just so you know, you made the nice list.'

'Huh. So you're finally seeing what a good guy I can be.'

'It's a different kind of nice list, Hamish.' She stepped past me, her shoulder brushing my arm as she made her way to the printer and slid out a sheet of paper. 'That was a list of people it'd be nice not to have in my life.'

Brutal.

'Tell me, do you break every guy's heart the way you so casually do mine?' I called after her as she walked down the hall.

She didn't reply.

She didn't need to.

Those swinging hips said it all.

It seemed that no matter how hard I tried, how many accounts I landed or how many bonuses I scored, Claire wouldn't give me the time of day, niceness be damned.

'Damn, she's cold.' Zeb gave a low whistle, coming to stand by my side.

'She's ... defrosting,' I said, slowly.

'Well, I'd sure love her to heat things up over in my corner of the office.' He slapped me on the back, then followed Claire down the hall.

I cringed. 'This isn't *Mad Men*.'

'What do you mean?' he asked, stopping in his tracks.

'Maybe you've heard of this little thing called equal rights,' I said, choosing my words carefully. Zeb had been working there a lot longer than I.

'Ha! Yeah, mate, of course.' He started moving again, heading towards the boardroom. 'Come on, mate. I want to get to this meeting on time.'

'*Me too*,' I muttered, the irony of the words clearly lost on him.

A low hum of noise reached my ears as I entered the room. Twelve employees sat around the long oval table, some talking, some looking through their notes. I took a seat between Zeb and Claire at the back, and as Frank walked through the door, I glanced at my wristwatch. Eleven am. Right on time. Looked like my lunch date would stand after all.

'Got somewhere better to be, Christianson?' Claire asked in a low voice.

I flicked a glance at her. Legs for days stretched under the table beside me. Goddamn. 'Nowhere I'd rather be than here with you.'

'Ha!' She snorted.

'Morning,' Frank muttered, waving hello to the room at large as he shuffled past the black swivel chairs to an empty seat at the head of the table. He pushed his glasses up his nose, the thin frames so at odds with his broad shoulders, his tall physique. 'How are you all today?'

Murmurs of 'good' and 'can't complain' went around the room, and he nodded.

'Right. Excellent.' Frank glanced at a sheet of paper in front of him. 'I have our sales tallies for the month just gone, and you'll all no doubt be unsurprised to know that once again, Hamish has come out on top. Congratulations, Hamish.'

Hell yeah! That made it three months in a row. I beamed. A few polite claps went around the table. Claire stiffened beside me.

'That means you'll get the November bonus. Coming in second was of course Claire—nice work.' Frank nodded in her direction, and she smiled. 'Then Zeb, and the rest of you lot.'

'Congratulations,' I whispered to Claire.

Her eyes didn't move from the man in the front of the room.

'Before we launch into your reports, I want to let you know that there's an opportunity up for grabs at the start of the new year,' Frank said.

I straightened. Opportunity?

'One of you will be promoted to senior accounts manager. Now, in the past we haven't utilised this role, but as we continue to expand I'm beginning to see how it would be an advantage to put one of our top salespeople in a position to motivate and lead others in the team,' Frank continued. 'The person who is awarded this position will be smart, driven, and motivated. Not only will they have excellent and consistent sales figures, but they will be good when it comes to teamwork and skill development.'

I puffed up my chest. It was like he was reading my résumé.

'Of course, there are a few of you I already have in mind for this role, but during the month ahead I will be watching you all closely to see how you perform. I'll announce the promotion Christmas Eve, the day after our Christmas party—which I expect you all to attend, mind you.' He nodded, taking the top piece of paper and moving it to the bottom of the pile. 'Right! Now let's talk budgets.'

Papers shuffled. Voices whispered.

I leaned forward in my seat, my eyes on the man in the front of the room, but my mind on one thought and one thought only.

I had to get that promotion.

Chapter Two

Claire

I had to get that promotion.

Not just because I'd worked here for five years, or because I was good at my job, or because I knew I deserved it.

But because it was getting to the point where I couldn't pay the rent.

'I'm sorry, baby,' Chad had crooned through the phone earlier that morning. 'Just one more month.'

'That's what you said last month. And the month before that,' I'd whispered, glancing over the top of my computer to make sure Hamish wasn't listening. His eyes were focused on his mobile phone. Probably scrolling through social media. 'Chad, this is getting out of control.'

'I know, I know it is. But it's almost a new year! And you know what they say—new year, new you.'

I did. I knew it because that was what he'd said the year before—*new year, new you*. Right before he walked out the door of our shared apartment in the middle of the city, taking the contents of my bank account and my engagement ring with him.

'Chad, please. This is getting out of control. I can't keep covering for you.'

'I don't know what you want me to say. I'm sorry? I'll pay you back?' he'd asked.

'I want you to say "I have the money. It's going into your account next week, and then the bank won't chase you for the overdue amount",' I'd snapped.

'But that would be a lie,' he'd replied, and I'd rested my head in my hands. A lie. Just like our relationship had been. 'I'll have something to you soon, I swear it. On my life, Claire.'

'You better,' I'd replied, trying to inject menace into my tone but no doubt failing miserably.

Now, all I could think about was that promotion. If I landed it, it might be enough to cover the excess debt, at least short-term, or maybe to hire a lawyer and get me out of this mess.

When I took out the loan in my name, I'd thought things between Chad and me were solid. We'd met at work and had been dating for three years, living together for two, and he'd just proposed.

Turned out the money I'd borrowed to finance our wedding and a new car, he'd blown gambling. Right before he blew me off, quitting his job and leaving me with a broken heart and broken bank account courtesy of the debt he'd accrued in my name.

Now I was struggling. A year of making those repayments with little to no help from him, and my purse strings were drawn tight. This was the sort of thing they didn't tell you to look for when you dated. Look for a man who's nice and funny. Someone who pays attention to you and makes you feel special.

No one ever said that a man could be those things, but he could have another side too. One addicted to the rush of gambling, the thrill of risking it all—an affair he'd found all too easy to commit to.

Around me, the room broke into casual chatter as Frank closed the meeting, wishing us all luck for the weeks ahead. December was a busy month, yet one where it was notoriously hard to bring clients in.

'You going to apply for that promotion?' Vi asked as she stood to follow him.

I smiled. 'Definitely.'

'You'll be a shoo-in,' she replied, squeezing my arm. 'I can't think of anyone better suited to the job.'

'Thanks.' I smiled, but I could.

I chanced a quick glance at the man pushing out of his seat to my right. He turned so his butt was eye level, and for a moment, just one moment, I let myself look. I let myself stare at those round globes that I'd heard the women from marketing gossip about on rainy afternoons in the office.

Then I stopped.

Because men who looked like that only broke your heart, and your bank account too.

'You've got time on your side, Claire,' Vi said, pulling my attention back. 'He's only been here three months.'

Three months he'd consistently come out on top when it came to landing new clients.

'Oh! One more thing!' Frank said, commanding everybody's attention once more. 'We have our office Secret Santa on again. I encourage you all to please get involved. Leave your name with Vi by close of business today if you're interested.'

He turned and left the room, with other members of staff following in dribs and drabs. Vi stood, rushing after her boss. Frank liked a double-shot latte before lunch, but he did not like to be kept waiting.

I stood, collecting my notes and holding them close to my chest. If I wanted a chance at landing that job, I had to work hard, and work fast. There were several new leads I'd been researching, and now was the time to act.

I stopped in the kitchen and placed my notes on the cabinet. Tea. I'd be able to strategise the best game plan with a nice hot cup of tea in my hands.

'Are you going for the promotion?'

I looked up. Hamish leaned against the doorframe, his blue eyes sparking with humour. His tousled dark hair was a devil-may-care twist to his good-boy office attire.

'Yes. Obviously,' I replied, head held high. No point beating around the bush.

'Me too.' He stepped over to the cupboard and pulled a mug out, placing it next to my notes. 'Ah, what's this here? A list of potential—'

'A list of none of your business.' I snatched the folder away. I couldn't afford to let him land any client on there. If they were thinking of coming to our firm, they had to come to me.

'I see you have Actron Energy written down. I actually have a meeting lined up with them myself. Would you like to come?' he asked.

I raised my eyebrows. What was the catch?

'Maybe we could go for a drink after. Get rid of some of this animosity between us,' he continued, and there it was. A date.

Business and pleasure should never mix.

Not even at Christmas.

'I am not going to have a drink with you.' I poured the hot water over my teabag.

'Fine then.' He stood next to me, mixing coffee and sugar in the bottom of his mug. 'Dinner.'

'No!' I turned to stare at him. He was hot—the kind of man women threw themselves at. He had an air of danger about him, wrapped in a shirt and tie.

I glanced down at the knee-length dress that felt a little too tight on me this season, hugging all my curves just that bit too closely. If he was dangerous and sexy, I was girl-next-door and frumpy. We were polar opposites—and men like him didn't go for women like me. All they saw was a meal ticket, someone to play house for them while they went after the next big thing.

Chad's such an arsehole.

I dished sugar into my tea and stirred it angrily.

'I don't know what I have to do to get you to see that I'm a nice guy, but I am.' Hamish held his hands out either side of his body. 'Give me a chance.'

'A chance? A chance to steal my clients out from under me?' A chance to break my heart? 'No way!'

His face darkened. 'If I was worried about stealing clients, I'd just—'

'Hamish. Claire.'

Hamish whirled around. I dropped my spoon.

Frank stood there, his mouth twisted into a scowl of displeasure. 'What's this about stealing clients?'

'It's nothing.' Hamish sighed, turning back to his coffee. 'I was just asking Claire if she wanted to come to a meeting with me this afternoon, and she mentioned that she was concerned it might look like she was stealing my client.'

My grip on my mug tightened. How dare he? Actron was—

It was a client I wanted, yes.

But if Hamish already had a meeting, technically, the client was more his.

'Working together. I like that.' Frank nodded, stepping between us to take his own mug down from the cupboard. 'You know, I think you both are strong candidates for the position we have coming up. But I want to see more from you. More teamwork. More office spirit.' He smiled at me. 'You used to organise all the social goings-on around here.'

My chest panged. Used to.

Back when Chad worked at the firm, and I'd been excited about socialising after work.

Back when drinks after meetings with clients weren't a bad thing at all.

'I'll ... I'll make a bigger effort.' I smiled, hoping it was more convincing than I'd thought. 'I'm actually just about to sign up for the Secret Santa.'

'Oh good! Hamish?' Frank asked.

Hamish gave a wide grin. 'Of course. I love Christmas.'

'Don't we all?' Frank chuckled. 'Now, I'll leave you two to prepare for the meeting with Actron. If it does come off, I'm sure we can organise with accounts to split the commission, make it nice and fair.'

He strode out of the kitchen, mug in hand.

I looked up at Hamish. 'Why did you say that?' The client was his, fair and square.

'I thought you might need the extra incentive. To realise I'm a nice guy. That you can trust me,' he said, and there was that word again. *Nice*. Why was he so obsessed with being nice?

'Well, you didn't have to do it. And if you want to take the client for yourself, I'd be okay with that. Obviously.'

'It might be fun to work together for a change.' Hamish shrugged. 'You know—instead of you spending your time trying to break my heart with your constant rejections.'

'Ha!' I rolled my eyes. 'I'm sure there are plenty of ladies to keep that heart intact.'

'No.' He shook his head, that twinkle in his eye again. 'No ladies.'

'No girlfriend?'

'No.'

'No lover?' I pressed.

'No.'

No?

How could a man like Hamish be single?

'If you already have a presentation for Actron, let's use that,' he said, taking his mug and walking out of the kitchen. 'Saves me having to put one together.'

And there it was.

That was how he was single.

He was the kind of guy who made you feel special, wanted, unique—only to get you to invest more into the relationship than he was ever willing to give.

Hamish Christianson was just like my ex.

So why did I find him so attractive?

Chapter Three

Hamish

She was stunning.

There were no two ways about it.

As she stood in front of the two men from Actron, gesturing to the presentation behind her, fire in her eyes and passion in the words that came from her mouth, I knew inviting her to come to this pitch with me was either the best or the worst idea I'd ever had.

The best, because I wanted her. Lust stirred in my veins as she leaned across the table, handing the men and then me a printout, her cleavage hovering right in front of my face.

The worst because she wasn't interested. Not only that, but she was my primary competition when it came to the promotion at work.

That was why I'd invited her here—to show Frank I was all about working as a team. That I wanted the best for the company, not just for my own personal gain.

And I did.

It was just that I wanted my own gain, too. Was that so very wrong?

'And that's why you should choose In The Lead for your marketing in the year to come,' Claire finished up, taking a seat beside me.

'Thank you.' Enrique nodded. 'We appreciate the demonstration. But I have a few questions I was hoping to ask you.'

'Shoot,' she said, smiling.

'Right. As a firm, what would you say your weak points are?' Enrique asked, and I couldn't help but notice that he made eye contact with me as he spoke.

'I'd say our weakest point would be that we care too much.' Claire nailed the question like a pro. 'We want the very best for our clients, so if something isn't working, we put in the extra hours and pull out all the stops to turn it around for them.'

'I see. Hamish?' Enrique pressed.

'Yes?'

'What do you have to say about it?'

My skin prickled. Did it matter what my answer was? 'I agree with Claire. We care a lot about our clients—that's no doubt why we have a ninety per cent retention rate year after year.'

'I see. And what about your strengths? Your ... assets?' He lingered on the word, and for the briefest second his eyes dipped to Claire's chest.

The hairs on the back of my neck rose. Did she see?

'Well, as I said in my presentation, we have a very talented team of people who can meet your needs,' Claire spoke confidently, her eyes never leaving his, but she turned her body slightly towards me, as if protecting herself.

'So that's why I should go with you instead of a bigger firm like Murphy's?' Enrique's eyes lingered on Claire again.

'Actually, Murphy's is downsizing,' I filled in the info on my old place of employment. Looked like I'd left in the nick of time. The EA to the CEO had called to tell me the news on the way to work—how they'd marched a bunch of staff out in the middle of the day, no questions, no pleasantries, and no Christmas bonuses. 'I heard they made some significant staffing cuts this week.'

'I haven't heard anything of the sort.'

'I doubt they'd include it in their pitch. Which company would it make you more likely to sign with? One worried about internal budgets? Or one focused on ensuring your marketing budget received the biggest bang for each buck spent?' I asked.

Enrique's black eyes glittered. 'I see. And if this was to go ahead, who would be my point of contact? You?' Enrique looked at Claire, and something in his gaze … 'Or you?' He turned to me.

'We …?' Claire paused.

'We both would,' I offered.

'Sounds confusing,' Enrique replied.

'Sounds like between the two of us, there'd always be someone available to help you with your needs.' I leaned forward across the table. I'd met guys like him before—ones who'd already made a decision but wanted you to jump through hoops. 'Listen, I know you're a busy man, and we have other clients to see too. How about any further questions you pop in an email, and we can discuss it further?'

'So you're too busy for me.' Enrique leaned back in his seat.

'Never too busy,' Claire rushed. Damn it! Didn't she know that made us look desperate?

'Then why do you have to leave?' Enrique asked.

'As I said, I have another meeting this afternoon. But let's chat in the weeks ahead,' I said. *If you haven't found another marketing agency who'll let you squeeze them like a snake first.* Clients like him were hard work, and rarely worth the pain.

'Can we be flexible on price, Claire?' Enrique asked, as if I hadn't spoken a word.

'We could certainly look at tailoring the plan to suit your budget,' she said, gathering her things. 'We'll talk about it over email, or—'

'Claire,' I growled. We were a team.

'I would be happy to talk to you on the phone,' she finished, flicking me a look that was definitely not so nice.

'Thank you for your time today, gentlemen.' I extended my hand for the two men to shake, and Claire followed suit.

Frosty silence walked with us all the way to the lift, then the whole ride down to the taxi rank.

When we were seated inside a cab headed back to In The Lead, she finally spoke.

'You blew it in there. Too busy to answer a few questions?' she asked, her full lips tightened to a thin line.

'It was strategy, Claire. Men like that like to be kept waiting. They think they're all-important, and if you give too much at first, they dig for more.'

'If that was the strategy, why didn't you tell me before we went in?'

'I didn't know that was what they'd be like till we met,' I replied. 'What do you think I am? A mind-reader?'

'Clearly not,' she snorted. 'But you cut me off when I was speaking! You made me look like a child.'

I opened my mouth to protest, then snapped it shut. I hadn't meant to—had I done that? I'd been so caught up in the moment, and then when Enrique had stared at her chest ... Anger boiled my blood. I couldn't exactly tell her that.

I turned to stare out the window. 'For one minute, can you just give me a break?'

Traffic merged into a single lane as we wound around tall buildings that stretched up towards the sky like long grey fingers.

Overhead, grey clouds were moving in. 'Silent Night' played on the radio, a small hint of warmth in an otherwise frosty environment.

'You made me feel like an idiot.' Her voice was small. 'And I don't like being spoken to like that.'

I glanced over. Gone was the stormy veneer from moments earlier. Her eyes were soft, vulnerable. Her chest rose and fell slow, deep, as if each breath cost her a lot. My fingers itched to touch her, run my thumb over that rosebud mouth and kiss the smile back on her face. Where was the woman from half an hour earlier, the one who owned that boardroom with her fiery passion? She'd been prepared to give her all to win that client. She'd been *alive*.

'You were amazing in there, Claire,' I said, keeping my hands in my lap. 'Your presentation was great. If they don't sign based on that alone, they're idiots.'

A small smile lifted her lips. 'Thank you.'

We rode in silence the rest of the way back to the office.

Chapter Four

Claire

I loved Christmas.

I loved the way it smelt—like pine trees, and spun sugar, and women's perfume in the air.

I loved the way it tasted—like nutmeg, and ginger, and sparkling wine, a combination of richness and celebration all at once.

I loved the way it sounded—like bells, and laughter, and the Health Direct Christmas Carols that played on television every year.

I loved the way it looked—like fairy lights, and bright red gift-wrap, and mistletoe.

But mostly, I loved the way it felt.

Like *home*.

Like a home I missed so very much.

'Have you finished all your shopping for the year?' Vi asked, stopping to hold open the door at the grand old department store in the mall.

I followed her inside, the building's air-conditioning a pleasant relief from the sultry summer heat. 'Mostly. I just need to pick up something else for Mum …'

'Perfume?' Vi gestured to the pinks, purples, golds, and greens of the bottles dotted over the glass counters in front of us. 'Everyone loves perfume.'

'Maybe ...' I picked up the nearest one—Wild Rose. My finger pumped down the nozzle and the scent of old-lady potpourri filled the air. I coughed, choking on the pungent aroma, and put the bottle down. 'Definitely not.'

'How are you feeling, anyway? I know this is only your second Christmas without Chad—'

'I'm fine.' I shrugged the question off.

'Are you sure? You were together three years. And holidays like this—they can make you wish you had someone.'

'Well, not me. I'm fine.' I pressed the button for the lift.

'You never want to talk about him, but I know he's still a big part of your life.' Vi's eyes were kind as her hand touched my arm. 'Don't you want to vent? To let someone in?'

I shrugged. I'd let Chad in. That had been problem enough. 'Vi, you are too good to me. But honestly, I'm doing okay. It's just Christmas.'

The lie tasted sour in my mouth.

As the lift shot up to the building's fourth floor, Vi took out her phone. I kept my eyes on the little numbers above the door.

'Oh! Secret Santa emails are in!' She nudged my shoulder as the doors opened, taking us out to the womenswear department.

'Already?' I'd forgotten about that. Just one more hoop to jump through to try and get this promotion.

'Yeah.' She made a face. 'Ugh. I have Frank. What am I supposed to get him?'

'A Christmassy tie?' I offered.

'Oh God! Yes, I should. Something ridiculous. Who'd you get?'

I slipped my hand into my bag and pulled my phone out. We strolled past a rack of long, slinky black dresses, and Vi paused, pulling one out to admire.

'What do you think? I can see you in this at the Christmas party,' she said.

I looked up. Red beading decorated the neckline, making the dress look as if it were alight. The dress scooped low in the back, then dropped to the floor in a combination that was somehow sinful, sweet, and sexy all at once. *I love it.*

I glimpsed the price tag.

I hated it.

I hated it more than I hated Chad, and debt collectors, and men who tried to stop me from getting what I wanted.

'I don't know. I think I'll just wear something I already have,' I hedged, focusing back on my phone, eager for the distraction.

'What? But this would look amazing on you,' Vi said.

My heart stopped.

My Secret Santa email had arrived.

'I got Hamish.' I held my phone out miserably. 'But I presume you already knew that.'

'It's a random generator. I may have taken the names, but I had no idea who ended up with who.' Vi held up one hand. 'Scout's honour.'

'Ugh,' I groaned. 'What on earth am I going to get him?'

I pressed my eyes closed, stared up at the ceiling. Could this week get any worse?

Today, four days after the meeting with Actron, the client had called—called Hamish, not me—and asked if he could come meet with them a second time. *Alone.*

Of course, I'd told him to go. After all, it wasn't like I could force them to work with me.

But the snub still burned, reminded me that he was my main competition for this promotion, and at the rate he was going, he'd blitz me when it came to the finish line.

What I needed was a big win. Someone bigger than Actron. Someone like—

'Health Direct!' I exclaimed, shoving my phone back in my bag.

Vi looked at me as if I'd lost my marbles. 'Uh … you okay?'

'They would be the perfect client. Health Direct,' I repeated.

'The Christmas Carols sponsor?' Vi asked, and I nodded. 'But they've been with Murphy's for years, haven't they?'

'Yes.' I grinned. 'But Murphy's is downsizing. Maybe they'd be open to a move.'

'They would be amazing,' Vi's eyes widened. 'You know, I have a cousin who works there. I could try get you a meeting.'

'That would be amazing,' I gushed. 'Thank you.'

'No worries.' Her eyes sparked with amusement. 'As for Hamish … you could always get him a lump of coal. He's the sort of man I wouldn't mind putting on my naughty list.'

I rolled my eyes. 'Well, you can keep him there,' I said, running one hand along a silk scarf my mother would love. 'He's not the sort of man I'd date—now or ever.'

'Okay.' Vi shrugged, but even though she didn't speak, I felt the full force of her argument.

Chapter Five

Hamish

Half past twelve.

Time for my standing lunch date.

Only she was running late, and at this time of year, with this much on the line, I didn't have time to lose.

I glanced out the window, past the Christmas lights twinkling there, and to the street. A mass of people walked past, but I couldn't see her. No wild red hair. No loud voice calling across the room.

'Sorry, sorry, sorry.'

I looked left.

Renee rushed towards me from the elevator. She navigated around a few people, stopped beside the menu outside the cafe and pressed a kiss to my cheek. 'I couldn't get a park, and then by the time I dropped Harry off—'

'It's fine.' I waved her apology away. 'I ordered you the Caesar salad.'

'Hold the anchovies?' She narrowed her eyes.

'Do you think I'm some kind of sadist?' I asked. 'Of course I held the anchovies.'

'Thank goodness.' She swiped at her forehead, as if the narrowly escaped Death by Sardine was truly a moment for concern. 'You know if they'd been left in, I'd have to order again.'

'That or call the poison squad.' I nodded sagely, holding out her chair for her before sitting at the place opposite.

'Obviously,' she replied.

'How is Harry today?' I asked.

'Good. He's just having a quick check-up with the doctors upstairs; nothing serious, all routine. Oh! And he loves the new car you bought him last week.'

I smiled, thinking of the cute kid's face lighting up when I'd presented it to him as an early Christmas present. I'd give him the world if I could.

It was just a shame the one thing I most wanted to give him was out of my reach.

'So tell me, how's the quest for the promotion? Going well?' Renee asked, changing the subject.

'I think so.' It was only one week after Frank had made his big announcement, but already I'd signed on a new client, and renewed another. The problem was they'd both been small fish. What I needed was an Actron, a monolith, someone with big marketing dollars to spend, to really get me across the line.

That and a reprieve from my guilt.

Ever since Enrique had asked to see me, and me alone, I couldn't shake the feeling of wrong from my shoulders—as if I were betraying Claire by going solo.

'Uh-uh. I know that look.' Renee circled her finger around my face. 'There's a girl.'

'The only woman in my life is you. You know that.'

'Hamish ...' Renee placed her hand over mine, resting it on the table. 'There's a girl.'

I grinned. 'There might be a girl—'

'I knew it!'

'—but she's my colleague, and my primary competition for the promotion at work,' I said. 'And to top it all off, she's immune to my charms. My nice ways. There's no chance of anything happening there.'

'Oh Hamish. Ye of little faith.' Renee shook her head dramatically, just as the waiter hovered over our table, two plates in hand.

'One Caesar salad, and one turkey toastie.' He placed them down in front of us, then left.

'You got turkey?' Renee wrinkled her nose.

'It's Christmas.' I shrugged. 'Turkey is festive.'

'I forgot how much you Christianson boys love Christmas.' She smiled, and a wistful expression crossed her face. 'There's so much I forget sometimes.'

'Hey.' I reached over the table and squeezed her shoulder. 'You're allowed to forget things like that. That's not important.'

'It is.' She shrugged me off. 'That's the kind of thing that *makes* a person.'

'No.' I shook my head. 'What makes a person are the bigger things. Like being kind. Caring. Nice.'

'You're too broad scale.' She smiled, but her eyes retained that sad sheen. 'They're not specific—those terms could apply to anyone. What makes a person is loving Christmas. It's running into the waves at full speed because you don't want to chicken out in front of your family.'

I smiled. *Josh, running into the waves, Renee standing on the beach and squealing as the cool water lapped at her toes.* 'He always did love to do that, didn't he?'

She smiled. 'He did. He used to say it was the ultimate battle of mind over matter.'

Mind over matter.

That was my brother's motto, right until the end.

'Anyway, all this is beside the point. Tell me about the girl.' Renee waved the conversation away.

'Like I said—there isn't really a girl.' I picked up a piece of my sandwich. 'At least, not in the romantic sense, anyway.'

'I don't know.' Renee stabbed at a piece of lettuce with her fork. 'You said she's competition for the promotion. That must mean she's ambitious, talented—aren't they qualities you'd look for in a partner?'

'Well, yes.' I frowned. 'But in an ideal world, my ambitious and talented hypothetical girlfriend doesn't want my job.'

'But this world isn't ideal, Hamish.' Renee sighed, and for a moment, I saw the pain of losing her husband painted on her face. So strong. She was the strongest woman I knew.

Thirteen months ago, my brother and their four-year-old son, Harry, had been in a car crash. The other driver had been on ice. He was sent to jail for five years and suffered a broken leg.

Harry had had lacerations to his liver, and internal bleeding that still required constant check-ups even to this day.

My brother had died.

The world was far from ideal. We knew that better than anyone.

Renee pasted on a smile, moving the conversation along. 'As for her being a colleague, that just makes things more interesting. Does your work have a policy on dating?'

'I don't think so.' I couldn't remember reading anything about it in the employee handbook. 'But are policies like that ever set in stone? I thought it was just understood: thou shalt not date thine colleague.'

'And "thou shalt not eat the yoghurt in the fridge if thine does not own it".' Renee's eyes sparked.

'And "thou shalt label all thine food in case thine tuna sandwich looks too similar to Jerry's".' I laughed along with her.

'But see, these commandments—they're not losing-your-job-over offences. That's why they're not in the handbook,' Renee said.

'That doesn't mean you should do them.'

'And it doesn't mean you should not.'

I took a bite of my sandwich, mulling over her words. Did she have a point? Maybe, but there was still one vital problem—Claire didn't like me. It was as simple as that; she'd made it abundantly clear. And while we seemed to have formed some kind of truce since that moment in the car on the way back from Actron, I still wasn't sure where I stood.

I blinked. Was that—

Claire.

There she was.

She stood at the entrance to the cafe and clutched a manila folder to her chest, those touchable curves that I ached to caress. Her green eyes roamed over the tables before stopping on one near the back. She waved at a woman with dark curly hair and shrewd beady eyes, and I watched her walk over, shake her hand, and sit down.

'Hello? Earth to Hamish?' Renee waved a hand in front of my face. I hadn't even realised she was talking.

'Sorry.' I took one last glance at Claire. She opened her folder, tucked a lock of hair behind her ear. Hair that I could imagine splayed out over my sheets. Hair I wanted to tangle my hands in again and again.

'You're looking at that woman like she's the tastiest thing you've ever seen.'

'That's her. That's Claire.'

'The one talking to the hospital's marketing manager?' Renee asked.

I jerked my head back to her. 'What?'

'That's Marie Foster. Health Direct's marketing manager,' she replied, matter-of-factly. 'I know, because she came to ask us to sign a waiver the other day for Harry to appear on television. They're filming the weather segment here or something.'

Claire was meeting with Health Direct Hospital.

She was trying to land their marketing.

That was ballsy. Health Direct had been with Murphy's for years. To get them on board would be a big coup, and one that Frank couldn't miss.

But it was also dangerous. When I'd worked with Murphy's, their contracts had been watertight. Even if they had downsized, there wouldn't be a way for Claire to bring this hospital over without someone at Murphy's making a very big mistake—and Murphy's staff rarely made mistakes.

I needed to let Claire know. She needed that information in order to form a strong plan of attack.

'I'll be back.' I stood, my chair scraping over the tiled floor of the cafeteria.

'You go break those office commandments, Hamish!' Renee called as I walked away from the table, but I didn't smile.

I wouldn't let anyone hurt Claire Roberts.

Not if I could help it.

Chapter Six

Claire

'Is this seat taken?'

I froze. Every hair on my skin, every nerve ending in my body, stood on end.

What fresh hell was this?

I looked up. Hamish towered over the table, that charming smile in place, his blue eyes twinkling brighter than the Christmas lights draped around the windows of the room.

'Hamish,' I said, pasting on a wide grin. 'Fancy seeing you here.'

Subtext: there's nothing fancy about it, and how the hell did you know where I'd be?

'It's strange who you meet in hospital cafeterias, isn't it?' He cocked his head to the side, then held out his hand to the woman sitting across the table from me. 'Hi, I'm Hamish. Hamish Christianson.'

'Marie Foster,' the woman simpered, and it was all I could do not to roll my eyes. *Yes, he's good looking, but that doesn't mean you have to turn into a puddle of goo when he makes eyes at you.*

'I work with Claire,' Hamish continued, entirely focused on Marie. 'We spend a lot of time together.'

'I can imagine that would be quite pleasurable,' Marie said, and why was she still holding his hand?

'It certainly is.' Hamish finally—*finally*—drew his fingers from her grasp and gestured to the empty chair again. 'Would you mind if I joined you?'

'Of course not.' Marie pulled the corner of the seat from the table, allowing Hamish to just slide right in. *Jerk*. 'Any partner of Claire's is more than welcome.'

'He's not my partner,' I blurted out. Both heads snapped at me, as if I'd dragged them from their flirty reverie by the ends of their hair. 'We just work together. In the same office. Near each other.'

'My desk is right *over* from hers,' Hamish said, and I could practically see the wheels in Marie's head turning. *Over her*. What would Hamish look like, naked and hovering over her?

'Marie and I were just talking about a possible move to In The Lead,' I said, filling Hamish in. 'I was outlining some of the many benefits of working with our group.'

'She mentioned you have great personal service and attention to detail.' Marie directed that line at Hamish.

I was going to be sick. I was going to vomit the sandwich I'd wolfed down in the cab on the way over here all over the two of them.

'I assure you, we cover everything so our clients are completely satisfied,' Hamish played right into her hands. 'But tell me, isn't Health Direct already in bed with someone else?'

Warning bells sounded. Marie's eyes flashed with something—concern?—then she straightened, a frosty expression taking over her face.

'We can talk about that later,' I said, because that had been my plan. Win her over with our services, then bring her back to reality—you can't have any of this unless you let go of Murphy's and sign with us.

'I don't know. I think we should put all our cards on the table now.' Hamish rapped against the white tabletop with his knuckles. 'You're with another marketing company. We're better. I used to work at Murphy's, and I can say that unequivocally.'

'You're cocky,' Marie said, her eyes now clear of that lust haze.

'No. Just honest.' Hamish shrugged. 'But because I used to work there, it means I also know what sort of contract they'd have you tied up in. I don't know that you'd be in a position to just up and change firms at the drop of a hat.'

Marie seemed to consider his words, nodding slowly.

'But the firm she signed with isn't the firm she's getting,' I blurted. Why was he doing this? Surely Health Direct had a legal team who could sort out those sorts of details.

'It is, Claire. The number of staff may be different, but trust me, those contracts are watertight,' he said.

Marie's back stiffened. She directed her icy gaze on me. 'When you set this meeting up, you said you knew my situation.'

'I did, I—'

'So what you're saying is you organised this meeting to waste my time.'

'What? No!' My jaw dropped.

'It was lovely to meet you, Claire. Hamish.' Marie nodded to each of us as her chair screamed along the tiled floor.

I rushed to my feet, stepping into her path. 'Please, Marie, let's talk some more.'

'Let me look at the contract,' Hamish said, seemingly unfazed.

Marie's glare was withering. 'Why would I do that?'

'Because I know Murphy's. I'll help you get out of the contract without any legal ramifications,' he said, cool as you like.

'I'm sure Marie's legal team are more than capable of handling a little thing like contracts,' I said.

Marie sighed, shaking her head. 'They are, but we're a hospital. Our legal team is run off their feet, especially at this time of year.' She paused. 'I have to say, I did like a lot of your ideas, Claire. And I think your team is certainly appealing.'

Hamish dipped his head graciously at the compliment.

'Why don't I have a copy of the contract emailed over for you to have a look at? If you can find a way around it, we can take discussions from there.' Marie slipped her hand into her black pantsuit, pulling out a small white card. 'Here's my email and phone. Get in touch when you have a concrete package with a concrete solution.'

'Thank you.' Hamish got to his feet, pocketing the card and extending his hand once more. 'It was lovely to meet you.'

'Lovely to meet you too.' She smiled, then turned to me, shaking my hand before marching around groups of people towards the lift.

I turned my glare on Hamish, my arms folded across my chest. 'What the hell was that?'

'I was looking out for you before you made a promise you couldn't keep,' he hissed, a cold light in his eyes.

'I didn't promise anything.' I gathered up my folder, tucking it under my arm, and strode towards the lift.

'You didn't, but you could have put her in a really difficult position. She works for a hospital, Claire. What if she signed with us and put her company in breach?'

I made a face, jabbed the button for the elevator to go down. 'She's a grown-up. She has lawyers. She would have figured it out.'

'But at what cost?' Hamish shook his head. 'There are hundreds of different companies in the city. I don't know why you had to go after this one.'

The elevator dinged open and I strode inside, pressing the button for the parking lot below. 'And I don't know why, with hundreds of companies in the city, you had to go after the one client I wanted to get.'

'I didn't! I was just trying to help!' Hamish raised his voice as the doors closed, leaving us trapped in the small space.

'By following me! By stalking me through the city and trying to steal what's mine!' I protested, whirling on him.

'You think I followed you?' His eyes glittered. 'I'm not crazy!'

'No, you're not. You're a guy who thinks he can use his good looks to get away with whatever the hell he wants.' I stepped closer, poking a finger at his chest. 'I've met guys like you before, and let me tell you, you won't come out ahead. These underhanded tactics—'

'Underhanded?'

'—never work,' I snapped.

My gaze dropped to my hand, still against his chest. His hard, solid chest. I looked up, and his eyes were softer now, without the fire that had flamed there before. My mouth felt dry, and the words that had been just there on the tip of my tongue fell away to nothing.

'Don't tell me what to do.' His voice was low, predatory. His hand grabbed the back of my head, threaded through my hair.

'Then don't—'

His lips crashed into mine.

I froze. What was he—

His mouth, so hot, so warm, kissed me. He grasped me to him, pulled me closer as if I were his oxygen and he was desperate for air.

Want unfurled inside me, a hungry beast ready to be unleashed. My folder dropped to the floor. I ran my hands over his back, those broad shoulders—divine. His tongue traced across the seam of my lips, and they parted, granting him entrance. The hand at the small of my back jerked my body forward until I felt his need hard up against me, and I shivered. More. This. *Yes.*

'Claire,' he groaned as he kissed along my jaw, tangling his hand in my hair. A ferocious cocktail of pleasure and pain shot through me, and I moaned my want, my need, my—

'Mummy, what are dat man and wady doing?' a small voice asked.

Oh, no.

I pushed at Hamish's chest, then jumped to the other side of the elevator. We'd arrived at our destination—only neither of us had seemed to realise.

A woman and a little girl stood in the parking lot, open-mouthed.

'They were just getting out of the lift,' the woman snapped, her gaze pure murder.

'Sorry,' I murmured, running a hand over my clothes. I scrambled to pick up the scattered paper, my folder, and walked out of the lift, my head held as high as I could.

'Sorry.' Hamish's voice sounded behind me, but I didn't look as I marched towards my car. My cheeks flamed. How embarrassing.

What had I been thinking? I wasn't even attracted to the man and his smarmy ways, his cocky attitude, and his—

That tongue, lashing against my own. The way he'd felt against me, all hard, all man.

'Claire, wait.' He gripped my arm, and I turned around.

His eyes were still dark with desire, and I wanted to give in—wanted to grab him by the tie and drag him into my car. Wanted him to take me because need, raw and feral, raged through my body like I couldn't remember it doing before. For so long, I'd been focused on work, and I'd turned off these feelings—now it seemed they'd all come unstuck.

'I'll meet you back at the office,' Hamish said.

My stomach turned to lead.

Of course.

The office.

It was just a kiss. It wasn't the start of something more, and even if it had been, was that what I really wanted?

No.

Yes.

My heart went into freefall. 'Fine,' I said, holding my head high. 'Make sure you send me that contract when Marie emails it across to you, too.'

His eyes searched my face. I could see the 'sorry' in his expression. *He's going to apologise.*

No.

He couldn't do that.

That would make that one kiss, that one mistake, seem even worse than it already did.

'Claire, I—'

I held up my hand, shaking my head. 'Just don't.'

He scrubbed a hand over his stubbled jaw, looking into my eyes for the longest time. Then he turned on his heel and walked away.

I headed towards my car, keeping my head high, but I hated the sting that pricked at the backs of my eyes. I hated Hamish. I had ever since he came to work at In The Lead. One kiss had been a mistake—a moment of weakness after three months loaded with tension, with push and pull, with give and take.

One kiss didn't mean anything.

But as I unlocked my car, I couldn't quiet the other voice in my head.

One kiss meant the world.

Chapter Seven

Claire

Every time I closed my eyes, it was there.

That kiss.

That kiss I wanted so badly to forget and relive all at once.

I glanced around the living room. An empty bucket of Ben & Jerry's rested on the coffee table. My bra was draped over the arm of the living room chair, and an open packet of Doritos beckoned me from the table, the lights from my Christmas tree turning the foil green then red as they flashed. In the background, the television played reruns of *The Bachelor*.

My stomach churned, not just from emotional queasiness but from actual overindulgence, and I groaned. Ugh. Why did I do this to myself?

My phone rang from its spot on the coffee table, and I groaned again. Of all the times ...

'Chad. Hi,' I said, trying to inject a sense of normalcy into my tone.

'Are you okay?' His voice was full of concern.

'I'm fine.'

'Are you sure?' he asked.

'Positive.'

'How many tubs of ice cream before you took off your bra?' he asked, and damn it. That was the downside to dating someone for three years—they knew you well, even when you didn't want them to.

'Just one. But it was diet.' *Lies.*

'I'm sure it was.' Chad chuckled knowingly. 'It's nearly Christmas, babe. You love this time of year too much to be spending your days surrounded by junk food and bad reality TV.'

'It's …' I shook my head, clearing the junk-food-induced haze. This was my ex—a man who'd betrayed me. He didn't get to lecture me on what I should and shouldn't be doing in any aspect of my life. 'Chad, if you'd just pay me some of what you owed me, maybe I'd never have had to end up in a position like this.'

'I'm sorry, Claire. Really, I am. It's why I'm calling.' He paused, as if leading to some big news. 'I have a new job.'

'Really? That's great,' I said. 'So you can start repayments soon?'

'Yes. Next month I'll be golden, I swear it.' The excitement in his voice was contagious. 'I'll pay double from then until the end of the loan, then I'll keep up the repayments until you're square. Not only that, but I'll send you some money next week, just before Christmas. Like a bonus, to say thanks again for helping me out this past year.'

'That would be …' *Great. Amazing. A dream come true.* 'Just see how you go, Chad,' I finished with instead.

'I won't let you down, Claire. Not this time. This time, things are different,' he said, energy in his voice. In the background, a car honked. 'Shoot, I gotta go. Just wanted to call and tell you the good news.'

'Thank you.'

'And whatever happens, just remember that you can handle it, okay?' he asked, and I forced a smile.

'Okay,' I said.

We ended the call, and I placed the phone back on the table, my heart somehow heavier than it was before.

This wasn't the first time I'd received a call like that.

It was the first time I didn't believe his promises though. He'd let me down too many times before.

Still, he was right about one thing.

I could handle it.

I'd been handling things before, and I could do it again. I just needed to focus on work. To land Health Direct. To get this promotion.

And to forget all about my sexy co-worker.

That item was top of my list.

Chapter Eight

Hamish

> Hamish: *Hey Claire. Sorry to bother you on the weekend, but I just wanted to let you know that Health Direct sent the contract through. I'll look it over tonight.*
>
> Claire: *Thanks for letting me know. Give me a call if there's anything you need.*

I stared at the blinking cursor on my screen. Anything I needed.

I could think of one thing I needed right now, but it had little to do with contracts and paperwork, and everything to do with the sexy co-worker I hadn't been able to get off my mind all week.

Her hot body. Those delicious curves pressed up against me …

I closed my eyes, savoured the memory for what had to be the hundredth time since it happened. That kiss had been explosive. Everything I could have wanted.

But ever since it happened, Claire had been even more closed off than usual.

Back at work, I'd tried to bring up the subject of the kiss more than once and each time, she'd shut me down, quickly. She'd made it abundantly clear—that kiss was something she didn't want to speak, think, or hear about, ever again.

Or maybe it was me. Maybe I'd done something to piss her off. Maybe she'd wanted to take things further once we got into the parking lot, finish what we'd started in the back of her car.

I stifled a laugh. There was wishful thinking if ever I'd heard it. A woman like her was too good for a one-and-done in a car. A woman like her would be used to champagne and roses, lovemaking on thousand-thread-count sheets.

I glanced across at my own bed. When was the last time I washed those?

I lifted up one corner of the linen, took a sniff.

Too long.

Way too long.

Still, as I balled the material up and stuffed it in the machine, Claire lingered in my mind.

I sank onto the sofa, pulling my phone from my pocket once more, and typed out another message.

Hamish: *The only thing I need is …*

I stopped before I hit send. What I needed was her body, pressed against mine. My hands under that tight shirt. Her coming undone around me as I kissed along the creamy skin of her neck.

Hamish: *The only thing I need is your gratitude when I help land you the biggest client our firm has ever seen.*

Better. Not entirely true, but better.

Claire: *You may have helped, but you also hindered. It was you who brought this whole contract thing up in the first place.*

Hamish: *I just didn't want to see you in trouble. I was trying to be nice.*
Claire: *What is it with you and nice? Always so nice.*

I sighed, walked to the fridge, and grabbed a beer. What was I supposed to say to that?

I spent the next three hours studying the Murphy's contract. As I'd suspected, it was tight—watertight—and I didn't see how Health Direct could get out of it. Claire was going to be disappointed. She couldn't sign them—not now. Not until the Murphy's contract finished in six months' time.

By then it will be too late.

Too late for the promotion, and likely too late for Claire.

I forced a smile. That should have been good news for me. I needed that job more than she did. It had to be mine.

I grabbed some clean sheets from the hamper, laid them out on the bed. With Actron under my belt, Claire would find it hard to top my sales for the month. The only way she could beat me was if Health Direct came on board, and as per usual, it looked like Murphy's had locked their client down behind an impenetrable wall. Health Direct wouldn't be able to get out of it unless Murphy's made some kind of mistake.

But what if they already have?

I flicked the top sheet over the mattress. It didn't matter. It didn't matter if they already had, because I wasn't going to pursue that—not for Claire. Not when it put something I wanted, something I needed, in so much jeopardy.

What if a mistake has been made—a breach of contract—and the client just hadn't realised?

I grabbed my phone, tapped out a message. Darcy and I had once been pretty close—and better yet, the beautiful executive assistant for Mr Murphy himself owed me a favour.

Hamish: *Hey, Darc. I'm doing some investigating into Health Direct. Remember that favour you owe me?*

Seconds later, the reply came in.

Darcy: *You ask someone to feed your cats while you go on holidays once, and they laud it over you for the rest of your life.*
Hamish: *A pretty pussy deserves a pretty favour.*
Darcy: *Uh-uh. No. Your flirting is no good here.*
Hamish: *That wasn't flirting. If I was flirting with you, you'd know it.*
Darcy: *If you were flirting with me, I wouldn't just look into Health Direct for you, I'd book you an appointment, because you'd obviously need your head read.*
Darcy: *I'll log onto the online system and look into Health Direct for you. But please, never sleaze near me again. You make me feel so dirty.*
Hamish: *Thanks, Darcy. You're the best. And don't worry about the dirty thing—I'm sure Veronica will help wash you clean again.*

I sank back into the couch. Hopefully, she'd be able to dig up something good.

I wanted to help Claire—wanted her to land this account.

But I need that promotion.

Not someone else.

Not Claire.

I tried to push down that voice in the back of my head, but it was there.

So were the bills on the end of the coffee table. I lifted one up, my eyes fixed on the five figures down the bottom of the page. A red *overdue* stamp was printed over the top. Damn it. This one couldn't wait much longer.

Flickers of red teased me from farther down the pile. Neither could any of them. It might have been Christmas, but debt collectors didn't believe in the season for giving. There was no give—it was all take, take, take.

I sipped at the beer, but it tasted too bitter, too sour in my mouth. What was I doing? Why was I giving a perfectly good lead to a woman, just because she'd somehow become stuck in my head?

'Damn it,' I whispered, pinching at the bridge of my nose.

Bed. I'd go to bed and deal with this—sort out some kind of game plan for what would happen if I didn't get this job—in the morning.

As I placed the most pressing bill back on the pile, the letters shifted. Behind them, the silver corners of the photo frame caught the overhead light.

Don't do it. You don't need to do this.

With one shaking hand, I pulled the photo closer.

Two smiling faces looked up at me from the frame, identical grins that stretched wide across sun-loved faces. Slowly, I traced one finger over my brother's nose, his blue eyes, the freckles that dotted his cheeks—the only difference between us.

My chest constricted, that familiar ball of pain always lurking under the surface. I pressed my eyes closed tight for a moment. Christmas.

Lights draped around trees.

Presents in brightly coloured paper.

Carols in the park, in buildings, on the television.

Family.

It was always so much harder at Christmas.

I dropped the photo on the couch. Fuck that. Fuck Christmas, and fuck the world.

As I made my way to the bedroom, my phone beeped.

Darcy: *Found something interesting. Am sending you an email now. Consider all pussy-related favours coming to a close.*

A small smile flickered on my lips.

Hamish: *Thanks, Darcy. You're the best.*

This was what I needed. And maybe I could talk to Claire about going halves in the commission. If Darcy was as good as her word, this client would only be signing with us because of something I'd brought to the table. Fair was fair, after all.

But as I brushed my teeth, splashed water over my face, and stared at those tired, unsmiling eyes in the mirror, I couldn't stop the doubt racing through my mind.

Would I really ask that?

Would I really do it?

I walked into the bedroom, slipped off my clothes, and tossed them in the hamper. I had to. I had to do it, or everything would fall apart. I needed the money, goddamn it. This was no time for playing nice. You didn't leave Murphy's to come to In The Lead and fail.

Health Direct was mine. There were no two ways about it.

Yet as my head hit the pillow, my fingers typed the message anyway.

Hamish: *Got some news about Health Direct. Want to meet tomorrow morning for coffee to discuss?*

Claire: *That's fantastic! Maybe you really are a nice guy after all.*

I stared at those words. You really are a nice guy.

If only she knew just how how nice.

Chapter Nine

Claire

What did you wear to a coffee meeting on a Sunday with a man you hated but had accidentally kissed in a moment of weakness, who you now owed a favour to?

I glanced down at the sky-blue wrap dress, the frill on the skirt dancing in the summer breeze.

Apparently, you dressed as if you were going on a date.

Why did I choose this? I should have worn a shirt, letting him know I meant business. And a jacket. And maybe a chastity belt.

But what if it is a date?

I pursed my lips. I hated that thought.

But it was there. And I couldn't stop thinking about just what coffee on a Sunday was really supposed to mean.

I glanced at the busy cafe, searching for a familiar face in the crowd. White tables were strewn across the sidewalk, crowded with people sipping their lattes and soaking up the gorgeous morning sun. Waiters bustled from group to group balancing plates and menus and mugs. *It's probably busy because everyone wants to get their caffeine fix before Christmas shopping.*

Christmas shopping—Secret Santa.

I winced. Damn it. That would be exchanged this week, Christmas Eve, the day after the office party. I had to think of a present for Hamish, and soon.

'Are you okay?'

Hamish. 'Hi.' I placed one hand over my eyes to shield them against the sun and looked up at him.

He'd got the memo about how to dress for coffee with a colleague. Dark blue jeans were moulded to his body, hinting at the shapely thighs that lay underneath. A white T-shirt stretched across his chest, those broad shoulders, and he had a slim black folder tucked under his arm. He looked fresh. Like summer. Like the perfect mix of casual and business, wrapped in one delicious package.

'Are you okay?' he asked again, concern in his blue eyes.

Damn it. 'Fine,' I said, and did that sound mean? Aggressive? I softened my tone. 'I mean, I'm okay. Doing … whatever.' I waved my hand as if it could say the words I couldn't. Words like *You look good enough to eat* and *What was that kiss, anyway?* and *Is this a meeting or a date?*

Ever since the kiss, Hamish had tried to bring it up with me in the office, but I'd shut him down each time. He'd kissed me, then walked away. Not only that, but getting involved with a colleague was a bad idea.

Case in point—Chad.

Hamish gestured towards the cafe. 'Let's get you some caffeine and talk, then you can be on your way.'

Yes. A meeting.

It was most definitely a meeting.

I followed him into the sea of crowded tables. Miraculously, a couple stood just as he reached the middle of the mass, as if everything really was that easy for him. Tables opened up. Clients handed over their business.

Colleagues threw themselves at him in elevators.

'Breakfast, or just some coffee?' the waitress asked, wiping down the table as we sat.

'Just coffee—'

'Breakfast,' Hamish said at the same time.

Heat flushed my cheeks.

'How about I grab you some menus and then you can decide,' the waitress said, rushing off and returning a few seconds later with two cardboard printouts. She took our drink orders then disappeared again as she was called over to another table, more hungry and thirsty patrons desperate for her attention.

'You can have breakfast.' I shoved the menu towards Hamish. 'I just thought—'

'It's fine.' He gave an easy smile. 'You want to get down to business. I get it.'

I don't know what I want. 'Sure,' I replied, nodding to the folder still tucked under his arm. 'So what'd the contract say?'

Hamish placed the folder on the table. 'As far as I can see, the client can't get out of it unless Murphy's make a mistake.'

My smile fell. 'That's bad news.'

A twinkle lit his eyes. 'But I reached out to a contact I still have there—and it turns out, they have.'

Oh my God. They'd made a mistake?

Could I be about to land the biggest client of my career?

'That's amazing!' I blurted. 'Seriously, Hamish. That's just—wow. And you're sure?'

He nodded, his grin reflecting my own. 'Absolutely. I've got the details for you here, but if you pass this back on to Marie, she should be able to action a contract cancellation effective immediately, enabling you to sign this client before the Christmas deadline.'

I shook my head, amazed. He did this—he did this for me. So I could get a key client. And at a time when so much was on the line. 'Thank you,' I said. 'I just—wow. I can't believe you did all this when you didn't even have to. When you won't even get anything out of it. It's for me. I just—thank you!'

Something flickered in his eyes. His smile faltered. He opened his mouth as if to speak. Was everything okay?

'Any breakfast?' the waitress asked. She placed our drinks down on the table and the delicious chocolatey scent of coffee hit me.

'Yes,' I said, suddenly hungry for more time with this man. Why shouldn't we have breakfast? He'd just done me a favour that would potentially change the course of my career, and would certainly change my imminent financial problems—the least I could do was share a piece of toast with him.

I quickly scanned the menu, ordering the Bircher muesli, and Hamish asked for a BLT. The waitress disappeared, and we were alone again, in the midst of hundreds of others.

I sipped at my coffee, studying the man opposite me.

When he first came to In The Lead, I'd decided we couldn't be friends. He was sexy, ambitious, and flirty—too flirty. Every word that came out of his mouth had sounded good, but I'd seen him for what he was: looking to come out on top. Putting himself first.

He was exactly like Chad.

And I wasn't going to make that mistake again.

I'd ignored his attempts to charm me, brushing him off as just another blow-in trying to climb the corporate ladder.

But what if he was more?

What if he wasn't just about getting himself ahead—but about wanting me to get ahead too? He'd shared Actron with me, after all. What if he was nothing like my ex, who'd always put himself first?

'What are you thinking?' Hamish asked, that easy smile back in place.

'Just ... about you.' I shook my head. 'You're not who I thought you were.'

'I take it that's a good thing,' he said, leaning forward.

'It's a very good thing.' I took another sip of my coffee. A woman carrying too many bags of shopping bustled past, knocking into my shoulder.

'Sorry, love.' She winced, pulling the unruly bag back in line.

'It's fine.' I waved her away. 'It's Christmas.'

She nodded her thanks and kept moving.

'You really like Christmas, huh?' Hamish asked when we were alone again.

'I do. I love it so much—have ever since I was a kid.' I beamed. 'It just reminds me of spending time with my family, and eating too much, and long, lazy afternoons spent lying on the beach ...'

'Eating prawns and then somehow finding room to fit in a roast dinner?' Hamish smiled.

'Yes! And pavlova and pudding for dessert.' The hot and cold, the past and the present—the perfect mishmash of cultures in a meal that somehow fit the day and our country so well.

He gave me a cheeky look, a dimple popping in his cheek. 'Do you have any weird family Christmas traditions?'

'Ha! What do you mean?'

'Some people have them. Zeb, at work?'

'Yeah?' I asked.

'He goes skinny-dipping with his cousins every Christmas Eve.'

My jaw dropped. 'You're kidding. But he seems so straitlaced.'

'I know.' Hamish nodded. 'It's always the quiet ones you have to watch.' He gave me a look that was laced with something more, something that made my skin buzz. Something that said he was watching me.

I leaned closer. 'Well, I don't know if it's really weird, but when I was a kid, Mum used to buy me a new decoration for my tree every year.'

'Like a bauble?'

'Yes, but an extravagant one. She'd find something unique, something special, and she'd add it to my gift. Her way of trying to ensure each Christmas was more beautiful than the last.' I smiled, thinking of the gold Christmas angel she'd given me last year, the quilted turtle dove the year before that.

'That's a really nice idea,' Hamish said, thoughtful.

'Does your family do anything like that?'

'Not really.' He paused, then his face split into a wide grin. 'Well, actually, there is this one thing.'

'What's that?'

'My brother and I used to play Christmas pranks on each other. We'd find the worst-taste gifts we could and put them under the tree.'

I laughed. 'That sounds horrible!'

He shrugged. 'It was never anything mean. Think ugly Christmas sweaters—lumps of coal—that kind of stuff.'

'Sounds … kind of fun.' I made a face. 'I think I prefer my mum's tradition, though.'

'I think I do too.' He laughed, and the full, rich sound made me want to laugh along with him. 'Do your parents live around here?'

'No.' I shook my head. 'Every Christmas Eve, I fly up to Cairns and spend the holiday there.'

'That would be hot,' Hamish said, then quickly held up his hands and added, 'The weather, I mean. In Queensland. I'm not trying to be sleazy.'

I laughed. 'It is.' And what if I wanted him to flirt a little now? What if things had changed?

We'd kissed. He'd run away.

But maybe that wasn't because he realised he'd made a mistake. Maybe he was worried I thought he'd pushed things too far.

I took a deep breath. 'Maybe I was too harsh on you that day back in the office, when I said you were a sleaze. You're not a sleaze. You're—you're not that bad.'

'Not that bad?' Hamish widened his eyes. 'Don't go too far with the compliment. I might get the wrong idea.'

'Maybe you're more than not that bad.' I looked down at the caramel-coloured drink in front of me, biting my lip before meeting the heat of his eyes again. 'Maybe you're actually really … nice.'

'I knew it.' He leaned back in his chair, a wide grin on his face. 'I was sure I could win you over with my charm and good looks.'

I rolled my eyes, laughing. 'Well, you've done some really nice things for me these last few weeks—first Actron, now Health Direct. I appreciate it, Hamish. A lot.'

'I haven't done much at all.' His gaze darkened. 'And the truth is, you're good at what you do. With or without me, you'd have found a way to land those clients. You're a damn talented woman, Claire.'

Heat buzzed through my veins. Something about the way he said those words …

I wanted him. I wanted to feel that scorching-hot kiss on my mouth again. I wanted to pull at the edge of that T-shirt and run my hands over the firm skin underneath, explore the lines of his body with my hands.

'One Bircher, and one BLT.' The waitress slid the plates on the table, unceremoniously interrupting my fantasy. 'Enjoy.'

Hamish.

I was enjoying him—enjoying everything about this unexpected date.

And when we finished our meal, the conversation every bit as delicious as the food, I knew without a doubt.

I had feelings for Hamish Christianson.

Work on Monday couldn't come soon enough.

Chapter Ten

Hamish

Claire.

Her smile, so wide, open and free.

Her laugh, infectious and completely unstoppable.

Her body, so tempting, all luscious curves and invitation to touch.

I glanced up over the top of my computer screen at her. Once, I'd have done that and she'd have shot me a look, one that said she hoped I rotted in hell.

She met my eyes.

This look didn't say *leave me alone.*

This look said *desire.*

I opened my email screen to a new message.

To: Claire.Roberts@inthelead.com
From: Hamish.Christianson@inthelead.com
Subject: Christmas party
Dear Claire,
Will you be attending the Christmas party tonight?

From Hamish

To: Hamish.Christianson@inthelead.com
From: Claire.Roberts@inthelead.com
Subject: I'll be there with bells on
Dear Hamish,
Of course, I will. I love Christmas, and it is a party celebrating the event's very nature, right?
From Claire

To: Claire.Roberts@inthelead.com
From: Hamish.Christianson@inthelead.com
Subject: What else will you be wearing?
Dear Claire,
You do love Christmas. I have to admit, you're bringing me around to the event, too. It's been a while since I found myself looking at ugly Christmas sweaters, but you brought that joy back to me. Thank you.
From Hamish

To: Hamish.Christianson@inthelead.com
From: Claire.Roberts@inthelead.com
Subject: Why do you want to know?
Hamish,
I must apologise to your poor brother in advance then. When he sees the torture you no doubt now plan to unleash on him, he's going to wish I never reminded you of your twisted tradition.
Claire

To: Claire.Roberts@inthelead.com
From: Hamish.Christianson@inthelead.com

Subject: Because it's my dream to unwrap you. And I want to know what I should imagine tearing from your body, Claire. You won't have to apologise to my brother.

The cursor blinked, waiting for me to finish the email. Finish what I'd started.

Was I ready to tell her? Could I go there?

I glanced up at those green eyes again. They were fixed on the screen, the picture of concentration.

I ran one hand through my hair, sighed. It had been so long since I'd done this—flirted, hoped, wished for something more—and I'd forgotten that it would come to this point. The point where it became more than just thoughts of hot kisses. The point where it became more than laughter over brunch. The point where it became *more*.

I glanced at the date. *A little more than a year …*

Nausea churned my guts. Pain, raw and real, stabbed me in the chest, a physical ache just as deep and twisted as the emotional one. *Damn it.*

'Claire? Hamish?'

I looked up. Frank waltzed over, dwarfing a piece of paper in his giant hands.

I minimised the email screen. There was no point dwelling on the past. I had to move forward—take action. Just like I'd done ever since the accident, and just like I'd keep on doing. I focused on my boss, my eyes trained on his dark eyes. On now.

'I just got the signed Actron contract. Well done, you two! Commission has been split, and it's a neck-and-neck race for who'll come out on top this month.' He slapped the piece of paper against the corner of my desk. 'Maybe you'll let Claire come first, hey?'

I have every intention of it. When I explore her body with my mouth, trace those curves with my fingers, she will be the first to come, there's no doubt about that.

I give him what I hope is my best 'good ol' boy' smile. 'She's a very deserving lady.'

'That she is, that she is.' Frank clapped me on the back. I glanced at Claire. Her cheeks were the colour of candy canes, all red and white together. I stifled a smile. So she hadn't missed my innuendo. 'How are things coming along with Health Direct?'

'Good,' Claire said, her voice pure professionalism. 'We have sent them the contract and outlined the schedule Murphy's failed to meet. It's just a matter of time before they sign on with us.'

It was little more than a technicality—just a glitch in their social media programming, I had no doubt. But they'd promised daily posts on social media, and on the day of the layoffs, one had been missing. It was enough to get them out of the contract, and enough to get us in with the client who could truly make or break us.

I just had to hope Claire would share that with me, as I had with her.

'I see. Well, keep up the good work, you two, and I hope you manage to relax a little and enjoy the Christmas party tonight. It's great to see what you can achieve as a team.'

He walked away, humming under his breath.

His words lingered. *As a team.*

Memories flashed in my mind. The passion in her voice as she gave her presentation.

The laughter on her lips as she teased me about my Christmas tradition.

The fire in her eyes as she moved close to kiss me.

This was more than just flirting. More than just an accidental kiss after months of heated tension.

It was time to see what we could achieve as a team.

To: Claire.Roberts@inthelead.com
From: Hamish.Christianson@inthelead.com
Subject: Confession
You won't have to apologise to my brother.
He's dead.

Chapter Eleven

Claire

You won't have to apologise to my brother.
   He's dead.
   I read the words over and over. A chill ran through my body, just as it had back in the office, and I rubbed one hand against my upper arm to ward off the department store's air-conditioning.
   Hamish's brother had died.
   I couldn't begin to imagine how hard that must have been.
   When he told me, our flirty email exchange had stopped. I didn't know what to say—did he want me to ask for more information? Did he want to talk about it?
   In the end, I did the only thing that felt right. I walked to his desk and placed my hand over his, hoping he could read all the words I wanted to speak in my eyes. All the *I'm sorry*. All the *no one should have to go through this*.
   I bit down on my lower lip, studying the gift items in the department store. Secret Santa exchange was tomorrow, and I finally knew what to get him. I just hoped he knew that I meant it as something ... nice. Something that would make him smile.

As I walked the gift up to the counter, my phone buzzed in my purse and I pulled it out. Vi.

'Hey hon,' I greeted her, twisting to squeeze past a giant bauble display.

'Hi. Where are you?'

'Getting my Secret Santa present all wrapped up,' I said, standing at the end of a five-deep line. Ah, the Christmas rush. Even waiting didn't make me mad. 'You?'

'I'm just heading for a blow-wave. Wanted to see if you were interested in getting your hair fixed before the party tonight.'

The party.

The work Christmas party—something I put in a cursory appearance at, then left well before the clock struck twelve. It was possibly the only part of this time of year I didn't love.

But not tonight.

Anticipation hummed in my veins. For the first time in a long time, I was actually looking forward to the Christmas party.

Tonight, Hamish would be there.

And I couldn't wait to talk to him again.

'Claire? Your hair?' Vi pressed.

'Shoot, sorry. I'm going to leave it—thanks anyway,' I said, stepping forward as the line moved. 'By the time I get home, I won't have long to get ready.'

And I can't afford it.

I didn't want to say it aloud in case she worried, but my bank account was looking scarily low. Thank God Mum and Dad had paid for my flights back home for Christmas. I needed Chad to come through with that money, and fast.

'No worries,' Vi said, her voice light. 'Besides, I guess what's the point in getting your hair done when Hamish is just going to mess it all up when the party ends?'

Heat flushed over my chest. 'Vi!'

'What?'

'Hamish and I—it's not like—We don't—' How did she even know?

'Claire, it's written all over your face every time you two make eye contact. There's so much sexual tension between the two of you, the rest of us go home and have cold showers.'

Oh, God. Was it that transparent?

'Besides, he's made it pretty clear from day one that he's been interested in you. It hardly comes as a surprise,' she continued, hammering those final nails into the coffin of my embarrassment one at a time.

'So everybody knows.' I tried to keep the waver out of my voice. 'Do you think Frank does?'

'Frank?' Vi snorted. In the background, I heard the beeping of a pedestrian signal at a traffic light. 'No. God no. He's clueless at the best of times.'

'Good.' Relief rushed through me. What if this affected my chance at the promotion? What if everyone found out, and the good reputation I'd worked so hard to gain was ruined?

Chad had left not just me, but the company, when he'd walked out of my life. I'd been the one who had to walk into a room just as the whispers stopped. I'd been the one who'd been overlooked as other staff members were promoted or formed teams to acquire new clients.

It had taken me a long time to establish my credibility after my ex left In The Lead in the lurch, and I wasn't about to let that slide now.

Not even for a man who just opened up and let you in?

I bit my lip. Damn it. No. In the list of priorities, work came first. It had to.

'Okay, I'm almost there. I gotta go. See you tonight, okay?' Vi asked.

I nodded, even though she couldn't see me, and hung up the phone just as I reached the front counter.

The woman behind the desk eyed the item as if it might poison her, but smiled sweetly at me as she folded it in two. 'Would you like it gift-wrapped?'

'Please.'

Christmas. Presents. Giving.

They were three of my favourite things.

And yet somehow, the idea of this perfect imperfect gift didn't fill me with the joy it had only a few moments before.

I walked into the crowded bar just off Oxford Street, and followed the signs with In The Lead written on them to a room off at the back. Black leather chairs lined the walls, with some of the guys from accounting lounged out in the group closest to me. Clusters of people stood, drinks in hand, talking around bar tables. Overhead, the lighting was low, dark shadows filling empty spaces in the corners.

I stopped at the entrance, running a hand over the bottom of my dress. No one so much as glanced in my direction, all too busy focused on their own conversations, their drinks, each other. *This is so not my scene.*

'You look good enough to eat.'

The voice was low and hummed against my ear. Vibrations thrilled through my body.

Hamish stepped around in front of me, and he might have worn a shirt and tie to work every day, but tonight, in jeans that hung low on his hips, and a blue shirt that looked like heaven on his golden-brown skin—my mouth watered. I wanted him. Wanted him so much my skin burned.

'You look ...' His gaze trailed slowly up my body, starting at my red heels, lingering over my legs, my hips, then up to where the lace of my dress met my chest before resting on my face. *He's devouring me with his eyes.* 'You look incredible.'

'Thank you.' I smiled. 'Should we get a drink?'

'Lead the way.' He gestured to the group in front of us, and I stepped out, taking a glass of champagne from a waiter and heading to one of the deserted leather lounges in the back corner.

Here, away from the main group of people, it felt quieter, more intimate somehow. I crossed my legs under the table and placed my drink down as Hamish slid in beside me.

'So this is what the In The Lead Christmas party looks like, huh?' he asked, scanning the room.

'Pretty much. The guys from accounting spend the night comparing stats from the latest NBA games. The women in marketing fail to add up that only eating lettuce for lunch means they shouldn't drink as many wines as they plan to.' I nodded towards a group of five ladies standing around a bar table. One already had her heels off. Another swayed slowly to the upbeat music that blasted through the speakers. 'And Frank will wait until everyone's had a few, then give some speech about how he's so proud of us and thinks this has been the company's best year yet, and how excited he is about things to come in the times ahead.'

'Wow.' Hamish nodded, taking it all in. 'So Christmas parties here are pretty much like Christmas parties everywhere.'

'I guess so.' I took a sip of champagne. The bubbles danced in my mouth. I sipped again.

'What about kisses?' Hamish asked.

I stiffened. My head whipped to face him instead of the crowd in front of us. 'What about them?'

'Do any of the staff members do things they shouldn't at Christmas parties?' A naughty twinkle lit his eye.

'Things like kiss,' I said slowly. Memories from the parking lot flashed in my mind. *That kiss.*

'Things like kiss.' He nodded. His hand slid to the top of my leg. Heat scorched a path from it all the way up my thigh.

'I guess ... I guess sometimes they do,' I said, then took a forced breath. *Keep it together, Claire. Just because a guy touched you, even if he is insanely good looking, even if he is the first man to touch your bare skin in more than a year ... oh, Lord.*

His hand inched up, his fingers skimming the hem of my dress. 'This material is nice,' he husked.

A shiver ran through my body. 'Hamish.' *Don't stop.* 'We can't—people might see.'

'See what?' he asked innocently. 'The table is blocking their view, and even if it wasn't, all they'd see was a man unable to keep his hands off an incredibly beautiful woman.'

'No.' I chanced a quick look out at the party again. No one seemed to so much as glance in our direction. 'They'd see two people who worked together behaving in a manner that was extremely inappropriate.'

'You think this is inappropriate?' His eyes widened in innocence. His hand shifted under my dress, up my thigh. Fingers brushed over my panties. Lust shot through me like lightning. 'So this would be considered ...'

Oh, God. *Hot. Everything. Turning me on.* 'Highly inappropriate,' I said. *Keep cool, Claire.*

'Oh yeah?' he asked, his lips against my ear. His fingers danced over the lace of my panties again. 'Because it seems to me like you want this. You want this very …' He slid aside the edge of my underwear. 'Very …' A whimper escaped my lips. 'Much.'

I took a deep breath, and placed my hand on his upper arm. 'Hamish, no.'

As soon as I said the word, he withdrew, his face all serious. *He respects that.*

'I'm sorry,' he said, his expression sincere. 'If you don't want this, I—'

I placed my hand on his arm. 'I want this.'

That easy smile spread across his face again. 'Thank Christ.' He took a sip of his beer, his head tilted to the side. 'So you're just not into risky sex?'

I haven't had sex in a year! I'm into any sex, I wanted to scream. 'I—I can't do sex here. Or kissing here. What people think of me is important. This job is important,' I said, licking my lips. 'And while I don't mind the idea of—'

'Don't mind?' He raised one eyebrow with a cheeky grin.

'Okay, I really like the idea of us,' I admitted with a laugh. 'But be that as it may, these are my colleagues. It took a long time for me to build respect with them, and I don't want them to see me as just some cheap floozy who'll let a guy take her in the back of the bar.'

'You'd let me take—'

'Focus, Hamish.' I rolled my eyes, his teasing smile lighting his face once more.

'Sorry. I get it. I really do.' He rested his hands on the table—both hands—and signalled for another round of drinks. 'But I don't understand why you think you have something to prove. Everyone here thinks you're amazing.'

'They do now.' I shrugged.

'What's on your mind?' he asked, finishing his beer and handing it to the waiter as he brought him a new one.

'I …' I looked into those deep blue eyes, so focused on me. There was no laughter there now, no teasing, no flirting. Just sincerity. Just kindness. 'My ex used to work for In The Lead. One day, he packed up and left—no notice, no warning, no …' I took a deep breath. 'No money. He took all our savings and fled town.'

'What?' Hamish's jaw hardened.

'It's fine.' I held my hands out to placate him. 'I mean, I'm fine. I'm over him now. But at work, people … I don't think they blamed me, exactly, but all the loose ends he hadn't tied up, combined with a few deals that looked a little shady …' I shrugged. 'I'm just lucky Frank took my word for it. He believed that I genuinely knew nothing about what had happened.'

'Your ex is a dickhead.' Hamish's knuckles whitened as he lifted the glass to his mouth.

'He made some stupid choices. But that's why this promotion is so important to me. I want to stop being poor little Claire, the woman her ex left high and dry, and start being … someone to be respected. Claire, who's good at what she does. Claire, someone to beat in the monthly sales meeting. Claire, who's better than all that. Not Claire, the woman stupid enough to fall for a man with a gambling problem.' I glanced nervously across at Hamish. Did he think that was weird?

But all I saw was understanding in those crystal blue eyes. All I saw was kindness in the set of his jaw.

'Attention, everyone!' Vi called from the centre of the room, tapping her champagne glass with one of the girls from marketing's heel. 'Our commander-in-chief would like to say a few words.'

Bodies turned towards her. Hamish stood, offering me his hand, and I took it as he led me out of the booth and closer to the centre of the room. We lingered at the very back of the group, Frank's mistletoe-themed tie just visible in between heads and shoulders of other In The Lead staff members.

'Thank you for coming here tonight. You've all worked very hard this year—don't think it doesn't go appreciated, because it does,' he said, nodding, his eyes landing on each and every employee in the semi-dark space. 'And I can't wait to announce the big promotion tomorrow, Christmas Eve—after our Secret Santa, of course.'

Oh. I let out a breath. Looked like we'd have to wait even longer to find out who'd be getting the promotion.

'But it wouldn't be a Christmas party without a recap of the year, so let's discuss some of the highlights.'

A small collective groan filtered through the group.

'Let's start with January. What a month that was …'

Hamish's fingers brushed my leg. Even through the material, lust danced under my skin. How did he have that effect on me?

As Frank started in on February and the campaign that saw Valentine's Day reel in some boutique romantic clients, Hamish leaned closer and whispered in my ear, 'You don't do sex at office Christmas parties, right?'

'Right,' I whispered back.

'But how do you feel about sex outside of office Christmas parties?'

I looked up at him. 'Like … when?'

'February twenty-six was a particularly good day for us. That's when I hired Amanda, and Mandy, your strict rule of thumb has really helped eliminate some problems around the office, like smoking too close to the building, and parking in illegal spots. Well done,' Frank prattled on.

Hamish raised his eyebrows and looked down at me. 'Like now.'

I shouldn't.

Relationships with people at work never ended well—my own story was proof of that.

But as I looked up at that incredible face, only one word left my lips.

'Yes.'

Chapter Twelve

Hamish

'Yes,' she breathed as I pressed her up against the wall in the deserted alley outside the club. My thigh wedged hers apart, our bodies together. I pinned her hands above her head and kissed down her neck, my lips trailing a scorching path against her soft, creamy skin.

'You're so fucking hot,' I groaned, my face moving down to her breasts. Desire owned me—consumed me. I had to have her. *Now*.

I ran my hand over lacy material. Her nipple jutted out, crying for my touch. I consumed it. My mouth covered it through her dress, my tongue flicking, licking, making love to that bud, and she shuddered under my touch, her hands threaded through my hair and pulled me closer still.

'Hamish,' she breathed. Her hips thrust towards me, and I wanted to make her mine. Wanted to have her right here, and right now.

No.

I tried to push the voice away, but it was there, in the back of my mind.

I couldn't.

Claire deserved a lot of things, but cheap sex in the alley outside her work Christmas party was not one of them.

Using superhuman strength, I fixed her dress in place, stepped back. Her eyes met mine, the unspoken question lingering in the air between us.

'Come back to my place.' I shook my head. 'I'm about a fifteen-minute drive away, and—'

She gripped my hand. 'I'm closer.'

She marched to the street, pulling me along, and this was a different side of Claire—one I wasn't used to. I'd only ever seen her display this kind of authoritative passion in the boardroom, and seeing it now, her taking charge—it was a huge turn-on. I couldn't wait to see her taking charge in the bedroom.

She flagged down a cab and we slid into the back seat. She gave the address to the driver and the vehicle wound its way downtown.

We didn't speak—I couldn't. If I opened my mouth, the temptation to use it to kiss her, to take her right then and there in the back of the car would be too strong. Instead, my eyes focused on the skyscrapers flashing past, the other vehicles moving along the city streets.

We might not have whispered dirty promises of desire, but our hands stayed linked together tight, our grip never faltering. Our fingers made promises our bodies would later keep.

When we reached her building, I threw a note at the driver and we walked inside. She waved to her doorman, and he nodded in greeting.

The elevator took too long. It was the slowest damn thing in the entire world, but when it finally arrived and we walked inside, I stepped closer to her, caging her into one corner of the lift.

'Now, I finally have you all to my—'

'Hold the lift, please!' a voice called from the foyer.

I took a deep breath. Goddamn.

Claire smiled sweetly up at me, her eyelashes batting, all innocent temptress. 'Sure,' she called out, reaching around my body and pressing the 'doors open' button. As she stepped back, her hand brushed against my dick. I took a deep breath. Everything about her expression told me she'd goddamn meant to do that.

We rode the elevator to the tenth floor in silence, the little old lady who'd joined us offering polite smiles every now and then. Claire just kept that cheeky grin, her eyes on mine the entire time an unspoken challenge. Tension simmered in the air between us. When we got to her room, I was going to make Claire pay for that little stunt.

Nicely.

In the nicest way possible.

Finally, the lift opened, and Claire walked ahead, stopping at the third door on the left and unlocking her apartment. She pushed the door open, stepping inside. 'Come in. It's not much, but it—'

My lips were on hers before she could speak any more.

The door slammed behind us, and I slammed her up against the wall, our mouths a mash of teeth and tongues and lips all desperate for more. I made love to her mouth as she ran her hands over my chest, my shoulders, as if she were as ravenous for each and every part of me as I were for her.

'I need you,' she whispered, her hands on my belt.

I flipped her around, her body flat against the wall. One hand stopped at the top of the zipper to her dress. 'Do you know how many times I've thought about doing this?'

'No,' she breathed, looking over her shoulder at me. 'How many?'

'I've thought about it since the first moment I saw you in the office,' I said, jerking the zipper down and exposing her body from the delicate lines of her shoulder blades to the curve of her back.

'I've thought about waiting under your desk until you came in and then taking you with my mouth as you tried to work.'

'Yes,' she groaned.

I pulled the dress from her shoulders, down her body until she stood there in her G-string and bra. One hand followed that thin line of lace between her cheeks around to the promised land.

'I'd be turning you on like you'd only ever dreamed about,' I husked against her neck.

She clutched at the wall as if it could keep her upright, her eyes a challenge as she met my gaze over her shoulder. 'Guess it's time to see if dreams really can come true.'

As the night turned into the early hours of the morning, she proved to me that they did time and time again. Our time together wasn't a wild flash fire. This didn't just speak of desire and passion—it spoke of that, and emotion, too. Of *maybe this isn't just a physical attraction. Maybe this is something more.*

I rolled to my side and pressed my lips to hers in a kiss fierce with everything.

Lust.

Care.

Passion.

Love.

And as we lay there, both sweaty, satisfied, and satiated, all I could think was that this was the beginning of something truly special.

Chapter Thirteen

Claire

I woke from the most delicious dream—only it wasn't a dream.

A smile curved my lips as memories of the night before washed over me soft and slow. Hamish, kissing my neck. His arms holding me close. The understanding in his eyes when we spoke.

This was the start of something—something big.

I stretched one arm out, ready to pull that gorgeous body back in—

Cold.

Cold, empty sheets.

My eyes flashed open. What the hell?

White light streamed through my window. *I forgot to close the curtains.*

I pushed back the sheets, slipped my nightgown over my head and padded through the house, carrying so much weight with each step. *Maybe he's in the bathroom. He couldn't sleep, so he went out on the balcony. He's fixing breakfast in the kitchen.*

But no telltale rush of water from the shower, no cool breeze from the open balcony door, and no tantalising scent of coffee reached me.

Hamish was gone.

Up.

Vanished.

'Idiot,' I muttered to myself. How had I been so stupid?

I ambled into the kitchen and flicked the coffee machine on, dejected.

A note.

A note on the fridge.

Claire,
Sorry, something came up.
Last night was really something. You are amazing.
Hamish

I ripped it from its spot behind the magnet, reading it over and over as if perhaps some hidden meaning would come through. Something came up? Before seven in the morning? What kind of 'something' came up then?

Regret.

I pushed the negative voice away. No. Last night, I decided to take a chance on this man because he was genuine. Because he was more than what Chad had been. Hamish wouldn't have slept with me unless he was sure about it—surely.

But the voice lingered as I sipped my coffee on the small balcony.

It lingered as I jostled with commuters on the train into work.

And it lingered when I stowed my handbag under my desk to no gleaming blue eyes at the seat opposite, no charming smile as I turned on my computer.

The day passed in a daze. The Health Direct contract came through and I signed it and handed it to Vi to give to Frank, but I didn't feel that usual thrill I did when I landed a big deal, that rush of pride when I thought of my numbers displayed on the board.

You're better than this. You don't need a man to make you happy.

I knew this, and yet it didn't stop that empty feeling in the pit of my stomach. Didn't stop that ache in my chest whenever I looked at Hamish's vacant chair.

Late in the day, my desk phone rang.

'Hello, Claire speaking,' I said.

'Claire, hi. It's me.'

My heart sunk. That wasn't the 'me' I wanted to be on the other end of the line. 'Chad, are you okay?'

'No, I ... no.' His voice was strangled, as if he'd been crying. 'Claire, I'm sorry, but I can't get you that money. Something's come up, and I—'

'But I need it.' I tightened my grip on the phone. 'It's Christmas Eve, Chad. I have to buy presents for my parents. And I don't have time to try and organise a loan to cover the repayments you can't seem to make.'

'I'm sorry. I'll make it up to you, I swear.' He sniffed. 'It's just been a rough month. That job fell through. Things have been tight.'

I pinched the bridge of my nose. 'Okay.'

'Okay?'

'Okay, I guess. I don't know what else I can do. I can't exactly force you to give me the money, can I?'

'If I had it, you wouldn't need to force me. I'd hand it over gladly.' He rushed the words, but it didn't make me feel any better.

'I'm sure you would. I—'

Hamish.

He walked past me, his shoulders tense against the crisp material of his shirt. He sank into the chair opposite mine, his computer whirring to life, but he didn't meet my gaze. Bloodshot eyes focused on the screen in front of him. *What's happened?*

The dread that had lurked inside my stomach increased.

'Chad, I have to go. Just—'

'I'm sorry again, Claire,' he said in that sad-sounding voice. Who knew what kind of debt he'd got himself into this time?

'Just keep in touch about the repayments, okay?' I finished, then ended the call. Ugh. What a nightmare. How was I going to manage this?

By getting the promotion.

It came with a bonus, and I needed that bonus more with each passing moment.

I pushed back in my chair and walked over to Hamish's side. 'Hey.'

'Hey.' He looked at me, but his eyes were cold—devoid of life.

'Are you okay?'

He shrugged.

You're not. You're clearly not.

'I don't really want to talk about it.' He licked his lips, turned his head back to the screen. 'Sorry, Claire.'

'That's ... fine.' I pasted on a smile, so false. He didn't want to talk about what? Whatever had caused him to disappear this morning? Or us?

Was there even an us to discuss?

'Secret Santa time! Get into the boardroom, please,' Vi called as she walked past our desks, looking remarkably fresh.

I walked away from Hamish's desk, trying to inject some spring into my step.

When I took a seat in the boardroom, Hamish moved into the one next to me. He didn't make eye contact, didn't so much as glance in my direction. *Does he even know I'm here?*

'Afternoon, afternoon,' Frank said, squeezing past the chairs to the front of the room. A jaunty red Santa hat was balanced on top of his head. 'Thanks, all, for coming to the party last night. I'm sure you'll agree it was a roaring success, am I right?'

Several nods, murmured yeses filtered through the room. One of the women from marketing buried her head in her hands, her skin a tepid green colour. Apparently, the night had been bigger for some than others.

'So I'm sure you're all wondering about the big news—the promotion,' Frank said. I straightened, leaning forward. *Come on. Make it mine.* 'I'll announce that after we do our Secret Santa, but I can officially confirm that the sales leader for the month in December ...'

My fingers tightened into fists. *Please, please, please.*

'Is a tie! Hamish and Claire, you both came in first,' Frank said, and a few people clapped.

I glanced at Hamish. It would have been nice to beat him, but sharing the top spot with the man I'd just shared so much with was great, especially since I still got that one thing I wanted more than anything—respect. Applause from my peers for a job well done, instead of being 'that screw-up's lady' again.

Hamish stared straight ahead.

He didn't so much as flinch.

'Of course, the big game changer was Claire bringing in Health Direct. Without that, Hamish might have taken the crown for the fourth month running.' Frank chuckled. 'And now, it's Secret Santa time! When I call your name, come and collect your gift.' Frank gestured to the pile of gaudily wrapped presents in the corner of the room. The low buzz of conversation started.

'Hamish, are you okay?' I tried again, but it was like talking to a wall. He didn't seem to hear—it was as if he were on another planet.

'Oh! A set of wine glasses.' The hungover girl from marketing displayed her gift, and a few people snickered. 'Don't think I'll be using those for a while.'

More laughter, and Frank moved onto the next present.

'Is this about Health Direct?' I whispered to Hamish.

'No,' he said, short.

I took a sharp breath. Okay, then. 'Look, I'm here for you if you want to talk, but there's no reason to be an arsehole about it. I—'

'Hamish.' Frank gestured to the present I'd chosen, calling him up.

'I'm sorry, Claire.' He pushed back his chair and walked over to the pile.

My heart pounded in my throat. Sorry for what?

For snapping? Or for what happened last night? For the fact that he was shutting down, walking away—

Just like Chad did.

I took a deep breath. No. Hamish was nothing like my ex. I had to remember that.

Even if they both worked in ad sales.

Even if they both seemed to shut me out when I needed them the most.

Hamish took his gift back to the chair beside mine, and I held my breath as he unwrapped it. *Please, like it.*

He tore at the paper, then froze.

His face was a stony mask.

He looked at the ugly Christmas sweater with contempt in his eyes, a hatred I'd never seen there before.

'That is one hideous top, my man.' Zeb clapped Hamish on the back, but Hamish didn't move. Why didn't he move?

I'd thought the present would remind him of his brother. I'd thought it would be a nice gift, something to honour the tradition he'd had in the past.

Maybe I'd read the situation wrong.

Maybe I'd read it so, so wrong.

'Hamish, I'm sorry,' I whispered. 'I thought you'd think it was sweet—nice. I—'

'Please,' he said in a low voice, his eyes full of torture when they turned to stare at me. He gave a small, almost imperceptible shake of his head. 'Just stop.'

'And Claire, this one's for you.' Frank held out a small package in a white box, a large red bow on the top.

A sense of unease prickled my skin as I walked to the front to collect my gift, then made my way back to my seat. What was going on with Hamish?

'Open it.' Vi nudged my shoulder, her eyes on the gift.

I pulled at the ribbon, and it fell in long drapes on the white tabletop. I lifted the lid and—

My God.

Lace.

Red lace, bright as a fire engine.

'What's that then?' Frank asked, his fists knuckled on the table as he leaned across to get a better view.

A G-string.

A red lace G-string with mistletoe right in the middle of it.

Tears pricked the backs of my eyes. Anger, shame, hurt—they rushed through me like an avalanche. A few people around the table tittered.

'Who did this?' Frank asked, eyes wide.

Silence hit the boardroom like a sledgehammer. Blank faces met more blank faces.

Except mine.

Heat fired through my cheeks. Memories rushed me. Embarrassment, hurt, *regret*. All the weakness I'd felt when I'd wanted to be strong after Chad left.

'This is not acceptable. I will be taking this further,' Frank said, his eyes dark. 'Now, who do we have next?'

He kept calling out names, trying to move things along, but I felt it—their eyes on me, the laughter, the whispers. Just like I had when Chad left, and I had to front for his mistakes.

I couldn't tear my eyes from the scrap of red material. The *personal gift*. Humiliated—I was absolutely humiliated. No one would ever take me seriously. I would always be the woman who got taken for a ride by her ex.

I shoved out of the chair. Tears blurred my vision as I pushed towards the door.

'Claire?' Vi—her hand brushed my arm, but I shrugged it off.

'Claire!' Hamish called, but I didn't stop, couldn't stop. I grabbed my handbag and my phone from my desk then raced out to the street, desperate for air, for relief, for something to make the pain stop.

Sorry. He'd said sorry ... for what?

And as I ran to my apartment, hurt heavy in my heart, I couldn't help but wonder if perhaps the man I'd thought of as sweet and caring wasn't quite so nice after all.

Chapter Fourteen

Claire

I didn't answer my phone.

When the fifth text came through from Vi telling me I needed to call her back, I switched the stupid thing off. I felt like an idiot—a complete and utter mess.

There was no reason to think that Hamish had given me the lingerie. It could have been anyone who worked at In The Lead—but one night after he'd seen me naked, when he knew just how important my reputation was to me ... it seemed too much of a coincidence.

And even if he hadn't, he clearly wasn't interested in anything more than what that gift represented—a cheap, flimsy affair that you could leave behind in the office. Something you'd never take seriously.

I grabbed the note from the fridge, screwed it into a little ball and tossed it in the trash. *Something. Last night was really something.*

Obviously, it was something he'd like to laugh about with his colleagues.

Something he never planned on doing again.

I stomped across to the fridge, pulled out a bottle of wine, and poured myself a too-tall glass, one drink to take the edge off before I had to call a cab and head to the airport. *Now's not the time for moderation.*

Not when I felt like this.

There was still an hour before I had to leave. I grabbed a block of chocolate from the fridge, kicked off my shoes, and turned the television on to a cheesy Christmas movie. The kind where the man and the woman were meant to be together. The kind where there were no bills to pay, no co-workers laughing at you, no men who slept with you and then left—only happily-ever-afters. Only love.

Love. Something I didn't have.

So much for a merry Christmas.

Hamish

The call had come at five in the morning.

'Hello?' I'd whispered, sneaking through Claire's house and into the kitchen so as not to wake her. We'd fallen asleep sometime in the early hours of the morning after more sex, more laughing, and more talking. She was perfect. She was everything.

'Sorry, I ...' Renee had sobbed.

My heart stopped. 'What's wrong?'

'It's Harry. He's—his liver infection has played up again, and we're at the hospital, and—'

'I'll be there.' My hands were already grabbing at my jeans, pulling them up and over my legs. 'I'm coming to the hospital now.'

I'd raced to the hospital after scribbling a note for Claire and leaving it under a magnet on the fridge.

'Renee, you okay?' I'd asked, holding her close.

But she wasn't okay.

Not in the slightest.

Tears stained her cheeks. Her shoulders shook as she gazed at the poor little boy in the bed in front of her. He tossed and turned, his eyes closed but his body wide open to the pain that tore through it. *Harry.* I ached for him.

'He's just—they can't take him too, Hamish,' she'd sobbed, clutching at me as if for dear life. 'They can't take him too.'

I didn't ask who they were, or what she meant—I knew. They were death, and the future, and whatever came after that. They were the forces that stole her husband in that brutal car accident, leaving her to raise their son who suffered severe damage to his liver during the crash. They were the enemy, a being greater than she could fight because right now, every second she had was spent holding on to the one shred of good she had left—Harry. A son she loved more than life itself.

A son I loved more than life itself.

'How can I help?' I asked, pulling back and studying her.

She took a deep, fortifying breath. 'Nothing. You already do too much. All the bills … the rent—'

'It's the least I can do. You know that.' I shook my head.

'But we should have had insurance. I don't know why we thought we were invincible, but we did.' It wasn't the first time she'd said the words to me, and I had no consolation to offer. Life was expensive—but as Renee and I had come to learn, death cost even more. That was why I'd jumped ship from Murphy's when the offer at In The Lead came up. That was why I needed that promotion. Because one wage wasn't enough to support me,

Renee, and my cute-as-hell nephew who still needed medical assistance.

One man just wasn't enough.

'Mrs Renee Christianson?'

We both looked as a doctor stepped into the room, a clipboard under his arm.

'Yes?' Renee asked.

'I'm Dr Charlton, and I want to talk to you about your son's care. Are you able to step into my office for a moment?' he asked.

She looked to me, a question in her eyes.

'I'll stay, of course. Go.' I ushered her out of there and sunk into the seat next to the little boy who looked so much like the brother I'd lost.

As I waited for Renee to come back, I pressed my eyes closed for a moment. My mind felt as if it had been to hell and back. How was it possible that just a few short hours ago I'd been making love to Claire?

Reality hit home. We could never work.

I needed that promotion. She needed that promotion.

Only one of us could win.

One of us would get hurt.

And maybe, sure, we'd overcome that. Maybe we were stronger than I'd thought, but I'd seen the look in Claire's eyes when she spoke about her ex taking what she believed was hers. How could I be the man she wanted, the man she needed, and also the one to take from her what she was rightfully owed?

'A liver transplant.'

I blinked, looked up at Renee.

She walked over to my chair, a grim expression on her face. 'They want to do a liver transplant. But Hamish, he's so young ...'

'Renee.' I pulled her tight into my arms, holding her there until her shoulders stopped shaking, her sobs subsiding. No one should have to go through what she had. No mother of any child.

If only Josh were here.

The thought had never seemed louder than it did right then.

'Hamish.'

I looked up, dazed. Frank had called my name, the Secret Santa present in his hand. Huh. Like that mattered.

In the grand scheme of things, none of it mattered.

I collected the parcel and took it back to my chair. Slowly, I unwrapped it, moving as if on autopilot.

A sweater. Red and white, with a big reindeer face on the front. It was loud, garish, and screamed *deck the halls.*

My brother would have loved it.

A lump formed in my throat. Damn it. *Claire.*

I swallowed down the pain that had lodged in the pit of my stomach all day. I wouldn't fall apart—not here. I couldn't.

'That is one hideous top, my man.' Zeb clapped me on the shoulder, and I didn't move—couldn't move. I had to be a rock.

'Hamish, I'm sorry,' Claire whispered. 'I thought you'd think it was sweet—nice. I—'

'Please,' I said, shaking my head. *Please, don't remind me how sweet you are. How you care—you listen. How one of us is going to hurt the other very goddamn soon.* 'Just stop.'

She opened her mouth as if to say more, but Frank called her up front to open her present, and she left without a word.

When she opened the box, her face fell. I glanced inside. Lingerie.

I frowned. Who the hell would have gotten her that?

Around the room, a few people laughed. One let loose a wolf whistle. Frank made some awkward comment, but it only seemed to make the red in Claire's cheeks flame brighter.

Her eyes shone, and she stood, pushing past me and flying from the room.

'Claire!' I called. Shit. I had to go after her.

I stood to leave, but Vi grabbed me by the shirtsleeve.

'What have you done?' she hissed, her eyes full of fury.

'Nothing.' I shook my head.

'Really? Because she's been miserable all damn day, and I can't help but think it's because of you.'

'I didn't do anything, okay?' I shrugged the angry woman off.

'You looked pretty mad at her in here a few seconds ago,' she hissed, and what was she talking about? I wasn't mad, I was—

Furious.

Crazed with anger.

Because how could my nephew need a liver transplant when he was only five years old? How could it be Christmas Eve, and yet my sister-in-law be spending more time waiting in the hospital? How did the season for giving equate with mounting bills and unanswered debt?

And how could the first woman I'd felt something for in years be standing in the way of me getting what I wanted?

I was an idiot. I was behaving like a petulant child—what was wrong with me?

Claire wasn't stopping me from getting that promotion. Whether she got it or not—it didn't matter.

Renee's words from a few weeks ago at lunch came back to me. The things that made a person.

Why was I fixated on something so little as a promotion when it came to Claire?

Why didn't I focus on what counted—on us?

'I've got to go.' I stepped around Vi and raced from the room, headed down the empty hall to our desks. Was she okay? She'd worked so hard to build up her reputation—this must have devastated her.

'Hamish. Wait,' Zeb called, and I slowed my stride as my co-worker jogged down the hall after me. 'She left. Ran out the front doors just a few seconds ago.'

'Oh.' I'd missed her. I'd been too slow.

I turned on my heel, ready to go after her. Ready to be there for her when she needed me.

'You're leaving?' Zeb asked, following my about turn.

'Yeah. She's upset.' And I wanted to make that hurt go away. Whatever idiot had given her that present didn't have half a brain in their heads.

'Huh. But Frank's about to announce the promotion.'

'I don't care.'

'Your call, man.' Zeb's footsteps stopped outside the boardroom. 'Talk about overreacting though. If I'd known giving her that cheap G-string would freak her out so much …'

I stopped.

Gritted my teeth.

'What did you say?' I growled.

'The lingerie. She overreacted—typical chick. It was meant as a joke—her ex used to say the only thing she liked more than Christmas was sex, and I thought—'

I didn't think—my body went on autopilot.

I whirled around, drew my fist, and punched Zeb in the face.

'Fuck!' He staggered back, clutching at his nose. Blood oozed between his fingers.

Oh no. What had I done?

'What the hell was that for?'

'Don't talk about her that way,' I said.

People poured out of the boardroom, a clamour of noise with them. My fist throbbed.

'I think you broke my nose over that bitch,' Zeb groaned.

'What is going on?' *Frank*.

I turned to the man in question, shaking my fist to relieve the pain. I shouldn't have done that. But disrespecting her like that— I'd let my emotions get the better of me. And this wasn't the time or the place. 'I'm sorry for doing that.'

Frank raised his eyebrows. 'I see. Zeb?'

'He's a psychopath! Turned around and hit me for no goddamn reason.'

Frank sighed, a long exhale through his nostrils. 'We have a zero-tolerance policy for violence in this company, Hamish. Zero.'

I pressed my eyes closed. No. No, no, *no*. How had I gone from nearly having it all to losing it all in a few minutes?

'This is inexcusable.' His cool eyes met my own. 'It's a shame, Hamish. You were an asset to this company, but I can't condone violence. Not ever.'

I tightened my lips into a scowl. 'I understand.'

I made my way to my desk, and packed my personal effects into a box. I shouldn't have been so stupid. I should have thought things through.

But as I pictured Zeb's face, heard the tone in his voice as he laughed at the woman I cared for so much, I couldn't find the regret I should have. He'd disrespected her, and that wasn't something I could stand and let slide.

I walked out of the building, a box of personal belongings held tight to my chest. Four months. I'd never had such a short stint of employment before. Where to next?

'Hamish.' I turned. Frank strode towards me, something red and white in his hands. He held the Christmas sweater out. 'You forgot this.'

'Oh.' I took it, placed it on top of the box. Damn it. Claire. I needed to make things right with her asap. 'Thanks.'

'It's okay. For what it's worth, I'm sorry to see you go.' He pursed his lips. 'I don't know what went on back there, but I have my suspicions. And if it's what I think it is …' He took a deep breath, shook his head. 'Well, I'll have lost two good employees in a short space of time, but I can't look past either offence. It opens a gateway for what's right and what's wrong.'

He thought that? Of course, I did too, but in the world of media, so many boys still played to those *Mad Men* ways.

Frank paused, and something like regret flashed over his face. 'You know, about that promotion. You were—'

I held up my hand. 'Don't say it.'

It didn't matter anymore.

All that mattered was what happened next.

As I flagged down a taxi, the day's events replayed in my mind.

That call from Renee.

Harry needing so much.

Claire, hurting me with her bittersweet gift and me shutting her out when all she wanted was to get in.

Me punching Zeb in the In The Lead hall.

Maybe I wasn't quite so nice after all.

Chapter Fifteen

Claire

I stood at the end of the line at the departure gate. Only ten more minutes until we were supposed to take off—if things ran on time.

In front of me, a little girl jumped up to grab her mother's arm, distracting the woman from her phone. My hands itched to check my own, but I stopped myself. I hadn't turned my phone back on since I'd left the office, and while I missed it, it also felt strangely freeing. There was no reminder that deals still needed to be made, work matters still needed to be signed off on. There was no Chad to call me and let me down once again.

There was just ... me.

Me and the holidays.

My chest panged. Me, my parents, and no sexy interludes with Hamish Christianson.

The woman in front tucked her phone in her pocket and turned her attention to her little girl. *Family*.

It wasn't just me and the holidays. I was going home to see my parents—people I loved. Sure, it would have been amazing to be in a relationship, to not be spending the season alone, but was my life really that bad?

That G-string.

The whispers.

The laughter.

I swallowed down the hurt. Yes, that had been horrible, but had I made the situation worse than it needed to be? What if I'd tried to laugh it off? Would they have laughed so hard?

Am I the only one who still thinks of myself as the woman Chad took advantage of?

Once, I would have answered yes, unequivocally.

But as I stopped to really think, I found myself wondering. In the last year, I'd worked hard to rebuild my reputation. I'd consistently placed second or first when it came to account management.

There was one person who consistently thought of me as Chad's ex, though.

Me.

That had to change.

That had to change right now.

I glanced at the clock. Nine minutes to go. *Still time.*

I reached into my purse, pulled out my phone, turned it on and dialled. There was something I needed to do—something I should have done a long time ago.

'Hey, Claire.' Chad's voice was crestfallen, as if someone had just murdered his pet rabbit.

'Hi.'

'What's up? I'm kind of not feeling my best right now, so—'

'Chad, I know you're not well. That's why I'm calling.' I kept my voice clinical, businesslike.

'You … are?'

'Yes.' I sighed. 'Ever since you left me in debt, you've been *not feeling your best.*'

'It's true! I've struggled to catch a break.'

'Be that as it may, I can't support you anymore. I can't keep picking up the pieces of your mess.'

'Claire, it's not like that.' His voice hardened a little. 'And let's not forget, the loan was in your name.'

'But you took all the money!'

The little girl in front of me whipped her head around to look at me, raised her eyebrows. Oops. Too loud.

But I wasn't backing down. 'Chad, this is a courtesy call to let you know that I'm going to take this further. I'm not letting you bully me into paying the debt anymore. I'll hire a lawyer, get someone to look into it, and prove that this is not my problem—it's yours.'

'You won't do it. You're bluffing.'

'I will, and I—'

'Excuse me, sir, no phones at the blackjack table, please.' A foreign voice came down the line.

I dropped my jaw. He was at the casino? 'I thought you didn't have any money.'

'I don't! But you can't expect me to live off nothing.'

'Chad, you need help. I want to see you in rehab, or I want you to come with me to the bank and clear things up. Anything less, and I'm taking you to court.'

'Sir, no phones—'

'You're such a fucking bitch, Claire.' Chad's voice was hard, cruel. 'What happened to the caring woman who loved me?'

'Rehab, or a trip to the bank first thing in the new year.' I issued my ultimatum. 'And as for the woman who loved you? She's still here.' I stepped forward as the line moved closer to the plane. 'Only now I love someone else.'

I clicked the button to end the call. *Me.* I loved myself, and I had too much self-respect to let this arsehole get away with taking advantage of me again and again. I was better than that. I had to be better than that.

I looked down at my phone screen. Four minutes to go.

There was someone else I should call. Someone who deserved the benefit of the doubt.

He ran out on me this morning—he brushed me off at work—but maybe the gift I gave him was too soon. Maybe he felt about that like I had about the lingerie—as if it was shining a spotlight on my insecurities for the world to see. As if it made me less.

I had to do it—I had to call him.

Nervous energy raced through my body as I dialled Hamish's number.

The phone rang.

The noise sounded so very loud in my ear.

'Hi. You have reached the phone of ...' The automated recording clicked in.

'Damn it,' I whispered. I'd have to call back when we landed. The line shuffled forward.

'Claire!'

I froze mid-step.

Was that ...?

'Claire!'

I turned around.

Hamish.

He rushed towards me. He ducked past families huddled around suitcases, businesspeople talking on their phones, and slowed at my side, his chest rising and falling at a rapid pace.

'What are you ...?' I shook my head. 'Hamish, I tried calling you. I—'

'No. Whatever you're about to say, just let me speak first.' He shook his head, a deep earnestness in his eyes. 'Claire, I haven't gone about things the right way when it comes to us. Last night, I got carried away—but that's not how a woman like you deserves to be treated. You deserve the respect you told me you wanted from the people you work with, and I didn't honour that.'

'It takes two, Hamish.' She gave a small smile. 'I don't seem to remember suggesting we stop.'

'Maybe so, but I rushed in. I was so sure of how I felt that I didn't stop to think about the future. And when I did—I didn't handle it well.' He shoved his hands in the pockets of his suit pants. Had he come here straight from work? 'I left early this morning because I got a text from my sister-in-law saying my nephew was sick. I've been supporting her and my brother's son ever since he passed away last year.'

'What?' My God. His brother had left behind a wife and child? 'I'm so sorry to hear that.'

'And that's just it.' He met my gaze, scooped his hand along my jaw to cup my cheek. 'You don't need to be sorry. But you needed to know that—that I'm supporting another family. That my life will always be twisted with theirs, no matter what.'

'That's okay.' That was more than okay. It was who he was—a part of him.

'And that I'm not over my brother's death. I try act like I am, but sometimes, days like this—I can't handle it. I don't open up, and I should have told you. I should have told you I wasn't coping.'

'It's okay—'

'I want to be with you, Claire. This is me, putting my cards on the table.' He shrugged, holding out his hands in display. 'I'm not all nice. I'm not all perfect. But if you'll let me, I'll be all yours.'

My breath caught in my throat. This beautiful, broken and giving man—he was offering me the greatest gift I ever could receive.

And I was finally in a position to accept. 'Yes,' I whispered. Tears pricked at the backs of my eyes, and I blinked them away. 'Yes.'

He stepped closer. One hand clutched at the small of my back, pulling me closer to him. The other hand tangled in my hair as his lips met mine in a kiss so scorching hot, a kiss that said *I need you, I want you, I love you* all at once. I lost myself in his embrace, letting him share the load with me—but not take it entirely. We were a team—a partnership of the very best kind.

'Mummy, why is dat lady licking dat man?' I heard the small child in front of me ask, and I pulled away, my cheeks hot for what felt like the hundredth time that day.

'Sorry,' I mumbled my apology.

The woman in front raised her eyebrows, but shrugged and turned away. Looked like the Christmas spirit wasn't lost on her.

The line moved again, and the woman in front handed her ticket to the hostess.

'Can I see you when I get back?' I asked Hamish, not wanting to let go—not yet. Not when I finally had him in my arms.

'Actually ...' He winced, pulled a piece of paper out of his pocket. An airline ticket. He was—he was coming with me? 'I was hoping I could see you sooner than that.'

'Yes!' I squealed, and threw myself into his arms. 'Yes, a thousand times yes.'

And as our lips met in a kiss that I was sure the little girl in front of me would have disapproved of, I couldn't stop my smile. I had it all. I'd stood up to my ex; I'd fought for what I wanted; and now, I was taking home the reward.

Looked like Christmas had come to me after all.

Epilogue

Hamish

Nice was my specialty.

But sometimes, you needed to be a little naughty too. Sometimes you needed to be selfish.

That was why I'd told Renee the truth about Claire. Of course, once my sister-in-law found out I'd left the bed of the woman I loved to meet her at the hospital, she'd insisted I book the next available flight to join Claire in her hometown at Christmas.

'But you need someone,' I'd said. I couldn't leave Renee alone—not at this time of year.

'I have someone.' She'd shrugged. 'I have my son, who I love more than life itself. I have you, only a phone call away, and always so willing to help when needed.' She took a deep breath. 'But I also still have your brother. He might not be here, but he's still with me. And I think we both know he'd kick your butt for missing this opportunity when it's someone you care about so much.'

I left Renee with the presents I'd bought for her and Harry earlier. He was out of hospital, and the two of them would be spending Christmas in their family home—the one they'd shared with my brother. Harry still had to have a transplant—no Christmas miracle could put an end to that. But he had time, and his pain had subsided. For the time being, he was happy, safe, and surrounded by the woman who loved him the most in the world.

I'd flown to Queensland with the woman I loved after telling her about my newly unemployed status, and just how it had happened. I'd booked a room in a hotel, but after her parents met me over Christmas lunch, they'd insisted I sleep in the spare room, and even though I really would have preferred to bunk down with their daughter, I did as they requested—because I was a nice guy, after all.

Now, as I sat on the balcony of Claire's parents' home one week later, the sunset casting golds and pinks and oranges across the sky, I let out a long sigh. Perfect. There was nowhere else I'd rather be.

My phone buzzed beside me, and I picked it up.

Darcy: *I know you're happy where you are right now, but I thought I'd let you know a senior position's opened up back here at Murphy's. Derek laid off too many staff, and now he needs someone to raise morale. You'd be perfect for it, and I'm sure he'd welcome you back in a heartbeat. Interested?*

I grinned. Looked like things might just work out after all.

'What are you smiling about?' Claire padded barefoot across the wooden balcony before settling in my lap, her hands around my neck.

I showed her the text.

'Hamish! That's perfect!' She kissed me on the lips, once, chaste, then pulled away. 'Wait—is that perfect?'

'Yes.' I grinned. 'Looks like we're both starting the new year with new promotions.'

'Looks like it.' She grinned, resting her forehead against mine. 'I know it's a little early …'

'But you want to sneak into your bedroom before your mum realises we're gone?' I clutched her tighter, laughter bubbling in my throat.

'No!' She slapped playfully at my chest, then paused. 'Well, yes, but that's not what I was going to say.' She pressed her lips together. 'This Christmas has been the best ever, but it's the new year I'm really looking forward to.'

'And why's that?'

'Because …' She pressed her eyes closed for a moment before meeting me with a confident gaze. 'I love you, Hamish Christianson. And I can't wait to spend as much time as possible in the new year with you.'

'I love you, too.'

And as we kissed on the deck of her parents' property, the sun setting on the last day of the year, my thoughts were filled with naughty and nice ways to please this woman.

Because sometimes you just had to be both.

Christmas in Ghost Gum Springs

NICOLE FLOCKTON

*To Paula Jeffrey and Tania McLean,
my football supporting sisters.
Go Purple Haze!*

Chapter One

Take a trip, her work colleagues said.

You've earned it.

Enjoy your newfound wealth and freedom.

Do all the things you haven't been able to do over the last few years.

All great ideas that were of little comfort to Diana as she stood by the side of the road in the middle of nowhere with the scorching sun beating down on her back.

'Oh yeah, go visit Australia and experience a warm summer instead of another Christmas under fifteen feet of snow. Maybe you'll meet your very own Hugh Jackman.'

Fabulous idea. She'd rather be freezing under all that snow than where she was right now. What was the point in having an overflowing bank account when she couldn't access it to pay for help? As for finding a Hugh Jackman—there was only one and he was taken. The chances of her finding her very own Hugh were slim, especially when she had no idea where the hell she was.

Diana kicked the tire of her useless rental car. Steam poured out from underneath the hood. How did she get stuck with a lemon of a car? Was this her dear old grandmother's way of getting back at her for having the audacity to use some of the money she'd inherited? Probably, Grandma Mary-Lou was petty enough to somehow arrange for her car to break down from heaven. Or maybe it was from hell. Being vindictive seemed more of a devil emotion than a heavenly one.

For the tenth time since the car crapped itself, Diana wondered why she hadn't decided to just stick to the city and not venture out into rural Australia. It definitely wasn't like rural USA where there were many blink-and-you-miss-it towns dotted along the major state highways. Or at the very least large gas stations with a few fast food joints next to them. And to pile on to how crappy her day and life was, her cell phone had died so she couldn't even call anyone for help.

Maybe sitting in the car would be better than standing out under the baking sun. Sure, she wanted to get a suntan, but she didn't want to be fried like a chicken drumstick.

She opened the door and immediately closed it as a draft of hot air swept out to meet her. Nope, definitely not sitting in the car. Guaranteed heatstroke in there.

Diana gazed up and down the road again, wishing against all hope that a car would magically appear or a cowboy would come riding up on his horse and rescue her. She snorted at the thought. Did they even have cowboys in Australia? And since when did she believe in fairytales and Prince Charming coming to her rescue? She'd given up on that ideal when Grandma Mary-Lou threw away her book of fairytales—the only link she had to her parents—and replaced it with Emily Post's etiquette book. Now *that* was fun bedtime reading. Diana firmly believed her grandmother hoped that if she instilled certain morals her granddaughter wouldn't travel down the path her daughter had. Maybe if Grandma Mary-Lou had loved her daughter in the first place, her granddaughter wouldn't be stuck in the middle of nowhere–Australia baking like a cake. She'd be home in the snow-capped mountains of Montana enjoying a family Christmas.

'Hey, are you okay?'

Diana jumped, her heart racing a million miles a minute. Lost deep in her thoughts she hadn't heard the purr of the car.

'Do you need some help?' The driver asked with a hint of laughter in his voice.

Hot, annoyed and scared out of her wits she raised her eyes to the sky, blinded by the bright yellow orb and spoke before thinking. 'Do I look like I'm okay? I'm standing on the side of the road with steam and God knows what else pouring out of my rental. Of course I need some help.'

He chuckled and she flashed him a look Grandma Mary-Lou had used on her many a time. A look that had scared the bejeezus out of Diana but rolled off this man like water off a duck's back. 'This really isn't a funny situation.'

'Look, why don't you come and sit in my car. The aircon is on and you look like you need cooling down.'

Diana didn't know if she'd just been insulted or if this stranger was trying to be nice. It didn't matter if it was an insult or not, getting out of the searing sun and into a cool car was beyond temptation.

Don't let a man sweet-talk you. I don't want you ending up like your mother.

Diana faltered and stopped mid-step. It was like Grandma Mary-Lou's ghost was sitting on her shoulder, warning her like she'd always done. During college Diana had managed to mute and ignore the voice. That first semester she'd partied hard and had done all the things her grandmother hoped she wouldn't. Waking up in her room with no recollection as to how she'd got there had been the come-to-Jesus moment she'd needed. That as well as just scraping through on her end of semester exams. Come second semester, she'd quit the partying, buried her nose in the books and finished her degree. She'd even had a couple of serious relationships.

Now she was about to get into a stranger's car, in the middle of nowhere, in a country that wasn't her own. Maybe she should listen to Grandma Mary-Lou right now.

'I know what you're thinking,' her stranger spoke as he got out of his car. She looked at him, like really looked at him, not the quick glance she'd given him at first.

Damn, he may not be Hugh Jackman, but he was mighty fine to look at. Tall, at least six foot, wearing a blue t-shirt that hugged his broad shoulders and defined the expanse of his wide chest, khaki shorts that finished just above his knee. His eyes were hidden behind mirrored sunglasses perched on a straight nose. One corner of his mouth was raised in a yeah-I-know-you're-looking-at-me smile. It didn't detract from its fullness, if anything his lips tempted her to step closer so she could trace them with her finger.

Diana jammed the brakes on her thoughts. The sun was messing with her, but she remembered his comment and the fact she hadn't answered it yet annoyed her. Never in her life had she been struck dumb like she was at this moment. Pulling herself together, she straightened her shoulders and tapped her fingers on the fabric of her skirt. 'So, big guy, what am I thinking?'

'You're wondering if it's safe to get into a stranger's car. In a strange country.'

'How do you know this isn't my home?' she countered, surprised at how close to the mark he was.

'Your accent is a big hint. Along with the fact you look like you don't belong.'

The story of her life. She hadn't belonged in her grandmother's house. Hadn't belonged in the town she'd grown up in. Hadn't belonged at the school she'd taught at before she'd quit and come on this trip.

What she should do was march over to his car, slide into the driver's side and zoom off down the road, leaving him in her heat infused dust. Only she wasn't that petty, that had been her Grandma through and through. 'Fine, you've got me, aren't you a smartypants?'

He threw back his head and laughed, the sound trickled down her spine making her wish they'd met in different circumstances. When she wasn't covered in sweat and smelled like the gym at the high school she'd worked at.

'How about this,' he offered and closed the distance between them. 'Hi, I'm Connor Shetland, you look like you're having car trouble. Can I be of assistance?'

He stuck out his hand towards her. The manners instilled in her by Grandma Mary-Lou, the same ones she tried very hard to ignore, compelled her to grasp his hand. The second she did she wished she hadn't. If she thought she was hot before, one simple touch had her flesh tingling as if lit by a thousand flames.

Diana pulled her hand away and almost rubbed her palm down the side of her skirt. She didn't want him to think she was wiping away his touch, but she wanted to get rid of the sensation still lingering from their connection. Crap on a cracker, she really must be suffering a form of heatstroke to be having all these emotional highs and lows from a simple conversation.

Realising she was standing mute again, she mentally slapped her cheeks and concentrated on the here and now. All she wanted was to get off the side of the road and the man in front of her was her way to the nearest town. Or back to the city.

'Hi, Connor Shetland. I'm Diana Jenkins and you're right, I'm having car trouble and would appreciate a ride back to the city.'

'Pleasure to meet you, Diana. As for taking you back to the city …' He paused and her heart sank, he was just going to call for a tow truck or something and leave her here while he drove off in air-conditioned comfort to wherever he lived. No doubt to a woman who would give him a hot kiss before handing him a cold drink. A guy as good-looking as Connor wouldn't be single.

Why the hell was she wondering about his relationship status?

'… will that be okay?'

Crap, she'd drifted off again and hadn't heard what he said. Not wanting to look like a complete dimwit she pulled a smile out of nowhere. 'Yep, that's fine. I appreciate it, thanks.'

Connor watched the woman standing in front of him and bit back another laugh. She had no idea what he'd just said to her. He could go along with her and let her think he hadn't noticed the way she'd drifted off the second he started talking to her. Or he could call her out on it. The last thing he'd expected to find on his drive back to Ghost Gum Springs was a damsel in distress. Although from the short interaction he'd had with her, calling Ms Diana Jenkins a damsel would go down like a lead balloon.

'Are we leaving?'

As his damsel sauntered towards him, his eyes were immediately drawn to the long length of leg. Her skirt was pale purple in colour—Alice, his fashionista sister, would probably call it lilac or some other fancy name—and it finished a couple of inches above her knee. Her white blouse had the top two buttons undone and he could see a hint of the curves beneath, ones he wouldn't mind checking out if she didn't run the second he pulled into town. Her brown hair glinted with gold highlights in the bright Australian sun. Her facial features were delicate, but she definitely had kissable lips.

Now he was acting like the person Diana was concerned about: a lecherous creep who picks up women on the side of the road so he can have his wicked way with them. Definitely not his modus operandi. True, it had been a while since he'd been with a woman, but he didn't need to resort to kidnapping one.

A cockatoo squawked as it flew past, reminding him they were standing on the side of the road and he'd yet to answer her question. 'Yeah. Why don't you get all your stuff out of the car and I'll put it in the boot?'

'The boot? How is my suitcase going to fit into a boot?'

Her brow furrowed in confusion and he jammed his hands in his pockets to stop from reaching out and smoothing the lines away. Maybe he should've gone and got laid while he was in Sydney checking on his house and picking up more Christmas decorations for the pub. If he'd done that, perhaps he wouldn't be so drawn to this complete stranger.

'Not a boot, boot, but this.' He walked to his car, leaned in and pressed a button which popped the lid of his boot.

'Ohhh, the trunk.'

Connor chuckled. 'Right, that's what you call it in the States. What do call the bonnet?' he asked as he pointed to the front of his car.

'Hood and I'm not putting my bags in that,' she huffed as she rounded to the back of her car and opened his *trunk* wider. The sight of her bent over, her skirt stretching enticingly over her arse, had his body twitching to life. Time to change his view if he wanted to be able to drive back to Ghost Gum Springs without sporting a hard-on.

Connor moved to the front of her car, steam still rising from the radiator. A mechanic he wasn't, but at least he could look like he knew what he was doing. As expected the engine was covered as most new car engines were these days. He remembered Sunday afternoons whenever they visited their grandparents house: Grandad was always in the garage tinkering with his ute. At six he was eager to spend time with him, but his mother said he was too little and he would have to wait until he got a bit older. Unfortunately, his grandad had died a year later and he never got the chance to know his way around an engine. Today he wished he had, then he could look impressive when he was able to tell her exactly what was wrong with the car.

'So, hot shot, what's wrong with the car?'

Connor took a moment to centre himself before turning to face her. She'd practically drawled the words out and he found it extremely sexy. Normally an American accent annoyed the shit out of him, but Ms Diana Jenkins could talk to him all day.

Whoa, settle down, fella.

He was taking her to town, which was a half-hour down the road. She could call the rental company from there and sort out the car for herself. They'd send a car or something for her and she would be gone and he could get on with his life. If he only had some idea what his life entailed now. He slammed the brakes on those thoughts as well. Concentrate on the here and now.

He backed away from the engine and pulled the bonnet down. 'Looks like your radiator is shot.'

'Great, just fantastic. What the hell was I thinking to come to the ass end of the world for a vacation.' She muttered her annoyance, but loud enough for him to hear her.

'Seeking adventure?' he asked and was rewarded with another death glare. He laughed and cocked his head towards his car. 'Come on, let's get you some place out of the sun where you can get a drink and cool off.'

'Second sensible thing you've said since you turned up here,' she commented as she strode to his car.

He observed the sway of her hips in her short skirt, her long legs eating up the small distance from where they stood to where he'd parked his car. It wasn't long enough, he'd decided when she disappeared inside.

Giving one last check over her car to make sure she hadn't left anything behind, he walked to his own vehicle and slid into the driver's seat. 'What was the first sensible thing I said?'

'That you're going to take me back to Sydney.'

Conner laughed. 'I'm not taking you back to Sydney. I'm not driving three-and-a-half hours back to the place I've just come from.'

'Wait. What? Where are you taking me?'

As he'd suspected she hadn't heard a word he'd said when he told her where their final destination was going to be. 'I'm taking you to Ghost Gum Springs. A little town about thirty minutes down the road.'

Chapter Two

Diana had walked into a nightmare. Maybe she'd fainted from the heat and was now having a dream. All she wanted to do was get to a hotel, shower, order a bottle of wine and drink until she passed out. It was the only way to end the day.

She swivelled in her seat and looked at her *rescuer*. 'I want to go to Sydney. You told me you were taking me back there.'

'No, I didn't. I said the closest town is thirty minutes away and I would take you there.'

Diana shut her eyes and bit back a groan as realisation sunk in. She'd totally flaked on him when he was talking to her. Her mind had wandered off and she hadn't heard a word he'd said. Something she had no doubt Connor Shetland was more than aware of. Another side-eye glance at him confirmed her suspicions. Smugness didn't begin to describe what was on his face. Arrogance and assurance, a trait most of the guys she'd grown up with in small town Packenridge, Montana had worn around her.

She was the girl who lived with her grandmother because her parents had overdosed. Not like they'd wanted her. Neither had her grandmother, but that was beside the point. She was tired of being the girl no one wanted. 'Look, how much money will it take to get you to turn the car around and drive me back to Sydney?'

'I already told you I'm not driving back there. I have a job to get to in Ghost Gum Springs. You're going to have to suck it up, princess.'

The urge to argue the point further built inside of her, but the way his hands gripped the steering wheel, as though he wanted to grab her by the shoulders and shake some sense into her, had her biting back the retort.

Fine, she'd get to wherever they were going and ask someone else around town to drive her back to the city. If this place was anything like the town she grew up in, most folks didn't have two pennies to rub together. She was sure someone would like a nice injection of cash, especially seeing as it was so close to the holiday season. Everyone liked to have extra cash then. She hated Christmas though. Grandma Mary-Lou always thought it was a waste of time and money and the only gifts she'd ever got had been practical: cotton panties and socks. Not once had she ever got a toy or even chocolate for Christmas.

Thinking about the holidays reminded her of what she'd seen in the trunk of Connor's car. 'What's with all the Christmas decorations in the back of your car? I could hardly fit my suitcase in.'

'You didn't squash any of the boxes did you?'

His response appeared frantic. If he was so worried about the decorations he should've offered to put her case in the trunk himself. 'I may have dented a box or two. What's the big deal?'

'Oh geez, I hope you didn't break anything.'

'Guess you'll find out when we get to the town in the middle of nowhere.'

God, she sounded like a bitch. Just because her plans weren't working out as she'd hoped, didn't mean she had to take it out on

Connor. He hadn't had to offer to drive her to a town, he could've called for someone to come and get her and then driven away.

One thing about her, she wasn't a petty bitch, even if she was doing a good impression of one right now. Grandma Mary-Lou may have been grumpy, but she had imparted manners into Diana, through Emily Post's etiquette book of course. It was time to woman up and admit she'd taken her frustration out on Connor. 'I'm sorry, Connor, that was uncalled for.'

He brushed off her apology with a wave of his hand. 'Which boxes did you dent?'

His obsession with the Christmas decorations seemed over the top, but whatever. It would be just her luck to meet a cute guy, and not only be a diva bitch, but for the guy to turn out to be nutty about Christmas. The one holiday she disliked the most out of all of them. 'I don't know, the top two maybe. I didn't pay much attention.'

'Okay well those are probably the boxes with garland and window clings. Should be fine,' he muttered as though doing a mental inventory of the items.

Diana turned in her seat to look at her rescuer. His eyes focused on the road in front of them, an endless strip of black tar that looked like it was melting in the summer sun. His profile was attractive though, a hint of stubble shaded his cheeks. How rough would it be beneath her touch? She curled her fingers until her nails dug into the soft flesh of her palm. Seriously, she wasn't going to be hanging around long enough to find out.

'Why do you have so many decorations? It looks like there are enough boxes to decorate at least five trees.' If she hadn't been watching him, she would've missed the faint sheen of red dusting his face.

The guy was embarrassed?

No way.

He shrugged his shoulders, before reaching out and turning the volume on the dial up. Static filled the car.

'Shit,' he mumbled. He fiddled with the touchscreen in the middle of the dashboard and a few seconds later the familiar sounds of one of her favourite songs filled the car. Clearly, he didn't want to talk to her anymore, which was totally fine.

Diana transferred her gaze out the window at the passing landscape. It was so different to Montana. There wherever you looked you could see mountains, here there was nothing but great swathes of barren land.

How did anyone survive out here?

She shuddered and breathed out a little sigh of relief when in the distance she saw what looked like a couple of structures. She hoped the town they were going to had more than two buildings. A glance at her watch showed it was getting late in the afternoon.

'I'm going to be stuck in the middle of nowhere tonight, aren't I?' she asked, instinctively knowing the answer.

'Yeah, I don't think the hire car company will be sending anyone out tonight,' said Connor as he flexed his fingers over the steering wheel, like he was releasing tension in them. 'I reckon you'll be lucky if they even make it out by the end of the weekend.'

'Seriously? Please tell me you're joking. What about this place we're going to, Ghost Tree Lake, is there a mechanic there?'

'Ghost *Gum Springs* and as for a mechanic, I'm not sure. I'm still fairly new to town.'

'Perfect.' She sighed and slumped in her seat. This really was turning out to be a nightmare of a vacation. She would bet her newfound fortune that Grandma Mary-Lou was looking down at her with a smug I-told-you-so look. The same one she always directed to Diana when she'd tried to go against her grandmother and failed.

Yeah, she totally should've stayed in Montana.

'Here we are,' said Connor as he pulled into his spot at the back of the pub.

'Where is here exactly?' his prickly American passenger asked.

A normal sane guy would dump her and run away as fast as possible—except he wasn't feeling particularly normal or sane at the moment. Beneath all the prickles, Connor sensed Ms Diana Jenkins was a little lost. Like him he supposed.

As a lawyer he'd always had to judge a person's character quickly when choosing jurors. Normally, he was spot on. The last case he had, he'd been way off and his client had paid for it. His gut churned in remembrance of how badly his client had paid and how similar her persona matched Diana's.

Stop it.

He couldn't change the past, no matter how much he wanted to. Now here he was, in rural Australia re-examining his life and his future. He'd been grateful when his mate Shane 'Smithy' Smith had offered him the chance to work at the pub in Ghost Gum Springs while Shane and his new wife took a three-month-long honeymoon around Australia.

He'd only been in town himself for six weeks. But, so far, he was enjoying working behind the bar and getting to know the locals. It was a far cry from the courtroom and exactly what he needed.

'I didn't realise my question was so difficult.'

Yeah, that's right, Diana asked where they were. 'We're at the pub. The hub of the town.'

'And why are we here?'

'Well this is where I work and after standing out in the sun for as long as you were I'm betting you're pretty thirsty.'

'Right. So long as this place has a working phone then I'll be happy.'

'Yes, there's a phone and you don't even have to crank it to get it working.'

A smile tugged at the sides of his mouth as she rolled her eyes. 'Well that's good to know.'

'Come on, the sooner you make your call, the sooner you'll find out how long you'll be here. You never know, you may find you like this place and decide to stay here longer than a night.'

'Oh, trust me, I don't plan to even stay the night.'

Connor studied his companion. Her complete and utter distaste for her current situation seemed to be a bit over the top to him. Sure, breaking down in the middle of rural Australia was scary, especially for a tourist. But he'd come upon her and now she was safe.

'You may not have a choice. I told you it's getting late, the hire car company aren't going to drop everything and bring a car out to you tonight.'

Her composure crumpled and for a moment he thought she was going to start to cry. Instead she took a deep breath and when she released it, her face returned to the impassive mask she'd been wearing since she'd got in his car.

Diana Jenkins was a chameleon and she intrigued him. He wanted to know why she put on a brave face and appeared scared to let her real self shine through. Was Diana like Melanie, never letting the people who could help her close? If she had, maybe she'd still be alive.

Perhaps he could persuade Diana that Ghost Gum Springs was exactly where she needed to be instead of going back to the city.

Maybe they could be each other's distraction over Christmas.

Yes, he kind of liked that plan.

Chapter Three

Diana walked into the pub and halted mid-stride. 'Oh my God, it looks like Santa vomited in here.'

The only other place she'd seen so many Christmas decorations was in the Christmas Shop in the town over from the one she'd grown up in and had worked in until recently. Every viable surface in the main room was covered with garland. There wasn't just one tree in the space, but three.

Three.

Who put three Christmas trees in a bar?

'Santa didn't vomit, Santa moved his entire workshop to rural Australia. He should've stayed in the North Pole.'

Diana had to squint to see who'd spoken. She spotted an older man sitting at the shiny wood bar.

'Oh, quit it, Fred, you know you like it,' said Connor as he walked in rolling her suitcase and holding one of the boxes she'd seen in the trunk of his car.

'Tell me that box doesn't hold more decorations?' The man Connor called Fred grumbled.

Diana wandered over to where Fred sat and plonked herself down on the stool next to him. 'There's a whole trunkload of boxes.'

'Smithy'd pitch a fit if he saw what Connor was doing to his pub. Christmas decorations don't belong in a fine drinking establishment as this one.'

'I tried my best to dent as many boxes as I could,' she commented as she looked around the *fine* establishment. Beneath all the greenery and shiny baubles the interior of the pub looked similar to the bars she'd visited her first year of college.

'Fred Gates,' he held out his hand towards Diana and she took it, giving it a brief shake. 'What's a pretty lady like you doing with Santa's Elf?'

'Diana Jenkins. I think I'm being punished by the big red guy for being naughty throughout the year.'

Fred roared with laughter and slapped his hand on the bar. 'I like you. How long ya staying?'

'Just long enough to call the rental company and tell them to come rescue me.' She leaned closer to Fred, enjoying having a fellow Scrooge to grumble with. 'Do you think if I tell them I've been kidnapped by Santa's Elf, they'd come get me quicker?'

'Nah, it's a Friday, they'd have all knocked off and started their Christmas parties. Probably already three sheets to the wind.'

Not the news Diana wanted to hear, and she had no idea what *three sheets to the wind* meant but it didn't sound good. Fred might be friendly enough, but she'd been around small towns all her life and could bet the rest of the town would be judgemental of her. A stranger. An American. And she probably dressed wrong.

Or they'd be nice to her face while gossiping about her behind her back. Just like when she'd been a teenager, she'd get invited out for coffee only to be stood up and she'd end up looking like a gullible fool when she'd arrived excited to have finally made some friends. After the fourth time it had happened, it sunk in she'd never be welcome anywhere in the town she'd grown up in.

Being judged wasn't anything she wasn't used to, she'd had her fair share of it while growing up. Not only by Grandma Mary-Lou but also by every single person in town because of who her parents were and what they'd done.

There was every chance she could be completely wrong, but she didn't think so. Small town mentality was the same all over the world.

'I was beginning to like you Fred, but not so much now with that piece of information.'

Fred shrugged his shoulders and took a swallow of his beer. 'Sorry, love. Just the way it is. It's Christmas and a Friday, not the best combination.'

'Rental car companies should skip Christmas. Don't they know emergencies happen all the time?'

'I can tell you're not from around here, love. Things work differently in Australia. If you're planning on staying for a while, you might want to get used to it. Lots of places close over Christmas and New Year.'

The thought of being stuck in Ghost Gum Springs horrified her. Man, she could kick herself for thinking her life needed adventure and listening to her well-meaning colleagues. She was beginning to wonder if they really were 'well-meaning' after all. Obviously, she hadn't learned from her teenage years. She just figured grown women weren't as petty. She should've known better. She'd bet half her new fortune they were hoping she was going to fail. After all, this was the first time she'd ever travelled anywhere out of continental USA. No doubt they'd started a *Watch-Diana-Fail* pool the second she'd climbed into the cab for the airport.

'Again, not the news I want to hear.'

'Don't worry, you'll be fine here. Maybe you'll find someone who is heading to Sydney and they could give you a lift.'

Yeah, from Fred's tone, Diana could guess the chances of that happening were unlikely. Yep, she was right, small towns were the same all over. No one in Packenridge, Montana ever ventured into Bozeman or any of the other more populated cities of the State very often.

This was turning out to be a fantastic vacation … not.

Before she could question Fred further a tall glass of clear liquid was placed in front of her. The bubbles fizzed away excitedly, and a bead of condensation slid down the glass.

'What's this?' she asked and looked up to find Connor watching her closely. His green eyes were assessing her, and she wondered how much of her conversation with Fred he'd heard.

'Lemonade.'

'This isn't lemonade.' The lemonade she knew wasn't a clear liquid, it was cloudy and yellow and tart.

'It is here.' He nudged the glass a little closer to her. 'Trust me, you'll like it.'

Diana leaned forward and closed her lips around the clear straw being pushed out of the glass by the gassy bubbles. She took a couple of tentative sucks. 'This isn't lemonade, this is Sprite.'

'Sprite is lemonade here.'

She shook her head, a little gurgle of laughter growing inside her. 'You people are weird.'

A crooked smile broke out over Connor's face. 'Weird is good.' He winked and walked away from her.

Damn he really was good-looking. She supposed if she was going to be stuck somewhere, at least there was one decent guy she could look at. A guy who had very kissable lips. Not to mention a strong body. He'd hauled those boxes in as if they weighed nothing, which could be likely because Christmas decorations weren't exactly heavy. Would he be puffed if he carried her in through the doors?

Whoa. Don't go there, Diana. Nothing good can come from travelling down that road. Look at what stepping outside of your comfort zone has brought you. Trouble.

Why the hell not? She countered the voice in her head. She was a grown ass woman. It had been a long time since she'd been reckless and lived in the moment. There was no one here to judge her. She wasn't going to stay in this place forever. Perhaps her car breaking down and being rescued by sexy Connor Shetland was exactly what fate ordered for her. A holiday fling on the other side of the world where no beady eyes could criticise her sounded ideal.

Question was, did she dare take that leap and, more importantly, could she tempt Connor to leap with her.

Connor hauled the final box out of his car and slammed the lid shut. Maybe he'd gone a bit overboard at the store, but he couldn't help himself. His mum had loved Christmas. Every corner, open space or flat surface had been covered with Christmas paraphernalia. His friends had loved it and his dad had smiled indulgently and kissed his wife under the mistletoe every chance he got.

This was the first year he wouldn't be spending Christmas with his parents and siblings. Mum, Dad and Alice were currently visiting his younger brother who'd moved to Houston for his job. They'd been gone two months and were planning on staying until early February. In a way he was glad they weren't around to see what had transpired with his case and what had led him to Ghost Gum Springs and his job behind the bar at Smithy's pub. There was something relaxing about pulling beers and shooting the breeze with the locals. Completely different from standing in front of a judge and trying to convince him to do right by his client. He hadn't done right by Melanie and she'd paid the ultimate price.

With a determined shake of his head he pushed thoughts of his old life out of his mind. He had until the end of January to make a decision about his future. He would worry about it in the New Year.

In the meantime, he planned to show his temporary home town exactly what Christmas should look like. Little did Fred and his friends know he'd snapped some pictures and sent them to Smithy. His friend had responded with a laughing emoji and told him to have at it. The guy was in the middle of his honeymoon. He was thinking about his new wife and enjoying their time together. Smithy didn't give a rat's arse about what Connor was doing to his pub.

He shouldered his way through the door, his eye immediately going to the woman still perched on a stool at the bar. Fred was telling her something and she was watching him with genuine interest in her eyes. The expression surprised him. From the snarky comments she made in the car she gave off the impression of being a diva. It confirmed his thoughts that there was more than met the eye with Diana Jenkins. He liked a challenge and a challenge was exactly what he needed to keep his mind off his law career.

Diana wasn't short of a penny either; her suitcase was a top quality brand, and there was the Louis Vuitton purse perched on the stool next to her.

He'd made decent money as a lawyer and liked good quality things. His healthy bank account had given him the opportunity to step back from his career in law and reassess what he wanted to do. Smithy's offer and the salary he was being paid to manage the pub in the owner's absence was the money he lived off while he stayed in Ghost Gum Springs. Not that there was a lot of things to spend his wages on.

'Jesus, Connor, more Christmas decorations? Don't you think there's more than enough here already?'

Connor glanced over his shoulder and smiled at Jarod Owen, the local policeman. 'I got some just for the police station.'

Jarod shook his head. 'Please tell me you're joking.'

Connor hefted the box a little higher and made way for the police constable to get out of the entrance of the pub. 'Don't you think a little bit of Christmas cheer will make it so much easier to deal with the criminal element of the town?'

'I'm going to pretend this conversation never happened. Besides it would be a waste of time decorating the station. Don't want to make the place seem too friendly ...'

Connor laughed. He hadn't planned on decorating the police station, but it wasn't that bad of an idea. Come to think of it, he should check with Cindy Green who was the practice nurse for the town doctor, see if she wanted some help decorating the place, even though Christmas was only a couple days away.

A low whistle sounded from beside him and he followed Jarod's gaze. He was looking right at Diana. 'Well, well, who's that? She certainly doesn't look like she belongs around here, but maybe I could persuade her to stay.'

Connor carefully placed the box down on the table next to him, all the while attempting to control the overwhelming desire to punch Jarod in the gut. An extreme reaction to a flirty comment and a reaction he didn't quite understand. He'd met the woman just over an hour ago. He had no claim on her, but he almost wanted to go back to the good old days in school where you could put 'dibs' on the hot new girl.

However, there was no way Ms Diana Jenkins would take to being *dibbed* on. 'Don't get your hopes up. Her car broke down on the highway, I picked her up and brought her here. She's only staying long enough to get the hire car company to come and bring her a replacement car.'

Jarod burst out laughing. 'Good luck with that happening this time of year.'

'Yeah, I tried to tell her, but I don't think she really believed me.'

At that second, she threw her head back and laughed out loud at something Fred said. Her face lit up with joy and Connor wanted to know what Fred had said so he could say it again to keep her smiling like she was right now.

'Ahh, I see how it is,' murmured Jarod. 'She's all yours, mate.' He clapped Connor on the back and made his way to the bar, taking the empty stool next to Fred and not Diana.

Chapter Four

Diana downed the rest of her *lemonade* and listened with half an ear as Fred talked to the guy on the stool next to him. He'd been introduced to her as the local policeman, Jarod Owen. Hope had risen inside of her when she heard what he did for a living. Surely he would be able to get her back to Sydney, but he'd looked at her and, even before she'd asked, told her he couldn't drive her to the city.

For a second she pondered why he would blurt it out when she hadn't asked, then she spied Connor carrying another box out of the corner of her eye and had her answer. Anger flared in her and the temptation to flirt with Jarod fired through her senses, but the anger left her as quickly as it had arrived. Sure, Jarod was good-looking, he had that quintessential Australian surfer look she'd seen when she'd been cruising the internet planning her trip. In fact, he and Connor could almost pass as cousins, their looks were that similar, yet it was Connor's blue eyes she wanted to see flare to life when she flirted with him, not Jarod's.

Diana mentally facepalmed herself. She was here for one night, two at the most, flirting with her rescuer wasn't on her agenda. Forget about her plan to see the countryside, once she got back to Sydney she was going to look at changing her flight and head back to Montana. If people thought she was returning with her tail between her legs, she didn't care.

'Hey, you okay? Would you like another drink?'

Pulled from her internal thoughts she looked up into Connor's blue eyes, concern for her shining in their depths. Why would he be concerned for her, he'd only met her a short time ago? Unused to having that emotion directed to her, she pulled her shields around her. Too many times she'd been suckered in by people purporting to be concerned about her. Only one person looked out for Diana Jenkins now, and that was Diana Jenkins herself. Not some good-looking Australian bartender who probably lived from paycheck to paycheck. 'I'm fine. What I need is to get out of here.'

'So, you keep saying.' He tossed a cordless phone on the counter. 'Here you go, call the company. Good luck getting the answer you want.'

He walked to the other end of the bar to attend to some customers who had come in while she'd been lost in her thoughts. The rectangle device mocked her. Taking a deep breath she picked it up and clicked on the green telephone button. The buzz of the dial tone greeted her, waiting for her to dial. For a reason she failed to understand, she couldn't bring herself to dial the number. How stupid was that. All she'd wanted to do from the moment her car broke down was to get back to the city; now she had the means and she couldn't pull the trigger.

'Forgotten the number, love?'

Diana twisted her head and looked at Fred. 'The number's in my purse, but there really isn't any point is there? You said it yourself. I'm basically stuck here for the weekend.'

'Trust me, love, when I say there could be worse places to be stuck in.' He lifted his beer and took a long swallow. 'Ghost Gum Springs may not be big, but we've got everything you need.'

'A five-star hotel?'

He chuckled. 'No, but the rooms upstairs are clean and well maintained. I'm sure you'll be comfortable for a night or two.' He slid a look Connor's way and she followed his gaze. Connor looked the quintessential bartender, a towel tossed over his shoulder as he conversed with some patrons. 'Maybe you'll even decide to stay a little longer,' he finished quietly.

Nope. Not happening. Come Monday she was going to be placing the call and getting her ass back to Sydney.

She really wasn't cut out for adventure.

Connor closed the door, clicked the lock into place and walked back into the main room. Silence descended over the bar along with a sense of well-being. The work maybe hard, but he couldn't deny he was really enjoying playing barman.

'Do you need some help cleaning up?'

Startled he looked over his shoulder and saw Diana hovering in the doorway connecting the main bar with the hallway leading to the upstairs room. He'd shown her to a room a couple of hours ago. He figured she'd be asleep by now. She'd changed into some leggings that enhanced the long, lean length of her legs even better than the mini skirt she'd been wearing earlier. Her tank scooped low in the neck and even from where he stood, it didn't hide the upper curves of her breasts.

He shook his head in an attempt to control the fire burning through him.

'Oh, okay, well goodnight.'

Lost in the red mist of desire creeping over him, it took Connor a couple of seconds to process her words. He threw down the dish rag he was using and ate up the distance between where he was working and where she'd been standing. When he got to the doorway, she was almost to the stairs.

'Diana? Wait.'

She paused but didn't turn around. The way her shoulders slumped, as though she'd been wounded by his words surprised him. In the whole time she'd been sitting at the bar, she'd appeared confident, like nothing would bother her. Had it all been an act?

He closed the distance and laid a soft hand on her shoulder, squeezing it gently. Half a heartbeat later she swivelled her head to look at him over her shoulder. 'I didn't mean to bother you.'

'You didn't, trust me, you surprised me that's all. Usually once a guest heads upstairs that's where they stay.' His hand slipped off her shoulder when she took a step away and turned to face him. He caught the aroma of apples and noticed the dampness still lingering in patches of her hair. The fresh scent enticed him to lean forward and breathe in to find out if the apples came from her hair or her skin.

His dick tightened against his pants. Bloody hell, he never reacted this quickly to a woman. Sure, it had been a few months since he'd bedded one, but he'd left the spontaneous erection stage of his life a long time ago.

Connor breathed through his nose, big mistake, all that did was give him another lungful of her delicious aroma. It also did nothing to calm his raging body. 'Can I …' his voice broke and he coughed to clear it. 'Can I get you another drink, something to help you sleep?'

A light pink hue coloured her cheeks. Hmm, what was that all about.

'I wouldn't mind another glass of lemonade, please.'

'You mean Sprite,' he teased her.

A smile lit up her face. This time a genuine one and he found himself wanting to find out how to keep it on her face, instead of the defeated look he'd seen when he'd stopped her in the hallway. His earlier suspicions were correct—there was definitely more than met the eye with Diana. That little hint of vulnerability he'd seen intrigued him. It had been a long time since he'd been intrigued by a woman. It was refreshing. 'Come on,' he canted his head. 'I think I can scrounge up another glass for you.'

He waited until she walked up next to him before he started for the main bar area.

'It really does look like Santa vomited in here.'

He paused on the threshold, a smile spreading out over his face. 'It does, doesn't it. Looks fantastic.' He'd added some of the decorations he'd collected in Sydney. He'd spoken to Cindy earlier and planned to take the rest over to Doc Bateman's surgery in the morning.

Diana shook her head and walked into the room in front of him. He admired the soft sway of her hips and the way the material lovingly cupped her arse.

Jesus Christ, he needed to get a hold of himself. He could honestly say in all his life, he'd never been so instantly turned on like he was right now. He took a couple of deep breaths and willed his dick to control itself. He'd definitely be taking a cold shower later on.

'What's the deal with you and all these decorations,' she asked and waved her hand around. 'I can understand a woman going over the top, but not a guy.'

Connor walked behind the bar, at least his lower half would be hidden behind the length of wood. 'Christmas was always a big deal in my family. My mum loves it and pretty much decorates every inch of the house. What's not to love about it?'

'Commercialisation and the fact not everyone can afford to have Santa vomit all over their house.'

Bitterness underlined her comments, giving him another tiny glance into her life. He planned to dig a little deeper and as a lawyer, he could draw out information from the most reluctant witness. 'You don't like Christmas?' He'd start with an easy and, yes, obvious question.

A perfectly shaped eyebrow arched. 'What gave me away?'

He chuckled. 'I take it Christmas wasn't a big thing with you? Which surprises me considering all the Christmas movies that come out of the States every year.'

'As I said, it's all commercialisation, don't believe everything you see on television. Or hear. If that was the case, then I'd be expecting kangaroos to be hopping down the streets of central Sydney.'

'True, although if you're lucky you might see one tomorrow. They've been known to stroll down the street then pop in here for a cool bevy.'

She rolled her eyes. 'I think you're making fun of me. And what the hell is a bevy?'

He reached beneath the counter and pulled out a clean glass. 'A bevy is …' he started and finished filling the glass with lemonade. 'This.' He placed the glass in front of her.

'A drink? Or a lemonade?'

'A drink.'

She lifted it to her lips and he bit back a groan as she swallowed down some of the contents. 'Why don't you just say a drink?'

'Because it's more fun to confuse you.' As her eyes narrowed he could tell he was pushing his luck with his teasing. 'Tell me, did you grow up having a white Christmas?'

'More like a black Christmas,' she muttered and placed her hands on the counter as though she was about to push away and head back to her room.

Not thinking, he reached out and laid his hand over hers. 'I'm sorry. I'll stop asking questions.'

If any of the opposing lawyers he'd conquered in the courtroom saw him now their jaws would probably drop to the floor—he never gave up on a witness this easily. But Diana wasn't a witness and didn't deserve his cross-examination, even though he'd planned to find out what he could about her. Every now and then she let her prickly guard down. It must be hard to constantly feel the need to protect oneself. Hide who you really were. Why did she do that? More to the point why did he want to delve beneath the prickly skin and see if he could find the true woman beneath. He should just drive her back to Sydney himself. Only, if his mum was here she'd open her house to a stranger and welcome her with open arms. Christmas was the season to be around people, not by yourself, especially when you were in a strange country. He was pretty sure his mum would be happy he was doing everything he could to make Diana feel welcome.

'Which part of the States are you from?' Okay, maybe he couldn't stop being a lawyer.

'I thought you weren't going to ask any more questions.'

Connor shrugged as he picked up a tray to collect the glasses still resting on various tables. 'I'm a barman, I ask questions and everyone tells me their problems.'

'They train that into you at bartending school?'

Connor laughed. 'It's more something you pick up as you go along.' If only she knew where he'd got his questioning skills. For some reason he didn't want to mention his profession, just like she didn't want to talk about herself. He probably should respect that. But they were alone in a big pub. It was almost midnight and he couldn't deny he wanted to get to know this American beauty he'd picked up on the side of the road.

'Well I'm from Packenridge Montana, where everyone knows your name and your business.'

Connor nodded. 'Sounds like here.'

'Oh no, Packenridge is nothing like this place. I may have only been here for a few hours, but the people are very different.'

'How so?'

Perfect white teeth pulled at her plump bottom lip, as though if she said something she'd be struck down by lightning. She released her grip on the pink flesh and shrugged her shoulders. 'They just are.' She picked up the drink, signalling that was all she planned on telling him.

Diana sat at the bar while he collected up the glasses and placed the tray on the counter.

'Do you want some help?' she asked when he went to move away again.

'Thanks, but I've got it under control. I've got it down to a fine art now.'

With efficient movements he wiped the tables down.

'You know I don't think I've ever seen a man look so domestic,' said Diana as he rinsed the cloth out.

'I've been living by myself since I was eighteen. My mum made sure I could do the basics and then I improved over the years by myself.' It was on the tip of his tongue to ask Diana if she cooked with her mum, but he refrained.

'Kudos to your mom. Not many men would admit to being so domestic.'

He winked at her. 'I'm not most men.'

'I'm beginning to see that.'

Chapter Five

Diana stepped out of her room the next morning. After a good night's sleep she was ready to call the rental company and get back on the road to Sydney. Even though Fred said they probably wouldn't be open she didn't quite believe that. Rental companies had to work on a Saturday.

She skipped down the stairs and stopped when she saw Connor. She'd hoped her annoyance at her situation had given him an extra spark to his handsomeness. But no, if anything, he was even better looking first thing in the morning than he was last night wiping down the tables like a pro. Today he had on a pair of cargo shorts that finished just below his knee and was again wearing a snug-fitting polo shirt. His muscles bulged as he lifted a box off the ground and put it on a table. A box that looked suspiciously like one of the boxes he'd had in his trunk when he'd picked her up the previous day.

'Oh my God, please tell me you're not putting more decorations around this place? Or the upstairs rooms.' She shuddered at the thought of her room being 'Christmassed' out.

His laughter rumbled across the room. A warmth began to form in her belly and spread out, heating areas she'd sworn had been frozen up from Grandma Mary-Lou's habit of emasculating every man who'd tried to date her after college. Not that there were many in Packenridge, most usually kept away from her. Not to mention after what she went through during her senior year of high school. Just because Connor was being nice didn't mean anything. Remember, once burned twice as shy.

She so didn't need this inconvenient attraction to Connor Shetland. It was too much of a risk. The sooner she got out of this place the safer she'd be.

'Diana? Did you hear me? Do you want to come?'

The sound of Connor's voice practically in her ear jolted her back to the present. 'Pardon?'

Again he laughed. This time she didn't let it overpower her sense of hearing and focused on a spot over his shoulder while he spoke to her. 'You didn't hear a word I said, did you? Is this a normal habit for you?'

Indignation rose up inside of her at the suggestion she was 'flaky'. She was the least flaky person on the planet. Although around him, she couldn't deny he caused her to lose her equilibrium. 'No, it's not and I'm still …' She tried to clutch onto a reason for her supposed flakiness.

'Jetlagged?'

'Yes.' She practically shouted the word, even though it wasn't anywhere near the truth. 'It's a long flight to Australia from the United States.'

'Right.' How he managed to inject a wealth of scepticism in five little letters she had no idea, but he did.

'You were saying?' She pointed to the box on the table.

'I'm packing up some decorations to take to the local doctor's surgery. They're not open today, but Cindy has agreed to meet me there. I wanted to know if you'd like to come with me and meet her. She's nice and friendly. I think you'll like her.'

An irrational spark of jealousy pierced her belly, deflating the bubble of desire his laughter had caused. Who was this Cindy? Was she his girlfriend? Is that why she was opening the practice especially for him?

Why did it even matter?

'Well I know you're not staying and are champing at the bit to get out of here, but I thought you might like to meet her. Doesn't matter, you can stay here.'

Connor turned away and picked up the box in preparation of walking out the door. 'Wait? What?'

He paused and looked over his shoulder. 'You said to me *Why did it even matter?* I took that as a message that you didn't want to come with me.'

God, she'd spoken that out loud. She was going right back to living up to the vague impression Connor had of her. Grandma Mary-Lou would be chortling loudly at this. The last thing she wanted was to be stuck in the pub by herself. Maybe she could call the car rental place from the doctor's surgery? Offer to leave a couple of quarters to pay for the call.

Before she could do any of that she needed to fix this mess her irrational shot of jealousy had dropped herself into. 'Sorry, Connor, I didn't mean that at all. I admit, I'm all out of sorts, nothing seems to be working out like I hoped. If the invitation still stands, I'd like to come with you.'

His eyes narrowed, as though trying to confirm she really did mean the words or if she was just playing nice. In the end he shrugged and hefted the box a little higher. 'Okay, let's go.'

She blew out a breath, minor crisis diverted. Pulling herself up to stand a little straighter she followed Connor out of the pub and into the bright morning light. 'Damn,' she muttered.

'What?'

'It's bright out, can I run upstairs and grab my sunglasses?' She noted that he was sporting a pair and she had no idea where he'd conjured them up from.

'Sure.'

'Thanks.'

Within two minutes she was back, and Connor was standing where she'd left him, the box on the ground beside him and his phone in his hand.

A dart of anger arrowed through her. 'Hey, I didn't think you had a cell phone. Why didn't you give it to me yesterday when you stopped to help me? I told you I needed to make a call?'

He glanced up from his device and looked at her. She wished she could see what he was thinking but his eyes were hidden behind his glasses. 'There was no point mentioning I had a mobile yesterday. There's no reception out where you were stranded. By the time we got into town, where there was reception, you were annoyed with me.' He shrugged his shoulders. 'Besides I knew there was a landline inside and you could make your call that way.'

Diana hated that what he said was pretty much how things had gone down. She hated that he was right. And she hated that he looked so delectable, that she wanted to see what it would be like to be held by his strong arms. The same arms that were now hefting the box of decorations up.

'You ready to go now?' he asked, and she caught a flash of an eyebrow as it rose above his sunglasses line.

'Yes.'

God, it was tiring being so petty and angry. How had Grandma Mary-Lou gone through her whole life like this? Generally speaking she was a cheerful person, it had annoyed the people in town who had tried so hard to bring her down with their snide comments about her parentage.

Plus, she did enjoy life. She wanted adventure and well, she guessed she was having an adventure now. She needed to embrace it, even if it wasn't as smooth as she wanted it to be.

As they walked down the main street of Ghost Gum Springs, Diana took the time to look around. They walked past a café, and the aroma of freshly baked goods wafted out, teasing her senses. Underlying it was the scent of brewed coffee and her mouth started watering. Her day wasn't complete without a strong cup of joe. On the other side of the main street was a grocery store and post office.

As she suspected, this place was like every small town in America, yet there was a different feel here compared to home. Here the town almost appeared welcoming. As though it was opening its arms and bringing her into its fold. Which was absolutely stupid and maybe she was still suffering from sunstroke after her spell in the hot Australian sun. Or the jetlag she'd lied about having.

'Here we are,' Connor said as they stopped out the front of a large white building. It had a peaked roof with red tiles. The words *Dr John Bateman, GP* was stencilled on the door.

There had been no doctor's surgery in Packenridge. If anyone was sick they had to travel an hour and a half to a bigger town to get treated. Most people became adept at dealing with minor injuries and only making the long journey if it was really serious.

Diana glanced around. Ghost Gum Springs didn't look much bigger than the place she'd grown up in, how did they have a doctor? How busy was the guy too? 'This Dr Bateman must have a pretty good life.'

'What do you mean?' asked Connor as he shifted the box to one arm, his muscles bunching beneath his shirt.

'Well this town isn't huge, how many people would he see on a regular basis? I'm just surprised the town has its own doctor.'

'From what I've heard, John's been here for years. There's a decent-sized hospital about an hour away and I think he does clinics at outlying towns on a regular basis.'

'Packenridge could've benefited from a system like this,' she muttered as the door opened and a pretty woman who Diana recognised from the bar the previous evening opened the door.

'Hey Connor, come in, John is excited to see what you've brought us. He popped the tree in the corner already for you.' She stepped back to allow Connor to walk inside. Diana wasn't sure what to do. Connor hadn't introduced them, and she wasn't one to foist herself onto people if she wasn't welcome. She needn't have worried as an arm filled her line of vision. 'Hi, I'm Cindy Green, I saw you last night at the pub, but didn't get a chance to meet you.'

She took the offered hand and shook it. 'Hey, I'm Diana Jenkins. It's nice to meet you too.'

'Oh, you're from the States, which part?'

'A small town in Montana. Nowhere special.' It was impossible to keep the cynicism out of her voice.

'Okay then, let's get these decorations unpacked,' Connor said, and Diana sent him a silent thanks. Answering questions about her home wasn't high on her agenda of things to do while on vacation.

'Are you sure you want to let Connor loose on your waiting room?' asked Diana. 'You have seen the bar, haven't you?'

'I have, and I love it. It looks perfect. I didn't get a chance to decorate last year as I had just moved here. John doesn't do much decorating either. Just the bare minimum,' Cindy commented as she peered into the box Connor was opening.

'You mean Santa's little helper wasn't here last year to spread holiday cheer?' Holy shit, did she sound as cynical as she thought she did? Yep, if the look Cindy was sending in her direction was anything to go by. She really needed to get herself under control. Cindy didn't deserve her attitude.

'No, Connor's only been here just over a month. Is that right?'

'Yeah, I arrived here towards the end of November.'

That surprised her. The way the locals had given him a hard time in the pub the previous evening, she'd thought he'd been here for a few years.

'Hey Cindy, do you think Diana can use your phone? She wants to phone the rental place in Sydney to see if they can come and get her. Her car broke down on the side of the road about half an hour out of town.'

'Oh wow, that's not good. For sure you can use the phone, follow me,' the other woman beckoned. 'I'll get you sorted with an outside line. Don't go too crazy in here, Connor.'

He winked at the pretty doctor's assistant. 'Can't make any promises.'

Diana's feet appeared glued to the ground, her reluctance to move away surprising. She wanted to get away from the small town, didn't she?

Yes. An emphatic yes.

Then why was she so reluctant to follow Cindy and make that call?

Giving herself a mental shake she got her shit together and followed Cindy. She wanted out of here and she wanted out now.

Maybe.

Connor whistled to himself as he draped tinsel over the reception counter. He could hear the soft murmur of voices and then Cindy's laugh. The practice nurse was very pretty, but she didn't make his blood zing whenever he saw her, unlike what happened when Diana got within three feet of him.

However, it didn't matter what sort of feelings he imagined Diana's presence conjured up. No matter how tempting it was to dig beneath the surface and try and find the real Diana hidden beneath the prickles, she was arranging to get as far away from this town as possible right now.

Cindy walked out as he was standing back to judge his tinsel handiwork. 'Wow, how did you get the tinsel to hang in perfect semi-circles? If I tried to do that, one side would be longer than the other.'

'It's a secret. One I can't share with you.'

Cindy rolled her eyes and shook her head. 'Right, didn't realise you and Santa were such good buddies.'

'Don't you know, it's Mrs Claus that controls all the decorations.'

Cindy giggled. 'You really are a hopeless Christmas addict. Please tell me you don't go crazy on Valentine's Day.'

'Nope. Christmas is the only time I bother with decorations. When you're with the right woman every day is Valentine's Day.'

'Not only a Christmas elf, but a hopeless romantic too. I never would've guessed.'

Connor turned to find Diana standing in the doorway. 'There's a lot you don't know about me.'

As Diana held his gaze, everything in his peripheral vision faded. Tension sizzled through the air, like the moment before lightning flashed through the sky. 'I'm beginning to see that,' she murmured.

'Hmm, well, uh. I think I'll leave you to it. I need to, uh, check out the storeroom.' Cindy rushed off before Connor could stop her.

Diana broke the silence that had cropped up between them. 'Well that was awkward.'

Connor cleared his throat and grabbed a box of ornaments.

What the hell was that?

How could he lose himself in a pair of eyes like he'd done when he and Diana looked at each other? It had never happened to him before.

It's Christmas, you deserve a little holiday cheer.

He slammed the brakes on that voice. As tempting as the idea was, Diana was probably leaving today. He grasped onto that like a lifeline. 'Did you get through to the rental place?'

'Yeah.' How she managed to inject a wealth of dejection in one word was beyond him.

'I take it, it's not good news.'

'No. They can't get anybody out to me until the day after Boxing Day. Whatever day that is. Plus, they wanted to know where the car is and my *stuck in the middle of nowhere* wasn't helpful.' She shrugged her shoulders. 'So, it looks like I'm stuck here.'

Connor put down the box and walked over to where she stood. He put his hands on her shoulders. 'Boxing Day is the day after Christmas so the day after that is the twenty-seventh. It's only a few days. And your car is here, I arranged for a tow truck from White Hope to go pick it up. It was delivered to the pub last night. I'm surprised you didn't see it when you walked out this morning. You looked right at it.'

At the mention of her car, her demeanour changed, brightened up as if she'd been given the best Christmas gift ever. 'It is? That's great, maybe it's going to be okay to drive now. I should go check it out.'

She went to rush past him, but he took hold of her hand as she walked past. 'What?'

Speaking was a lost art form as Connor concentrated on the warmth radiating up his arm from the simple contact between his fingers and Diana's bare arm. 'You're not going anywhere.'

His words came out harsher than he intended, and she pulled away from him. 'Really? I don't think you get a say in what I can and can't do?'

'Sorry,' he rubbed a hand through his hair. 'That came out harsher than I intended. Robbo, the tow truck driver, is also a mechanic. He said a stone had pierced the radiator. The only way that car is getting to Sydney is on the back of a truck.'

The fight drained out of her and he pulled her into his arms, hugging her to his chest. 'I'm sorry. Ghost Gum Springs isn't that bad.' He brushed a kiss across the top of her head. Her body softened against his and his dick twitched at the way she wiggled her hips against him.

'This was supposed to be a fun vacation. Now it's a disaster.'

Connor pulled back and the action had Diana looking up at him. 'It's not a disaster. It's a different adventure.'

Her lips pursed, and he bit back a groan. He smoothed a hand across her cheek and then lowered his head. His lips lightly swept across hers. The touch quick, but sweet. Connor began to pull away, but Diana followed until their lips connected again. This time for a longer touch and taste. He tightened his hold and widened his stance to brace the both of them. Her mouth opened beneath his and he slipped his tongue inside. Desire for more simmered to life through his blood.

It was insane, this instant attraction he had for Diana. Sure, he'd been drawn to other women in the past. He'd seen the pretty face and fabulous body and wanted to get to know them. Only it was always on a superficial level. He'd had long-term relationships, had even thought about asking one or two to move in with him. Those relationships had moved slow, and never with the strength of need as what was flowing through him now with Diana. A woman he'd known for less than twenty-four hours.

Sensibilities returned, and he broke the kiss, stepping away from her. Her ragged breathing reached his ears and he knew if he looked at her, he wouldn't be able to resist taking her in his arms again.

'I probably should get back to this,' he said vaguely pointing to the bare tree.

'Yeah, I think I'll walk back to the pub.'

'I can walk you back and then return here to finish up.'

Diana rolled her eyes and he smiled—there's his sassy girl. *No, she's not your girl, she's a guest.*

But you'd like her to be more than just a guest.

Since when did he have arguments in his mind?

'I don't think I'll get lost, it's just down the street.'

He reached into his pocket and tossed a set of keys at her. She caught them in one hand. 'You'll need those to get in. Just leave them on the bar, everyone knows the pub doesn't open until midday on a Saturday. You're the only guest staying at the moment, so you won't be disturbed.'

'Thanks.'

He watched her walk out the door, memorising the way her hips swayed slowly left to right. He was still gazing at the closed door when Cindy walked out.

'Well I kind of expected the tree to be finished, but it looks like you haven't done much since I left you.'

'Right, yeah, sorry. I'll be out of your way in a flash.'

Cindy laughed. 'I just bet you will.'

Connor ignored the unspoken meaning of her words. Had she seen Diana and him kissing? Jesus, did it matter? He didn't answer to her. He didn't answer to anyone but himself.

What he should do was ignore the voice in his head telling him he wanted Diana and listen to the voice that said she wasn't his to have. Only problem was, he badly wanted to listen to the devilish voice that promised more pleasure to come.

Chapter Six

Once again, Connor's eyes darted to the door leading from the hall to the pub to see if Diana was going to walk through it. It remained firmly shut. He hadn't seen her since she left Dr Bateman's office. The keys lying on the wooden bar indicated that she'd made her way back safely to the hotel.

When he returned from decorating the doctor's surgery, he'd been busy organising the lunch and dinner menu with the pub's cook, Chook. Connor didn't know what his real name was, but in the country if someone says their name's Chook, that's what you call them.

For a Saturday, the lunch crowd was big. It could be because it was another hot day and everyone enjoyed the cool air-conditioned comfort the pub offered. Connor didn't mind, the more profits he could secure while Smithy was away on his honeymoon the better he felt. It had been a generous offer from his friend to take over the running of his business. His experience had been limited, but he learned fast and loved a challenge.

He looked at the door again while he was pouring a beer, willing it to open.

'Connor, I want beer, mate, not bloody foam,' Gary from the grocery store grumbled.

A quick look down confirmed he'd fucked up. 'Sorry, mate.' He dumped the contents in the drain and grabbed a fresh glass. This time there was less than an inch of foam in the glass when he placed it on the coaster.

Gary took a swallow and then looked over at the door. 'Why you watching the door so much?'

'He's looking to see if his American girlfriend is going to show,' piped up Fred from the other end of the bar.

Great, just what he needed, comments from the peanut gallery. 'Can it, Fred. Diana's not my girlfriend, but she is a hotel guest. I'm just looking out for Smithy's business. Don't want to get a bad Yelp review or something.'

'What are you yammering about?' asked Fred.

'Nothing,' he muttered as he grabbed a damp cloth and went off to wipe down some tables. There it was, the hazard of living in a small town. Everyone always had an opinion and loved sticking their noses in where they weren't wanted.

The next couple of hours passed in a flurry of meals and drinks. Connor's feet were aching by the time the only two people remaining were Gary and Fred. Both were looking a little worse for wear.

Normally, Fred was pretty good at controlling his beer consumption, but he seemed to be keeping pace with Gary.

Connor leaned forward on the bar, hoping to take a little pressure off his feet. 'So why are you still here, Gary? Why aren't you home.'

'Missus and I had a fight. I'm waiting for her to cool down.'

Connor chuckled. 'Returning home drunk is sure to win you a few brownie points. How about I get you a coffee before you head out?' He looked over to Fred. 'You want one too, Fred?'

'Nah, it's only me dog Blue at home. He won't care if I turn up three sheets to the wind.' He let out a large belch. 'See ya, Connor.'

He staggered to the door and almost ran into Diana as she finally appeared. 'Sorry, love,' Fred slurred before looking at Connor. 'Your girlfriend's here, Connor.'

He shook his head at Fred's attempt at being funny. 'Bye, Fred, don't trip on your way out.'

The other man waved his hand and disappeared through the door.

'Thanks for the offer of coffee, but I'll pass,' Gary mumbled as he too stood, swayed then staggered towards the door. 'Mattie will have left the pot on. We fight. I get drunk. She makes coffee. I sleep and all's well in the morning. Been that way for twenty years. God, I love that woman.'

He tipped his head as he walked past Diana and she looked at him as if he had ten heads. The door slammed behind Gary and it was only him and Diana—again.

'Will they be okay?' she asked as she swung a look at the door the men had left through.

'Yeah, they'll be fine.'

She sauntered up to the bar, her hands in the pockets of her pants. She'd changed since he'd last seen her. She was now wearing a short-sleeved sweater. The dip at the front highlighted her curves and the sky-blue colour looked amazing on her. 'You know you're not a very responsible bartender if you keep serving them when they're drunk. How do you know they won't try and drive home?'

'Easy,' Connor said as he reached underneath the counter and pulled out a square box. Inside were two sets of car keys. 'Normally I wouldn't let them drink so much, but it's Christmas.'

She crossed her arms, the movement pushing up her breasts. His body responded immediately, and he tightened his hold on the box to stop himself from reaching over and running his finger over the tantalising swell. 'I still don't think it's a responsible thing to do. Drinking is an addiction. Addictions kill.'

He studied Diana closely. Her face lost all animation as she spoke about addiction and he could hear the pain in her voice. Knowing it wasn't the most sensible thing to do, because he didn't know how she'd react, he walked around the end of the bar until he stood in front of her. Close but not touching. Her perfume teased him, like it always did when he got near her.

'Did you lose someone you loved to an addiction?' It seemed the logical conclusion to come to. Unless she'd been addicted to a substance. Perhaps her trip to Australia was her reward for being sober or drug free for a year.

'Doesn't matter,' she said.

Clearly, she didn't want to talk about it and regretted bringing it up. He'd give her a pass. Something like an addict's recovery was their own personal journey. At the end of the day she probably wouldn't be around here long enough for him to enquire more about it.

'What have you been doing today?' he asked as he moved away to collect some used coasters from a nearby table.

'Not much.'

'Look, I know Ghost Gum Springs is small, but you don't have to stay in your room the whole time you're here. Why don't you look around? It's not a bad town, as towns go.'

'Are you an expert on towns? Cindy said you only arrived in November, how much experience with small towns do you really have? Trust me I've had plenty.'

'Okay, fair point, this is the only small town I've lived in.' An idea formed in his mind. An idea he should squash because nothing good would come of it. Only it had taken hold and he couldn't let it go now. 'How about I show you around tomorrow. The pub doesn't open until five on a Sunday.'

What he said was true, Ghost Gum Springs was small, but a few kilometres west there was the natural spring that gave the town its name. He could go to Beryl's café and pick up some sandwiches and some of her famous cream buns. That is if Diana agreed.

'How about you drive me back to Sydney instead?'

Damn, he should've thought she'd counter with that. 'Okay, how about we make a deal?'

'I'm listening.' Well at least she hadn't completely nixed his idea and he could see she was interested in what he had to say.

'Give me tomorrow to show you that staying here is a great way to experience a Down Under Christmas. If you don't feel that way, we'll get up at the crack of dawn on Christmas Eve and I'll drive you to Sydney.'

Her shoulders picked up and a small smile curved her gorgeous lips. Lips he wouldn't mind sampling again. 'You'd do that?'

'Sure.' He hoped he could convince her to stay though, he didn't fancy spending eight hours in the car before one of the busiest days in the pub, but for her he'd do it.

She held out her hand. 'Deal.'

He grasped and instead of shaking it brought it up to his lips, kissing the top of her palm softly. 'Deal.'

What was she thinking?

Diana smoothed her hands down the sides of her capri pants. It was only five minutes until she had to go downstairs and meet up with Connor and his let-me-convince-you-small-towns-are-good tour. No way was that about to happen.

She'd deliberately stayed in her room the whole day after their kiss at the doctor's surgery. A kiss that had played on repeat in her mind all through the day and into her dreams.

Not leaving her room had been the only way she could protect herself from falling under the town's charm. Cindy had been super friendly to her in the short amount of time they'd spent together. Fred was how she imagined a grandfather would be, fun and inappropriate. But she'd been burnt too many times by people pretending to be her friend only to turn their back on her. They'd say the cute footballer wanted to dance with her, and then she'd walk out on the dance floor to find it vacant and everyone staring and laughing at her. Humiliated didn't begin to describe her emotion at that moment, but she decided on that lonely dance floor to pull a cloak of indifference around her. Smile and be happy and not show how hurt she really was underneath.

Unfortunately, her grandmother's secret keeping had angered her more than she was willing to admit. Today she would make the effort to not be such a bitch to Connor. He didn't have to take her out. And secretly, a part of her was thrilled to know she was getting to spend the whole day with a good-looking guy.

While she was being brutally honest with herself, sitting alone in her room for another day didn't appeal. Time would tell if she'd made the right decision to spend it with Connor instead.

'Okay, Diana Jenkins, you're a grown ass woman, stop acting like Grandma Mary-Lou still controls your life.'

Straightening her spine, she collected her handbag, checking that she had her sunglasses, lip balm and camera. Connor said to wear a swimsuit, so beneath her t-shirt and pants, she wore her black bikini. The chances of her stripping down to it were slim. No way was she swimming in front of Connor. Oh, she wasn't body conscious, it was just she'd heard the stories about crocodiles taking people who took an innocent swim. The last thing she planned on being was a crocodile's Christmas dinner. Besides, they were in the middle of rural Australia, she hadn't seen any sign of water. Nor had she seen a community pool. Nope, her clothes were going to stay firmly on. No showing off her bikini clad body to the sexy bartender.

'Let's do this.'

Diana opened the door and walked down the stairs, screeching to a halt when she spied Connor's ass sticking up in the air as he bent over a cooler. A sense of déjà vu swept over her. This set up was so similar to when she'd come down the stairs the previous day.

Damn, why did he have to be so delicious looking? It would be better if he was ugly as sin. Then again, she probably wouldn't have wanted to spend the day with him.

Whoa, she wasn't normally shallow, but her last thought was so catty Grandma Mary-Lou would've been proud.

Right, she was going to make the most of today because she was determined to stick to her plan and return to Sydney tomorrow. So what if that meant she'd be spending Christmas by herself. Nothing new for her. Christmas was always just another day to Grandma Mary-Lou. How could you get excited when you stopped getting gifts when you were thirteen?

'Morning Diana, you ready to go?'

Lost in her thoughts she hadn't seen Connor straighten or turn and face her. Once again he was wearing a shirt that highlighted the blue of his eyes. It hugged his broad shoulders and looked soft, so soft her fingers itched to reach out and touch it.

He quirked an eyebrow and she wanted the floor to open up and swallow her. God, she was standing there like a lump of coal. She wracked her memory to try and recall what he'd said to her. Oh right. 'Yep, all ready.'

'Great, I've got some drinks in the esky. I'll just load it in the car and then we'll be on our way.'

Diana worked out the *esky* was the cooler he was bent over when she'd come down the stairs. 'Do you need help with anything else?' she asked, not wanting to seem like she wasn't going to make an effort.

'All under control.'

Her stomach grumbled. Dinner had been a long time ago. 'Can I go grab something to eat from the kitchen? Like an apple or something else.'

Connor hefted up the cooler, his muscles bunching and bulging with the movement. 'Nope.'

He disappeared out the door before she could question him further. No, that wasn't happening. He wasn't going to dismiss her like she was a piece of trash. She stomped out the door and followed him to the SUV he was loading the cooler into. A car she didn't recognise. The car he'd picked her up in was a mid-sized sedan. This vehicle looked like it was made to handle the tough Australian outback terrain she'd heard so much about.

'What do you mean I can't get anything to eat?'

Connor glanced over his shoulder. 'I'm taking you out to breakfast. It's all part of the tour. If you eat something now, you'll spoil your appetite.'

'Oh.' The indignation dissipated out of her.

He walked up to her and she held her breath. 'I'm not mean.' He leaned in and kissed her cheek. 'I'm going to show you the best time. Convince you to stay.'

A shiver rippled down her spine. She had to fight these feelings, remain strong and not get pulled under his spell. 'Why would you try to convince me to stay?'

'I think, if you give it a chance, you might be surprised.'

Familiar words. Words she'd heard so many times over the years. Each time she started something with the hope of *being surprised* the biggest surprise she ever got was how terrible it was. Not how fantastic.

There was no reason for her not to expect this time to be any different, even if the guy she was with was completely different to anyone she'd ever met. Connor didn't *know* her or know of her parents and what they were like, and she had no plans to share any of that with him. She'd already shared too much.

'We'll see,' she murmured as she brushed past him to go to the passenger side of the car.

'You'll need the keys if you're planning on driving.'

'Huh?' Seeing as she had no idea where they were headed why would he say that to her.

Connor canted his head to the car, his smile lighting up more than her face, the warm glow from his peck on the cheek was turning into a full-on inferno. 'You're standing by the driver's side.'

'What? No, I'm not.'

'Honey, we drive on the right-hand side of the car.'

Diana peered into the car and saw the steering wheel. 'Oh, right.'

Connor slung an arm over her shoulder. 'Easy mistake to make. Come on.' He led her around to the passenger side of the car.

Yeah, this was going to be a fantastic day … maybe.

Chapter Seven

Connor gripped the steering wheel to prevent himself from reaching over and taking Diana's hand in his. A sign to reassure her that everything was going to be okay. She seemed to enjoy herself during breakfast at Beryl's café. Fred had been there and so he'd spent some time joking with her. Never before had he seen the crusty older man smile as much as he did when he'd been talking to her.

Connor could admit to himself that a little dart, well okay more than a little, a huge dart of jealousy had stabbed him in the gut. He wanted to make Diana smile and laugh like that. He wanted to find out what made the woman tick. There were so many secrets to her he had no idea if he'd ever uncover them all.

'How much further?' she asked.

'Not much,' he replied as the SUV jolted left to right as it went over another pothole. The road they were travelling to get to the springs wasn't the smoothest.

'Great, although not sure my teeth are going to last. If I've got any cracked teeth, I'm going to send the dentist bill to you.'

He loved the way her snark came out every now and then. Most guys would get annoyed with it, but to him, it showed him under all the layers Diana had a good sense of humour. She seemed to rarely let it out though.

'I can guarantee if you break a tooth I would be more than happy to pay your bill. A smile as beautiful as yours shouldn't be marred.'

'That's very superficial of you, Connor Shetland. There is more to a woman than her looks. And my smile is far from beautiful, you did notice my crooked front tooth didn't you?'

'Yes, and you're right my comment was inappropriate. A broken tooth would only enhance your ugly smile.'

Diana burst out laughing, and his heart leapt at the carefree sound. Even more natural than the laughs she'd shared with Fred.

Score one for Team Shetland.

The large ghost gums the town was named for thinned out and a few seconds later they drove into a clearing. His body relaxed naturally at the gorgeous sight of the blue spring. There were only little patches of green among the expanse of brown from dried out wildflowers and other grasses natural to the Australian outback. Instead of detracting from the beauty of the lake, it only highlighted Mother Nature's handiwork.

A gasp sounded from the woman riding next him. 'Oh wow, this is stunning.'

Before he'd even turned the engine off her door was open and she was out, striding down to the spring. He studied her for a few moments, admiring the curve of her arse beneath the tight black capris she was wearing. Around her neck he could see the strings of her bikini top tied into a neat bow. His body twitched at the thought of seeing Diana in her bathing suit, running his hands over the smooth expanse of her back, cupping her rounded cheeks and bringing her close to him, her breasts crushing against his chest as he kissed her.

Great, now he had to stay in the car for a little longer until his erection subsided. Unless ... he eyed the spring. Having swum in it before, he was well aware of how cold the water was. Just what his body needed. Opening his door, he yanked his t-shirt up and over his head. He kicked his shoes off before removing his socks.

He jogged to where Diana was standing, picking up speed as he got a little closer to her. 'Last one in's a rotten egg.'

The cold water clung to him as he dove into the spring, refreshing, revitalising and reducing his hard-on almost immediately. He popped his head out of the water shaking it, droplets spraying around him in a perfect circle.

'Man, this feels awesome,' he grinned and looked at Diana. The joy slipping out of him at the look of horror on her face.

What the hell?

He waded through the water as quickly as he could to get to her side, grabbing her hands. They were ice cold on an almost forty degree Celsius day. 'Diana? What's wrong?'

'Croc-crocodile.' She said the word so softly he wasn't sure he'd heard her correctly.

'Did you say crocodile?'

She nodded.

When Smithy had told him about the springs he'd assured Connor that no crocs lived in the water. It wasn't the right climate for them, but still he turned back to the water. His eyes scanned the shoreline but couldn't see anything to suggest there had been a crocodile. Not even beady eyes and a long nose marred the surface of the spring.

'It's okay, Diana, there's no crocodile. We're safe.'

'How do you know, they could be lurking at the bottom of the spring, waiting to grab you when you least expect it.'

Connor pulled her into a hug. 'Honey, I can assure you there are no crocs here in Ghost Gum Springs. We're too far south for them. And the most dangerous crocs are up the north east and west of Australia.'

'Are you sure?'

He brushed his lips across the top of her head, inhaling her fresh apple scent combined with sunshine. It was a smell he could definitely get used to. 'I promise.'

Connor took a step back; his body already reacting again to being so close to her. He didn't want to give her another reason to be skittish around him. 'Do you want to come in the water? It's really refreshing.'

'I don't think so.'

'Okay.' As much as he'd like to swim with her, he wasn't going to force her into doing something she didn't want to do. After all, he was supposed to be convincing her that staying for Christmas was a good idea.

Fuck, had he ruined it by bringing her to the one place he'd been convinced would sway her into staying?

Diana plucked at the hem of her t-shirt. She was hot, even though she was seated under a tree and there was a slight breeze in the air. The distant sound of splashing teased her.

A swim would be so good right about now, yet she still hesitated about getting in the water, even after Connor had assured her there were no crocodiles hiding in the bush surrounding them or lurking in the depths of the water.

This was his second swim. Following her mini meltdown, Connor had gone to the car and brought out a blanket. He placed it under the tree and had returned to get the cooler. He'd sat down next to her, but she could tell he was itching to get into the water. She couldn't blame him, it did look inviting.

God, why was she sitting here being such a scaredy cat? She'd come on this trip for an adventure. How much more adventurous could she be than swimming in an outback lake? Now that was a story she could tell her friends. And she used that word loosely. Sure, they'd encouraged her to go on a trip, but they'd only become friendly towards her when it came to light that Grandma Mary-Lou had been the original Scrooge and had millions in the bank. Millions that were now Diana's. A fact she still had trouble comprehending.

With distance she could fully see how she'd been used. So many dinner invitations that hadn't been forthcoming before her grandmother's death. So much well-meaning advice from people telling her how she should invest her money. She'd grabbed at their attention as greedily as they were trying to grab at her money.

God, she was being so stupid. She was holding Connor at a distance, treating him badly because she was worried he was using her like what had happened to her in high school and yet she'd fallen into that trap before she'd even come on this trip.

Connor didn't know how much money she had, yet he was going out of his way to include her. Even Fred was treating her in a way she'd never been treated before. And both the men had only known her for two days.

At the end of the day, she didn't need to ever return to Packenridge, Montana. There was nothing keeping her there. No familial ties. She'd quit her teaching job, a job she hated with a passion, but was a good solid occupation according to her grandmother.

The world was at her feet, she could do whatever she wanted, including swimming in an outback spring.

Decision made she stood and stripped out of her clothes. Connor was swimming and diving under the water. He wasn't aware of her approach. She got to where the water floated up the dirt shore. Taking a deep breath she took a tentative step forward.

'Shit, that's cold.'

The sound of laughter rumbled through her and a cool hand touched her shoulder, causing her to jump. 'It gets better when you're fully immersed.'

Her heart beat out a rapid tattoo in shock. 'God, you scared me. How did you even know I was about to get in the water? Last I saw you were under the water paying no attention to me at all.'

A finger trailed down her cheek, her skin tingling beneath the touch. 'I was watching you all the time. Did you really think I would bring you here and not be aware of what you were doing and where you were?'

For a second Diana wondered if she'd been dropped into the middle of a romance movie, because that's what every word coming out of his mouth sounded like. 'You could've fooled me. I was watching you and you appeared to be oblivious to me.'

Connor closed the distance between them and pulled her up against him. Her hands landed on his shoulder. 'Believe me when I say I've been aware of you, Diana Jenkins, from the second I saw you standing on the side of the road.'

Sunlight disappeared as he captured her lips. They were cool at first, before heating up and making her hotter than she'd been sitting under the tree. Releasing her grip on his shoulders she wound her fingers through his damp hair while opening her mouth to welcome his tongue. With minimal clothing between them, it was impossible to miss the hardening of his dick against her belly. She ground her hips, eliciting a moan from him. A sound she wouldn't mind hearing over and over again.

A groan ripped out of her as his hands clasped her ass and took over the grinding. Her nipples hardened against the soft lycra of her bikini top. Her core pulsed in need, wanting his fingers to slip beneath her bottoms and stroke her until she cried out her release. His lips roved over hers before beginning a delicious journey along her jawline.

What would it be like to make love in the outback?

'Uncomfortable.' Connor muttered against her neck.

'What?' The spell broke the second Connor spoke.

'Making love in the outback would be uncomfortable, especially as the blanket is pretty thin.'

Mortification swept over her as it sunk in she'd spoken out loud, again, and Connor was responding to it. She twisted out of his hold, surprised when he didn't try and haul her close again. In a daze she walked towards the spring, shivering as the water lapped her knees. If Connor followed her she didn't know, nor did she care.

When she thought it would be safe to do, she dived in, the chilly water embracing her. Diana pushed the thoughts of the kiss out of her mind as she held breath and swam underwater. An impossible task when all she could remember was the sensation of being held by him. The way his lips caressed hers. Even in the water her body heated and yearned to experience it once again.

She broke the surface and took a big gulp of air. She was losing her mind. No matter how beautiful this location was. No matter how welcoming the people of Ghost Gum Springs appeared to be. She had to protect herself, she'd been hurt too many times. Tomorrow she'd be back in Sydney, surrounded by people who wouldn't look at her too closely to see if they could find out all her inner thoughts.

'Are you okay?' Connor asked as he glided up beside her.

Tentatively she lowered her legs to see if she could touch the ground, sinking a little before finding purchase. 'I'm fine, but I think I'd like to head back to the hotel.'

Connor shook his head and droplets of water sprayed in the air. 'You really don't.'

If she was standing on solid ground, she'd have put her hands on her hips, but with only the tops of her shoulders and head showing above the water the gesture would be totally lost. 'Yes, I really do.'

Connor shrugged. 'You just think you do. Take a look around,' he lifted his arm in a wide sweeping arc. 'This is Mother Nature at her finest. A natural spring in the middle of nothing but sun baked soil. You travelled halfway around the world for adventure. This is adventure, not staying in an impersonal hotel in the city. Getting on a stop-and-go tourist bus with a bunch of strangers isn't fun.'

His impassioned speech surprised her. There was nothing remotely country about the way Connor spoke or acted. His speech inflection was completely different to what she'd heard from the locals when she'd been in the bar on her first night.

She braced herself, as best she could in the soft soil on the bottom of the spring, as Connor moved slowly towards her. 'I'm sorry about kissing you. If I promise not to do it again, will you let me continue with my plans for the day?'

It should've made her happy that he was taking responsibility for the kiss, but she was with him every step of the way. She'd wanted it as much as he did. As for continuing the day, she could let him continue with his idea to show her the finer points of country living. It wasn't like he'd succeed in changing her mind. Her fear of letting herself believe he wouldn't let her down, like so many others had, would ensure she maintained her desire to return to Sydney. 'Sure, I suppose I can do that, but I'm also pretty certain that come tomorrow night I'll be sipping a cocktail in a city bar.'

He grinned, the whites of his teeth shining in the sunlight. 'We shall see.'

An hour later Diana's belly was full and she had no doubt that if she closed her eyes she'd drop off to sleep. After their swim, they'd returned to the blanket and Connor proceeded to unpack a mountain of food.

'I don't think I can move,' she moaned, and her eyes drifted shut, unable to keep them open any longer. Sleep was within reach.

'Come on sleepyhead, it's time to get going.'

Of course he'd be full of energy while she felt like a sloth. 'I'm not moving anywhere.'

'No can do, princess, you promised you'd let me continue on my keep-Diana-in-Ghost-Gum-Springs tour.'

'Such a silly idea for a tour. It should be stay-at-spring-for-rest-of-day tour.'

He chuckled and with her eyes shut, her sense of hearing intensified the sound, causing ripples of pleasure to flow through her. The sound of his laughter was something she found herself wanting to hear more and more.

'How about another swim before we go?' he asked as a shadow fell over her.

'You're blocking my sun, and if I swim now I'd likely sink after all the food you made me eat.'

'Oh no, I'm not taking the blame for you enjoying some of Beryl's tasty treats, that's all on you.'

Enjoying the light banter was making this day better and better, but she still wondered why Connor was trying awfully hard to convince her to stay. 'Why is it so important that I stay here instead of going back to Sydney?'

Connor crouched down in front of her. He flicked his sunglasses up so his blue eyes blazed brightly. 'Because no one should spend Christmas by themselves.'

Well, shoot, how can anyone resist a man when he says that to you?

Her breath whooshed out of her and her gaze flicked from his eyes to his plump lips. Lips that a little while ago had been glued to hers. Her tongue darted out to moisten her dry ones. With her eyes trained on his lips, she saw him swallow. Drawing on the need to taste Connor again she leaned towards him. For a fraction of a second he copied her action before jolting upright as if he'd been stung by a bee.

'Nope.' He took a couple of steps back and she battled down the rejection building in her. 'I promised I wasn't going to kiss you. No matter how much I may want to.'

Oh, the promise he'd made was the reason he pulled away, not that he didn't want her. Which was such a silly thought considering she'd witnessed how affected he was by her closeness. 'Right. Okay.' Standing she brushed herself down. 'Well, let's get going then.'

An awkward tension had sprung up between them. An awkwardness that was new and she found she didn't like it. She'd rather go back to the light-hearted banter they'd been sharing. What she really wanted was to be wrapped up in his arms, kissing him senseless again. How silly was that when she'd been fighting her growing attraction to him not too long ago?

The sooner she got back to Sydney the better she'd be. Or would she?

Connor tapped his finger on the steering wheel as he drove them to the next destination. It had been so hard to resist capturing her mouth with his when she'd leaned towards him on the blanket. But he was a man of his word and he promised he wouldn't kiss her.

'Where are we headed now?'

'If I told you, it wouldn't be a surprise.' He glanced over in time to see her roll her eyes. Over the course of the day he'd observed Diana fight an inner battle with herself. If she was laughing or enjoying herself she pulled herself back and shut down her smile. As though she'd been mentally slapped down for having a good time.

What had happened to her in her past that prevented her from letting her hair down and enjoying life?

In all the time they'd been together, whenever he broached the subject of her family she shut him down quickly, and as much as he wanted to question her now, he didn't want to spoil what was left of their day together. He had to convince her to stay. He'd meant it when he'd said no one should spend Christmas by themselves. It also could be because this was the first year he wasn't spending Christmas surrounded by family that was pushing him so hard to have her stay. Then again, he had the Ghost Gum Springs townsfolk to spend the day with, but they weren't Diana. They didn't make his world seem brighter.

Lost in his thoughts he almost missed the turn off to the lookout. It wasn't an *official* lookout but one Reg, the town solicitor, had mentioned to him in passing.

'You really like taking me on rough roads, don't you?' Grumbled Diana as, once again, his SUV traversed the potholes and small rocks on the road.

'I'm giving you the full outback experience, love,' he laid on a thick Australian accent.

Diana groaned. 'Don't give up your day job to go into voiceover work. That was the worst accent I've ever heard.'

'And since when did you become an aficionado on Australian accents?' he asked grinning, glad they were back to the joking from earlier in the day.

'Well I can definitely tell you haven't been in the *outback* long. Your accent is more cultured than say Fred's or some of the other people I've heard in the bar. Plus, Cindy said you'd only been here since November, remember.'

'Busted.'

'Yep, you can't fool this girl.'

Connor turned a corner and pulled to a stop in a large clearing. 'We're here.'

Diana's brow furrowed as she studied the landscape beyond the windscreen. 'Okay, what's so special about this place?'

'Just you wait and see. I have it on good authority that you are going to be blown away by it.'

'Hmm, we'll see.'

Damn, she was a tough nut to crack. Her determination to stick to her guns and head back to Sydney was admirable. While he'd be disappointed if she asked him to take her to Sydney tomorrow, he wouldn't renege. He'd given her his word and what sort of man was he if he went back on it.

Connor unbuckled his seatbelt, opened the door and got out, moving around to her side in time for her door to swing open. He jumped back so he didn't get slammed with the hunk of metal. 'You know your way back, do you?' he asked as he held out his hand to her.

'What do you mean?' she asked as she placed her hand in his, with no argument. He considered it a small victory.

'You practically took me out when you opened the door. I was trying to be a gentleman and get to your door first so I could open it for you.'

She rolled her eyes again, a habit he normally thought cute, but in this instance, it was a little annoying. 'I'm quite capable of opening my own door, you know.'

'Never said you weren't.' He shouldn't be upset at the way she constantly fought him on every little thing. Hell, she'd travelled to Australia by herself; if that wasn't a sign of an independent woman, then he had no idea what was.

He stumbled as she tugged at his hand. Connor turned to face her. Diana stood inches from him, her lips taunting and tempting him. 'I'm sorry, Connor. I'm being a bit prickly aren't I when all you're trying to do is show me what I came to Australia for.'

It took everything in him not to pull her close for a hug. If he succumbed to the urge he wouldn't stop at hugging. He'd have to kiss her again. And while he had a suspicion she wouldn't mind it, their next kiss would definitely be one she instigated. 'Yes, you are.'

They stood for a few quiet moments, both looking into each other's eyes, as though they were both trying to figure out what the other was thinking. He knew what he was thinking: how much he wanted to keep her smiling. Shadows hid within her. Shadows that prevented her from embracing life to its fullest. He hoped, before she left, he could get rid of some of those shadows. If only she'd let him try.

Chapter Eight

Diana watched the scenery as it whizzed by on their drive back to town. Their stop at the lookout had been amazing. Standing on the rise she could see the little town in the distance. A mass of structures amongst a plateau of barren landscape. The spring they'd swum in wasn't visible but she'd found the copse of ghost gum trees that surrounded it and hid it from prying eyes. When they'd been there they'd been locked in their own little private oasis and it wasn't until she was looking down on it that she realised how special the natural spring was.

'Is there anything else left on my little tour?' she asked tiredly. What she'd really like to do was take a bath and then sleep. It had been an exhausting but wonderful day.

'There is, but if you're not up to it then we can give it a miss.'

The temptation to tell Connor that she'd like to pass was squashed when she looked across the cabin of the car and found him looking intently at her, a ray of hope shining in his eyes. He was doing everything he could to convince her to stay and she couldn't fault him. He really was like Santa's elf. But she couldn't waver and fall under his Christmas spell. It would be better for all if she headed back to the city. Although she should see what his last tour item was. 'Yes, I'm tired but I'd like to see this last stop.'

He smiled brightly and her own lips stretched in response. He really was handsome as sin. 'Well we have a little time, what I want to show you doesn't happen until the sun sets.'

Diana fought back a yawn. 'So, I have time to shower and change?'

'Yep, and you can do that in about five minutes' time.'

Looking out the windshield again she could see the outskirts of Ghost Gum Springs. She couldn't deny the town was sweet, just not for her.

They arrived back at the pub and she headed upstairs to her room while Connor unpacked the car. The bed looked so inviting. Maybe she could get a little catnap in.

Sleeping before dinner is a bad idea, Diana Louise.

Grandma Mary-Lou's voice sounded loud in her head and she wanted to slap her away. How, after nearly four months since she died, was Diana still letting the old lady rule her life? If she wanted to become independent, she needed to cut the ties to the woman who'd done everything in her life to hold her back. Had squashed every dream she'd ever had. Had squashed every possibility of friendship by encouraging the town gossips in thinking the apple doesn't fall far from the tree, and it was only time before Diana fell into the same pit her parents had landed in.

'You don't control me anymore. It's time for me to control my life,' she said to the invisible binds surrounding her. Diana didn't know what she expected by saying it out loud. That some magical bang would happen, and she'd feel freer?

Of course, it wouldn't happen but maybe if she said it out loud often enough she'd begin to believe it. Once her trip was over she'd return to Montana and sell the small house she'd spent her whole life in. A clean break. She'd find somewhere else to start over. The world was full of opportunities and she had the financial means to take her time to find the right place. Oh, she wouldn't waste the money she'd been given. She wasn't entirely stupid. The firm who'd been handling Grandma Mary-Lou's finances had done a sterling job. So well, in fact, that Diana trusted them to continue doing it. Although, unlike her grandmother, she planned to use it and not live her life scraping by above the poverty line.

A new opportunity could be right here in Ghost Gum Springs with a certain hot bartender.

The little devil voice she'd forgotten lived inside of her sparked to life. 'Oh no,' she said to the empty room. 'I'm not going to fall for the first man I see. Especially someone who works behind a bar, no matter how hot they are.'

There was nothing wrong with being a bartender. It was an honourable occupation, but she wanted to spend her life with a man who had ambitions.

Diana pulled her thoughts together. Nothing needed to be decided right now. All that was required of her at this moment was to get through the evening. Then tomorrow, when she was back in Sydney, she could plan.

Connor adjusted the lights on the tree in the corner of the bar's main area. They really didn't need fixing, but his nerves were stretched thin. Why he was so determined to convince Diana to stay was beyond him. Her reactions to the spring and lookout hadn't been over the top. He thought she'd enjoyed the day, but he didn't want to assume anything.

His lips tingled as he remembered the kiss they'd shared. The way her body had fitted nicely against his. His dick twitched in his pants, letting him know what it would like to happen.

'You and me both,' he muttered talking to the part of his anatomy he hadn't talked to since he was a kid. He was really losing it.

'Will you stop fidgeting with that damn tree, it looks fine. The whole damn town is going to be lit up. Such a dumb idea,' grumbled Fred Gates as he strolled up to where Connor stood.

Connor slung an arm around the older man. 'Aww come on, Scrooge, you're going to love it. I'm pleased everyone got on board with the idea.'

'Like we had a choice. You've come into town and turned this place into Santa's bloody village. I'm sure Smithy didn't have this in mind when he asked you take over from him.'

Connor laughed taking Fred's ribbing in the vein it was given. 'He's too busy enjoying his honeymoon to worry about what's happening here.'

Which wasn't quite true. When he'd gone to check his emails after he and Diana had returned from their venture, Shane had presented him with an offer to sell him the pub if Connor was interested. Never in a million years would he have expected his friend to sell the bar. He'd been living in Ghost Gum Springs all his life, but after seeing other parts of Australia, he and his new wife had decided they wanted to do a world trip. And to fund it he wanted to sell the pub. Surprisingly, Connor was seriously considering the idea of becoming a *publican*. He couldn't deny he'd been burned out with his career in law. Having his client lose her life because her deadbeat ex had managed to find her had hit him hard. Connor felt he'd failed Melanie. Failed her in ensuring that her ex was off the streets. But a technicality had set the loser free and Melanie had paid with her life.

It was a guilt he had to live with for the rest of his life, and it soured him on the career he'd always loved.

But life presented you with obstacles that you overcome and learn from and the six weeks he'd spent in this small rural town had shown him another side of life. If he wanted to keep using his law degree, he could always offer his services to Reg as a consultant.

Connor was learning life was full of possibilities and change was good. He would talk it through with his financial adviser to see if it was a worthwhile proposition. Although the pub did a cracking business with the locals and trivia night always pulled in a crowd from the surrounding areas, it was always best to do his own due diligence. But if Smithy could make it work, then so could he.

'Jesus, Connor, you're away with the Christmas elves, aren't you. You've been staring at that tree for the last five minutes.' Fred tapped him on the arm.

Connor pulled his thoughts inside where he could examine them later. 'I'm just going through everything in my mind, making sure it goes off without a hitch.'

'You're sure going to a lot of effort for someone you've just met,' he mused.

Connor couldn't deny the truth of his words. 'You're right, but, Fred, Diana's all alone in a strange country on the other side of the world to her home. It's Christmas. The season of goodwill and good cheer. It's a magical time of year and everyone deserves to have a Merry Christmas.'

A faraway look entered Fred's eyes. 'My Stella always made a fuss over Christmas.'

Stella? Who the hell was Stella?

As far as Connor knew Fred was a crusty old bachelor. In the time he'd been running the bar, Fred had always been alone and the only thing he talked about was his dog, Blue. Never before had he mentioned a woman. But with the look in the old man's eyes, this Stella person had to have been pretty special to him. Before he could ask, Fred continued on with his reminiscing.

'I'd come home on the first of December and the tree would be up. There'd be gifts under it too.' Fred studied the tree Connor had been working on. 'She went out on Christmas Eve telling me she wanted one last thing. She never came home, bloody roo jumped out in front of her car.'

The older man's voice broke and Connor laid a hand on his shoulder offering him silent support. 'I've hated Christmas ever since then.' Fred shook his head. 'All this reminds me of her.'

'Shit, I'm sorry, mate. I didn't know.'

Fred shook off Connor's hand and fixed him with a hard stare. 'Of course you bloody didn't, I just told you. But,' he paused and gazed around the room again. 'I have to say seeing all the effort you've put in has reminded me of the good times Stella and I had together. Times I'd forgotten, so I have to thank you for that. Never loved another woman. No one measured up to my Stella.'

'That's what my dad says about my mum,' Connor mused. 'He said he took one look at her and that was it. He never wanted anyone else. Luckily for him she felt the same way.'

'Your dad's right, when you find the right woman you know. If Diana is that for you, hang on tight and don't let go.'

Fred wandered away, leaving Connor standing there mute. He wasn't in love with Diana. He'd met her two days ago. Sure, he was attracted to her and if he'd seen her in a bar in Sydney he definitely would've gone up and flirted with her. He also couldn't deny he was drawn to the side she kept hidden. The side he had no doubt existed beneath the prickly coat she donned. Someone or some people had let her down. He'd let down one woman and she'd paid for it with her life. He wasn't going to let that happen to Diana. She was a puzzle he was determined to solve. But no, he wasn't in love with her. It was ridiculous, and Fred was dreaming. He didn't believe in love at first sight.

Then why are you trying so hard to convince her to stay?

'Shut up,' he muttered to the voice in his head. He glanced at the large clock over the top of the bar. It was time to collect Diana.

He strode out of the main room and took the stairs two at a time. He was a little puffed when he found himself facing Diana's door.

Nerves jumbled in his belly. How pathetic, he wasn't a novice in the dating game. He'd been around the block a few times. But tonight was special. He was excited and hoped that at the end of the evening she'd stay with him.

No, in town, not with him.

Fred's comments were stirring his mind in a mass of knots. Determined not to give his conversation with Fred another thought, he rapped his knuckles on her door. Connor's jaw dropped when it opened.

A vision in red greeted him. His heart rate kicked into overdrive. Diana's hair was freshly washed and hung in loose curls around her bare shoulders. Her lips glistened from the gloss she was wearing, giving them a plump look, and he badly wanted to sample them again. Her dress had shoestring straps and the top fitted snugly against her figure before flaring into a soft skirt which stopped just above her knee. Her feet were encased in matching red heeled sandals.

'Wow you look amazing and very festive.'

She laughed. 'Thank you and yes, I admit I'm wearing red because you seemed determined to get me in the Christmas spirit.'

He crooked his left arm out. 'Shall we?'

'Lead on, Santa's Elf.'

Connor led her down the hallway to the staircase. Her light mood was in such contrast to the way she'd been acting since he'd picked her up on the side of the road. He couldn't deny he hoped it meant she was going to stay for Christmas.

They reached the bottom of the stairs and he continued towards the front door.

'We're not going there?' she asked and pointed to the main room of the pub.

'We will, later. We're going for a walk first.'

She stopped, forcing Connor to halt his progress. He looked over and raised an eyebrow in question.

Diana lifted her foot and her dress slipped up, giving him a nice view of her thigh.

Was she trying to kill him with lust here?

Did she even know how beautiful she looked and how much willpower it was taking him to not grab her close and kiss her?

'Do these shoes look like they're suitable for taking a stroll?'

His eye was drawn to her shoes again, he'd like to do a lot of things with those shoes still adorning her feet. Walking down the street, not so much, but that was what they were about to do. 'Well I suppose not, but I promise not to let you fall.' He winked at her. 'And you know I keep my promises.'

Once again she rolled her eyes and he laughed. He tapped her on the nose. 'You know you're cute when you do that?'

'Do what?' she asked.

'Roll your eyes. You've done it a lot since you met me.'

'Maybe because you annoy me.' She did an exaggerated roll of her eyes, taking the sting out of her words.

Connor laughed out loud and opened the door. 'Your words don't wound me. Now are you ready for the next part of Diana's Stay-in-Ghost-Gum-Springs Tour?'

'As ready as I'll ever be. Lead on, Santa's Elf.'

A quick nod to Jarod who was waiting on the corner and, with a flicker, all the shops on the main street lit up with Christmas lights. In some of the windows there were illuminated Santas, snowmen and Christmas trees.

'I know you said that Christmas in some towns isn't what's portrayed in Christmas movies, but tonight, Ghost Gum Springs is putting on a light show just for you. You want to go take a look?'

Beside him Diana appeared to be in a trance. Her eyes wide and glistening with tears. Shit, he'd hoped to make her smile not cry. He'd hoped to show her that, even though they'd only known her for a short time, the town was welcoming her.

He needed to go into damage control.

'It's okay if you don't want to. We can go back inside.'

She blinked away the tears and looked at him, a smile tugging at her lips. Relief swept through him. Maybe he hadn't fucked things up. 'No. I'm speechless. This is beautiful. I've never seen anything so pretty. Grandma Mary-Lou didn't let me enjoy anything about Christmas.'

There it was, another little preview into her past. Would she be more open as the night progressed? He just wanted to understand her, to know her better.

'Come on, I think you're going to enjoy our walk.'

Diana swallowed hard against the lump in her throat. Why would the townsfolk go to so much trouble for her? There was nothing special about her. She was a visitor. One who was anxious to leave.

The first place they stopped at was Beryl's café. A small Christmas tree stood in the corner of the store, its lights flashing on and off. On closer inspection she worked out some of the decorations were bakery items—a large slice of chocolate cake, a cupcake and a whisk. They were some of the cutest ornaments she'd ever seen.

They walked slowly down the street. If a store didn't have a tree or window decoration they had strung up lights around their doors or on their awning.

'Do they do this every year with the lights?' she asked after looking at a Christmas Village display in the window of the town's hair salon.

'No this is the first year.'

Diana looked at him suspiciously. 'Did you have something to do with this?'

His eyes widened in mock surprise. 'Who me?'

She shook her head at his feigned innocence. 'Yeah, you.'

'Maybe.'

A warm glow simmered to life in her blood. How could a total stranger make her feel welcome after a couple of days when her grandmother had spent her whole life making her feel unwelcome. There was something wrong with this picture and she didn't know how to take it.

'Thank you,' she whispered.

Connor reached out and brushed his thumb gently across her cheek. 'You're welcome.'

They finished the rest of their walk down the main street in silence. When they reached the pub she sighed that their little adventure was over. She walked inside, surprised to find the main room was empty.

'Where is everyone?'

'Told them all that we were closed for the night.' He led her over to the only table set in the room.

'Isn't that bad for business? You don't want to upset the owner. I'm sure he'd be wanting to maximise profits during the holiday season.'

He winked at her. 'I have it on good authority the owner won't mind. He knows the pub is in safe hands with me.'

'Not if he finds out you closed the night before Christmas Eve.'

He sighed. 'Can you please just accept that it's fine and that I'm doing something nice for you?'

He was right, she'd reverted back to being a bitch about things after he'd gone out of his way to do something wonderful for her. It wasn't anything she was used to and she couldn't believe Connor had done this without an ulterior motive in mind.

As quickly as she thought it, she squashed it. Connor wasn't like that. She had to believe he had no other motive than to make her smile. She walked over to where he was standing by the bar. 'I'm sorry, Connor,' she said as she touched his shoulder. 'I have no right to question you about what you're doing with the pub.'

'It's fine,' he said and walked around to the other side of the bar. Her arm fell uselessly to her side. How could she have been so insensitive to question what he was doing? It was exactly what Grandma Mary-Lou had always done—made snap judgements. If whatever the person was doing wasn't within her ideals, she always berated them, making them feel like they were less than an inch tall. It was what she'd done to Diana her whole life.

Diana wandered over to the set table, taking in the red tablecloth, the arrangement of flowers sitting in the centre. Gold napkins lay across the white china plates. Having eaten at the pub before, the plates weren't the normal ones served to patrons. These plates were thin and sported a gold trim.

He'd gone to so much effort. And it scared her. The feelings growing inside her were ones she wasn't used to experiencing. No one had ever made her feel special. The few guys she'd been with, ones who hadn't grown up in her town, had been more concerned with what they could get out of her and not what they could give her. Of course, when they each met Grandma Mary-Lou they ran away faster than a fox running from a bear. Leaving her disappointed again when she'd thought someone liked her for who she was. Eventually she stopped dating. There was no point.

'Take a seat,' Connor called out. 'I'll bring over some wine before getting our first course.'

Diana followed his instructions and sat. He appeared a few seconds later with two flutes of champagne. He handed one to her.

'To a wonderful night,' he said and held his glass up. She tapped hers against his, and a light ting sounded.

After taking a sip, Connor leaned past her to place his glass on the table, brushing his arm against hers. A little snap of electricity sparked between them. She didn't think the touch was accidental. Before she did something completely stupid, like grab his arm and kiss him, she sat down and waited for him to bring their food to the table.

The lights had been dimmed and the glow from the Christmas trees lent a very romantic atmosphere to the room.

'Here you go,' he said appearing beside her like a magician. A cocktail glass was placed on the centre of her dinner plate.

'What's this?' she asked as she looked closer to the dish. 'Is this shrimp?'

'Yep, this is a prawn cocktail. Or maybe a shrimp cocktail, seeing as you call them shrimp.'

Diana had never had a lot of seafood, Grandma Mary-Lou always said it was an unnecessary expense. The one and only time she'd had shrimp she'd loved it. She picked up her fork and pierced the soft white flesh dipping it into the creamy sauce. She took a bite and moaned in delight at the burst of flavours across her tongue. The tartness of the shrimp blended beautifully with the sweetness of the sauce.

'I take it you like it?' Connor asked, amusement lacing his tone, before he forked some of the dish into his own mouth.

'It's so good. Why isn't this on the menu? I'm sure everyone would love it.'

Connor finished chewing. 'Chook likes to prepare meals with super fresh produce and meats every day. Prawns generally have to be freeze packed so they don't go off while they're being transported from Sydney. But I convinced him to order some for Christmas lunch.'

'Are you saying we're eating shrimp that should've been saved for Christmas lunch?'

'Sort of. We're kind of his guinea pigs too.'

Diana swirled her last piece of food in the sauce and popped it in her mouth. When she swallowed she addressed his last comment. 'What did you mean about us being your cook's guinea pigs?'

Connor placed his fork into the dish. 'Chook was trying a new sauce. If we didn't like it he'd go back to the more traditional cocktail sauce that's used on prawns. But this is the best sauce I've ever tasted.'

'I agree. I still don't get why he's cooking in a country pub. He could cook in any quality restaurant he wants to if this first course is anything to go by.'

'He says he's been there done that and never again. It's his story to tell. He's happy to be a cook in a country pub. Less stress he says.' He pushed his chair back and stood. 'You ready for the next course.'

'If it's anything like the first, I sure am.'

An hour later Diana laid her spoon in the bowl that had held the most delicious piece of chocolate cake she'd ever tasted. 'I don't think I can move. After the picnic today and tonight's dinner. I've probably put on ten pounds.'

Connor chuckled. 'Chook really outdid himself, although Beryl created the dessert.'

'These people are hiding away in a country town when they should be living in the city. They'd make a killing.'

'They like living here. I think they like the laid-back nature of Ghost Gum Springs. Beryl is more than happy to run her café here. And I already mentioned Chook's past.' He shrugged his shoulders. 'I have to admit, they're not wrong about staying here instead of living in the city.'

'Did you run a bar back in Sydney?' Diana asked. They had spent the whole day together and yet she didn't know a lot about her dinner companion's history.

'No. I'm a lawyer.'

Whatever she'd expected him to say, it certainly wasn't that. He looked so natural behind the bar pulling beers. 'You're a lawyer? What the heck are you doing running a bar?'

Connor picked up his plate before standing and getting hers. 'Let's just say I needed a change and Smithy offered me the chance to take over for him while he was away. I said yes.'

He walked away before she could ask him anything else.

A lawyer.

Wow, that still shocked her. She never would've picked him as one, although now that she thought about it, the first day he had peppered her with a lot of questions. It didn't take much effort to conjure up an image of him in an expensive suit standing in a courtroom.

'Would you like a coffee?' he asked as he returned to stand beside their table.

'No, thanks.' Having sat down for most of the evening, Diana pushed back from the table, stood and stretched. Her muscles popped in release.

Warm hands encircled her waist and she found herself resting against Connor's hard chest. Gooseflesh bubbled over her skin when his lips brushed the curve between her neck and shoulder.

Her head fell to the side to grant him more access and her eyes drifted shut. 'What are you doing?' she asked quietly.

'I'm not sure.' He turned her so they were facing each other. She put her hands on his shoulders. In her high-heeled sandals their height difference was not noticeable. All she had to do was lift her chin and their lips would be on the same level.

After the kiss they'd shared at the springs, Connor had been the ultimate gentleman. He'd kept his promise to not kiss her again, until now. 'You broke your promise,' she murmured.

'I did.'

Diana leaned a little closer to him. 'I should tell you off. Then go to my room.'

'You should.' His arms tightening around her contradicted his words.

Their bodies were aligned so closely it was impossible not to feel the evidence of his desire. An answering warmth pooled between her thighs. God, she wanted to kiss him again. 'I release you from your prom—'

Her lips were captured by his and she sighed, opening her mouth to allow his tongue entrance. Her arms tightened around his neck, anchoring his lips in place. His hands travelled down her back, her skin tingling to life.

She wanted more. More than his hands cradling her ass. More than his lips roving over hers. More than her arms around his neck. She wanted it all.

As reckless as it was going to be, she didn't care. For once she was going to take life by the horns and go for it. She had no one to answer to. No petty-minded townspeople to judge her. Distance had given her the courage that Packenridge, Montana had suppressed within her.

Diana broke the kiss. 'Take me upstairs, Connor.'

'Are you sure?'

'Yes.'

Chapter Nine

A wide grin broke across his face and he entwined their fingers together. He flicked off lights as he led her to the staircase.

Their footsteps whispered on the carpet runner as they climbed the stairs. When they reached the top Connor led her to the right, not the left, which was the direction of her room. During the short time she'd been staying at the hotel, she hadn't even considered where Connor slept.

He stopped at the door at the end of the hall and pulled her close. She looked up at him, a smile playing on her lips. 'No doubts?' he asked.

She rose on her toes and brushed her mouth across his. 'None.'

With a twist, the door was opened and he swept her inside. Before she could even take a look at her surroundings he had her back in his arms and his lips crashed down on hers.

An urgency to be close to each other replaced the languid exploration they'd shared downstairs. Her fingers were busy on his shirt, while his found the zipper of her dress and pulled it down.

A cool breeze from the air conditioner brushed against her heated flesh as the material pooled at her feet.

'We need to slow down,' he whispered against her neck.

'No, I don't need slow. I want this as much as you do.' To prove her point her hands went to the waistband of his jeans, his breath hissed across her cheek when she brushed against his hard length.

She took a moment to trace his flesh and Connor groaned long and low in her ear.

'You're killing me here.'

She laughed and unbuttoned his jeans. 'Can't have that can we.'

This brazen side of her was new and she liked it. She planned to embrace it when she returned to Packenridge. Her fingers faltered for a second at the thought of returning to her home town, but she pushed those thoughts aside. The long flight home would give her plenty of time to think. Besides, she was selling everything and moving to a bigger city where it didn't matter what anyone else thought. She was done with country living.

'Hey, where did you go?' Connor asked, lifting her chin. His eyes serious as if trying to delve into her tumbled thoughts.

Clearly, he'd picked up on her momentary lapse into her thoughts. 'Nowhere important.'

They both stood in their underwear. The chest she'd admired while they'd been swimming was right there in front of her. Waiting for her to touch it. What was she doing thinking about the future? She should be living in the moment.

Reaching behind her she unhooked her bra, shook her shoulders and the straps coasted down her arms. She tossed it aside and straightened up, thrusting her breasts towards him.

'You are beautiful,' Connor whispered as he trailed his fingers from her neck to the gap in between her breasts. Her nipples puckered in anticipation for the moment when he touched her.

Her head dropped back when his mouth closed over a nipple, his tongue teasing the bud before his teeth nipped at it.

Her legs buckled beneath her and she would've collapsed to the floor, but Connor scooped her up and placed her on the bed.

Excitement buzzed through her, something she'd never felt before when she'd been with any other guy. Her encounters had been all about them getting in, thrusting a few times and then withdrawing, leaving her wondering if that was all there was to sex.

Tonight, however, no way would Connor do that to her. The way he'd kissed her breasts had shown he was all about making sure she got maximum enjoyment out of their time together.

The rustle of foil pulled her out of her past memories. Connor stood by the bed, condom in his hand. His erection straining against the fabric of his boxer briefs.

Diana reached out and grasped him through the fabric. His flesh jerked against her hand as she began to rub him.

His hand closed over hers. 'Sweetheart, your touch feels incredible, but I won't last if you keep doing that.'

'Can't have that can we,' she murmured as she scooted back and patted the sheet beside her. 'Come join me.'

In a flash he was beside her, his arms around her pulling her so that she lay over the top of him. Her breasts crushed against his chest as their lips meshed together in another hot, hard kiss. Their legs entwined and his hands moved to her ass, stroking it before slipping beneath the thin fabric of her panties.

Diana ripped her mouth away from his. 'Please, Connor.'

'Please what?'

'Make love to me. Fill me.'

She gasped when she was flipped over. Connor's hands pushed down his briefs before repeating the action with hers. His heavy erection lay against her thigh and she couldn't wait to have him inside of her.

Connor grabbed the condom and protected himself. Anticipation fired through her and she lifted her hips, encouraging him to take her.

'Not yet, sweetheart,' he breathed against her breast. 'I have so much I need to explore.'

Her protest died on her lips when his mouth closed over her breast and his fingers found her pussy and stroked her.

A million sensations zoomed through her. Her breasts tingled beneath his mouth and her core clenched and unclenched with every pass of his finger. It wasn't enough though. She didn't want his finger inside her, she wanted him.

Reaching between them she wrapped her hand around his hard erection, guiding him to where she wanted him.

'Impatient, aren't you?' He nuzzled her neck.

She moaned, he'd found a sensitive spot she didn't know existed on her neck. It only fired her desperation to have him take her. 'I know what I want, Connor. And I want you. Inside me. Now.'

Never before had she demanded the guy she was sleeping with to do anything to her. It empowered her and gave her more confidence than she'd ever felt in her life.

He placed a final kiss on her neck. 'Don't let it be said that I don't do what I'm asked.'

Connor removed her fingers from his shaft and placed her hand above her head. He nudged her legs further apart before he settled at the juncture between her thighs.

She wriggled a little closer and with one thrust Connor slid inside her. Her eyes rolled back in bliss at the sensation of him filling her.

Diana found his mouth and kissed him as he began to move. Their tongues mimicked the thrust and retreat of his lower body action. Her legs hooked around his waist to deepen the penetration. They found a rhythm that worked for them and tension coiled inside of her so tightly she thought she was going to break.

She broke the kiss and gasped for air as she shattered around him. Her legs shook and lost their grip on Connor as her orgasm overpowered her. A couple of thrusts later Connor stilled above her, and his hips jerked his own release as he cried out her name.

As they came down from the heights of their lovemaking, Diana didn't want the night to end. She wanted to experience this over and over again. She never wanted to leave Connor's embrace. Panic set in with the road her thoughts were travelling and it replaced the pleasure flowing through her. She couldn't let herself fall into this trap. Without a doubt in a couple weeks' time Connor would grow bored and dump her. She'd be stuck in the middle of nowhere and people would look at her, shaking their heads in disappointment. No way could she let that happen.

She had to get out of here. How big of a mistake had she just made?

Connor pulled Diana tight against him. His chest heaving from the intensity of the moment they'd just shared. After a few seconds it registered that instead of being relaxed, like she should be after the orgasm she'd just had, Diana was stiffer than a piece of wood.

'Everything okay?' he asked, instinctively knowing it was anything but okay.

'Um, yeah. I need to go back to my room. It's going to be a long day tomorrow.'

Connor sat up and pulled Diana with him. 'What do you mean?'

She pulled away from him, opening up the distance between them. 'Well the drive back to Sydney will take a while. I figure you'll want to head off early so you don't get caught up with traffic.'

Connor couldn't believe his ears. Even after one of the most magical nights of his life, Diana still wanted to leave. 'You still want to go to Sydney?'

'Yes.'

He opened his mouth then closed it again. He was having trouble forming a sensible sentence. He'd been so confident that come tomorrow morning they'd share breakfast together before getting ready for Christmas Day. He was so sure he'd be able to change her mind. To show her that no matter what she thought, living in a small country town wasn't bad. That she was safe with him. How had he got it so wrong? 'What about tonight? What about what we just shared?'

'I, uh. Look, Connor, I uh. I need to go.' She jumped out of the bed, gathered up her clothes and was out the door before he could process it all.

'What the hell just happened?' he muttered out loud. Whatever it was, it wasn't over. There was no way he was going to let her get away with announcing she was still heading back to Sydney, not after the magic they'd created in this bed.

Determination fired through him and he got out of said magical bed. He went to the bathroom, disposed of the condom and splashed water on his face. What he needed to do was not act like a wounded boyfriend who'd been rejected by his girlfriend, but he did deserve an explanation.

He returned to his room and pulled on some shorts. He was out the door and standing in front of Diana's door before he thought more about what he was doing.

He knocked on the door. 'Diana, can you please let me in?'

'Go away, Connor, I'm tired.' Her muffled response irritated him, but he wasn't giving up.

'Please, Diana, I just want to talk.'

He counted up to ten before the door opened a crack. 'What is it, Connor?'

'Can I please come in? I don't want to have this conversation standing in the hallway.'

There weren't any other guests at the hotel, so it wasn't like their conversation was going to be overheard, but he still didn't want to talk to her through a four-inch crack.

'Fine.' She opened the door and walked away. He took note of the expensive suitcase sitting in the middle of the bed, clothes thrown haphazardly in it.

'What's going on, Diana? I thought we shared something wonderful today.'

Her shoulders slumped, and he willed away the urge to pull her into his arms. Minimal physical contact was called for. If he got too close, he would be tempted to kiss away her doubts and he had an idea she wouldn't appreciate it.

'Connor, today was wonderful. The walk around town and dinner tonight was amazing. What happened in your room was out of this world. An experience I'm never going to forget. But it doesn't change the way I feel. I want to go back to Sydney.'

He appreciated her honesty even though it wasn't what he wanted to hear. 'I still don't understand it.'

'I've grown up my whole life in a small town. My Grandma Mary-Lou took me in when my parents died of a drug overdose. She didn't want me but when CPS contacted her she had no choice.

'Even before I arrived the whole town had judged me on the sins of my parents. They were all waiting to see if I'd slide down the same slippery slope, Grandma Mary-Lou leading the pack. We lived a frugal lifestyle. The boys tried to tempt me into drinking and smoking. I refused because I was still trying to win Grandma's approval.' She sat on the bed and plucked a t-shirt out of her case, twisting it in her hands. 'When I went to college I was away from the prying eyes, and because I'd tried so hard to be a good girl, I was ripe to fall off the wagon. I don't think I remember my first semester.'

She tossed the t-shirt down and stood again, pacing around the small space. Connor crossed his arms to stop himself from grabbing her and pulling her close.

'Anyway,' she continued. 'I got my degree and instead of staying away I moved back home in the hope that the time apart would've made Grandma Mary-Lou miss me and enjoy having me back. I was dead wrong. Nothing had changed. Grandma Mary-Lou still looked at me like a piece of dirt. The townsfolk still made fun of me and talked about me behind my back. I tried to ignore it all, but I was stuck in a job I hated and everything was getting too much for me to take.'

'What did you do for a job?'

'I was a teacher. I thought by becoming a teacher Grandma Mary-Lou would be happy I'd chosen an occupation where I was always guaranteed of a job. And she was, *education is a steady employment* she said, but I was in a terrible school and it wasn't what I hoped it would be.'

The despair in her voice reached into his soul and he couldn't fight it any longer. He pulled her close. 'I'm sorry, sweetheart. You are a beautiful, wonderful person. If your grandma can't see that then her life is poorer for it.'

Diana scoffed and pulled out of his embrace. 'I'm sure she's laughing in heaven at all the misfortunes that have happened to me on this trip. I'd be surprised if she didn't orchestrate all my issues because I had the audacity to use some of the money she left me on a frivolous vacation.'

Enlightenment hit him like a lightning bolt—being in Ghost Gum Springs reminded her of the life she was trying to escape. As much as it would hurt him to do it, he couldn't make her stay. He wasn't cruel. He had to accept they were mere ships passing in the night and even though he'd tried to help her, he couldn't fix everyone. No matter how much he wanted to.

He'd tried his best to ensure Melanie was safe from her abusive ex, but the system he'd admired for so long finally worked against him. He couldn't change the outcome no matter how much he wanted to. Just like he couldn't change Diana's mind.

Decision made he walked up to her and kissed her softly on the forehead. 'I'll drive you to Sydney tomorrow. We'll leave at 6 am if that's okay?'

Her eyes widened in shock, as though she had expected him to try and talk her out of her request. 'Thank you.'

He tempered the urge to pull her close and kiss away the sadness. Once he started touching her, he wouldn't be able to stop. 'Sleep well, sweetheart.' He brushed his lips across the top of her forehead and walked away.

When he reached his room, he sat down on the bed, the aroma of her apple perfume wafted up to him. It was going to be a long night.

Chapter Ten

Diana sat at the bar and sipped her glass of wine. People surrounded her and yet she was all alone. The guy next to her bumped her arm and the wine glass clinked into her tooth.

'Sorry, love,' he slurred. 'You alright? How about I buy you another drink. It's Christmas Eve after all.'

'Thanks, but no.' She turned her back, hoping he got the message that she wanted him to leave her alone.

How ironic, here she was in the city, where she had thought she wanted to be, but she yearned to be back in Ghost Gum Springs sharing barbs about the Christmas decorations with Fred. She looked around the room and found a small tree in a corner, looking a little worse for wear as people brushed up against it continually.

How could everything she thought she wanted turn out to be everything she didn't want? The city sucked, it was so impersonal and not one person, apart from the drunk who'd tried to buy her a drink, had smiled at her or asked her how she was.

To make matters worse, she hadn't been able to find anywhere decent to have a Christmas meal. Most places were closed or the ones that were open were already booked up.

'Merry fucking Christmas to me,' she muttered and gulped down the rest of her wine. Might as well go back to her hotel room, order room service and stare at the four walls in her room. No point turning the television on, it would only be playing sickly sweet Christmas movies.

As she walked back to her hotel she couldn't believe she wished she was back in a town four hours away. Back in Connor's arms.

The drive to Sydney that morning had been tense and quiet. She'd pretended to be asleep most of the trip. It saved her from trying to make small talk. She'd had no idea what to say anyway. Connor hadn't even got out of the car when he'd pulled up at the hotel. A valet had opened the door and one look at Connor's face had her swallowing her invite to see if he'd like to grab a coffee before he drove back. His eyes were forward, and his hands were clenched on the steering wheel as if it was a life preserver. The only chink in his impersonation of a statue was when she leaned forward and kissed his cheek. He'd flexed his fingers and for half a second she thought he was going to release his grip, pull her to him and give her a proper kiss goodbye. Instead all he did was nod and she had to fight back the tears.

Now she was fighting another set of tears as the entrance to the hotel loomed in front of her. She walked through the double glass doors and a huge Christmas tree stood in the middle of the foyer. It was beautiful, yet cold. She wanted the explosion of decorations that filled a pub in a country town miles and miles away.

'What am I doing?' she asked herself. 'I don't want to be here.'

Swiping away the tears, she strode towards the elevators, a plan forming in her mind. As she punched the disc for her floor, doubts crowded in. What if her plan blew up in her face? Had she thrown away her chance to experience something she'd only ever seen in movies because of her fears?

But there was no reward without risk and if this gamble didn't pay the big dividends she hoped it would, then she'd just continue with her plan to try and find a new place to settle down in. Even though she was pretty sure she'd already found it in the unlikeliest place.

Christmas morning dawned bright and the temperature was already rising, but the glow and excitement that usually filled Connor was absent.

As he marched downstairs the aroma of freshly baked bread assailed his senses. It didn't matter that he'd left a part of himself in Sydney when he'd dropped Diana off. When she'd kissed him on the cheek he wanted to grab her and kiss her until she changed her mind and asked to return with him. But he didn't, and he'd let her walk away. It was a miracle he hadn't crashed his car on the drive back. His attention certainly hadn't been on the road.

Pushing thoughts of Diana to the back of his mind, he strode into the kitchen with a big smile on his face.

'Merry Christmas, Chook.' He hoped he'd injected enough enthusiasm so the hotel cook didn't pick up on the fact he was anything but festive.

'Merry Christmas to you, mate. Although you look like you got a lump of coal under the tree instead of the present you wanted the most.'

Damn, he hadn't been convincing enough. He'd have to work on it. 'Nah, just got a lot on my mind. We've got a few people coming for lunch. I want it to be a big success.'

'Why?'

Connor wasn't sure if he could trust the cook to keep the news of a possible sale to himself, but he needed to voice it out loud to make it seem more real. Of course it wouldn't happen until he'd done a comprehensive review of the books. Plus, he needed to tie up his life in Sydney and he couldn't start doing that until his former office opened up after the New Year.

'Look, what I'm about to say is between you, me and the gatepost. You understand?'

Chook nodded. 'You can trust me. I've got plenty of secrets no one knows about.'

'Smithy's looking at selling the pub and he asked me if I'd be interested in buying it.'

Chook tapped his wooden spoon against the pot he'd been stirring. 'Is it something you want to do? You don't strike me as a guy who'd be happy pulling beers for the rest of his life. You're a lawyer, right? Won't you be itching to get back into putting the bad guys behind bars?'

'Sometimes the bad guys walk, no matter what you do. I was getting burned out. The stress was getting to me. I like it here. I like the people.'

'I think you'll be great if it happens, and I'd be okay with it because you're willing to let me try different things on the menu. Smithy's always like, *the locals don't like change. It's been this way for twenty years.*'

Connor laughed at Chook's poor impersonation of the pub owner. 'Well it's not set in stone. But we can make one night a week Chook's Night where you wow us with your culinary skills.'

They chatted for a few more minutes about the menu and timing for Christmas lunch, before Connor walked out to start decorating the tables. He'd advertised that Christmas Lunch was going to be held at the pub for those who didn't want to cook or weren't going to a family member's place for lunch. The response was good, and they had over thirty people coming.

He decorated the tables and Christmas music played over the speakers, but it still didn't get him in the mood. He loved Christmas. His mum had instilled her love for the holiday in him. He needed to find the joy that usually filled him on this day, and he needed to find it fast.

Most of the townsfolk had grumbled about his over the top decorations in the pub, but deep down they loved them as much as he did. From what he'd been told by some of the locals, this year they were all excited about Christmas. He was glad he'd been able to help some people enjoy the holiday. Pity the person he wanted to spend time with was over four hours away from him.

Stop it. You're acting like a lovesick fool.

Okay, whoa. He wasn't a lovesick fool. He'd known Diana for all of three days. People don't fall in love in three days.

Dad said he knew the moment he laid eyes on mum that she was his. Fred said the same thing as well.

He wasn't his dad, but he could acknowledge to himself Diana stirred feelings inside of him he'd never experienced before. It was deeper than attraction, even though that was part of it. Their one night had been amazing and he wouldn't mind repeating the experience. But it was more how he wanted to get to know her on a deeper level. How, when she'd told him about where she'd grown up, he'd wanted to go and tell them how stupid they were. How their lives were poorer for not knowing her. He wanted to champion her like he'd never wanted to do with any other woman he'd spent time with.

The door opened, and a crowd of people walked in. He dragged his mind back to the task at hand—creating a wonderful Christmas lunch for the town who'd welcomed him and his love of all things Christmas.

An hour later everyone was seated at the table ready for the first course to be served. Connor gazed at the people gathered around the long table he'd created and noticed a gap in the middle.

'Where's Fred?' he asked.

Beryl broke off the conversation she was having with Cindy from the doctor's surgery and looked at him. 'Not sure, I knocked on his door before I came, but there was no answer. Either he's playing Scrooge or he's off somewhere. He usually keeps to himself Christmas Day.'

A seed of worry planted in his mind, especially after what Fred had told him about losing the love of his life on Christmas Eve. Connor had gotten fond of the old man and had been happy when Fred had agreed to come to lunch. 'Should we go check again?'

Beryl shook her head at his question. 'Leave him be, he'll come when he's ready.'

Connor thought about ignoring Beryl, but she narrowed her gaze, daring him to defy her. If the plan to take over the pub came to fruition, the last thing he wanted to do was upset the lady who baked the best cream buns he'd ever tasted. He nodded and proceeded to go to the kitchen to collect the plates.

He lost count of the times he went back and forth between the kitchen and the guests, but finally he and Chook joined the table. Fred was still missing. Perhaps the older man found it too difficult to join in with the festivities, the memory of losing his wife on Christmas Eve too much to overcome.

He forked the delicious meal Chook had prepared into his mouth, conversation swirling around him, but he didn't pay attention to it. He was just glad everyone was having a good time.

'Connor.' Chook elbowed his arm.

'What?'

The pub's cook canted his head towards the door. Connor looked where he indicated and was glad he'd finished his mouthful, otherwise he likely would've choked on it. He had no idea what shocked him the most: Diana standing in the doorway of the pub or Fred standing next to her, a huge smile on his face.

Connor pushed away from the table, his chair clattering to the ground. He was at the door in seconds, facing the woman he thought he would never see again.

'What are you ... What's going on?' He couldn't form a coherent thought. He was sure he'd fallen into a post-Christmas lunch food coma and was dreaming Diana standing in front of him.

'Merry Christmas, Connor.' A flash of pink darted out to moisten her lips. Man, how he wanted to lean in and trace the path of her tongue with his own.

He became aware the occupants of the room were staring at them. The last thing he wanted was to have his conversation with her in front of the main players in town.

'Fred, go see Chook, I'm sure he can set you up with some food.' Fred nodded and leaned over to kiss Diana on the cheek.

Huh? What is that all about?

He reached out and took Diana's hand, a shock of electricity vibrated through him, and led her into the hallway where they could talk privately.

'What's going on, Diana? Why are you here? What's with Fred giving you a kiss on the cheek? Why aren't you in Sydney?' He fired out the questions like he would when he was cross-examining a witness. She pulled her hand away.

Her mouth opened and closed a couple of times, as though she was struggling to think about how to answer his questions. 'I thou—'

Connor angled his mouth over hers, giving in to the urge to taste her. It had only been one night since he'd seen her, but it may have well been years. He couldn't believe she'd come back. He almost didn't care about her reasoning, she was here and that's all that mattered.

Diana moaned and pulled away from him. 'What was that for?'

He laughed. 'We're asking a lot of questions and not getting any answers, aren't we?'

'Yeah.'

'Okay, I'll start. I kissed you because I wanted to. I didn't expect to see you again.' He reached out and tapped her nose. 'I had to see for myself you were real and not a Christmas dream.'

She rolled her eyes, he loved seeing it. 'I'm real for sure.'

'Why are you here? Why are you back in Ghost Gum Springs when you seemed so determined to leave?'

She shrugged as though standing in the pub was no big deal. It was to him. A huge deal. 'Sydney wasn't what I thought it was going to be.'

'What do you mean?'

She looked away from him. 'I was just another person sitting in an impersonal bar. It was loud and there was no atmosphere. There was no Christmas spirit. No Christmas decorations.' She breathed deeply before turning to look back at him. 'But most of all there was no you. No Santa's Elf to make Christmas magical.'

'What exactly are you saying here, Diana?' He needed clarification because what he was hoping for was almost too much to believe.

She placed a hand on his face. 'I'm saying you were right, Connor. Christmas isn't a day that should be spent alone. In a few short days you showed me possibilities I thought only existed in movies.'

He pulled her into his arms, holding her close. He had no idea what was about to happen but having her spend Christmas Day with him and the people he'd grown fond of in his short time in Ghost Gum Springs was as natural as breathing.

After a couple of minutes he pulled away. 'How long are you staying?'

'Until I have to fly back.'

'How long is that?'

'End of January.'

He smiled. 'Then I have a few weeks to convince you of the benefits of living in a small town.'

She returned his smile and he could see the shadows slipping away from her face. 'I guess so.'

Connor closed the gap between them and lowered his lips until there were millimetres from hers. 'Merry Christmas, sweetheart.'

'Merry Christmas, my Santa Elf.'

Epilogue

Four Months Later

Diana wished the people in front of her would hurry up and move down the aisle. After sitting on a plane for over fourteen hours she couldn't wait to get off.

Excitement carried her through the long process of getting through immigration and the collection of her bags. She knew the moment she walked through the glass doors and into Connor's arms her life was about to begin.

It had been so hard to get on the plane at the end of January and leave Connor behind. Even though they hadn't said the words to each other, Diana knew she was in love with him. Being apart from him for the last three months had been hard, but knowing that once she finalised everything in Montana she'd be heading back to Australia, and Connor, got her through.

The doors slid open and there he was, holding a bunch of roses. The people around her faded to nothing, her eyes glued to Connor and his broad smile.

She stopped in front of him. She swallowed a couple of times to dislodge the lump in her throat. 'Hey.'

He reached out and pulled her into a hug, the sound of cellophane crinkling near her ear. 'Hey yourself.'

Diana closed her eyes and breathed in the unique scent that was Connor. 'God, I love you.' That wasn't what she meant to say. She meant to say she missed him but as soon as the words left her mouth an overwhelming sensation of rightness flowed through her. Her only fear was that Connor didn't feel the same way.

They'd had numerous FaceTime conversations while they'd been apart. He'd been busy finalising the purchase of the pub from Smithy. Just like she was busy preparing for her move to the other side of the world. But they'd shared so much with each other. He'd shared about why he walked away from his law career in Sydney and how he'd approached Reg about doing some consultation work for him. And she shared with him the life she'd had growing up in Packenridge.

The one thing they hadn't shared were the words she'd just spoken.

'I love you too,' he whispered against her ear before he captured her lips in a kiss. A kiss she'd been yearning for, for three months. A kiss that cemented their relationship. A kiss that filled her heart to overflowing. The scent of crushed rose petals assailed her nostrils and she pulled her lips from his.

'We squashed the roses,' he murmured.

She chuckled as he plucked a ruined petal from her shirt. 'Yeah we did.'

'You ready to go home?' he asked as he grabbed the trolley holding her suitcases.

More ready than anything else in her life. 'Yes, let's go home.'

TINSEL
in a
Tangle

AINSLIE PATON

Dedication

*For women everywhere
who strategise, negotiate, shop, make, clean, cook, solve and
hustle to put the merry in Christmas and the happy in New Year*

Adam: Now

The only jingle bells Adam heard were the ones ringing in his ears.

That was a relief after suffering through Bing, Frank, Elvis, Madonna, and Mariah—even if it was a sign of concussion.

It could be concussion. The nurse said he wasn't allowed to leave casualty until someone saw to him, and that meant waiting until the muttering drunk guy, the Santa with a buggered knee, the woman wearing reindeer antlers, and the two little kids in candy cane PJs had been attended to.

It could be a long night.

It hurt to open his right eye and his left eye was swollen closed. His neck felt like a sumo wrestler had been trampolining on it, and there was blood all over his shirt. His brow might need stitching. His hands weren't shaking to look at, but deep inside the bones were clattering together like knives in a shaken cutlery drawer.

He'd never gotten into a physical fight before. He wasn't made that way. Books over brawling; movies before mauling—almost anything before being aggressive. Even assertive was sometimes too flagrant an attitude. It was no surprise he got on better with his workflow software than he did with his office mates, but tonight he'd discovered his tolerance had a limit, and he'd tripped over it with twelve months of aggravation stored up in his fists.

Felix might look like he was made of thick crust pizza dough, but he punched like a character in *Sniper Elite 4*. That's why Adam's arse was sore. He'd hit the floor so hard he'd bounced, but he hadn't stayed there. He didn't like the view, Felix standing over him like he bloody owned the place and everyone in it. Also legs, a lot of legs, a lot of bare legs in tall heels and short party dresses providing quite the unlooked for opportunity for up-skirting, had that been a thing he'd ever thought about doing.

Odd that he thought about it now. That's how radically out of order this situation was. He really should be focused on whether he had enough money for an Uber ride home, and what the hell he was going to do Monday morning when they gave him the flick.

Felt like he'd gone thirty rounds with Felix while Mariah sang about what she wanted for Christmas. Probably only lasted thirty seconds. Mariah was warbling *youooooo* when he'd put Felix down.

And Felix had stayed there.

Man, they sure knew how to throw a wowzer of a year-end party at LuxLife. Shame Adam's first would be his last. They could forgive karaoke mic hogging, bum photocopying, those beef jerky edible undies and sex toys in the Kris Kringle, but Adam was pretty sure decking the head of HR was a sackable offence.

Things were already grim, and then the only person in the company he'd rather lose a limb for than disappoint walked in to St Vincent's.

There could only be one reason for her to be here. His Christmas present was going to come with unemployment benefits, like not being able to pay his rent.

Shelby left a space between them and sat in the next orange plastic bucket seat in the connected row. She still wore holly in her hair and Christmas tree earrings, and she smelled like spice and vanilla, a human version of a delicious warm pudding. A reminder of good things year-round.

He tried to straighten up, but he'd been here over an hour already and he was moulded to the chair and everything hurt, but nothing more than the pinched concern on Shelby's face. He kept his own face averted and tried to focus on the blue and silver twists of tinsel strung along the opposite wall and the assorted non-farm animals in the nativity scene. There was a T-Rex, a Porg and a Groot watching over a LEGO baby Jesus.

'Are you okay?' she asked.

He didn't have to wait till Monday. He was going to get sacked in the casualty department of St Vincent's hospital at 10 pm a week before Christmas, while wondering if it was his wonky eyes and concussed brain or was Joseph really a Mr. Spock doll?

This sucked mightily, and he hated Shelby seeing him this way, but he'd brought it on himself. Might as well get it over with. 'You didn't have to come.'

'Someone had to check on you.'

'Not you.' *Urgh*, said that aloud, really, really didn't mean to, especially while sounding shitty when contrite was more fitting. None of this was Shelby's fault.

'Why not me?' she said.

Because she was going to ask why he'd hit Felix and he'd have to lie because the reason would make no sense to her and that would make this whole wrong episode of decking the halls even more pointless than it already was. 'I'd have thought someone, you know, on the executive team would need to do it.'

'Well, it would've been Felix, but he's somewhat incapacitated at the moment due to excessive Christmas cheer.'

That was a strange way of putting it. He'd half expected Felix to arrive at St Vincent's too. 'Is he all right?' The guy had dropped, out cold.

'He'll have a black eye and a headache but he's fine. No stitches required.'

Adam rocked forward and peered at the ground. It was a relief to hear Felix was okay. He could swear his tailbone creaked right before two fat ruby drops of blood fell to the puke-coloured flooring between his feet. He straightened up again and used the gingerbread men tea towel he'd swiped from the kitchen to mop his head.

He was a triple threat: assault, battery and theft. *Ho, ho, ho.*

He should look at Shelby, but he didn't think he was strong enough to take her disappointment even if he only had one working eye to see it with. He smudged the blood droplets with his foot. 'Might as well get on with it then.'

'Do you need anything? Can I call someone for you?'

She couldn't be kind. He didn't want her to be kind. She was always kind and fair and sensible. Always had a smile, always made you feel better. A sweetheart, everyone said so. He never had though. Never had the guts to openly admit how much he liked her for her sweetness and her strength. If she was kind now, then fuck, it might be tears hitting the floor next. He'd rather lose another fight than blubber in front of Shelby.

But then, he'd rather blubber than never see her again and that's what was going to happen.

It was better if she just got it over with, cold, professional, efficient. He'd seen her be that way on deserving occasions, so he knew she had it in her. It was part of her all-over awesomeness.

'You know I don't have family here,' he said. They were all in sunny Queensland and most of them could stay there as far as he was concerned.

'Your roommate?'

Okay, so cold wasn't a temperature setting Shelby used often, but she could try harder to twist that dial for the sake of his mental health and wellbeing. 'In Bali.'

'I know you'll have made other friends since you moved to Sydney.'

No one he wanted to call right now. Bad enough he'd come off the worst. The final humiliation of ending up jobless as well as beaten up in the freaking festive season was much better contemplated as a solo pursuit like picking your nose or squeezing pus from a boil. He risked looking at her directly. 'I'm fine.' As long as you quit being kind. *Bah-humbug.*

'I'll stay with you until they—' Her eyes went wide. 'Oh Adam, your face is all—and your hand, are you hurt anywhere else?'

He attempted a laugh because he couldn't take the shock in her voice or the way her forehead crumpled, her lips turned down and her eyes got glassy. 'Only my pride. You don't have to stay.'

'Of course, I do.'

He didn't have anything to say to that. It was probably in her job description, part of the LuxLife HR manual. *When an employee of Australia's favourite online luxury goods retailer is injured, even if it's their own phenomenally moronic fault, first sit with the dickhead before you sack him. This ensures the jerkface's mortification is complete.*

His body got heavier with defeat like there was a squad of sumo sitting on him. But Shelby didn't leave. He couldn't brood her out, no matter how hard he doubled down on his misery because she was tenacious. Right now he didn't love that about her.

For a time they sat silently while the two kids sniffled and poked at each other, their hassled mum tried to peace-keep, Santa played a noisy game on his phone, and the drunk guy muttered to himself.

Adam had lost more than his job tonight. He'd lost any chance he ever had with Shelby. If he'd ever had a chance that is. Women like Shelby who knew who they were and what they wanted in life didn't look twice at men who went at it like a bumper car that never won a race: stop, start, reverse, stall, cause an accident, crash.

When he couldn't stand it any longer he said, 'You don't have to wait to do it.'

She wore red shoes with candy cane striped heels. She had earrings for every holiday and major event. Flags for Australia Day, hearts for Valentine's Day, rabbits for Easter, crowns for the Queen's Birthday, popcorn for Eurovision and little sparkly jockey's caps for Melbourne Cup. She had encouragement for everyone, and none of the LuxLife crew liked making her unhappy.

Just by being interested in you, Shelby made you want to be a better LuxLife employee, but more than that—a better person. It was her special magic. She was part beloved team mascot brought to life for the exclusive benefit of cheering you on, and part walking advice column who knew how to help you succeed.

'Do what?' she said, her stripy heels lifting as if he'd suggested an exciting solution to a nagging problem.

'Sack me.'

Her heels went down, slowly, one at a time. Click, click, like a key turning in the lock that would define his immediately bleak future. 'Why don't we get you stitched up and home safe and we can talk about that later.'

Adam closed his eyes. 'I decked your boss.'

'And he decked you.'

'I started it.' There was no way Felix was the one looking for a new job in January.

'Why? I mean I'm all for exciting, memorable Christmas parties, but I like to plan the entertainment in advance and this was, well, out of the blue.'

Not for Adam. For him, it had been too long coming and the acid shame he felt eating the lining of his stomach wasn't because he'd inappropriately initiated a merry old smackdown in the middle of all the peace and goodwill on earth, but because it had taken him all year to do it. He'd had enough evidence Felix was treating Shelby badly when she wore the hearts in her ears and by the time she wore the crowns he'd have pledged his life for her if she'd asked.

Shelby had never asked him anything more personal than 'How was your weekend?' and 'Are you going home for Christmas?', and it wasn't like telling her how he felt now was going to save his job. If he told her the truth, it would only make her feel worse.

She angled the toes of her shoes his way. 'You're going to have to tell someone.'

'Not if I'm sacked. It won't matter.'

'Worry about feeling better first.'

He met her two chocolate eyes with his one squinty one. 'It's okay, Shelby, you can hit a man when he's down. I know the truth anyway. I know violence is never acceptable and I deserve the consequences, because right now I'm not sorry and I'd do it again.'

She shook her head and her Christmas trees bounced. 'I didn't come here to sack you.'

He passed a hand over his eyes. Maybe he was seeing things and his hearing was wonky. *Not here to sack him?* He had to be hallucinating, because if Shelby was here for any other reason, this was a deck the halls with boughs of holly goddamn Christmas miracle.

Shelby: Now

Shelby sat in the uncomfortable plastic seat in the casualty department of St Vincent's with her heart lodged in her throat. It had jumped up there and gotten stuck when she'd seen the damage to Adam's face. At least she was in the right place to have a major organ displacement emergency.

'I told you, I came to see if you're okay,' she said, squeezing her hands together to stop from reaching out to comfort him.

Adam broke eye contact and dropped his chin to his chest. 'You don't have to stay.'

She sure wasn't leaving. He looked terrible, the split brow, the purple bruised forehead, one eye totally closed, blood all through his hair. One of his hands was swollen and the knuckles were all torn, and the custard on the pudding was the cold vibe he was giving off. That's what had made her sit a little apart from him when what she'd wanted to do was put her arms around him and hug the hurt out.

He was the last person she expected to become violent. It was easier to imagine December Chen from customer service smiling and asking if you had a good weekend while stabbing you with a freshly sharpened pencil, or Rudy Christakis from billing trying to get you drunk on Christmas punch so you'd forget he still hadn't done the 'bullying in the workplace' training than it was to imagine Adam taking Felix, who was twice his bulk, down for no reason she could think of.

It was horrifying and amazing all at once. And it was messing with her head.

Adam was the man who noticed your water jug was empty and made it his mission to fill it for you, daily. He was the man who quietly worked back if he discovered you were the last person in the office because he didn't want you to have to be alone at night, even though your desks were nowhere near each other.

He was the man she'd developed a hopelessly inappropriate unrequited crush on that she'd resolved to act on in the smallest, and most easily discounted way tonight, by inviting him to her orphan's Christmas lunch.

That was before he decked Felix.

Now she was a mixed drink and uncertain about the taste. Was there too much of a kick in Adam's personality she'd failed to see? She had a habit of being too forgiving, and ending up disappointed. It was her kind of tipsy.

'I'm staying.' She didn't have to, this was beyond her job description and the only person who could decide what happened next was their CEO, Stella. Since her flight got delayed and she'd missed the party, Stella didn't know it had ended in black eyes and broken skin yet. It was hard to imagine that once she did, things wouldn't get worse for Adam.

He gave a full body sigh and that didn't help with her desire to hug him one bit. Meanwhile she needed answers. What would make Adam resort to fists? Maybe she'd just been too caught up in Christmas party planning to see trouble on the timeline.

In Shelby's experience, there were two types of office Christmas parties: the ones where people got sloshed, flirted too obviously, forgot themselves and did regrettable things behind potted palms, and the ones where only half the people show up, the catering is awful, everyone stands around wearing stupid hats and strained smiles, laughing at terrible dad jokes, and desperately hoping for someone to do something shocking before they made an excuse to leave early.

HR managers were supposed to make sure companies had their end of year celebrations without offending anyone, breaking anything, or getting sued, which was seasonal insanity when you consider all anyone wanted to do at a work party where there was free booze and food was act like they weren't at work. For some people that meant acting like they were at a rave or in an episode of *Romper Stomper*.

Over the years she'd done her best to encourage party committees to avoid fancy dress—someone always wore too little and showed too much; Secret Santa with a dubious theme—the least suitable person always got the edible underpants; booze cruises—the horror; curiosities like topless waiters—just, no; ice sculptures—what were they thinking, it was always stinking hot; and hiring Gabe in legal's cover band. An idea only ever pushed by Gabe.

There was always an argument with marketing who wanted something more fun, and with the management team who wanted safe and not too expensive, and all Shelby wanted was for it to be over.

Nothing in her six years of experience as a people manager had prepared her for seeing her boss out cold on the floor at the hand of her secret fantasy boyfriend.

People got silly at parties, their guards came down and they said inappropriate things. They danced like they thought they were

Beyoncé, when their moves where really more like The Wiggles. She'd repaired egos and mopped tears at Christmas parties. She'd sent people home to recover from imagined insults and counselled people over real ones, got people up to dance, and asked the disorderly ones to calm down, but she'd never had to clean up after a physical fight.

She wasn't entirely sure what the clean-up should be. As far as Christmas party behaviour was concerned, it was back of beyond naughty, a long, long way from nice.

'Never thought I'd see a nativity with a colour-change-hair Barbie as Mary,' she said to break the quiet they'd both sunk into.

'Thought I was seeing things at first. The Porg is a nice touch,' Adam replied.

He'd seemed angry when she'd arrived, well not angry so much as embarrassed and maybe a little ashamed. He definitely wasn't pleased to see her, but then he'd thought she'd come to make him more miserable.

'I've sent Stella a message, but she might not get back to me tonight. I'll stay with you until they fix you up and we'll worry about everything else later.' He didn't respond so she slid into the seat she'd left between them and ducked her head to look at his poor smashed face. 'Is that okay with you?'

'I can't stop you.' He shook his head, scrunched his forehead making his cut reopen. 'I'm sorry, that was rude and you're being nothing but generous and kind and I don't deserve it.'

She took the tea towel out of his hand and dabbed it gently on his brow. She hoped it was clean when he nicked it from the staff kitchen. He flinched away at first, relenting only when she clucked her tongue at him. She could mop his head, but she couldn't do anything to sort out what had happened especially if he wouldn't tell her why he'd gone after Felix.

'You want to know why I think you did it?' she said.

'Nope.'

She drummed her heels on the floor. Stoic, that was Adam. Man of few words. Responsible. Focused. Dedicated. Excellent reader of people. Good with detail, never missed a deadline. But he also kept to himself and he'd forced her to use her super stealth HR ninja skills to get any personal information out of him at all. What she knew about him outside of his resume she could write in a tweet and still have characters to spare.

Adam Tide. 29. Queensland born. Self-taught coder, UX wizard. Parents strict Catholics. Older brother recently married his male partner. All out family war. Escaped to Sydney. Ridiculously cute man bun. Deliciously lovely.

She suspected the man bun, artfully messy and worn low at his neck was a protest, a middle finger to his parents in the same way as the move to Sydney was, and maybe the tattoos. She didn't know if he had any, but it was a decent guess. What she really wanted to know was if she was right.

She hadn't asked him to be her orphan when she should have and now, now it was like hot cross buns appearing in Woolies right after New Year, all out of sync and just plain wrong.

One of the pyjama kids was crying, outraged, wet, snotty sobs. It was the sound Shelby would make if she wasn't on the job. HR professionals didn't itch to scratch their nails over the meticulously clipped beard hairs of crushed-on colleagues to see if they were soft. And they had no business imagining that the owner of the beard had decked their dickhead boss just for them.

A visit from the real Santa, not like the one waiting opposite who was sitting on a pillow that must once have been his additional tummy stuffing, was more on the cards.

In lieu of a snotty sob, she sighed. 'Felix can be a bit—'

'Of an arse.'

She poked Adam's shoe with her own. 'I was going to say, a bit difficult.'

'He's an arse.'

It wasn't easy to dispute that. She'd spent four years disputing it in her head because that's the only way she could keep working for Felix at LuxLife. It was the forgiveness problem in glorious flashing neon lights. Plus, she loved her job every day of the year except the day of the Christmas party, and she loved all the people she was responsible for, except Felix, because there was no more dodging it—Felix was an arse of the first order. If she kept on working for a man she had no respect for, who she made allowances for and apologised for, who she had to charm, placate and outmanoeuvre, one who she knew was an arse, what did that make her?

An arse whisperer?

Oh shit, no!

Adam took the tea towel out of her limp hand. 'I know you can't admit he's an arse. It's in the handbook. Don't speak evil of another LuxLife employee.'

It wasn't, but that was a good idea.

'I don't believe you don't know he's an arse,' he said.

A nurse came, and the crying kid and his family went with her to another room. The silence was holy, it prompted the truth. Kind of. 'He is what he is.'

'An arse.'

'My boss and there's nothing I can do about that. Did you hit him because he's an arse? That's not a great reason. Almost everyone wants to hit him for that.'

Adam groaned. 'Wish somebody else had.'

'Me too.'

She shoulder-bumped him gently, her bare forearm touching the soft cotton of his shirt, skin meeting skin where their sleeves ended. She did it without thinking. They'd never touched before, not deliberately for no reason. Back in January, there'd been a handshake. Their fingers had grazed passing a folder once, and she'd just mopped his head and poked his foot, but that was all business.

There was one occasion when her skirt had brushed across his knee and it'd done something to both of their breathing, and there was that time they almost collided outside the print room. She'd thought about that every time she'd printed a document for weeks. And then that moment in the lift where she almost trod on him, almost stumbled into him and he'd touched her shoulder to steady her.

She'd made up a whole fantasy about that incident. It was all about them being alone and stranded between level five and six and not minding at all, instead of squeezed in with a good half of the office including the volleyball team who stank of cold sweat and the lamb kebabs they'd brought back for lunch.

But this, it was like the time with the skirt, both of them stopped breathing. Adam didn't twitch away. If she wasn't imagining it, he leaned in a little, moved his forearm so that more of her arm aligned along his. There was a line of muscle and veiny cords on his arm, a light smattering of dark hair, and he wore a thin rubber bracelet at his wrist. How was it she'd never realised men's forearms could be so mesmerising? She simply couldn't take her eyes off his arm or believe he was a violent man.

He'd been filling her water jug for weeks before she'd realised it was him doing it. And he'd never admitted to staying behind so she didn't need to be alone on nights she worked back, and she didn't think it was a coincidence, but then she couldn't get enough oxygen to her brain, so she couldn't exactly trust her thinking. Plus, there was the forgiveness problem.

'Sorry, I shouldn't. Sorry,' he said and oh, freaking Father Christmas, he moved his arm.

She really had screwed up by not asking him to lunch. She'd had all damn year to do it. When she took stock, she'd screwed up all round. She'd spent another year enabling a man who was an arse, and she'd been too much of a chickenshit to ask a man she liked so much she'd almost passed out from the press of his forearm to Christmas lunch.

It was just lunch. It didn't say anything about the almighty inappropriate and unrequited crush she had on him. It wasn't even a hot roast. It was all cold: chicken and turkey, ham and prawns and scallops with five different types of salad with mango, cranberries and pomegranates, and yes, probably kale, and certainly avocado, but also soft rolls and nice wine and the frostiest beer. After that there'd be pavlova and fruit cake and maybe a trifle and a definite serving of having eaten too much and vowing never to eat again but still backing up for leftovers at dinner time.

She'd known she'd wanted to ask Adam to lunch way back in June when he made a comment in the staff room about how you didn't get to choose your family. With her Mom gone, Shelby and her sister Cassie did exactly that, chose their Christmas family, so Adam wouldn't be the only orphan.

'I hit him because he's an arse. That's all Stella needs to know.'

It was less than Shelby wanted to know. Adam wasn't drunk, and he wasn't a natural with his fists unless they were hovering over a keyboard, and truly at some time, everyone wanted to slap, kick, shove or punch Felix. She wanted to do it at least weekly. It was rumoured the only reason Stella kept him on was because his family had helped her raise the money to start LuxLife when no one else would.

'You're sure that's what you want to say?' she asked.

He studied the floor as if it had the answer written on it in fading blood.

She was here for all the wrong reasons and her heart was hopelessly dislocated over Adam. She really wanted to ask him to lunch. It was now, or her New Year's resolution would need to be something about chasing her dreams or personal courage, or maybe getting a new job herself so this didn't feel like it was wrong anymore.

'Can I—' she said, trying to push the words out over a tongue that'd gone soft and sticky like hot caramel sauce on pudding. Adam angled his face to look at her with his good eye and her back teeth stuck together. Neither of them saw the nurse.

'Adam Tide,' she said. 'You can come through now.'

Santa and the women in the reindeer antlers weren't the only ones who found that jolly annoying.

Adam: Before

The day Adam started at LuxLife was the day he hoped his own lacklustre life would kick up a gear. New city, a job he'd never expected to get, a company he was excited to contribute to, a chance to be his own person far from the stifling expectations of his family.

He almost got his hair chopped and shaved off his beard to celebrate. He almost got a new tattoo.

He almost lost his head before he even made it out of reception.

'Hi Adam. I'm Shelby Yule. Welcome to LuxLife. I'll introduce you around and take you through orientation. You can ask me anything.'

It wasn't the slam of introductions—he was good with names and faces—and it wasn't the whole LuxLife culture, a zero bullshit, truth and honesty, doona days, holiday on your birthday approach to work that spun him out, it was dark brown eyes, a boy haircut, a radiant smile, and that "ask me anything" that made him think about radically off limits non-work topics before he'd even sat at his own desk.

That shouldn't have been a shock, cute was his jam, but there was more to Shelby than tiny starfish earrings and an aqua dress with a swirly skirt that looked like something out of a costume box, and he knew that the moment he met her.

By the end of the day he was shockingly disappointed that his desk was at the other end of the open plan floor to hers, but since this was a new job and the start of a new life away from his feuding, take sides or die lonely family, he needed to have his head in the game. And the game wasn't an office romance.

'I hope you'll be happy here,' Shelby said, as she showed him how to use the electric standing desk. It was completely adjustable, with settings that could be personalised for his height and it was a revelation. At his last job his chair had been wedged on one setting and no amount of asking for it to be fixed had made a difference. He'd gone home most nights with a neck ache, but at this desk he'd be invincible. It was almost a metaphor for his life.

They were both peering under the plank of ergonomic wonderment at the attached wire basket designated for cords and cables when Felix arrived.

'I see Shelby is pressing your buttons, Adam.'

He straightened up to greet Felix, confused by the guy's greeting and Shelby's snort, unsure if it was a sound of amusement or frustration. Either way it was unwanted sexual innuendo and it made the hair on his arms spring to attention.

He'd met Felix during his final interview, but since that was online and he'd been more focused on trying to impress tech tycoon extraordinaire, Stella Wong, he'd logged only one fact about Felix. Bad cop. He'd figured that was all part of the interview rigmarole, but maybe it went beyond trying to fake out job candidates.

'Welcome aboard. Hope you enjoyed your orientation. Shelby has a knack for making people feel at home. That's why we keep her around,' Felix said with a laugh.

It was another confusing statement. It sounded like a compliment except for the part where it sounded like a threat and made Shelby wince. Yes, that was absolutely a wince, a flicker of distaste that quirked her shoulders and narrowed her eyes.

They exchanged a few banal pleasantries, Felix moved off and Shelby talked him through the employee reporting systems and gave him a lesson in the after-hours security access.

'So that's it,' she said. 'You're all set.'

'Thank you.' *I think your boss is a dick.* It would be bad karma on day one to say that. 'Today was great.' Also, it wasn't his business. He didn't know Shelby or Felix, and getting involved in office politics he didn't understand was like refusing to get involved in family politics he did; bound to be a pit of sorrow and a no-win situation. He'd had so much of that he'd moved states and changed his phone number.

This job was a huge step up and for the first time he was working for a CEO he respected and admired. He settled in to his routine at LuxLife far easier than he'd expected to. It wasn't hard to trace that back to the quality of his orientation. After a month, he actually did feel at home, though he was teased for being the new guy at every occasion possible and most of those included Shelby.

In February, she asked him to pick a glittery heart out of a bowl and send an anonymous card to the person whose name was written on it. His eyes nearly bugged out of his head.

She laughed at him. 'I forget this sounds weird to new folk. It's not a love letter. You just say something nice about the person. On Valentine's Day everyone gets a card that makes them feel special.'

It was a little hokey. 'What if I don't know the person well enough?' He might be able to wiggle out of this on a technicality.

She shook the glass bowl. 'That's why you're going to pick a heart that's folded in half lengthwise. They're for people you work most closely with.'

'Isn't that cheating?' Was Shelby's name still in there, had she folded her heart in half for him to find?

She smiled. She had hearts in her ears. 'What's a little cheating between colleagues, huh?'

'I thought LuxLife was all straight talk, truth and honesty.'

She sagged, her chin dropping towards her chest and her shoulders slumping, making him almost gasp. He'd meant that as a joke, but it came out like a complaint, like he was grumpy with her when she'd gone to the trouble of making this easy for him. He liked her so much he couldn't stand the thought of disappointing her. 'I'm sorry, I—'

'Sprung,' she said, grinning. *Cheeky kitten.* 'You're the first to pick.'

He looked in the top of the bowl, near overflowing with red paper hearts some folded in half to look like sail boats and others to look like they were waiting for their mate to be complete. Shelby's heart was in there, but you never won anything decent in a lucky dip and it's not like there was a strategy that would change that.

Unless it was rigged.

He plucked one off the top, the first lengthwise folded heart he saw, as if it had been strategically placed there for him.

It wasn't rigged. And why the heck had he thought it would be? He'd scored Dave Wilson in marketing. So much for wishful thinking. Dave had a loud laugh, a kiwi accent and liked to cook. He often brought delicious brownies into the office. It would be easy to say something positive about Dave, but instead of feeling relieved, he was oddly disappointed.

'Drop your card into the mail room and we do the rest,' she said.

It was hokey, but he went with it. He bought a card for Dave that had the words *I wish I could bake a cake filled with rainbows and smiles and the whole world would fall in love* printed on the front. Inside he'd written simply, *for the brownies, man.* Adding the *man* because he was vaguely bothered by the idea of sending a love note to another bloke he worked closely with, even though he'd been best man at his brother's wedding. Scott and his husband Louie would take him out the back and pummel him for feeling awkward about the card.

In his defence, he'd rather have bought a card for Shelby.

On Valentine's Day, Dave made a loud announcement standing on his desk. 'To the bro who bought my V Day card. You're all good, eh.'

Adam figured it was the *man* that earned him the 'bro'. The card that had been left for him had a rustic hipster look with the words *I would shave my beard for you* written in big fat letters that were decorated with hairs on the front. Inside, his office Valentine had written: *I really like the fact that you never speak over the top of anyone and you're always polite and courteous, but if I had a beard, I'd only shave it for money. You win some, you lose some.*

He'd laughed out loud. He had no clue who'd sent it, even eliminating all bearded colleagues, and it wasn't Shelby's handwriting. It put him in a good mood all day, good enough not to regret he wasn't the one who sent the roses he saw in reception with Shelby's name on the little envelope.

She deserved roses, dozens of them because the whole office had fun that day and nobody felt left out and there was nothing hokey about that.

The next company-wide fun day that rolled around was Easter. Chocolate and hot cross buns weren't unexpected, the hat parade was.

Shelby tracked him down in the kitchen where he was heating noodles, brewing jasmine tea and brooding about his five o'clock probation meeting. He'd been at LuxLife three months and while some parts of his job came easily, there'd been an angsty period over a change of procedure he'd initiated that had fouled up. To say he was nervous about having his position confirmed was an understatement. He'd been nervous for weeks, a low-grade anxiety that made it difficult to relax.

Felix had been on his case about it. 'This isn't a formality. We have a waiting list of people who want your job,' he'd said, and since it was Adam's error, he had to cop it on the chin. But he couldn't afford to be without work and if they boned him he'd have instant money worries.

Shelby made him nervous too. Nervous in a kind of rollercoaster, thrill-seeking way that had nothing to do with the fear he might lose his job and everything to do with how much he enjoyed talking to her.

'I need to tell you about the hat parade,' she said.

If he'd been paying more attention to her words and not the funky overalls she was wearing, that might've made sense.

'It's not exactly a parade in the march along sense,' she explained. 'It's just that on Thursday before we break for the holiday, if you want a hot cross bun you have to wear a hat. Basically, everyone wears a hat. No hat, no bun.'

'If I wear a cap, I get a bun.' It seemed like a fair exchange. It was easier than choosing a cheap card.

She scrunched up her nose. 'A cap will do the job.'

'Hang on.' Now he was listening as well as watching. 'You don't really think it will.'

'No, no, a cap is fine. Gets you a bun. It's just that some people go all out.'

All out in the hat department. He had a minor brain blank wondering what that could mean. 'What will you wear?'

'Oh no.' She shook her head, a mock serious expression on her face. 'I don't hat and tell.' The look she gave him, eyebrow wiggles, sucked in cheeks, and fish lips made him laugh. It made him think about hooking his hand into the strap of her overalls, pulling her close and giving her a kiss to tell about.

Except this was work and mostly he just felt a kind of queasy that noodles lunch wasn't going to fix. He watched Shelby leave the kitchen. It might be the last time he saw her.

'Hey,' he called.

She turned back. 'What do you need?'

To have worked out what the rest of that sentence was going to be before he opened his mouth. 'Sorry, I—' He felt his face get hot and itchy. To have a plan B if things went south, to have no more debt and savings in the bank, to quit arguing with Scott, to call his dad and try to speak civilly, to have a conversation with his mum without making her cry.

To have a friend like Shelby who made him laugh.

'Stella thinks you're a great addition to the team. If you're worried about your probation period, you don't need to be.'

'Felix,' *was a dick about it*, 'said you'd have no trouble replacing me.'

'If he told you we have a list of people who'd sell a limb to work here, he's right, but I'm sure he didn't mean to put you on edge. None of them are you.'

'I stuffed up.' He'd cost the company time and money. Oh, shit, he was going to lose his job. By the end of the day he'd be unemployed, short on rent, low on hope and long on fucked.

Shelby came closer. 'And you made things better in the end.'

That was true. He'd been right about the new process being more efficient, he just hadn't anticipated all the steps he needed to get there.

'Stella says sometimes you have to break things to see how they can be put together differently.'

He'd know if that was a theory she'd apply to him in a few hours.

Shelby's eyes got big. 'Oh Adam.' She slapped her hands on her sides. 'You should never have been worried about this. That's not how we do things. We're going to fix this right now.'

And she did. She marched him to Stella's office, interrupted another meeting saying this was urgent and in less than fifteen minutes his position was confirmed.

'I'm super sorry you were concerned, Adam,' Stella said after she'd outlined the projects she wanted him to focus on. 'I think you're doing a great job. I can't wait to see what you break and fix next.'

His noodles were cold, and Shelby had disappeared before he could thank her, but everything else was looking up. He sent her a private LuxChat message.

Thank you for sorting me out.

And immediately wanted to call it back because he'd made it sound personal and maybe a little suggestive. He went to make more tea and by the time he was at his desk with the pot, Shelby had responded with a winky face and the words *I'll sort you out anytime.*

That made his face get hot again, but he was blaming the tea.

The sunny feeling lasted all afternoon, but his temperature control was tested as he was leaving for the day.

'You went ahead without me.'

He heard Felix before he saw him, which was business as usual; the guy had a boomer of a voice, bested only by Dave.

'You interrupted Stella for no good reason and you know how jammed her calendar is.'

He cringed for the person being chewed out then he rounded the corner and saw it was Shelby.

'The meeting could've waited,' Felix said and looked at Adam. That's when it became obvious this was about him: his meeting with Stella that Shelby had pulled off on the fly and left Felix out of.

'Adam, congratulations. I'd like to have been at your confirmation meeting, but unfortunately Shelby didn't notify me that the time had changed. You have a new contract letter to sign. You'll need to log in to the employee portal. Make sure you do that before you leave tonight.'

Shelby had put herself out for him and now she was under fire. 'Shelby was helping me out.'

'Adam, you don't need—'

Felix talked over Shelby. 'Did you ask her to bring the meeting forward?'

He shook his head, but he didn't mind admitting he'd been sweating bullets. 'No, but—'

'Then Shelby was making life harder for Stella. As you've waited months to be confirmed, I'm sure you could've waited a few more hours.'

That was entirely reasonable, but it was also making a big deal of things. It's not like Stella didn't know how to say no when she needed to. 'I was anxious and Shelby—'

Felix cut him off again. 'Did a nice thing without thinking about how that affects other people. I need your contract paperwork now, Adam. Shelby should have told you that already.'

Shelby's eyes were down, her lips twisted. He'd caused her a problem and he didn't want Felix to have another reason to be shitty with her. He went back to his desk, logged on again and completed the paperwork. It wasn't the triumphant moment it should've been.

He opened LuxChat and brought up Shelby's name, then typed *Felix is a fucking dickhead. I'm sorry I made life hard for you.* He looked at the send button. He deleted the fucking because maybe that was going too far and since calling the head of HR a dickhead in writing wasn't smart, he deleted the whole first sentence and hit send.

He didn't hear back till morning and he might've predicted the result.

She responded: *You didn't make life hard for me. It was just one of those things. It's all good.*

After that he didn't see Shelby for days. Easter Thursday, he came to work in his favourite cap. It was black and had the word *thinking* embroidered on it in white letters.

The first person he saw was Dave who wore a plastic shower cap with pink flowers on it. 'Want my bun, bro,' he said.

December wore a hat she'd made herself out of a plush toy octopus. Its tentacles were tied under her chin. Stella wore a Sherlock Holmes cap. Felix wore a shiny top hat that made him look about seven foot tall. There were big fancy wedding hats and a bunch of berets and bucket hats; straw cowboy hats were big and so were Akubras, but the hat he most wanted to see was Shelby's.

He had to wait half the morning to catch sight of her. She wore a sloppy knitted beanie that came down low over her forehead and fell in soft folds over her head, into a woolly puddle at the back of her neck. It should've had the word *adorable* written on it. It was the kind of hat that was made for cold winter nights and snuggling by the fire, or late Sunday breakfasts at a favourite café. Maybe she'd get to wear it with whoever had sent the roses, whoever she sorted out in her life away from work.

He really liked looking at Shelby in the sloppy knit hat. Cute girls in adorable hats were his new porn. He admired her for the fact she'd brought spare beanies so that no one missed out on a bun. He didn't like the fact Felix had an opinion about that. Said it was cheating. No hat, no bun. He made Shelby frown and since her forehead was hidden under rows of stitches she was all down-turned lips, and narrowed, lowered eyes. He almost went to her, stopped himself because what was he going to say after I like your hat and Felix is a dick? Anyway, she shook it off and went about making sure everyone was enjoying themselves like it was nothing she wasn't used to.

She didn't ignore him, but she didn't seek him out either. And since he'd caused her trouble that was fair. That's when he started filling her water jug. It was no big deal. He was filling his own and if hers was empty it was an easy twofer. Because he normally got to the office before she did, he didn't even have to interrupt her, just swing by her desk on his way to the kitchen.

It was months later, in the middle of the year, when he learned that Shelby's roses had been from Stella. It was a LuxLife tradition. Every year Stella picked five people who'd made an outstanding contribution to the company to send roses to on Valentine's Day. The woman was a tech guru and an ace CEO.

If Shelby had an admirer, he was still a secret, and Adam had no reason to wonder about how she spent her time out of the office, except that it became a kind of game he played with himself. Did she like Netflix and pizza or was she more of a party hard girl? Was she into fancy restaurants or raves or home cooking? Was she a gamer or a reader, a festival fan or an exercise junkie? Did she collect teaspoons with those enamelled tops that said Innaloo,

Dondingalong or Useless Loop? Did she knit her own hat? Did she dream of backpacking Europe or climbing Everest or buying a new car, or having Stella's job one day?

What did she taste like?

That last one, ah, that vision lighting up his brain, about standing close to her, about asking for what he wanted and having her say yes, about flicking his tongue over the bow of her upper lip before taking her face in his hands and sharing a first kiss—that could get him into a lot of trouble.

The very same category of idea looked like it was going to get Dave into trouble. He was having a thing with Christina Alexiadas from product development. A hot and heavy thing that they both thought was secret and almost everyone knew about, on account of how they couldn't keep their eyes or their hands to themselves and then made the weakest excuses for when they got caught out.

You had something on your face.
Can you undo this clasp?
Your label was sticking out.
Could you open this bottle for me?
I was just checking you hadn't lost an earring.

Also, there was the fact that Felix thought it was funny to call attention to them, as if the time Christina sat on Dave's desk phone and engaged the intercom and the whole office heard him say, 'You were on fire last night, babe,' wasn't enough to do that.

They'd essentially all gotten used to Dave and Christina being a thing that could cause nausea when Adam's birthday rolled around in July and Shelby asked him to pick a day for his holiday. Since it fell on a Saturday he'd figured he'd missed out.

She'd rolled a spare chair up beside him. 'Hey new guy, do you want to take the Friday before or the Monday after off?' she asked.

Unexpected and very cool. 'The Monday.'

'Good call. You can snuggle in while all of us LuxLife wage slaves slog in to work on a cold morning.'

Someone to snuggle with would perfect the idea.

'Even better if your partner can take a day off too,' she said. Mind reader.

'It'll just be me and Feral,' he said and watched for Shelby's reaction. She'd made a move to leave, but he'd stopped her. Now he wanted to hold her in place a while. 'Feral's morning breath is like garbage rolled in sewerage.'

Shelby laughed. 'I don't know whether to suggest medical attention or worry about the fact your partner is called Feral.'

'Feral belongs to my roomie, but she likes me better.'

If she'd had a single doubt that Feral had fur, it was trash now. He could see the depth of amusement in her eyes. 'Feral sounds like a handful.'

Since Feral was a big, old, well-fed tabby cat who liked to sleep on Adam's feet, this wasn't far from the truth. You needed both hands to move her; she could make herself liquid.

'I hope you and Feral will have a great birthday together,' Shelby said, and this time he had no clever conversation to stop her leaving.

She rocked forward to stand at the same time as he moved to square his chair with his desk and their knees brushed and her skirt flicked over his thigh. A hushed second later their eyes caught, but before he could think of anything to say, she was gone.

And that was the best career move for both of them.

Shelby: Before

Christina wouldn't come out of the ladies. That wouldn't be such a problem if Dave wasn't in there too.

'If they were, you know, doing it, that would be one thing,' December said. 'But they've been in there arguing for the last half-hour and I don't want to poop in the middle of someone's crisis.'

It was a fair point. Not that it worked on Dave. His response to Shelby's request that he leave the ladies was met with him pounding on the door of the cubicle Christina was inside and shouting. 'It's not that I don't love you.'

'It's just that you love your mum more,' Christina shouted back. 'You should've stood up for me.'

The last person who'd stood up for Shelby was Adam. Adam who was secretly filling her water jug every morning, adding slices of lime and lemon, sometimes mint and strawberries. He'd pretended not to know what she was talking about when she asked about it, as if he didn't have the same things in his own water jug. The last thing she wanted to do was embarrass him. He was the guy least likely to call attention to himself. And in an office mostly full of look-at-me extroverts she cherished that about him.

'She's my mum,' Dave said.

'And you're scared of her.'

'Shit all I am,' he protested, or maybe that was agreement. It was a kiwi thing.

The cubicle door opened, and Christina came out. Her eyes were all smudgy. 'We're over.'

'What? Because my mum said you didn't need dessert?'

'Because, you dumbass brownie baker, when I said I'd love some you sided with your mum.'

'You can't break up with me over that.'

'It's not like I don't know I'm fat. You're fat too, but you get dessert and I don't. That's not how it works.'

'Babe, you can't break up with me over a piece of pav.'

Christina gave Dave a look Shelby knew stood in for the words *watch me*. She pushed past and left them standing there.

'Dave, you need to,' she made a gesture towards the door.

'She can't break up with me over something my mum said. That's fuckin' ridiculous.'

'You're in the ladies.'

He gestured to the outside world. 'I'm upset and I'm not ready to go out there. How are we supposed to work together now?'

That might be a problem. 'You're both professionals.' Although right now there wasn't much evidence of that. Dave looked like he might cry. 'You worked together before.'

'Yeah, nah, but now we've seen each other naked.'

Shelby put both hands up to stop him saying more. This was why office romances were a bad idea. This was why she kept her distance from Adam, because she could easily want more than a professional relationship with him and then she'd be the one crying in the bathroom because office flings came with a heavy serving of unnecessary scrutiny and, when they ended, the unhappiness was a toxic river of discontent that spread everywhere.

'Dave, please don't cry.'

He rubbed the back of his hand against his nose, so she grabbed some toilet tissue and thrust it at him.

'I thought, I thought she was, you know, the one,' he said, taking the tissue and blowing his nose loudly.

There was a knock at the door. 'Can I come in?'

'Give us a minute,' she called.

'Like I'm busting, hurry up.'

'Use the men's. Knock first.'

There was a rumble of agreement and the outer door banged. Sometimes being responsible for LuxLife's people came with unusual challenges. Like toilet triage.

The break had given Dave a chance to pull it together. He splashed water on his face and gave a big shuddery sigh. 'S'pose everyone will be laughing at me now.'

'You wore a shower cap at Easter. Since when have you worried about people laughing at you?'

'Since I got my heart broken over a piece of pav,' he said.

You're not supposed to hug employees, but she wanted to. Dave needed a hug. He needed a lesson more, and the part of Shelby that wasn't trying to get Dave to quit the ladies was high-fiving Christina for making her stand.

'She can't break up with me over meringue.'

'I think she broke up with you because you didn't back her choices. And if you didn't take her side over something simple like wanting dessert, it kinda suggests you might not be there for her for the big-ticket items.'

Dave rubbed his face. 'Shit a brick,' he said. Which had a way of focusing them on their location.

The next few weeks were a little rocky for Dave, Christina, and both of their teams since the couple reconciled only to fall apart again—fortunately not in the bathroom this time—and everyone had an opinion about them.

Dave was a dickhead.

Christina was a hardcase.

They were a car crash. Good thing they broke up.

They were made for each other. We should help them get back together.

There was a collective gasp when they argued across the tops of the workstation spine, and Shelby had to step in and remind them of their responsibilities. It was an uncomfortable conversation for everyone.

Back in the bad old days, companies banned office romances, but since you couldn't stop people being attracted to each other, affairs went underground. People snuck around and kept it quiet, and since the woman was always the one asked to leave if a romance was discovered, not being caught was once a serious thing, instead of a half-baked notion.

Shelby could never be sure the office didn't have its fair share of one-night stands and full-on flings, but if it did, the other couples had worked out how to do it on the sly. Good for them. So when Felix wanted to restructure the product development team, effectively demoting Christina, Shelby saw red.

'It's not a demotion,' he said when he showed her the new structure. On paper it certainly didn't look like one, and Christina wasn't about to lose salary, but she'd lose authority, and that was a demotion in whatever outfit you dressed it in.

'We can't do that,' she said.

'We have to do something, since you've failed to get the two of them to act professionally.'

Harsh but also real. 'I'm not a relationship counsellor,' she groused.

'HR is about relationships. Since you failed to create a solution to this and the two teams are dysfunctional because of it, I need a better suggestion than "we can't restructure",' Felix said.

'It will settle down.' Dave was due to take leave and that would help reset things.

Felix quit playing with his fidget cube and glared at her. 'Instead of finding a solution, your strategy is hope and a prayer. And in the meantime, we're losing productivity and morale has taken a hit. Stella and I didn't build this company on wait and see.' He slid the new organisational chart across his desk to her. 'Make this work.'

She'd have argued, but he had an infuriating way of being largely right about the big picture at the same time as he was wrong about the detail. He had a knack for making her feel ineffective and weak for not knowing how to make him see other sides to the story.

She stormed into the print room to make a copy of the org chart, taking her frustration out on the copier by poking the print screen extra hard. She'd talk to Christina first and then to Dave, one last time before she forced a restructure on both their teams. She wasn't weak, and she wasn't ineffective, but it was easy for a big, loud person who was higher up the chain than she was to make her feel that way. Felix's plan was almost as disruptive as the broken romance had been. There had to be another way and she'd find it. Not that he'd thank her for it.

Copies of the chart in hand she turned to leave the print room, eyes down on the page filled with little boxes, lines and arrows connecting them. She didn't see Adam until almost too late, his boots appearing in her line of sight right before they near collided, her printed pages smooshing against his stomach, her forehead almost bumping his shoulder.

'Whoa,' he said, so softly and so close to her ear it made her shiver.

Boots, blue jeans, a black shirt, the cuffs rolled back, the swell of his chest, the wide span of his shoulders. That neat beard lining his jaw and filling in his cheeks, the soft lips framed by it, the gentle eyes, and a brow wrinkled in expectation of her response. He'd put lime and basil in her water jug this morning. He smelled like green trees after a thunderstorm.

'Are you okay?' he said.

No, her inability to step back made her feel ineffective, and his long dark eyelashes made her feel weak, and that was incredibly irritating. She was allowed to have a favourite colleague, but she wasn't allowed to show it, and Adam had been her favourite since he started in January. By halfway through the year, the only way not to show it was to avoid being alone with him.

And yet she didn't step back, just breathed him in, weak in her resolve and ineffective in her will, and smiling all over her body, in all the secret places no one could see, where favouritism was allowed to grow ripe and flower and spark indecent thoughts in the quiet moments before she dropped off to sleep.

Adam shifted to put some space between them. 'Did I step on you? You came out of there like the room was on fire and I wasn't quick enough to avoid you.'

'I'm good.' A near collision shouldn't make her feel lighter and more capable. Adam shouldn't make her think about clandestine couplings away from gossip-greedy eyes.

'You're sure? Your printing got scrunched.'

Better that than her heart. 'Lime and basil.'

He shrugged and stepped aside. 'No idea what you're talking about.'

'At least let me kick in for the fruit and veg.'

He'd moved past her by the time she got that out and the only indication he'd heard was the slight turn of his head, the crooked hitch of his smile.

The fact she aced her meetings with Christina and Dave, got them to agree to a truce, a return to normal work behaviour instead of a restructure was no surprise, except to Felix. A half smile, given reluctantly, went a long way to making her feel unbeatable.

Half smiles from impossible crushes didn't make a career though, and they were about to enter the most anxious time of the year, the annual performance review period.

For Shelby it was three weeks of planning, working back late, chasing paperwork and soothing egos. For everyone else it was the dread of having to find constructive ways to give and take feedback without resorting to meaningless platitudes—*Muhammad always does excellent work*, or hurtful opinions—*Arnie needs to shut up about Mortal Kombat because no one is interested in violent video games about killing people.*

If she survived the reviews this year without an argument with Felix, it would be an outstanding achievement. Knowing that was unlikely should've meant it wasn't disappointing when a dispute smacked her upside the head.

It was early evening of week one, and the two of them were last in the office. When Felix suggested doing her own review then and there over a plate of guacamole instead of when it was scheduled in week two, she almost baulked, but it would be good to dry-run the process before everyone else did it, and the call of the avocado and sour cream was strong.

They settled in the kitchen, the guac and a bowl of corn chips between them. Everyone else would book a private meeting room for their discussion.

The first half of the review went well. It was mostly scores against key job competencies and Shelby's were as expected. Not five out of five, Felix was stingy and said no one's performance was ever perfect, but certainly in the above average category, which was pleasing.

The second half of the review was designed as a more fluid discussion. It was supposed to be the valuable part where people learned about how they could get more satisfaction out of their jobs, but it could also be where things went off the rails if the reviewer wasn't careful.

Careful to Felix was shark to crowded beach.

And Shelby was chum.

They went off the rails, ploughed up the sand, and got buried in salty verbal combat.

He opened with, 'Although your day-to-day performance is good, you need to adopt a more professional attitude.'

That was it for the guac, it was no longer delicious. She abandoned her pursuit of a corn chip. 'What do you mean by that?'

'You're too friendly.' Felix scooped, crunched, double dipped, then licked his finger while she waited. 'You have almost no authority. And you have obvious politics.'

This from a man who used his relationship with Stella as the basis of his own authority and had a cabal of mates who always had the inside track on what was happening in the company before it happened.

She used the line she coached others to use when their feedback was confusing. 'Can you give me an example of that?'

'You always side with the women.'

Their population was seventy per cent male. 'I don't think I do that.'

'You sided with Christina.'

'No, I was even-handed. There was no need to take a side. It wasn't even a real work problem.' He was steamed that she didn't execute his restructure plan, that's what this was about. And now she was steamed. Reviews were not about airing petty grievances. 'Can you give me an example of my lack of authority?'

He lunged at the corn chip bowl. 'I don't want to totally destroy your confidence.'

'I beg your pardon?' She had to cough that out.

With a full mouth and a slimy green tongue, he said, 'Half the time I have to finish your work for you.'

It came out mumbled, but it was a direct hit on her competence. Never, he never had to do that. 'That's not true. You're mad I didn't do your re-org.'

'Do I look mad?' He went for another corn chip as if he'd never borne a grudge in his life. 'I guess I expect too much from you. I shouldn't assume you can upskill to work you're not well-suited to. It's unfair of me.'

'What the hell does that mean?' That was some twisted mix of not about her, insulting, damaging and cruel to boot. But she'd made a mistake by raising her voice. She pinched the skin between her thumb and first finger as a reminder to keep it together. Shouting at Felix would only make him decide she was too volatile or too emotional or too whatever it was he didn't think was effective because—because—because, she had no idea what his problem with her was.

'Have you considered going back to uni for more training?'

'Wait, I don't understand what you're saying.' Her heart understood the conversation had moved into fight or flight territory, it was hiccupping hard against her ribs. 'What part of my job am I not suited for?'

He waved a corn chip. 'These are general comments. It should be clear I'm saying you have room to improve.'

Clear as the mucky water in Shelby's bucket when she'd mopped her kitchen floor. He'd given her above average gradings on all of her job performance criteria, and now he was casually attacking her in the vaguest way while he chowed down. 'How are you dissatisfied? Nothing you're saying shows in my scores.'

He pulled the bowl of guac towards him. 'You're taking it too literally.'

'This is my performance review and you're questioning my abilities, what other way is there to take it?'

He smirked and then stuffed his face with a clump of avocado. 'You need to practise your listening skills. They're bloody vital for a people person.'

'I'm listening, but I don't understand you.'

He gave a dramatic sigh and looked at the ceiling. 'Shelby, you're making this harder than it needs to be. I'm just saying you need to act more professionally.'

No amount of skin pinching was helping. She threw her hands up. 'How?' Up went her voice too, making her sound frantic—how she felt, but not the emotion she wanted to show him. She tried to never let him see he was getting to her. It only gave him more ammunition to work with.

He shrugged as if he hadn't considered he'd need backup data. 'You could dress differently.'

If her face got any hotter, she could roast the guac just by looking at the bowl. 'What does that mean?' They were a casual office, and even on the big event dress-up days she was careful not to look ridiculous because she knew she was held to a higher standard. She'd already planned her Melbourne Cup day outfit. Not a micro miniskirt or fascinator in sight. Jockey silks all the way.

'Aw, you're upset.'

He said that like it was one of the world's greatest mysteries, and he hadn't poked and prodded her into anger. He couldn't be that clueless, so it must be deliberate.

'You're not being clear, and it is upsetting me, and you meant it to.'

He scrapped a corn chip around the edge of the bowl, making it squeak. He didn't even look at her. She'd just made mistake number two by calling him out.

'Don't be such a big girl,' he said.

'You've got to be kidding me.' She shouted that. The lid was off her temper. 'You did not just say that like it means something. My gender has nothing to do with how I do my job, but you wanted to insult me. It's unfair and unreasonable,' and since Felix was snivelling, she said, 'and you know that, but you did it anyway. It's juvenile and—'

'Is everything okay in here?'

Mistake number three, thinking they were alone in the office. Adam stood in the doorway, a mug dangling from his fingers.

'I didn't know anyone was here,' she said, startled. How much had he heard? Embarrassment burned a hot hole in her chest.

Adam didn't move any further into the room. He was staring Felix out, but that didn't make her feel any better. Of all people to spring her in a situation where she'd lost her cool it had to be Adam, who never lost his.

'We're done here,' Felix said, standing.

Adam leaned on the doorjamb. 'I interrupted.' He was going to make it hard for Felix to leave and they were not done here, but she didn't want an audience. 'Shelby was speaking.'

'We probably interrupted you,' she said, getting to her feet and shuffling her papers into a pile. 'We'll finish this in Felix's office and let you make your coffee.'

Maybe the look Adam gave her said *are you sure?*, and maybe it just said, *great, I need my caffeine fix*. She much preferred the latter because she didn't need him as a witness to the fact she'd been ranting at her boss.

Adam moved first, going to the coffee machine and letting Felix shuffle around him and leave.

She took a second to clear up, taking the bowls to the sink and scraping the leftovers into the garbage. 'I'm sorry you heard that. It's nothing to worry about. Robust discussion,' she said with an attempt to laugh it off. 'We often argue things out.'

That would've worked on just about everyone else and just about anyone else wouldn't have made her feel like a dope for what was essentially a defence of Felix and what he'd done to her. But there was something about Adam and the way he quietly assessed the world and saw all the people in it, saw her, in a way no one else did, that made her squirm under his regard.

There was no misinterpreting the look he gave her this time. He wasn't buying. He'd made no attempt to make coffee either, had put his mug in the dishwasher. He took the bowl she was holding out of her hand. 'I've got this. Go do what you need to do.'

She couldn't get out of the kitchen fast enough and she was halfway across the room, chased by bewildering shame and rancid fury, before he said, 'Don't let the bastard get you down, Shelby.'

Which told her two things. He had heard more than her raised voice and he'd come to check she was okay. It was sweet, and it was also humiliating in a way she couldn't explain, except to realise she cared what Adam thought about her.

Quick as she was to follow Felix, he was nowhere to be found and she went home feeling like a Chinese dumpling steamed too long—congealed and sticky and stuck. If she backed Felix into a corner to continue the discussion he'd call her pig-headed, a dog gnawing a bone, or he'd pretend not to know what she was talking about.

It wasn't the first time they'd disagreed passionately and left things unresolved, but every time it happened it hollowed out a part of her enthusiasm for the job. Maybe it was time to move on. Find a boss who didn't have a problem with her being a big girl, who could celebrate her competence instead of fearing she might be after his job.

An office without Felix would be a delight. It would also be an office without Adam and his water-jug-filling, shout-investigating, gentle eyes and caring ways, and that shouldn't make any difference to her thinking.

It really shouldn't.

It took her the rest of the week working back to wonder what Adam was working on that had him working back too. For the next four nights, they were the last to leave, locking up and riding the lift to the street together. He never mentioned the fight in the kitchen, so she let it slide with him, the same way she let it slide with Felix, except that for the rest of the week she wore t-shirts with girl power slogans on them. Starting with *I run like a girl, try to keep up*, moving on through *Girls just wanna have fundamental human rights* and *The future is female*, to *Nevertheless she persisted* and ending with *Nasty women get things done*.

Felix got the point. Not that he was cured. He was still a gaslighter and a bully, but she felt a whole lot better about things, especially since her formal written review didn't mention any of her supposed failings. It did make that whole argument and t-shirt protest pointless, but she'd take it.

And Adam stopped working back late a week later, about the same time she did. Curious that.

It was another fortnight before she spoke to Adam again. She'd woken with a head cold and was seriously snuffly with a voice that was all Miss Piggy after an all-nighter of alcoholic nightcaps. He arrived at her cubicle with a hot lemon drink.

'You should be at home,' he said, putting the mug in front of her. How did he even know she felt bad? 'It's just a cold.'

'You're pale, you look like you didn't sleep well, and you sound terrible. You're a walking germ factory.'

She picked up the mug. She was so stuffed up she couldn't smell the lemon. It was a little unnerving that Adam had paid that much attention to her to know she felt sick. 'You just don't want to catch my germs.'

'You've got that right. Please go home. We promise not to trash the place while you're gone.'

A voice from over the cubicle spine said, 'Do what Adam says, Shelby, or it'll be a sickie fest and you'll have to fumigate the whole office.'

She sipped her hot lemon drink. It was soothing for her scratchy throat. She watched Adam walk back to his desk, spinning her chair around so she could thoroughly check him out and that was soothing too. Nice butt. Sexy little spring in his step. Those calf muscles would bunch. Look at those shoulders. Amazing hair. She spun back around. *Oh crunch, please nobody notice I did that.* She must be delirious.

She went home to bed and had a feverish dream about being married to Felix and Adam walking in on them during a domestic dispute about stacking the dishwasher. The most disturbing part wasn't that she was Felix's dream wife or that he never unstacked the clean dishes and always left a mess in the sink—that felt about right—but that dream Adam had been wandering around shirtless and she'd woken just as she was about to touch him for the first time.

Her t-shirt—*Cinnamon rolls, not gender roles*—was stuck to her and she was still snuffly, but it was almost worth feeling sick to dream about feeling up her inappropriate-office-romances-are-bad-unrequited-but-hella-thoughtful crush, who she really wanted to invite to her orphan's Christmas lunch.

She really, really wanted to do that when it rolled around to her birthday. Because Adam saved her.

She might have to put herself out there for everyone to see and listen to as part of her job, but personally she'd rather avoid being the centre of attention. That was something Felix never understood. The day before her birthday holiday was always fraught with cake, singing and stupid jokes about her advanced age—twenty-eight—impending incontinence and forever spinsterhood, that were intended 'affectionately', but always made her wish she'd falsified her staff record to be birthday-less so no one was reminded. She'd even give up the extra day off if she never had to fake it through the razzing again.

Last year, the joke had been to give her a blow-up walking frame. She'd put on a smile and laughed along, but as soon as possible she'd stuck a pin in it and binned it where no one would see. This year, Adam warned her.

He stopped her as she was coming out of a meeting. 'If you don't want a fuss about it being your birthday tomorrow, you could find an excuse to be out of the office at three.'

She was so shocked Adam guessed that about her, she didn't reply. This was different to hearing her shout or noticing she was sneezing and sniffling.

'Sorry, I'm out of line.' He shook his head, looked at his boots. 'Forget I said it.'

'It's just cake and a bit of joking around. We all endure it.' Adam had endured his. She'd made a note in his file to say he'd prefer something quieter next year with his closest team members, not the whole office.

'Felix got you a Gorillagram.'

Odd how you could feel the blood drain out of your body. It pooled somewhere around her knees, making her shiver. 'How do you know?'

'Everyone knows.'

They did now. How typical of Felix to use her birthday as an opportunity to position himself as the best, most fun boss ever. It was only a month since the guacamole performance review debacle and the war of t-shirt words. If he really cared, he'd have put a cupcake with a candle in it on her desk with a fancy coffee. He was well aware she hated a fuss. It was in her file too, if he'd ever bothered to look.

'I can't just not be here.' How bad could a Gorillagram be? Fifteen minutes in the spotlight. Excruciating, but she could do it. Grin and bear it and be grateful it wasn't something worse.

'It's Noel's birthday Friday. He'd love it.'

The expense wouldn't go to waste. Her circulation kicked into gear again and she smiled at Adam. 'That's excellent because I do have that root canal thing. Almost forgot about it.'

Adam smiled back. Nice butt. Sexy little spring in his step. Look at those shoulders, wide enough to let him see what others didn't. Hair that just begged for fingers in it. And a smile that was as good as curling on the floor with a pile of puppies. 'Thanks for reminding me.'

Best work birthday ever.

By the time Melbourne Cup rolled around it was Adam, not Dynamite Diva, the horse she drew in the sweep, she was barracking for. She hoped he got a win, but it turned out his horse was a dud like hers, though from his grin you'd have thought he came out ahead.

She found herself standing beside him while everyone stood around wearing fancy clothes, eating posh little sandwiches with no crusts, prawns on skewers, and the good kind of cheese with deluxe crackers. 'You look happy,' she said.

He'd worn a grey suit with a light blue tie and she'd never seen him so dressed up. She'd planned on dressing like a jockey but switched at the last minute to a proper Audrey Hepburnesque black dress, and heels that were making her feet sore. She'd had to make a decision not to stand near Adam, so they didn't look like a couple off to a wedding, but despite that resolve had found herself right beside him. Maybe the room had tipped as the race was called and they'd been shuffled closer by cosmic forces. That had to be it, because she didn't intend to tempt fate.

He flashed his phone screen at her. A picture of two men hugging with shocked expressions on their faces. 'My brother had a win,' he said. 'Enough for him to afford a proper honeymoon in Vietnam over Christmas.'

It was a busy time of year for LuxLife but Stella still wanted everyone who wasn't essential to customer service to have time off. That meant Shelby got to take a break between Christmas and New Year and since Adam worked on development projects he could too. It was time to end her fantasy of inviting him to her Christmas lunch with some practical details. 'Will you go home?'

'Not this year. Been feuding with my folks. It's the reason I moved to Sydney. They're not ready to accept my brother and Louie yet, and I guess I'm still not ready to forgive them for that. What about you?'

Pah rump a pum. Deck those halls. Merrily on high. She didn't need to hear that. It sat the fantasy down in a comfortable chair, plumped up the pillows, pulled up a foot stool and served exclusive cocktails.

'I spend it with my sister. We have this big lunch that we invite orphans and strays to. You know, people who have no family or get left out.' Or people they had inappropriate crushes on who weren't going home for Christmas. Adam would have his own friends, and if he didn't have someone special in his life to spend his Christmas day with other than Feral the cat, she'd be her own Gorillagram. 'We do it every year. We love it.'

He gave her one of those puppy-pile smiles that stroked her whole body and made it sit up and beg, and it was fortunate she got called away because he was good at reading her and she didn't want him reading that. No good could come of it *or* future cosmic room tilts. *Woof.*

It was useful the end of the year was always a rush. As though days were robbed of hours, time sped up and there weren't enough minutes available to get through the urgent tasks. On top of all that time-condensing stress, all her Christmas office party planning worries descended. The good thing was she thought she'd fully tamed her fantasy longings about Adam and his possible planless Christmas day—until that moment in the lift.

She knew he was there when she stepped in. Half the office was in that lift, coming back from lunch, from hasty shopping, from the volleyball league game. She should've waited for the next one, if only to avoid the food and body odour, but she was in a hurry to get back to her desk, almost late for a meeting, so she stepped in and stumbled on the strap of someone's bag. It was Adam who stopped her tumbling into a wall of sweaty bodies, into him, his fingertips to her shoulder.

He didn't say anything, didn't call attention to her, he simply steadied her with a fleeting touch that did riotous things to her pulse.

'Thank you,' she said softly, not sure he'd hear over the raucous recount of the team victory, not wanting to call attention to him either.

'Happy to sort you,' he whispered back.

Four words could make you glow. Those four words made being late, the fuss of Christmas planning and their busiest trading season melt off her. She felt brushed and soothed and fluffed up and bright and ready for anything.

She was first out of the lift, but they all piled through the office door together.

'Shelby Yule. You're late.' Felix stood in the entryway. 'Hurry up. The Christmas committee is waiting.'

Felix high-fived each of the volleyball winners as they came past. If she was late, well so was he. He could've started without her, but that would mean he'd actually have to run the meeting, not just take up space in it.

She went to move around him, giving him a hard look as she made for her desk to dump her bag and pick up her tablet, but his next words stopped her short.

'Ooh, judging from that look it must be that time of the month. Do you need to go change your tampon before you grace us with your presence?'

The expression *stunned silence* was nothing on the unearthly quiet that blanketed the space. She knew Adam was somewhere behind her. She knew he'd heard.

Her whole body went rigid, teeth clacking together loudly in her head. She stared at the floor willing it to open up and swallow Felix in a fiery cataclysm, and then nervous laughter broke the spell and Ravi said, 'Holy shit, Felix. Don't be such a jerk.'

'Ah Shelby knows I'm only kidding,' Felix said. 'But I won't be if she doesn't bloody hurry up.'

'If I said something like that to my wife, she'd stop feeding me for life,' Ravi responded. 'Pull your head in and apologise, mate.'

She didn't want an apology. She didn't want to be on the same planet, in the same office, room, existence as Felix. He had wrecked her glow and there was no way to make up for that.

'Sorry, Shelby,' Felix said, singsong. 'I don't even know if she wears tampons,' he said to no one and everyone, as if that made everything okay. 'Just hurry the hell up.'

She stopped herself looking for Adam. Because if he turned sympathetic eyes on her, if he said something to give her comfort or express his outrage, she might need to do more than invite him for Christmas lunch. She might need to put her head on his shoulder and sob.

She was frustrated and furious and disappointed and stuck. It was their busiest time and there were reports to finish, rosters to finalise, a party to plan. There were Christmas carols on repeat in her head, gifts to buy and meals to shop for. Tempers were short, and they predicted a heatwave. It was the usual overwhelming seasonal pressure cooker stuff. But for one thing.

She didn't need mistletoe as an excuse to want a kiss.

Shelby: Now

She'd ask Adam when he got back from being stitched up. What's the worst that could happen? It was lunch. If he said no, it's not like her whole world would spin in the other direction. It's not like she'd spent a year inappropriately focusing on how much she liked his work ethic.

Oh, stuff his work ethic, she'd mostly been inappropriately focused on how he smiled a little crookedly and made her want to lie in a pile of puppies. How much she wanted to see what he'd look like with his hair loose, and whether he really did smell like green trees after a thunderstorm or if she'd imagined that from their near collision events.

She'd learned something else about herself tonight. She wasn't that great at creating fantasies. To think she'd never tuned in to his incredible forearms when she'd imagined what his hugs might be like. She'd never be able to look at his arms again without feeling swirly inside in all the best ways.

It wasn't just lunch she wanted to invite Adam to. It wasn't just touch she wanted, a kiss she was secretly desperate to have. It was the idea of exploring what they might be like together as friends, as more than friends, outside work. It was the outrageous idea they might enjoy spending time together and sharing their lives.

But Adam had never done anything to encourage her to think this way, other than treat her with the same courtesy he treated everyone with. Filled water jugs weren't a declaration of undying affection. Steadying hands and words weren't invitations to anything beyond collegiality, much as she might want them to mean more. And especially after Dave and Christina's flame out, she'd been hyper wary of stepping over the boundary lines to attempt an office romance. It simply wouldn't do. Lunch was the compromise her dislocated heart could handle. She could be satisfied with that.

Liar, liar, Santa pants on fire.

He'd never done anything to encourage her and she'd never signalled she wanted to be encouraged. But this buzzing current of awareness she had, the one that let her know when he was near, even when she'd yet to catch sight of him, the cosmic room tilt that brought them close, surely meant something.

She loved her job. She'd loved it all the more this year, despite how awful Felix was, because seeing Adam, hearing his voice, sitting in meetings he attended where she could enjoy his thinking, even pouring water from the jug he'd filled, was a secret thrill, a twitch that ran under her skin, quickened her pulse and lightened her day.

So she was asking him when he got back from being fixed up because after tonight she might not have an excuse to see him again.

And that wasn't all she was doing.

She had to deal with her forgiveness problem, put it into perspective. Some people didn't do anything to deserve forgiveness, especially if they kept on making the same damn mistake. She was telling Stella exactly how she felt working with Felix, and exactly why she didn't want to do that anymore, and if that meant she talked herself out of her own job then she'd deal with it. Same as she'd deal with finding another man who made her feel good just by being in the same postcode if Adam said no to lunch and whatever might come after it.

With that resolve simmering she waited; posting a pic to her social feed of the most unusual nativity scene she'd ever come across and scrolling past other people's Christmas party pics, the potential harassment suits of which she happily bore absolutely no responsibility. That's when Stella walked in, dragging her suitcase.

LuxLife's founder, CEO and chief incredible person looked completely zapped after a month travelling to meet with investors, and yet she hadn't gone home. Shelby braced for impact as Stella collapsed into the seat beside her, making the whole row shake.

'Let's never do Christmas again,' Stella said.

'I'd vote for that.'

'Maybe we can leave it off the calendar, or take a moral stance against it, or I don't know, hit people with a designer forgetfulness drug that makes them fuzzy on dates till the new year. Just the dates, they get to remember everything else.'

Shelby couldn't help her smile. 'Did you just suggest drugging your staff?'

Stella groaned. 'It's been a long month. I'm a Buddhist. I don't even celebrate Christmas. And what happened to peace and goodwill to all men on earth? Where is Adam?'

'Getting stitched up. Felix is—'

'I know how Felix is. We've spoken. Joy to the world. I'd like to hear your version of—' Stella leaned forward and pointed at the nativity. 'Hey, that's Spock. Huh.'

Shelby winced. There was no way to tell the story without throwing Adam out over the shark net. He was fish food already. 'It might be my fault.'

'It's been a long year. Jesus is LEGO with Spock for an earthly dad. Do not even try that it's your fault thing on me.'

'Felix is an arse.' *Whoa.* She hadn't meant to say it quite like that, but there it was, no backstroking around it.

'That's more like it. He told me Adam threw the first punch for no reason. Is he lying?'

'No.' Felix was too clever to get caught out by telling a simple lie. He wove his misdirections out of elements of truth and strings of good sense and particles of trust that might be stretched thin, but rarely snapped.

'He was telling funny stories, you know how he is, life of the party.' He'd organised all the men to wear Christmas Hawaiian shirts, but he'd made it a secret, so a lot of the women were annoyed not to be included and had whinged to Shelby about it.

'As far as I know there was no specific trigger. Adam drew him away from everyone and punched him. Felix hit back, he put Adam on the floor.'

Felix had stood over Adam in his surfing safari Santa shirt swearing at him; 'The rest of us were stunned mullets. Adam didn't stay down. His eye was already closed, his brow opened, he was bleeding everywhere.' She shuddered at the memory; she'd been as gobsmacked as everyone else. 'He got up, and he hit Felix twice and Felix toppled over.' She snapped her fingers. 'Lights out.'

'I'm having trouble believing it,' Stella said.

She knew the feeling. 'I sent everyone home. I didn't know what else to do.'

'Hmm. Felix is an arse. What did you mean by that?'

The smart thing to do would be to tell Stella that since they were both tired and it was late, that the discussion could wait until Monday, but Felix had been an arse way too long. 'Felix is our office psychopath.'

Stella made a sound of surprise and Shelby tried to remember where she'd filed her resume. It would take no time at all to change her status to 'quick, I need a job' on LinkedIn. 'He knows how to manage up, so you don't see his worst behaviour. He has favourites, he gaslights, he undermines, and he plays office politics.' He could be rude, insulting and he sulked when he didn't get his own way, but he was clever. He rarely ever let any of that show to Stella.

'Why didn't you say something?'

That made Shelby squirm. She found Felix so difficult to deal with, so ready to put her down and find her work inadequate that she spent all her energy sucking it up and managing him. And that was a kind of forgiveness. She'd let a bully run her around and make her doubt herself. 'I was wrong to give him a free pass.'

Stella pushed her hair off her face. She was either irritated with her fringe or with Shelby. 'Why didn't you come to me?'

'I, um...' *Enough of defending him. No more free passes for Felix.* 'I didn't think you'd see it my way.'

'Why not?'

Oh crap. *Because you're a smart woman and you can't possibly not have known Felix is a two-faced rat, but you put up with him for years.* 'Because Felix has been with you since you started LuxLife and talked his family into investing. You couldn't have gotten it started without him.'

The blade-sharp look Stella gave her was the one she used to get difficult, never-been-done-before things completed on time and on budget. It forced a nervous cough out of Shelby.

'Who told you that?'

It was common knowledge. Shelby opened her mouth to answer and Stella shut her down with a raised hand, then walked across the room to the nativity scene and studied it, tapping one designer shoe in an exasperated beat.

So that went well.

She exchanged a strained smile with the reindeer headband woman and then Stella was back beside her.

'I have one more question,' Stella said.

Is it how soon can you pack up your desk?

'Why did Adam hit Felix?'

That wasn't much better. 'He said it was because—'

Stella finished for her. 'Felix is an arse.'

'I told him that wasn't a good reason, and I believe he knows there's no good reason for hitting someone, but he said he wasn't sorry and he'd do it again.' Oh God, it hurt to say that. Made her feel like she was betraying Adam with the truth.

'He's sweet on you, you know that, right?'

For a horrified moment, she thought Stella was talking about Felix. Nightmare scenario, not one she'd wake up from. 'Adam is sweet with everyone.'

'That's not what I meant. I want you to give me a Christmas present, Shelby.'

Oh, awkward layered on awkward. 'We had a Kris Kringle. I put your gift on your desk.'

'Not that. I don't give a stuff about another bath bomb, and I already know without asking that you bought a decent gift to give on my behalf. I give a stuff about LuxLife and making my best people happy and I can see I've not been doing a great job at that. I didn't know Felix was saying I can't do without him. I didn't realise he was being an arse, or maybe I did, but I didn't see it as a problem. That's on me. I see it as one now.'

A punch-up, someone decked in the office could do that. Change minds, redirect attention. Shelby was ready to interrupt, to remind Stella she was busy, and keeping people happy was her job, but Stella shut her down again, this time with a lip zip signal.

'I want you to start rating your own needs as important as everyone else's. I don't mean putting yourself first above others. But I don't want you to disappear under everyone else.'

'You want me to stop being a doormat.' At least she still had a job, even if it was ground floor level.

'I don't think you're a doormat, Shelby. I think you're the best HR person I've ever worked with. I know LuxLife would suffer if I were to lose you. I'm angry that I didn't know the truth, and given Felix is your boss, I can imagine you've had the worst of him to deal with.'

This was like being smacked and finding it tickled and you liked it. Weirdly delightful.

'I'm angry that it's come to this and I didn't see it. I know you don't lie to me. But you didn't come to me either. Are you protecting either Felix or Adam now?'

It was a fair question. 'No. Half the office wants to hit Felix for one reason or another but that doesn't justify Adam doing it.'

'No, it does not.'

They sat in silence, Stella brooding and Shelby feeling like her New Year's resolution was already in place. No more putting up with Felix. No more being agreeable to keep the peace with him. It wasn't going to be easy to stand up to him when she'd become accustomed to walking things back.

A woman arrived clutching her stomach. A man holding his arm close to his side. Somewhere behind the row of chairs, Adam was having his cut brow seen to and maybe starting to regret what he'd done.

'Stella, you don't have to stay.'

'One of my people is hurt. I'm staying.'

They were staying together. 'What are you going to do about Adam?'

Stella shook her head. 'I'm hoping LEGO Jesus has some guidance for me because this is a Christmas panto I wasn't expecting to be in. I don't like playing Scrooge.'

Adam: Now

Adam sat on an examining table while the doctor looked into his eyes and checked his hand, asking him to make a fist, then squeeze her finger. 'No sign of concussion. Nothing broken.'

She was wrong about that. It was only a couple of punches, but he'd broken something precious.

'Have you been drinking? Taken any drugs?'

Did a year's worth of stored up adrenaline and a raging inferno of dislike count? 'One beer.'

She held his jaw and turned his head left and right. 'Attacking or defending?'

'Does it matter?' He still wasn't sorry for putting Felix on the floor. The satisfaction of that would last longer than his bruising.

Peering into his face, she said, 'You tell me.'

'Maybe both.' There were other ways he could've handled this. He wasn't proud of himself. He'd shown a singular lack of foresight in starting a fight at a Christmas party. He could've talked to Shelby about it, taken his concern to Stella. He could've had it out with Felix using words not fists. 'I don't intend to make a habit of it.'

'Good, because next time, you might not come out of it so lightly.' She prodded his brow and he winced. 'Only needs a few stitches,' she said. 'Must hurt like a bad decision.'

What hurt was losing a job he loved and having that jeopardise the new life he'd built for himself during his year in Sydney, including patching things up with Scott and coming to terms with the fact there was no need for him be the tug of war rope between his brother and their parents.

It was only a superficial wound.

It might not be easy, but he'd find another job. He'd continue to enjoy the city and all it had to offer. His parents would eventually come around and if they didn't, he was cool with that.

What really hurt was how he'd lost his chance with Shelby.

She was like no one he'd ever met and someone he felt he knew, all at the same time. That didn't make any sense because what he did know about her wasn't even a hundred lines on a spreadsheet. He didn't know what her favourite things to do were, or what she dreamed about, or how she wanted her life to turn out, and that was an incredible failing. There was no formula for why he was so drawn to her. But it was a fact that his days were brighter if they'd shared a smile across the office, that filling her water jug gave him a buzz, and being near enough to touch her was a welcome tension, an aching kind of satisfaction.

'Sit very still. We want these to be neat so you don't scar.'

He'd managed to scar Shelby with his actions and for that he was heavy with regret. She was too smart and too sensible to want anything to do with him that she didn't see as a job responsibility now. He'd had a million chances to try to make something of their connection, and yet he'd never even asked her to walk out together to grab lunch.

He thought about putting his hands to her spikey hair, hauling her close, and kissing her so softly he transformed that ache he had into something they could share.

But they'd never even shared coffee.

It wasn't just that office romances were bad news, it wasn't that Dave and Christina had proven what a pain in the rear they were to everyone, or that for Shelby the decision to start something at work was complicated by her role. It was his old failing come to haunt him like the ghost of Christmas past.

A lifetime of not causing trouble, of not taking sides, of looking for the easy way instead of going hard after what he wanted and standing his ground. As a kid that had been his role. To be the brother who was easy to get along with, who didn't want for anything other than what came about with no effort. He was long overdue to start thinking like an adult, to own his ambition and build the life he wanted like Scott had. If he didn't start going after what he aspired to, it would always be like this: lost chances and unnecessary compromises, precious things broken.

He didn't try for Shelby's heart because he understood how devastating losing it would feel, and now the best thing he could do was apologise and get the hell out of her way before he disappointed her further.

The doc finished up, prescribed ice, paracetamol and peace on earth. He thanked her, wished her a happy Christmas and used the bathroom to clean himself up as best he could. Shelby would be waiting because she'd see it as her job to make sure he was all right. The least he could do was look like he wasn't dying a little inside.

There was nothing to be done for his shirt, but he washed the blood from his hair and left it loose to dry. It might finally be time to shave, to get a haircut, to get a new tattoo to go with what he'd learned from throwing punches. Something to remind him to use his brain to strike out instead of his fists.

Last person he expected to see among the sick and festively sorry in the waiting room was Stella. She shook her head and pointed to the seat in the row opposite where she and Shelby sat. 'Are you okay?'

He told her he was and sat, giving Shelby a grimace, getting one in return. This was it then. What he'd been waiting for since he squinted down on Felix in stunned amazement at what he'd done.

'When I said you could break things I didn't mean you should hit someone. Tell me what happened,' Stella said.

Shelby would've already told her, there was no need to elaborate. 'I decked Felix. This is my fault.'

'Why?'

'I don't like the guy.'

Stella looked at the neon tubing in the ceiling. 'There are a lot of people I don't particularly like, but I don't go around hitting them.' She waved a hand at him. 'It's not like you. What did Felix do to you?'

'Nothing. I just don't like the guy, don't rate him, don't trust him, don't want to know him.'

'Adam, you're an asset to LuxLife, but not if you can't tell me the truth. Why did you do something totally out of character?'

'I know it was the wrong thing to do. I'll apologise to Felix, and if you want, to the whole staff. I'm sorry you have to deal with this. Decking him wasn't the answer.'

'I'm not sure what the question was?' Stella said.

He glanced from Stella to Shelby and the concern on her face made him want to skip the paracetamol and take his licks without relief. 'It's not my place to say.'

With her elbows resting on her knees, Stella leaned forward and lowered her voice. 'If you don't tell me what's going on, *I'll* deck you, and I take boxing classes, so I know how to hit. We can take this discussion from casualty to police lock-up if you like.'

She'd do it. She was pocket sized and never made threats she couldn't deliver on. He had no doubt she could do him harm if she really wanted to. Still, it made him smile. She was fighting for him and he didn't deserve that consideration.

'It doesn't matter what the question is, violence isn't the answer,' he said.

Stella eye-rolled and slumped against the seat back. She didn't need to be here. All she had to say was 'don't come back Monday'.

'Did you do it for me?'

He'd been so focused on Stella, Shelby's words shocked a pained sound out of him.

'Oh, Adam. You did it for me. Oh no,' she said.

Shelby knew, and that just made things worse. It wasn't her fault he'd lost control and he needed to make sure Stella understood that.

Stella's glare bounced between them. 'Somebody tell me what this all means, before I get my tinsel in a tangle.'

There was no one event, it was the build-up over the year, but the tipping point was the way Felix humiliated Shelby before Christmas with his crass comments, singling her out for unwarranted attention in front of an unsuspecting audience. Adam had cleared out, so Shelby didn't know he was witness to that humiliation, but he couldn't let the fire it lit in him go out and tonight was gasoline.

'I've watched Felix make Shelby's life difficult all year. He puts her down, he makes sexist jokes, he dumps on her, he insults and humiliates her. I couldn't take it anymore.'

'So you punched him?'

'Felix had it coming.' He didn't spend nights and weekends plotting to take Felix down; he'd have been smarter about it if he had, chosen a more appropriate time and place for one thing before he knocked the guy's Santa hat off and put him on the ground.

He'd watched Felix holding court, life of the party, commenting to his inner circle about what people were wearing, and as if that wasn't bad enough, he made a snarky remark about Shelby being a worrier princess, and he'd simply decided then and there. Enough. It had to stop.

'There are no excuses. It was wrong, and I take full responsibility. Shelby certainly didn't prompt me. She had no knowledge I was going to do this.'

Stella stood, slapping her hands down on her thighs in exasperation. 'I'm jetlagged. I missed our Christmas party. I've just discovered Felix is a worse arse than I thought he was. We're supposed to be a no bullshit business. It's our busiest week of the year. I don't need this. I'm going for a walk to think. Neither of you move.'

They watched her stalk through the front doors into the warmth of the night and disappear between a couple of smokers and two ambos taking a coffee break.

'Maybe she won't come back,' he said, eyes still on the door.

'She has to come back, she left her bag,' Shelby said.

Getting sacked was proving to be a lot more complicated than he expected. 'She could phone it in.'

'She never phones it in. And you didn't either. You decked Felix for me.'

He could tell her he didn't do it specifically for her but because of how she and others were treated. He could toggle together some broader explanation so she didn't feel bad about it, but he couldn't have the last few things he said to Shelby be a lie.

'You deserve a better boss and you can't reason with a bully.'

'Oh jingle bells,' Shelby's hands went to her head as if she was trying to hold her thoughts in place. 'You really did do it for me.'

He nodded, watching her closely, wanting this to be a very different conversation, not one where she felt only disgust. If there was a way to soothe the concern from her face, to take the tension from her hands, stop the agitated jiggle of her leg, the rapid tapping heel, he would do it without a care for his own wellbeing.

But he was the reason for all those things.

'Hitting a man isn't like putting fruit in my water jug,' she said.

He made himself hold eye contact. She deserved that honesty. 'No, it's not like that.'

'It's not like helping me realise I was too sick to be at work.'

He looked down at the scuffed floor, and then back up to her face again. Only Shelby could give him absolution. 'No.'

'It's not the same as saving me from birthday embarrassment.'

'It's more like handing you a new reason to be embarrassed.'

'I'm not embarrassed.'

Not what he expected her to say. He stood to move across the aisle to her, needing to hear her say it again, in case concussion had set in, and the doors whooshed open and Stella came through them like a shooting star guiding the world to a new religion.

This was it.

He stopped himself from touching Shelby's shoulder, from reaching for her hand and imagining her fingers threaded through his. 'I'm sorry for this mess. You deserve everything you want, and I hope you get it.'

Shelby stood too, a stricken look on her lovely face as Stella pointed at the row of chairs and said, 'Sit down, both of you.'

They had to be causing a scene, drama for casualty's curious, but Adam didn't care. His head was thumping and his hand ached.

Whatever they'd used to numb his brow would start wearing off soon.

'You,' said Stella, pointing to Shelby and making her start. 'Make it a priority to hire more women. From now on everyone on the management team, including me, gets reviewed by the people they manage. And you start reporting directly to me.'

'What about—'

Stella ignored Shelby and turned to Adam. It was finally all over now. 'You.' She pointed the finger of joblessness in January at him. 'First thing Monday morning I want a public apology at a staff meeting. You need to explain yourself, admit blame and tap dance all over what a crap thing you did. And it better be good.'

He shook his sore head, glanced at Shelby and shared her shock. 'I don't—'

Stella pulled the handle of her wheely bag up with a snap. 'Merry Christmas. Here's your present. Felix is out. He's decided to spend more time with his family. Shelby you're the new HR director. Adam, if you ever raise a hand, a foot, a knee, an elbow, an inappropriate scarred eyebrow at someone, you are out the door without a reference so fast you won't have time to get your tongue around another word. I'm taking a risk on you and you'd better pay off. Questions? No? Good. I'm out of here. See you both Monday.'

For the second time, they watched Stella leave. She ploughed through the electronic doors at full speed without a backwards glance. He had questions. They queued in his throat, pushing and shoving to get access to his lips. He still had a job. He still had a chance. He was the luckiest guy in the world and he wasn't going to waste any more time not going after what he wanted, and doing it right.

Shelby stared at him, both hands to her cheeks. 'Congratulations,' he said, moving to sit beside her.

'You too,' she said and then laughed. 'I mean...' She shook her head, earrings spinning. 'I don't know what I mean. I just got a promotion for Christmas. It's like getting a puppy. And you got a second chance. But next time you want to stand up for me, we talk about it first and no fists ever, okay?'

'Not when there is any other way.' With his good hand he reached for hers and she took it, letting him fold her palm inside his. His second chance came with an enormous year-end bonus he was going to bank immediately.

They spoke together using the same words, their bodies angled towards each other, knees grazing. 'Would you—?'

Smiling at her hurt a little. In his cheek. At his brow. In his heart. 'You go first.' If she'd let him, he'd always stand up for her and put her first.

'Would you like to come to my Christmas day orphan's lunch? I should've asked you earlier. I've wanted to for months now. You probably have plans with friends, so I get it if you can't come, but I wanted to ask, and I thought I'd blown my chance, and I don't care that we work together, still work together. Oh Adam, I'm so glad we still work together.'

He'd never heard Shelby babble, or get breathless. He could feel the nervous tremor through her palm.

'I'd really like it if you'd come. It's nothing formal and it wouldn't matter that you don't know anyone but me, and—'

'I'd love to.'

The grin she gave him was everything Christmas should be. Hope and joy and peace and goodwill, the promise of love that could make the world a better place.

She squeezed his hand. 'You would? That's fantastic. I'm so pleased. It doesn't have to mean anything, just way too much food and a gut ache.'

The true ache was further up his chest and it was anything but unpleasant. 'What if I want it to mean more?'

She looked down at their hands. What if she did? 'What were you going to ask me?' she said.

There was a first time for everything and Christmas was the best time to reach for love. He'd decked a man tonight. Learning Santa was real and taking a sleigh ride to the North Pole care of Rudolph would've stunned him less. It was easy to ask for what he wanted.

'Would you let me kiss you?'

She took her hand away, lowered her eyes, and he swallowed his disappointment, only to have it switch to astonishment when she put her hand gently to the side of his face and pushed his hair back, fingers tangling in it before going to the back of his neck and holding him, still and warm and gentle and right.

'It's the season to be jolly,' she said, smiling as she leaned in.

And as their lips touched, bells rang, angels chorused, brolgas danced, boomers bounced, that damn partridge was firmly up the pear tree, and all Adam's Christmas wishes came at once.

Acknowledgements

The story *12 Days at Silver Bells House* wasn't on the cards and I hadn't even thought of writing it until I was asked if I could conjure up a story that would not only fit in with the Swallow's Fall series, but also have a country Christmas feel. Turned out I had a ball writing this story. So thank you Kate Cuthbert, Managing Editor at Escape Publishing. Thanks also (and again) to my wonderful, wise and witty writing colleagues who read everything I write and help it shine. Lily and Juanita, next time we're together, there will be wine (again). A huge, heartfelt thank you to all my readers who loved *The House on Burra Burra Lane*. Its success means so much to me. I hope you enjoy reading this Swallow's Fall story as much as I enjoyed writing it.

—Jennie Jones

With thanks to my fellow Rainbow Cove writers, Renée, Lorraine and Shirley. And special thanks to Shirley and Annie Seaton for helping me wrangle this story into great form.

—Susanne Bellamy

I'd like to thank the lovely team at Escape Publishing, including Kate, for choosing my book for publication. Special thanks also goes to Mimi, for the Christmas decorations, and my beautiful husband, for teaching me that it's always worth believing in yourself, even on the hard days.

—Lauren K. McKellar

A big thanks to Kate, Johanna and the team at Escape Publishing for loving my story. It's always a pleasure and privilege to work with you all. To my tireless PA, Jennifer Greeff, I couldn't write as much as I do without knowing I've got you in the background helping with graphics, social media and all the other little things I don't have time for. Once again, Abigail Owen, you helped me get this story written with our sprinting sessions. Finally, Jason, Skylar and Zane, my family, as always, your support means the world to me and I can't thank you enough for your endless encouragement.

—Nicole Flockton

About the Authors

Jennie Jones is a bestselling author who has sold over 50,000 copies and currently lives in a small country town in Perth, Western Australia. **Susanne Bellamy** is an Australian author of contemporary and rural romances, with a background as an English and drama teacher. **Lauren McKellar** grew up in a beachside town north of Sydney with a passion for romance and young adult fiction. *USA Today* bestselling author **Nicole Flockton** writes sexy contemporary romances, seducing you one kiss at a time. When she's not writing romance, **Ainslie Paton** works as a ghost writer.

talk about it

Let's talk about books.

Join the conversation:

 facebook.com/romanceanz

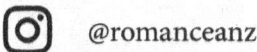 @romanceanz

romance.com.au

If you love reading and want to know about our authors and titles, then let's talk about it.